Praise for Beth Kery, Recipient of the
All About Romance Reader Poll for Best Erotica

"One of the sexiest, most erotic love stories that I have read in a long time."
—Affaire de Coeur

"A sleek, sexy thrill ride."
—Jo Davis

"One of the best erotic romances I've ever read."
—All About Romance

"Nearly singed my eyebrows."
—Dear Author

"Fabulous, sizzling hot . . . You'll be addicted."
—Julie James, *USA Today* bestselling author

"Action and sex and plenty of spins and twists."
—Genre Go Round Reviews

"Intoxicating and exhilarating."
—Fresh Fiction

"The heat between Kery's main characters is molten."
—*RT Book Reviews*

"Some of the sexiest love scenes I have read this year."
—Romance Junkies

"Scorching hot! I was held spellbound."
—Wild on Books

"Nuclear-grade hot."
—*USA Today*

Because You Are Mine series

BECAUSE YOU ARE MINE (ALSO AVAILABLE IN SERIAL FORMAT)
WHEN I'M WITH YOU (ALSO AVAILABLE IN SERIAL FORMAT)
BECAUSE WE BELONG
SINCE I SAW YOU

Titles by Beth Kery

WICKED BURN
DARING TIME
SWEET RESTRAINT
PARADISE RULES
RELEASE
EXPLOSIVE
THE AFFAIR (ALSO AVAILABLE IN SERIAL FORMAT)
GLIMMER

One Night of Passion Series

ADDICTED TO YOU (WRITING AS BETHANY KANE)
EXPOSED TO YOU
ONLY FOR YOU

One Night of Passion Specials

BOUND TO YOU
CAPTURED BY YOU

The AFFAIR

BETH KERY

BERKLEY BOOKS | NEW YORK

BERKLEY
An imprint of Penguin Random House LLC
375 Hudson Street, New York, New York 10014

Library of Congress Cataloging-in-Publication Data

Kery, Beth.
The affair / Beth Kery. — Berkley trade paperback edition.
p. ; cm.
ISBN 978-0-425-28075-1
I. Title.
PS3611.E79A69 2015
813'.6—dc23
2015003725

PUBLISHING HISTORY
Berkley trade paperback edition / September 2015

PRINTED IN THE UNITED STATES OF AMERICA

10 9 8 7 6 5 4 3 2 1

Cover photo of Vintage Box with Ring © iraua / Shutterstock.
Cover design by Sarah Oberrender.
Text design by Kelly Lipovich.

Penguin
Random
House

Week
ONE

Chapter 1

I walked into work and found myself in another world.

Emma Shore whisked aside curtains on a twelve-foot-tall wall made entirely of glass. The shock of sudden, blinding beauty disoriented her momentarily. The sun reflected brilliantly off an azure, beckoning Lake Michigan and filtered through a grove of white-trunked birches lining the water. Leaves fluttered like green-gold coins, fracturing the light in her dazed eyes. White spray flew into the air when a wave hit the black, jagged breakers in the distance.

The design of the house in which she stood was revolutionary, at least in Emma's limited experience. The mansion cascaded down the bluff to the sealike great lake, each layer of the house a steppingstone to the next, one level's roof the above story's magnificent terrace filled with picturesque outdoor seating and colorful pots of flowers. On the lowest level near the lake, a clear blue swimming pool tempted someone to pierce its serene surface.

Paradise. Out there it was, anyway.

She turned. Golden-green dappled light transformed the formerly shrouded, luxurious bedroom. Unfortunately, the other occupant of the room, Mrs. Shaw, appeared all the more disapproving in the sunlight. The rest of Emma's fellow nurses and nursing assistants from

New Horizon Hospice were already familiar with this assignment, having been at the Breakers for several weeks. Emma was the new girl on the block and bound to make a few missteps.

Apparently, she'd just made her first.

She studied the elegant, thin older woman with the blond bob, dressed in tailored chic as she crossed the suite. The woman had introduced herself a few minutes ago as Michael Montand's personal domestic assistant, whatever that meant. Emma's supervisor had labeled Mrs. Shaw more concisely as the housekeeper. Apparently, even a housekeeper of the Montand caliber could pass as an aging supermodel. Whatever her title, Mrs. Shaw had clearly decided Emma was trouble. Emma's reassuring smile as she walked to the empty bed was meant to quiet the other woman's anxiety. Emma was a nurse and a patient advocate, not a rebel. It wasn't her fault if the family or staff of her patients sometimes couldn't discern the difference.

"This is a sickroom," Mrs. Shaw said over the concerto playing softly on the stereo. "The way you're acting with all this sunlight and music, and having Mrs. Montand showered, you'd think you expected her to go to a party tonight."

"The sick appreciate beauty as much as the living. Usually more so."

"She's not sick. She's *dying*."

"Not yet," Emma stated unequivocally, ignoring Mrs. Shaw's shocked, outraged expression at her confident tone. She was a hospice nurse, true, but she'd also had her fair share of experience with death—much more than an average twenty-three-year-old. *No*. Her patient's time wasn't just yet.

"The doctors say—"

"I know what the doctors say," Emma interrupted, trying to control the edge to her tone. She glanced toward the adjoining bathroom and lowered her voice to just above a whisper, hoping Mrs. Shaw would do the same. Her patient was on the other side of that door. "I just mean that in my professional opinion, the end isn't imminent. Not today. Not tomorrow." She resumed making the bed briskly. "Cristina said she loved classical music when I interviewed her earlier, so I turned on the stereo. Who doesn't appreciate being clean? As for the drapes, has she complained of being bothered by sunlight before?" she asked, ignoring Mrs. Shaw's glare when she used her patient's first name. Cristina had given her permission to use it just an hour ago, and that was good enough for Emma.

"You speak boldly for someone so young," Mrs. Shaw said, her frowning face disappearing for a happy moment as Emma snapped the blanket into the air, blocking her vision of the woman.

"Has Mrs. Montand said she disliked having the curtains open?" Emma repeated quietly, bending to tuck in the blanket.

"I've never heard her say one way or another, but she's never had the opportunity to express her opinion. Mr. Montand has asked us to keep the curtains closed since Mrs. Montand returned to the Breakers to . . ."

Die.

Emma filled in the unsaid word in her head when Mrs. Shaw faded off. It never ceased to surprise her how people usually said the word so flippantly in everyday life, but refused to utter it when death hovered in the vicinity. Maybe they thought death would notice, and take them instead.

"We'll see how Cristina responds to the view when she comes back from her shower. It's easy enough to pull the curtains again. Cristina might find the sunlight refreshing," Emma finished the conversation with a friendly but firm tone.

When she heard the squeak of the wheelchair and muffled voices in the distance, she hastened across the room. She knocked and opened the bathroom door, stepping just over the threshold to assist Margie, the nursing assistant. Emma had been impressed by the sheer size of the bathroom, not to mention how it'd been sleekly updated to accommodate all of Cristina's disabilities. From what she'd understood, Montand had outfitted the suite for Cristina just months ago when he'd learned she'd been terminally diagnosed and was living alone and friendless in the city on a fixed income.

"Ah, a shower did you good, I see," Emma said when Margie

paused the wheelchair. Cristina Montand smiled thinly up at Emma from where she sat.

"It was better than sex. Certainly at this stage in my life, anyway," Cristina said in a husky, Italian-accented voice.

Emma grinned, glad to hear the wry humor in her patient's voice. The exotic accent suited her appearance and personality, somehow. Cancer was claiming her too young. Emma knew from the medical chart that Cristina was sixty-two. She had clearly once been a beauty. The wasting of the flesh combined with a slight swelling and discoloration due to an increasingly failing liver and kidneys couldn't entirely disguise the classic cheekbones and a swanlike neck.

"I've made your bed up nice and fresh and opened the curtains, but say the word and I'll close them again if you're tired," Emma said.

"Mr. Montand has given explicit instructions to leave the curtains closed," Margie said anxiously. Emma was puzzling out the nursing assistant's tense declaration, when the phone rang shrilly in the bedroom. Emma glanced around and saw Mrs. Shaw hasten to pick it up. The housekeeper looked at Emma, an ugly, triumphant expression spreading on her face as she listened to whoever was on the other end.

"Yes, I told her you wouldn't want them opened, but she seems to think *she* knows best. Yes, I'll see to it immediately," Mrs. Shaw said. Emma glanced uneasily at one of several surveillance cameras installed in the large suite. Had the enigmatic owner of the Breakers, Michael Montand, been the one to call?

Mrs. Shaw hung up the phone and marched over to the floor-to-ceiling wall of windows. She drew the drapes closed with a sweeping gesture, shrouding the room once again in darkness. Emma had her answer. Surely the nasty woman wouldn't be so smug if she hadn't been given permission to behave so dictatorially by her boss.

"What is that *cagna* doing here?" Cristina asked angrily when she saw Mrs. Shaw pass the door. Emma didn't speak Italian, but she had a pretty good idea that calling someone a *cagna* wasn't a compliment.

"This is *his* home. I do what he asks me to do." Mrs. Shaw cast one last glare in Emma and Cristina's general vicinity and exited the suite.

Emma exhaled the breath she'd been holding. "She's gone," she told Cristina quietly as she stepped aside so that Margie could push Cristina into the bedroom. "Do you want the drapes opened?"

Was it fear or anger or wistfulness she saw flicker across her patient's lined face at the question? Emma couldn't be sure, but one thing was for certain.

This family had some serious secrets.

"My stepson is the owner of the Breakers, and I'm dependent upon his charity. His father and the courts have made that crystal clear. I'll live by his rules," Cristina replied flatly.

"Nevertheless, the choice is *yours*," Emma assured.

"I'm very tired after my shower," Cristina said after a pause.

"Say no more," Emma said calmly.

Cristina gave a regretful glance at the drawn curtains after she and Margie had transferred her to the bed from her wheelchair.

"I caught a glimpse of the sunlight from there in the bathroom. Was it a very beautiful day?" Cristina asked Emma in a gravelly voice when Margie left the room.

"One of those days where the sunlight hits the water and is absorbed by the air, and you feel like it's a living thing, it's so brilliant."

Cristina smiled. "I remember days like those on the Riviera, days reserved for the young and healthy," Cristina said as Emma straightened the bedding around her frail form.

"A day like today is as much yours as anyone's."

Disease hadn't entirely erased the slicing quality of Cristina's smile. "Only someone young and beautiful would be so foolish as to think that."

Emma arched her eyebrows at the thrust but didn't respond. Cristina had an edge to her, there was no doubt about it. Emma figured if she was in as much pain as Cristina was as cancer slowly ate away at her flesh and pride, she might be a tad testy, too.

She had recognized Cristina's forceful character during their initial meeting earlier in the day. "You're not going to preach to me, are you?" Cristina had queried archly at that meeting.

"Preach to you?" Emma had asked, taken aback.

"About heaven and hell and all the good things I've got ahead of me whenever *this* gives out in a few weeks or days or hours if I repent." She'd glanced scornfully at her wasted body. "Your predecessor tried to, and that's why she's gone."

"I've never liked being preached to," Emma replied. "I don't do anything to anyone else that I wouldn't like being done to me."

"That sounds like a religious answer," was Cristina's reply.

"No. It's a commonsense one."

That had earned her a small, appreciative grin, but Emma was aware that she was still on trial. She might be for the remainder of her patient's life. She'd grown used to the jury being hung on many occasions before.

Mrs. Shaw certainly has her opinions, doesn't she?" Emma said quietly to Margie a while later. They sat in a luxurious living room off the bedroom, Emma doing some paperwork while Margie sipped a Diet Coke. Margie worked a regular eight-to-five shift, while the registered nurses had been hired to provide twenty-four-hour care for Cristina. Emma covered the three-to-eleven shift, Monday through Friday. It would be a change of pace to have a regular weekday schedule. Margie had paused to chat with her for a few minutes before she left for the day.

"Mrs. Shaw is the devil's minion. How else is she supposed to act?" Margie asked, shrugging.

"Devil's minion?" Emma choked back laughter. "You mean the

stepson's?" She'd already learned from her briefing with the night nurse, Debbie Vega, that Cristina had no close family to speak of beside the stepson, and that the stepson preferred not to be involved in day-to-day care. What had occurred this afternoon with the phone call and the drapes seemed to go against the idea that Michael Montand was uninvolved, however. Every family and patient was unique, but this entire situation with the Montands was singular for New Horizon Hospice. Hospice nurses typically provided palliative care and comfort to the dying patient as well as support and education to family members. They were only in the home three to fifteen hours per week or so, depending on what the family needed. Cristina's stepson had insisted upon twenty-four-hour care from fully qualified hospice nurses, however. Emma suspected he must have made a sizable donation to New Horizon Hospice to make up for the highly unusual circumstances.

What's more, Michael Montand and his family were famous, although not for something familiar to Emma's world. She vaguely associated the name Montand with fast European sports cars and commercials featuring impossibly gorgeous men and women doing things like sipping champagne at red carpet events and then racing across scenic highways in a high-performance Montand car just in time to catch a departing yacht. Now that she'd seen his house, Emma thought it might fit in to one of the Montand company's glamorous commercials.

"I haven't seen Montand in the two weeks I've worked here. I hear he's very busy, but still . . ." Margie's voice trailed away. She glanced toward the partially open door to the bedroom, but there was no way the patient could hear even if she were awake. The suite took up the entire floor. The rooms were large and draped with luxurious fabrics and several large paintings. Emma could hear her patient, of course, from a one-way monitor perched on the desk. "The maid told me there's another reason for his absence as far as Cristina. According to all accounts, Montand hates her with a passion."

"Hates his stepmother? I suppose it wouldn't be the first time in history," Emma said with a grin. "He certainly provides top-quality care if he dislikes Cristina so much," she said, closing the chart and sitting back in the chair.

"The rumor is that he relishes seeing her sick and miserable. I've asked the other nurses. He's never once been here to visit her, either while I've been on duty or during any of the other nurses' shifts," Margie said significantly.

"That would seem to negate the rumor, wouldn't it?" Emma asked drolly. Margie was a little prone to gossip and sticking her nose in where she shouldn't in family dynamics. Working in the mansion of an elusive billionaire sports car magnate was bound to amplify her sense of drama. Emma had learned to keep perspective in every new home where she worked, however. She was there to do a job and ease suffering, not take sides in family feuds.

"I just mean if Montand never comes to see her, he can't be relishing the sight of her misery too much," Emma explained when Margie just gave her a blank, non-comprehending look.

Margie's dark brown eyes went wide. "You saw what happened today with the curtains," she hissed, glancing significantly at a video monitor on the desk that showed Cristina's motionless form sleeping in the bed.

"You know families often use surveillance cameras when a loved one is this sick."

Margie rolled her eyes and took a swig of her soda. "Montand probably has a screen set up in his bedroom and office and private plane. Sick bastard. He's glorying in every second of his stepmother's death while he eats chocolates and sips champagne in bed."

Emma chuckled. "You make him sound like a depressed *Dynasty* character."

"It's creepy, I'm telling you," Margie said firmly, glancing warily at the television monitor and Cristina's image again. "It's not at all like our normal assignments."

"Every family has different needs," Emma said in an attempt at rationality. She glanced around the lovely living room. "Besides, there are much, much more uncomfortable and unpleasant places to spend one's last days and hours," she said mildly. "He must be rich as a Rockefeller to have a house like this. Maybe he's too busy making money to visit his stepmother."

"He travels a lot for work. Not that he has to work, of course. From what the maid tells me, he inherited this car company from his father that makes these superfast French sports cars."

"I've heard of Montand cars. Very exclusive. Very *expensive*."

"And he'd already started his own company here in the States before his father died. They make racecars, or something like that. He's got like a couple dozen cars in this megahuge garage that he had dug into the bluff. It's like some kind of billionaire playground or museum. At least that's what Alice, the maid, tells me. She says Montand is hot as Hades, but all that sexy goodness is a waste, because he's a cold, scary bastard."

"So Alice is around him a lot?"

"*Never*," Margie whispered. "He's paranoid. He doesn't want anyone in his private chambers but that scarecrow, Mrs. Shaw. Those two are cut from the same cloth. The cook hardly ever sees him, either. Mrs. Shaw collects the food and serves him or him and his *guests*," Margie said with a pointed glance, "in the dining room."

Emma sighed. "Well, if this Montand guy holds any animosity for Cristina, he's doing us all a favor by steering clear. I'm only interested in him if Cristina wants to—or needs to—see him during her last days."

"That's why I believe in Alice's opinion that he's the devil," Margie insisted before noticing Emma's cautionary glance and nod toward the bedroom. She quieted her voice. "Cristina says her stepson is the last person on earth she wants to see."

Both women blinked when Emma's cell phone buzzed where it sat on the desk.

"The tech nerd?" Margie asked, grinning.

"Yeah," Emma said, reading the message from her boyfriend, Colin. "He says he's *so* smoking Amanda's butt at Modern Warlord."

Margie rolled her eyes and grabbed her purse. "They hang around together even when you're not around?"

"All the time. They're both video game–aholics," Emma replied, rapidly texting Colin back.

She glanced up and caught Margie's sharp glance. "And here I thought your sister was cool," Margie said before she headed for the door.

The next night, Emma sat in an upholstered chair near Cristina's bed and read out loud from a 1986 version of *Vogue*. Cristina had chosen the reading material, and then grinned the biggest smile Emma had seen on her yet when Emma discovered the article featuring Cristina. It turned out that Cristina had been quite the fashion maven in her day. She'd twice been declared one of the best-dressed women in the world. She had owned a posh, renowned secondhand designer retail store in downtown Kenilworth. Fashionistas from all over the world used to throng to her shop not only to buy one-of-a-kind, barely used designer shoes, handbags, and apparel, but also to empty out their own closets—presumably so they could be filled all over again.

"I love it," Emma said, setting aside the magazine and standing to pull down the covers. Cristina had broken out in a sweat while Emma'd read. Her regulatory mechanisms were going haywire. Poor woman was freezing one second, boiling the next. Emma picked up a cool, damp cloth and pressed it to Cristina's forehead and cheeks. "I can't imagine having wardrobes like those women must have owned."

"They were bored," Cristina rasped. "I was bored. What else did we have to do but recycle our wardrobes? We couldn't change our lives, so we changed our clothes . . . and our makeup and our hair. It didn't work, of course, but doing it made us forget that. For a little while. How much does my stepson pay you?" she suddenly asked sharply.

Emma blinked as she set down the cloth. "Your stepson doesn't pay me. The hospice does. Are you asking me my salary?" she clarified amusedly as she stripped off a soiled pillowcase.

"Yes. I suppose. How much do you make in a year?"

Emma stated a figure, inclined to respond candidly to a candid question.

"That's not much."

"Thanks for reminding me," Emma replied dryly.

"Still, you told me you're not married and you have no children. You have no excuse for dressing like a camp counselor every day." She peered closer at Emma's outfit. "A *boy* camp counselor, at that," Cristina added raggedly before she began to cough. Emma held up a cloth beneath her patient's mouth, laughing at the woman's parry. She understood Cristina's reference. Cristina had commented on Emma's attire yesterday when they were introduced—jeans, a fitted T-shirt, and her favorite pair of red high tops. Her hospice was pretty good about letting the staff wear whatever they wanted for work. Most of the nurses wore scrubs, but Emma preferred her own clothing.

Emma placed the cloth in the overflowing red plastic bag of dirty linens.

"I don't have any children, but I live with my little sister. She's going to medical school this fall," Emma explained, talking as though the coughing fit hadn't taken place.

"And you've been helping her get by?"

"Her brilliance and the scholarships have done that. Still, she lived with me while she's been in undergrad."

"You said your parents are both gone. So you've paid for your sister's food and keep and whatever else her scholarship hasn't provided—which I'm sure is plenty? You don't have to answer," Cristina said after a short pause. "I'm getting the make of you."

"And here I thought I was so complex and mysterious."

"Martyrs never are. *That's* the reason you dress like a drudge, a pretty girl like you," Cristina decided with an exhausted air of finality. Her breathing was coming easier now, but the coughing had tired her. "You don't think twice about things like fashion. You look down your nose at we women who do."

"You're wrong," Emma said, quite unoffended. She found Cristina's sharp wit engaging, and sensed Cristina respected her for it. "And your logic is faulty. You call me a martyr because I'm a walking fashion mistake and because of the job I do."

"Who else but a martyr would do this godforsaken job?" Cristina sparred without pause, even though her speech had begun to slur.

"A person who loves it, of course."

Cristina snorted. Emma finished changing the pillowcase and lifted Cristina's head gently, slipping the fresh pillow into place. She settled with a sigh. Emma began checking her patient's pulse.

"And in fact," Emma continued when she had finished, "I am as vain as any female *can* be that works too hard, owns a car that's been long overdue for work at the shop, not to mention a perpetually clogged kitchen sink, a water heater that thinks 'hot' means lukewarm, and a stack of bills that never seems to shrink. Which is to say, pretty damn vain, from what I've noticed. Desire grows from lack as much as overindulgence."

Cristina gurgled a laugh and studied her figure narrowly. "What size are you? A four?"

"What has that got to do with anything?" Emma wondered.

"We're the same size—or at least we once were—although you are a little taller. I've racks and racks of clothes in my closet over there," Cristina said, nodding weakly at a door in the distance. "You take them. I want you to have them all," she finished imperiously, her accent now so thick and her exhaustion so great, Emma barely understood her.

Emma placed her hand on her patient's cold, trembling one.

"No. But thank you for the generous thought, Cristina," she said softly.

She kept her hand in place and watched as the older woman succumbed to sleep.

The repairman left without fixing the washer," Emma told Debbie, the night nurse, after they greeted each other in the living room of the suite. Debbie had arrived for her shift early. "He said the part probably wouldn't get here until Friday."

"What a slacker," Debbie said disgustedly. "What are you doing?" the other nurse asked when Emma stuffed down the linen in the bag with a latex-glove-covered hand, removed the glove, and then tied off a tight knot.

"The wash."

"What? You're taking it home with you?"

"Not a chance," Emma said with a grin as she headed toward the door. "I don't even own a washer and dryer."

She noticed Debbie's stunned glance and correctly interpreted it.

"This is a *mansion*," Emma said, waving her hand in a circular "look at reality" gesture. "There has to be another washer and dryer here. Probably a couple."

"You can't just wander around this house!"

"We're out of clean linens," Emma said firmly. That said it all for her. How could anyone do adequate nursing without clean bedding, cloths, and towels? "You're here early tonight. Start your shift a little early, I'll go a little late, and you'll have clean laundry before I leave," she said reasonably.

"No, we'll wait. I remember when I started, Mrs. Ring said that Mr. Montand had provided everything we needed in the suite," she said, referring to their nurse supervisor. "He specified there was absolutely no reason for us to leave this level."

"Did he?" Emma asked as she walked away, heaving the sealed red plastic bag over her shoulder. "It looks as if he was wrong."

Chapter 2

She descended another flight of stairs, feeling a little unnerved despite her earlier show of confidence with Debbie. She glanced around uneasily, but there was no one to ask for assistance. Hadn't Margie mentioned several house staff worked here aside from Mrs. Shaw? Perhaps they were all day employees?

Being unlike any house she'd ever been in, the Breakers defied intuitive navigation. There weren't really hallways, Emma realized, only stairs that led from one cascading floor to another. So far she'd encountered a fantastical futuristic workout facility featuring a gym, racquetball court, an indoor lap pool, and a landscaped outdoor terrace. She could make out the steam rising on the large outdoor whirlpool through the glass doors as she tiptoed through the silent, sleek facility. There had been no washer or dryer in the locker room that she could find, but she had located a chute that appeared to be for soiled linen. She just needed to locate where that chute ended.

It certainly wasn't on the next level, which opened to a stunning suite that featured a gleaming bar, a waterfall fountain, an elaborate entertainment center, and deep upholstered chairs and couches. She spotted yet another outdoor space through a wall made completely of glass panes. Several examples of graceful, sensual marble sculpture caught Emma's eye in the room. One made her do a double take and draw nearer to study it. Heat rose in her cheeks when she recognized the sexual act being portrayed. She guiltily recalled her mundane task and resumed her mission.

The straps on the heavy laundry bag were starting to dig painfully into her shoulder. She arrived on another floor and hesitated. Unlike most of the spaces she'd seen, this one opened to a wide hallway that led to a partially open, carved wood door. A possibility, she thought, shifting the bag to her other shoulder and grimacing, although probably just wishful thinking on her part. She peered around the door and sagged in disappointment. No laundry facilities here or anything remotely potentially useful to her. Unlike the rest of the minimalist, airy décor in the mansion, this room was decorated in dark woods, leathers, and rich fabrics in shades of burgundy and dark green. A large Oriental carpet covered the wood floor. She started to back out of what appeared to be a luxurious, masculine office.

She halted.

A television monitor sat on the carved desk, a slight flickering in the turned black-and-white screen capturing her attention. She glanced around cautiously and eased into the room. An appealing scent tickled her nose: leather and the hint of men's cologne—sandalwood and citrus. She leaned over the desk in order to fully view the screen. She saw the image of her patient, Cristina, her mouth a black, jagged slash against her white face, rising from a nightmare as she would from the depths of sucking water. Emma almost heard her scream, although the monitor was silent. Debbie's shoulder and dark ponytail blocked the view of Cristina a moment later as she bent to assist. Margie's voice echoed in Emma's head.

He might have one of those screens set up in his bedroom or office or private plane, for all we know. He may be glorying in every second of his stepmother's death.

Apparently not *every* second, Emma thought, frowning at the empty chair behind the desk. She glanced curiously around the office one more time. There was something odd in this scenario. She watched as Debbie settled Cristina and moved to the periphery of the screen. The stark fear and pain still lingered on Cristina's sagging face.

". . . how pleased I was when you called earlier. Why didn't I hear from you sooner?"

Emma started in shock at the woman's distant voice. For a confused second, she thought the sound came from the video feed.

"You called me," a man replied. "And I was away. I told you that."

Footsteps.

Adrenaline poured into Emma's blood, making her limbs tingle. Someone was coming down the stairs from the upper level.

Her heart stalled. *Shit.* She was in a private suite. Not at the threshold, but in the *middle* of the room. The hospice staff had specifically been told to remain on Cristina's floor. She imagined fumbling a lame excuse to two total strangers about why she was lurking about next to this desk.

My ass is so *going to get fired!*

Her heart resumed beating with an uncomfortable leap. Emma lurched with it, her gaze traveling wildly across the large office. There was a massive closed door that she considered entering, but what if that led her into deeper trouble?

"Of course," she heard the woman say. "France and Italy this time. Isn't that what you said at dinner?"

"You know I said France and Monaco," the man replied, sounding too distracted or impatient to be sardonic at full strength. The woman's laughter made hot blood flood into Emma's brain and her skin prickle with a need to flee.

"I suppose you were on that floating playground of Niki's with all of his *floatable* playthings?"

"I told you that Niki is here in the States, testing the new car and helping me with plans for the Grand Prix. Oh, I see," he said coolly. "You did hear me. You're just testing me."

Any second now they'll walk in and see me standing here like an idiot.

Emma transformed into a wild thing, her single objective not to get caught. Her gaze landed on a tall, regal armoire with drawers at the bottom and a large, deep cupboard at the top. She opened the door, wincing at the uncontrollable clicking sound, and carefully placed the knotted plastic laundry bag into the bottom. Fully in the clutch of fear and panic, she sat on the bottom of the cupboard and pulled her legs in, knees against her chest. The sleeves and legs of some sort of garments brushed across her face before she plunged into the depths of them. Using the latch at the bottom of the door, she swung it shut just in time.

"What, exactly, do you think you'll accomplish by trying to trick me into revealing a lie?" the man asked with dark amusement, his voice just feet away now. A door closed briskly. Another ominous sound came—the snick of a lock.

They were in the same room now with Emma. Locked in. Her heart roared so loud in her ears, she was surprised the man—was it Michael Montand himself?—didn't immediately throw open the cupboard and yank her out, shouting blistering accusations.

And dammit, she hadn't yet fastened the cupboard door. She'd been afraid the clicking noise would betray her presence as they drew near. Her hand started to ache from holding the metal fastening, keeping the door closed all the way but not latched.

"I'm not trying to trip you up. How ridiculous. I just missed you, that's all. France and Monaco? I would guess some uncivilized place. You look like a savage," the woman said, her voice lowering to a purr. Emma fully recognized for the first time that she had a light, melodious French accent. In her mind's eye, Emma imagined her entering the man's arms. Touching him. "A beautiful savage. Do what you do to me. Turn me into a savage, too."

"Why must you always overplay things, Astrid?"

Emma blinked her eyes open into the pitch black. Had she imagined his vaguely frustrated tone? Despite her near full-blown panic, she experienced a strong urge to laugh. It'd been precisely what Emma had been thinking she'd like to tell the fawning woman.

"Why are you so mean?" Astrid asked, attempting to sound unconcerned and sexily playful, and very nearly succeeding. Emma had the impression Astrid had some serious experience with flirting and seduction, yet was aware she was falling short in this instance.

"You didn't call me because you want me to be nice."

"No," Astrid breathed after a pause. "You're even meaner than me, Vanni. And we both know how bad I am."

Vanni? *Who is Vanni?* The woman had pronounced it like *Donny* but with a *V*.

Was she *not* trapped in Montand's suite then? Was she eavesdropping on one of his guests or a family member? Emma wondered wildly.

"Are you sure you want to do this again?" he asked soberly, ignoring Astrid's provocative language. "I've told you what I can offer you. It's the same I can offer any woman. It isn't much."

"You might change your mind someday."

"Never."

A pregnant pause followed his steely reply.

"Then the sex is enough. *More* than enough," Astrid breathed. "Ah. I *knew* you'd missed me."

Emma's anxiety ratcheted up another notch when she heard a jingle of metal. A belt buckle being unfastened? She waited in dread. Was that the subtle sound of a zipper being lowered? *Shit, shit, shit.* How the hell had she gotten herself into this—*her*—hardworking, practical Emma Shore?

The man gave a low grunt. "I suppose if you must use your mouth for something . . .

He didn't sound aroused. He seemed . . . *what*? Irritated? Or was that dark amusement tingeing his voice? Forgetting her anxiety for a second, she leaned her head out of the hanging garments and moved closer to the door. It bothered her that she couldn't picture him. It suddenly struck her that in her brief tour of the Breakers, she'd never once seen personal or family photos. Perhaps he wasn't family, though. Astrid's outline was clear in her head, despite the fact that Emma had never seen her. It wasn't her true appearance that gave her shape, but the character Emma had sketched however loosely by listening to her syrupy seduction. The man remained cast in deep shadow, however, despite the frantic working of her imagination to draw him. Was he old? Young? Stern? Bored? She wished he'd speak again to give her another clue.

Instead, only a tense, billowing silence pounded in her brain. Just when she thought she'd go crazy from the quiet, Emma began to hear Astrid's moans. They were low, excited . . . muffled. There was no doubt about it. He was in her mouth. Her throat, if the occasional gagging sound was any evidence.

Another unwanted noise entered her awareness, a wet sucking sound. She could envision the movements of the woman's head as she plunged back and forth on the man's—Vanni's—cock, her imagination fed by the cadence and volume of Astrid's muted moans.

Against her will, her sex prickled with arousal.

Her cheeks scalding, Emma clamped her eyes shut as if doing so would shut off all her senses. She felt both guilty at her violation of the stranger's privacy during an intimate moment, but also violated herself in some way. An intense longing welled up in her to throw open the doors and quit the place—and screw her job *and* her pride.

But she couldn't burst in on *that*.

The minutes dragged by. The woman's moans were growing louder and more excited. The man was right. She *did* talk too much. Or moan too much. *Why didn't she just shut up?* She *was the one giving* him *oral sex, not the other way around.*

And why was he silent as the grave?

"Enough," he said quietly, and again, Emma wondered at how he'd said her private thoughts out loud. The skin on her neck and forearms prickled with wariness and anticipation. Not knowing what would happen next—not seeing—was driving her mad.

Astrid's soft gasps penetrated the panel of wood.

"Go into the bedroom and get undressed. Everything off," he said.

"But—"

"I'm not in the mood to be the audience tonight for your usual lingerie fashion show. We all know you're beautiful, Astrid. I'll join you in a few seconds," he said more quietly after a pause, as if he'd regretted his sharp interruption and weary sarcasm.

Astrid didn't respond. Was she miffed? If she was, she didn't voice it. Something hinted to Emma that restraint wasn't typical for her. Vanni was supremely confident, but Astrid seemed almost as used to getting what she wanted. Her behavior wasn't the norm, or at least not completely so. She was holding her temper.

For him.

The sound of a door opening breached her awareness. So . . . the large office was attached to his bedroom suite? Emma leaned as close to the door as she could. *What is he doing out there*? The sooner he joined his bedmate and they got down to it, she'd be able to escape this ludicrous situation. She didn't think she'd even be able to confess this fiasco to Amanda or Colin, it was so humiliating, and she told her sister and her boyfriend almost everything.

Yet she'd never had something so incendiary to tell.

A moment later, she heard a slight squeak on the wood floor and footsteps. His stride was long. Fluid. Unhurried.

"Come over here. I'm going to bind you onto the sliding track, then use the flogger on you," he said.

Emma's mouth dropped open.

"Anything you say." Astrid's reply was only diffident on the surface. Beneath it, there was a dripping greed and hunger that shocked Emma to the core.

Oh no. What kind of twisted, kinky scenario was this? And why didn't that degenerate Vanni shut the goddamn bedroom door?

Yet she *didn't* want him to. And that made this whole situation even more incendiary than she could measure.

She heard something that sounded like heavy metal being moved and arranged on the floor. Emma's muscles grew so tight, they began to ache dully. Her hand screamed in acute pain, however, protesting from holding the catch on the door so tautly. She longed to let go. Curiosity was a sharp internal prod. Did she dare to peek out and ascertain the couple's location in the bedroom? They could be yards away by now.

The sound of leather against flesh was the next thing that penetrated Emma's tense misery. *Oh Jesus.* They were close. Much closer than she'd imagined. It was almost as if they'd barely moved away from the door. Emma bit her lip in rising agony. Another cracking sound. In the pause that followed, she heard Astrid moan.

"Oh, that feels so good. Yes, *give* it to me."

"Quiet," he demanded. Again, the sharp sound of a lash striking flesh. Another. Astrid cried out sharply.

Emma couldn't take this anymore. She knew about S and M. Almost everybody did in this day and age. It'd become almost a cliché in modern society. References to it usually earned a smirk or eye roll from Emma.

But sitting here, experiencing the sounds of a woman willingly being flogged with the intent of sexual arousal, hearing the taut crack of leather against bare skin and Astrid's moans, feeling the inexplicable tension and electricity in the air . . .

. . . none of it felt *remotely* funny.

What was worse and far more humiliating? A thick, warm sensation had settled in her sex. What was wrong with her? She and Colin had shared a satisfactory sex life for the past two years, but intimacy with Colin had never inspired this intense, undeniable, *uncomfortable* arousal.

It was humiliating, what he was doing to her. Wasn't it? Given Astrid's obvious excitement, it was a little hard to label it.

She began to ease the door open, telling herself that she needed to look if she wanted to escape. She paused when the lashing sounds ceased as well.

"Oh God, Vanni. *C'est si bon*," Astrid said shakily. Emma swallowed thickly. He was touching her. Pleasuring her, somehow. It certainly sounded that way.

"I told you to stay quiet," he said, his patient tone in these circumstances confusing Emma.

Again, the crisp smack. The sound was starting to tear at her, leaving a resulting throb in her flesh. It was unbearable. At all costs, she needed to get out of here. Holding her breath and sending up a prayer, she eased open the cupboard door a tiny fraction of an inch. Cool air brushed against her hot face.

She paused, frozen for a moment in horror. She could *see* them. Or a slice of them, anyway. Not really *them*. The woman. She was *right there*, maybe fifteen feet away. Emma moved her head, holding her breath, trying to get a more complete picture through the cracked armoire door. Astrid was naked and on her hands and knees, kneeling and bound with black rope to a sort of T-bar. The bar rose from a metal rack that sat on the carpet. Astrid's hair was long and dark—nearly black, lustrous and curled in loose waves. It her position, it hung over her face. Her naked body was voluptuous, the sun-kissed, golden skin gleaming and flawless in the soft lamplight. She clearly sunbathed topless. Her bottom was pale next to her gilded skin, but there was no evidence of a tan line around her breasts. A dozen or so black leather tails landed on a curved buttock, making Emma jump. Astrid cried out sharply. It all looked so alien . . . so *deliberate*. Astrid's almost palpable arousal confused Emma even further.

Curiosity nudged her. She craned to see the man holding the flogger. He must have been kneeling behind the bound woman, but the door to the bedroom suite blocked her view of him. The flogger fell again, lashing voluptuous flesh. This time, Emma made out the masculine hand and forearm holding the leather handle so surely. The leather tails landed again, the sharp sound twining with Astrid's loud moan. Emma didn't think it was a harsh lashing, although Astrid's bottom was taking on a rosy hue.

Vanni paused, resting the hand that held the flogger on the top of a buttock. Emma saw his other hand moving, rubbing the other cheek, as if soothing the sting. She bit her lip hard. The vision had sent a sharp spike of forbidden arousal through her, shocking her. The large, masculine hand moved, caressing hips and ribs. She saw Astrid visibly tremble in pleasure beneath his touch. His hand caressed the pinkened buttocks again and then lowered between Astrid's legs. Astrid made a muffled sound in her throat. She opened her mouth.

"Control yourself," he warned quietly. "You know it pleases me more than your hysterics."

Astrid bit off a moan. Burning to know what Astrid was experiencing in these bizarre circumstances, Emma moved her view in the small opening of the door. Astrid had turned her head, causing her hair to spill from her face. Emma had never seen a more exquisite woman aside from her sister, Amanda. But it wasn't just her physical beauty that struck Emma. Her face radiated pure ecstasy. What in the world was Vanni doing to her to evoke that much pleasure? Her eyes were clamped shut. Her dark pink lips opened as if in slow motion. She began to keen, the piercing sound startling Emma. Her hips began to jerk back and forth in a frantic rhythm, her generous breasts bouncing at the motion.

"Fuck me, Vanni. Fuck me with your beautiful cock."

The flogger fell, harder this time. It struck again and again. Emma strangled a whimper. Astrid forced herself into immobility, but the radiant glow on her face only seemed to grow stronger.

The flogger continued to fall, as if in retaliation for Astrid's lack of control.

Emma couldn't take this anymore. She drew her arm across her midsection and replaced one hand with the other, relieving the tension in the aching muscles. She pulled the door shut and buried her hot cheeks against her upper arm, praying for it to be over, when she was free from this wretched moment . . . this excruciating tension. Her sex had grown achy and hot. She longed to touch herself to alleviate the pressure, but the knowledge that she was aroused in these circumstances was horrifying enough without adding to her transgressions. It wasn't just shameful arousal that she experienced, however, but a wild desire to flee, to escape this untenable situation.

She'd never felt so helpless in her life.

The sound of the flogger ceased every once in a while, and Astrid's wild moans of arousal grew louder and more desperate, piercing Emma's unarmored consciousness relentlessly. She no longer needed to see them to be inflicted by their actions. He was touching her during those moments, building her pleasure.

She hated them. She hated *him* for forcing her to endure this, although she knew in some distant part of her brain that it was no one's fault but her own.

Worst of all, she wanted to see more. She longed to see *him*.

"Please, please . . . fuck me," Astrid pleaded wildly.

Emma lifted her head cautiously when the lashing ceased, rugged cotton fabric brushing her cheek, afraid to breathe in the taut silence that followed. She heard a sound like a piece of metal being moved . . . a clamp released.

"Oh *yes*. Yes," Astrid moaned wildly a moment later.

"This isn't for you," he growled. He sounded annoyed. Intimidating, but also . . . *resigned*?

Why?

Emma felt like she'd burst from boiling emotion she couldn't quite name. Her mouth had gone dry. Her throat hurt, perhaps from holding in a silent scream of frustration and excitement for so long now.

Astrid moaned loudly, but it was his rough, more restrained groan that made her head jerk up like someone had called out to her—Emma—specifically. The garments rustled at her abrupt motion. There was a slight jingle as metal hangers shifted on the rack, but Emma was too anxious—too focused—to be alarmed.

What was happening? What was he doing? It was growing so hot in the cupboard. Her throat felt parched and achy.

A strange sound began to enter her ears . . . a sound like . . . *what*? Moving, gliding metal? She heard Astrid's familiar moans, louder now. She immediately recognized the other sound: skin slapping against skin in a taut, primitive rhythm. Heat rushed through her, the product of the strange marriage of humiliation and arousal she experienced. She didn't give herself permission to move. Suddenly the door was cracked again and she was peering through the opening.

She stared for several seconds, bewildered as to what she was seeing. Astrid's bound, naked body jerked back and forth on the metal track in a hard, pistonlike rhythm, the action completely out of her control. The lewd slapping sound Emma had recognized rung in the air, impossible to ignore . . .

. . . the sound of hard, ruthless fucking.

When understanding finally dawned, Emma bit her lip until she felt pain.

The deliberateness of what was happening, the precision, the sheer lewdness was shocking. Astrid still was on the metal rack in a position that was almost on all fours. Her knees perched on a padded bench, her wrists restrained to an elevated T-handled, padded bar. His large, open hands gripped her hips. His skin was darker than hers—a golden brown. She could see his thick, long thumb sinking into the pinkened flesh of a buttock. He flung her back and forth onto his cock with fluid, mechanical ease.

Emma recalled what he'd said about the glider. The mechanism must have been locked into immobility while he'd flogged her, but he'd unfastened it. The device had been designed for this, for the exclusive purpose of allowing him total control of a woman's body while he fucked her. Astrid would have glided back and forth on the frictionless track with a twitch of his hand. Instead, Vanni hammered her onto his cock. He switched his grip, grasping two metal handles attached to the kneeling bench. Astrid rocketed back and forth against him, screaming in uninhibited, frantic pleasure.

Time seemed to collapse for Emma, and yet the moment went on forever. She still couldn't really see him totally with the bedroom door blocking him, despite her straining, curious gaze. As their excitement grew and time wore on, however, he moved forward slightly. Her breath burned in her lungs as she soaked in the partial image of him. She glimpsed the front of trim, thrusting hips and a ridged, taut abdomen. She saw his muscular forearms and flashes of a large, glistening, driving cock. She couldn't even see his face, and yet . . .

He was so beautiful.

Chapter 3

The thought seemed to come from somewhere else. Emma herself was too disturbed and confused to have thought it. She was too rapt to judge her admiration of a man who made love with such cold, methodical precision.

How can you possibly call it cold when not only Astrid but also you *are boiling hot?*

She moved closer, spellbound, her nose touching the hard edge of the wood door. Cool air brushed against her scalding face. He wore a condom that glistened either from lubrication or Astrid's juices. The latter, most likely, given Astrid's frenzy of sexual excitement. He'd removed his shirt, but hadn't even fully removed his black pants, she realized. She could see just the front of his fabric-covered thighs. Daringly—hungrily—Emma opened the door slightly wider, then immediately eased it back, panicked when Astrid spoke.

"Please . . . *please* . . . may I come?" she pleaded shakily, air puffing out of her when Vanni slammed her onto his cock without interruption.

"Do whatever you want," he grated out, and again Emma sensed his razor-edged tone contrasted with a weary resignation. She almost heard what he didn't say. *What difference does it make to me what you do?*

What difference does anything make?

He strained forward slightly and Emma caught a glimpse of his flexing, powerful biceps. What was that on the one farthest away from her? A tattoo . . . a simple one, some kind of Japanese or Chinese symbols?

Astrid began to wail in climax, thrashing her head. He increased the pumping action to a wicked pace. Only a very strong man could have done it. His hands fisted the metal handles, biceps bulging, cock pounding like a well-oiled piston.

He fucked himself, masturbated using a woman's flesh. But wasn't Astrid doing the same, selfishly pleasuring herself using his? It was so wrong, so beyond Emma's experience, so shocking . . . so exciting.

Emma's chaotic thoughts were cut off when he suddenly flung his head forward and growled. It was the most thrilling sound she'd every heard. His hair tossed forward as well, blocking his face. It was brown with sun streaks of gold, beautiful and wild. It probably would hang several inches past his chin when he held his head upright. He grunted, his arm muscles flexing hard and huge, his body going rigid. Astrid's shrieks and cries dissolved into the roar in Emma's ears. A great shudder went through his powerful body.

He didn't move, breathe, or utter another sound while he came.

Neither did Emma as she stared openmouthed at this man—Vanni—locking down the detonation in his flesh.

Her panic and confusion evaporated. Her sex continued to ache dully. Emma switched hands again, alleviating the pain from holding the door closed, and slumped back in the dark cupboard. She should have still been wild with anxiety in the ensuing moments, but something inside her had altered upon seeing that incomplete, disturbing, and yet highly compelling image of him.

She lost track of time and the bizarre reality of her situation. A numbness settled on her.

Something had happened to her in that armoire, and she didn't know what it was.

She still listened to them. How could she not, as close as they were and knowing their movements prevented or allowed her escape?

After an immeasurable period of time, their more distant, sporadic murmuring quieted. The minutes dragged by without Emma hearing a sound. She finally dared to open the cupboard a half an inch and peer out cautiously. Not only was the bedroom dark, every light in the office had been extinguished. The only exception was the monitor on the desk. It cast a dim, bluish, ghostlike luminescence on the shadowed room. All was quiet.

Now. Go.

Just when she'd galvanized herself into action, she saw a tall shadow suddenly appear in the bedroom entrance—there and then gone. She jerked slightly, her breath hissing into her lungs at the sudden shock of seeing him. She'd rustled the garments in her surprise. Her limbs tingled when she heard the subtle metallic sound of the hangers moving on the rack above her. His footsteps slowed just feet from the armoire.

Oh my God, he heard me.

She waited, horror settling on her like a mist, tingling and burning her skin, but she didn't move. She didn't breathe.

A second or two later, she heard the muted sound of the lock being released on the door to the suite, and the knob turning.

No. He didn't hear me.

It'd been her oversensitive imagination.

The door closing behind him sounded hushed and mysterious, like a lover's secret whispered in the darkness.

His insomnia was growing worse. It didn't matter how much he threw himself into his work, or fiddled around in his workshop, or exercised, he couldn't quiet his brain anymore. Sex used to help him rest, too. But the sickly residue that seemed to be permeating his life was now ruining even that primal, fundamental aspect of his existence. Oh, he still felt the physical pleasure, but it was like he was enacting a parody of the sexual act these days while part of him seemed to watch his uninspired performance, disgusted and amused by his lameness.

Cynical and bored . . . tired, and not yet thirty-one years old.

He'd had high hopes that like his father, full depression wouldn't settle in until his forties. But in all fairness, his father hadn't known Cristina when he was eight years old like he had. That was when she'd entered their life like a poison. By most accounts, he was the champion survivor of the Montand family in the post-Cristina apocalyptic world.

Not that there was much victory in that.

He walked silently through the living room and passed the bar, recalling he'd left the brandy decanter in the dining room earlier. A moment later he shut out the lights and stood before the floor-to-ceiling windows with brandy snifter in hand, gazing at the wide body of water that he couldn't really see because of the cloaking night.

The darkness pressed on him. Called to him.

A strange prescience distracted him. The bare skin of his torso tingled and roughened. In the reflection of the windowpane he saw movement. He went utterly still.

His morbid thoughts vanished as he watched the girl ascend the stairs in the distance. What was she doing? Where had she *been*? He'd specifically asked that the nursing staff remain on Cristina's level, he thought irritably.

Her figure was so light, her feet were so quick, her tread so silent he might have been catching a glimpse of a fey creature making an escape. He watched her fly up the stairs, her red fairy pack flung over her shoulder. Curiosity and amusement replaced his brief flash of anger. Her back and shoulders were held very stiff and erect, as if to say that although she was fleeing, she was doing so proudly. Defiantly? Silently thumbing her nose at the mortal world?

His stiff mouth softened and flickered at his uncharacteristic fanciful thought.

She wasn't entirely fairylike. No, he'd recognized her just now from the back—that erect carriage, that enticing, graceful curve that led from a narrow waist to round hips. He hadn't noticed her today because he'd been overseeing some new equipment installation at his plant in Deerfield, but he'd seen her yesterday on Cristina's monitor. Just in passing . . . brief glimpses before she'd cheekily opened those curtains.

Emma Shore.

He'd asked Mrs. Shaw for the offender's name yesterday and recalled it now.

He'd thought her unconventionally pretty before she'd irritated him by yanking open those curtains. Interesting looking. Her golden-blond hair was fairly short and reminded him of the style flappers used to wear, boyish and highlighting the shape of her skull. It suggested a nonconformist spirit—or at least a female who wanted others to *think* she was different, anyway. It touched her collar in the back while the soft-looking waves in the front ideally framed a delicate, piquant face. He couldn't tell the color of her eyes on the monitor, but he'd noticed they looked large and dark next to her pale skin and hair. She had a tilt to her chin and a bright smile that went well together. Most people couldn't pull off brash sweetness, but she did. Somehow. Or at least that had been his quick impression.

He'd certainly thought that her face looked far too young and fresh to go with the lush, ripe firmness of her ass. Her figure was light and supple, the gracefulness of her movement capturing his attention.

Not that he'd been staring. She was just difficult not to notice on the screen, that's all. Any straight man would have looked twice. Any straight man with good taste would have looked more than that.

He'd follow her now and demand an explanation for her intrusion into his home.

He remained unmoving, however. She'd annoyed him, but her appearance had lightened him somehow as well, freshened him like a lungful of sea air after a night of debauchery.

He stared out at the black lake, lost in thoughts that, for once lately, weren't bitter and morose.

Chapter 4

At the end of her shift the next night, Emma entered the bedroom to say good-bye to Cristina. Her patient had fallen asleep while Emma gave her report to Debbie, the night nurse. Emma paused next to the bed. Cristina looked even more shrunken than usual, her skin like dry, gray parchment stretched too tight over bone. A hospice nurse's main goal was to make the last days of her patient's life as comfortable and fulfilling as possible. Finding out what that meant for Cristina was proving to be a challenge for Emma. She sensed Cristina's soul was heavy. Shedding that weight—even a little—might help ease her passage from this world.

"Night, Cristina. Sleep easy," Emma whispered before she turned to leave the hushed room.

"It's your own fault. You knew what I was capable of and what I wasn't. *You* were capable of even less."

Emma blinked and spun around at the death-rattle voice.

"Cristina?" she whispered, confused to see that her patient hadn't moved from her sleeping position. She turned to go again after a pause. Cristina was having increasingly disturbed sleep, nightmares, and occasional hallucinations.

"It was too much for me. Not only one, but *two*! You knew as well as I do I wasn't cut out for it. So you found yourself a martyr. Is it my fault she died? And then you had the nerve to think I'd transform into *her* overnight and replace her, you bastard!"

Emma started at the venomous shriek. She hurried toward Cristina, who was now jerking and tossing on the bed, her mouth bared in a snarl, arms flailing.

"I've got her," Debbie said, appearing by Emma's side as Emma gently restrained the swinging arms and spoke in firm, soothing tones, calling Cristina back to the waking world.

"I think she's okay," Emma said after a moment when Cristina began to quiet and settle. Still, the invisible threads of her patient's nightmare seemed to brush against Emma . . . cling to her.

She waited until Cristina settled fully into sleep before she walked out of the bedroom and retrieved her purse. She noticed the stack of clean towels on a small table.

The vision triggered the memory of wandering around the house last night, of being trapped in that armoire. *Lots* of things triggered that memory. *Almost everything, in fact*, Emma reminded herself grimly as she searched for her keys in her purse. She'd finally escaped from that miserable experience and found her car, the laundry bag still slung over her shoulder like an inexplicable artifact she'd brought from another world.

She'd witnessed a lot of grief in her life, and understood the complexities and paradoxes of loss. Death transformed the living. It changed them, whether they wanted it to or not.

She'd been changed somehow last night, breathing the singular male scent that clung to the garments hung in the armoire, listening to the sounds of sexual excitement ringing in her ears. She'd been altered, but not by death, by something she found far more disturbing. The whole strange incident had upset her in a way she couldn't name. Something had rocked her comfortable world, and she resented the man—irrationally, she knew—for that earthquake.

She hadn't wanted Colin to touch her this morning when he'd stopped by before catching his train for work, a fact that bewildered her almost as much as it had Colin. She hadn't seen him since Saturday night, after all. Sure, their physical relationship had mellowed lately—and it had never been firework explosive since they'd started sleeping together two years ago—but she'd normally be glad to see Colin and eager to express her affection.

As a means of punishing herself for her odd behavior and her inability to shut off her brain in regard to the man at the Breakers and his perversities, she'd sentenced herself to labor. She'd gone to the Laundromat this morning, one of her most hated errands, and finished what she hadn't last night.

It'd been hard to return to the Breakers today following the "armoire incident," as she'd taken to calling it in the privacy of her mind. Once she was there, however, burying herself in work helped, like it always did. She hadn't slept well after she'd returned home last night. As good and exhausted as she was, all she could think about was dreamless, deep sleep, a rest blessedly devoid of the disturbing image of that man—Vanni—locking down his climax as though he thought he didn't deserve the pleasure.

Who was he? One of Montand's guests? A relative?

She constantly found her mind wandering, taking little imaginary excursions through the mansion, seeking him out. Was he in the mansion at the same time as her? What was he doing? She'd asked Margie this afternoon in a deliberately offhand manner if there were any other inhabitants of the house beside Montand. Margie had told her only Michael Montand lived there on a full-time basis—although he was currently away, to her knowledge—while Mrs. Shaw, two maids, a gardener, and the cook were day help. Alice, the maid, had told Margie that Montand was known to have guests there, though. Occasionally he threw lavish house parties, which affluent guests from all over the world attended.

Who was Vanni then, and how was he related to Montand? Or perhaps her original suspicion was right, and they were one and the same man?

No. They couldn't be. That didn't make any sense.

Stop thinking about him. He was cold and heartless about something that should have been intimate. He was a sick, strange man.

No, another voice in her head argued.

He was suffering. And something about him had called out to her . . .

A good night's sleep would end her stupid obsessions. She flung her purse over her shoulder and started for the exit. She came to a sudden halt and gasped.

"Oh my God, you startled me," Emma said to Mrs. Shaw, who stood in the entryway to the suite, unmoving.

"I've come to get you. Mr. Montand would like a word," she said unsmilingly.

Her mouth fell open. "With . . . with *me*? Mr. Montand? Why?"

"He didn't tell me his reasons, but I assume it's about your work here. He's very particular in regard to his stepmother's care," Mrs. Shaw said with a tiny smug smile.

"I see," Emma said, even though she didn't. To her knowledge, Montand had never spoken to any of the nursing staff individually. His expectations had been discussed with Dr. Claridge, who was the hospice doctor, and Monica Ring, the nurse supervisor. A flicker of anxiety went through her. What if this request was somehow associated with the armoire incident? Was she about to be called out or accused? Her heart started to beat uncomfortably in her chest.

There was only one way to find out.

"Okay. I'm ready," she said briskly, hitching her purse higher on her shoulder.

She followed a silent Mrs. Shaw down the hushed staircase, past the lavish workout facility and indoor pool, her heartbeat pounding louder in her ears with every step. Mrs. Shaw left the staircase behind on the next level. She led Emma into the luxurious living room she'd seen last night, the lush ivory carpeting hushing their footsteps. Emma could almost feel the housekeeper's disapproval and dislike emanating from her thin, stiff figure.

Mrs. Shaw paused before a door and swung it open.

"Ms. Shore is here," she said to someone in the room.

She stepped aside and gave Emma a glance of loathing before nodding significantly toward the interior. Her heart now lodged at the base of her throat, Emma stepped past Mrs. Shaw into the interior of the room. She had a brief, but vivid impression of a stunning dining room consisting almost entirely of black, white, and crystal. A huge white modernist china cabinet and wet bar structure dominated the wall closest to her. The long, grand dining room table was made of African blackwood and was surrounded by more than a dozen handsome blackwood and white-upholstered chairs. Two large crystal chandeliers hung above the table. The far wall consisted of warm brick in beige and reddish tones, offsetting the cool luxury and sleek lines of the room. On the brick wall hung a large painting that she recognized in a dazed sort of way was a modernist depiction of an engine.

She heard the door shut and glanced over her shoulder. Mrs. Shaw was gone.

Emma turned back to the single inhabitant of the room. He sat at the head of the table turned toward the glass wall that faced Lake Michigan. For a few seconds, she just stood there, speechless. He matched the room in almost every way. He wore a black tuxedo with careless elegance. His brown hair was not cut short, necessarily, but it wasn't long, either. A woman could easily fill a hand with the glory of it. It was thick and wavy and had been combed back from his face. A dark, very short goatee seemed to highlight a sensual mouth. He was all precision lines and bold masculinity: an angular jaw, broad shoulders, handsome Grecian nose. The only way he didn't match the immaculate, stunning room was the way his tie was loosened and the top collar of his white dress shirt unbuttoned at his throat.

He was even better looking than the actors hired to drive cars and drink champagne for his company commercials. Impossible.

"Well don't just stand there," he said, just a hint of impatience in his tone. He set down the fork he'd been holding on to a plate. Emma blinked. It hadn't even registered immediately that he'd been eating, she'd been so captivated by the image of him. "Come here," he prompted when she remained frozen.

She stepped forward, a surreal feeling pervading her. As she drew nearer, she realized that his eyes were the same color of the lake on a sunny day—a startling blue-green. The lake would serve to soften and warm the cool, sharp lines of the beautiful, austere dining room during the day. This man's eyes, however, would soften nothing. They seemed to lance straight through her.

His firm, sensual mouth quirked slightly.

"Why are you looking at me like that?" he demanded quietly.

"Am I looking at you a certain way?" Emma asked, surprised and set off balance by his question. "I hadn't realized," she fumbled. She yanked her gaze off his compelling visage and glanced around the room, wide-eyed. "I've never seen a room like this. It was a little like walking into a photo from a magazine or something." *Especially with you sitting at the end of that grand table in that tux.*

She looked at him when he laughed mirthlessly. "Cold and uncomfortable, you mean. I'll be sure to pass on your compliments to my architect and interior designer."

She matched his stare. "That's not what I meant."

He frowned slightly but didn't respond. Nor did he look away. "You're Michael Montand?" she prodded in the uncomfortable silence that followed.

He nodded once and glanced at the chair nearest to him. "Have a seat. Can I get you anything to eat or drink?"

"Would you mind telling me why you asked me here first?"

His eyebrows arched in mild surprise. They were a shade darker than the hair on his head and created a striking contrast to his light eyes. Clearly, she was just supposed to follow his command without comment.

"You're taking care of my stepmother. Surely you don't think it odd that a family member would want to speak with you about your work," he said.

"You haven't called anyone else from the nursing staff down here."

"Nobody else has directly disobeyed my orders."

She swallowed thickly at the ringing authority in his tone. Her heartbeat began to roar so loudly in her ears, she wouldn't be surprised at all if he heard the guilty tattoo. What could she say that wouldn't betray what she'd accidentally seen last night? Had that man—Vanni—told Montand something?

Was *he* Vanni? she wondered wildly. No, Vanni wasn't a nickname for Michael. Plus, the man she'd partially seen last night had long hair and it had been lighter, with gold streaks in it. She opened her mouth to utter some feeble excuse—she had no idea what—but he cut her off.

"It may seem random to you that I asked for the drapes to remain closed in my stepmother's suite, but I can assure you that I did so with a reason."

"I can explain . . . *What*?" she halted her pressured confession.

He gave her a nonplussed glance.

"The drapes," he repeated.

Relief swept through her. He'd meant the drape incident, not the armoire one.

"What did you think I was going to say?" he asked, eyes narrowing on her.

"I wasn't thinking anything," she lied. "Of course I'll respect your wishes about the drapes."

"I'd appreciate if you respected my wishes in regard to everything I have specified with your supervisor."

She held her breath for a split second. Had he emphasized the word *everything*, or was that her panicked brain jumping to conclusions?

"Of course," she managed.

He nodded once and then picked up his fork. Emma had the distinct impression that she'd been dismissed. She wavered on her feet.

"It's just that the sunshine . . . it might do Cristina some good."

He regarded her with glacial incredulity. Emma felt herself withering from the sheer chill.

"It's such a beautiful view. I see no reason to deprive her of it," Emma rallied despite his intimidating stare.

He set down his fork, the clanging sound of heavy silver against fine china startling her. He sat back in his chair. He possessed a lean, muscular . . . phenomenal frame, from what she could see of it. Clearly, he hadn't built that elaborate workout facility for show. Emma wasn't sure what to do with herself in the strained, billowing silence that followed.

"It may be beautiful to you," he said finally.

"It's not to you?" she asked, bewildered. "Why did you have this house built then? The view dominates every room." *At least when you're not in it, it does.*

One look at his frozen features and she knew she'd gone too far. His gaze dipped suddenly, skimming her body. If another man had done it, she would have been offended. In Michael Montand's case, it was like a mild electrical current passed through her. Her nipples tightened and something seemed to prickle in her belly, like a hook of sensation pulling at her navel. She shifted uncomfortably on her feet, her wisp of confidence evaporating.

"I didn't say it wasn't beautiful to me," he said. He glanced away and Emma knew she'd imagined that flash of heat in his eyes. He seemed to hesitate. "How is she doing?"

"Cristina?"

He nodded once and picked up a roll from a basket. Emma noticed he possessed strong-looking hands with long, blunt-tipped fingers.

"She's in a great deal of pain. It's getting worse. I've asked the doctor to increase her pain medications."

He looked up sharply.

"It's not uncommon, as the cancer spreads," Emma said, reading his glance of unease.

"Won't increasing her pain medication make her more confused?"

"Possibly. But it's better than forcing her to suffer. She's living the last days of her life. We're not talking about a headache here. This is severe, mind-numbing pain. When she's in the midst of it, she's not very cognitively sharp anyway. None of us would be," Emma said pointedly.

They stared at each other for a few seconds. Again his gaze dropped over her, so fleeting it might have been her imagination.

"Why do you dress that way for work?" he asked, returning to the task of buttering a roll.

Her mouth fell open. "I like to be comfortable. My hospice doesn't have an issue with it. Do you?"

He began slicing a filet of beef, his gaze averted from her. When he didn't reply for a moment, her anxiety ratcheted up, but it was accompanied by a spike of defiance. "Is it not *formal* enough for you?" she asked, as if determined to dig her own grave. He looked up, and she glanced down significantly over his tuxedo-clad form.

He gave a small, unexpected smile, white teeth flashing against tanned skin. Her heart paused.

"You're wondering if I put on a tuxedo to dine alone near midnight as a custom?" He raised his fork to his mouth and took a swift bite of beef, watching her as he chewed. Emma became highly aware of the movement of his lean, angular jaw and then the convulsion of his strong-looking throat framed by the stark white, open collar as he swallowed. He reached for a crystal goblet of red wine. "That would be pretty pitiful on my part if I did, wouldn't it?" he asked before taking a swallow of wine. Emma heard the thread of humor in his voice and didn't know how to reply.

"I just meant—"

"I know what you meant. And no, I'm not a formality hound. I just came from a public relations event in the city sponsored by my company. I didn't get hungry until now. I always lose my appetite at those things. All those cameras. All those vampires," he added distractedly. He took another bite of beef, and for a moment, Emma wondered if he'd forgotten she was there. "I didn't mean that I object to your clothing," he said quietly after a pause. "I just asked because I noticed it was different than the other nurses'."

His words seemed to hang in the air. *I noticed.* There was only one way he could have noticed since he never visited Cristina's suite. He'd taken notice of her on the surveillance camera. Maybe his thoughts went in a similar direction, because his expression suddenly grew sharp and then went carefully blank.

"I thought it might relate to your age," he said, picking up his knife. "You seem much younger than the others."

"You thought my dressing habits related to my age? Or my difficulty in not following your instructions did?"

"Both."

Her back stiffened at that. "I'm twenty-three."

His succinct nod seemed to say, *well it all makes sense then.* Irritation shot through her.

"You're not *that* much older," she said impulsively. The cool glance he gave her revealed she was mistaken; it made her feel about twelve years old. What she'd said was technically true. He didn't look much older than his early thirties or so, but he *seemed* decades older. Maybe her blurting out those words was her desperate attempt to even the playing field.

He took another bite of meat. "I'm thirty," he said with infuriating calmness after a pause. "And years are one thing. Experience another."

"I have a master's degree in palliative and hospice nursing. I'm very well qualified to take care of your stepmother. And I have *plenty* of experience," she defended.

That small smile quirked his lips again. "How did you manage all that in twenty-three years?"

She hesitated, frowning. She realized she was being defensive, but his aloof contempt annoyed her. "I have a late birthday. Plus

I did my bachelor's degree in three years," she mumbled, already regretting her outburst. Despite her flash of annoyance at his small, patronizing grin, the thought struck her that he had a very sexy mouth. He gave a small shrug.

"Even if you weren't as experienced as you are I wouldn't complain. You're very good with my stepmother. She likes you." He shot her a hard—or was it bitter?—glance. "And that's rare. Please just follow my instructions from now on," he said after a moment, picking up his water glass.

"I will," Emma said shakily. She wasn't sure what had gotten into her, to respond so defensively with a patient's family member. She normally let criticisms or suspicions in regard to her youthful appearance slide right off her. Her work always ended up being a testament to her worth.

"Good night," he said.

"Good night," she said under her breath.

Despite the fact that he'd been looking at his plate when he dismissed her, the prickly sensation on her back gave her the distinct impression his gaze was on her as she left the room.

After her shift the next night she exited the Breakers and walked out into a warm July evening. There were no stars or moonshine, and the air felt close. She inhaled deeply before she climbed into her Ford Focus, smelling rain. Heat lightning flickered on the distant western horizon. How fantastic would it be, to live here and be able to take a midnight swim on a humid night like this before a storm broke, to wash away the residue of the day in the cold, refreshing water?

The thought triggered an uncontrollable vision of slipping into that lovely pool that overlooked the lake and swimming toward the near-naked, sexy form of Michael Montand.

Get a grip.

Her fantasies were getting out of hand lately, she realized with disgust as she dug around in her purse for her keys. Her dreams, which had been dark and disturbingly erotic for the past few nights, were just plain out of control. Nor were they making for a restful night's sleep. She twisted the key in the ignition.

Nothing happened. She turned the key again.

"Oh no. Not tonight. *Start*, you bitch," she hissed heatedly. Her car seemed unimpressed by her cursing, however. Emma imagined it silently flipping her off for not having it serviced for months on end.

Sensing defeat, she placed her forehead on the steering wheel and sighed in intense frustration.

It was almost eleven thirty. Colin had been exhausted all week. He'd said on the phone earlier that he was determined to get to bed early tonight. He still hadn't gotten used to waking at six a.m. to catch a train into Chicago for his new job as a forensic science technician. Amanda didn't have a car. She took mass transportation almost everywhere, including to school and to her job as a waitress.

She'd just have to wake up Colin, she realized, feeling guilty not only for that, but the fact that she'd been so irritable and standoffish with him yesterday morning. Well, there was no help for it. She reached for her phone and started to dial.

Her head sprung up when someone tapped on her window.

"What's wrong?" came his muffled voice.

She stared in openmouthed surprise at the dark shadow of a stooping figure outside.

"Are you okay?" he demanded.

"Uh . . . yeah," she replied. Her already warm cheeks heated when she realized he probably couldn't hear her. She peered out the window, trying to see him better. The only source of illumination was a few lights in the house that were left on, but those were distant and filtered through tall trees.

It was *him*. Michael Montand.

Wasn't it?

She opened her car door a crack. The interior lights didn't turn on.

"My car won't start," she explained without getting out.

"Get out and I'll have a look," he said matter-of-factly.

She squinted, realizing he wore some kind of gray utility coveralls, like something a mechanic would wear. The garment stood in stark contrast to the tuxedo she'd seen him in last night, confusing her. She set aside her phone, unbuckled her seat belt, and got out of her car. He'd straightened. She realized he was very tall, maybe seven or eight inches past her five foot seven inches. Flustered, she moved aside as he strode past her with a single-minded purpose. He sat in the car, immediately moving the seat back to accommodate long, bent legs, the action practiced and smooth.

"Your battery is dead as a doornail," he said after only a second.

"I have jumper cables somewhere . . ." She faded off when he rose out of the car.

"I'll set you up," he said, his deep voice striking her as slightly different than last night. It was still cool and brisk, but tonight his utter confidence reassured her.

"Oh . . . that's . . . okay, thanks," she fumbled when she realized he wasn't even listening to her as he started toward the house. His booted feet scraped against the concrete when he came to an abrupt halt. She squinted, trying to put form to his shadow. It was *definitely* Montand. She could just make out the outline of his broad shoulders and singular, bold profile against the night sky.

"It'll only take five or ten minutes," he said. "This is the garage level, all my stuff is right here. Do you want to go back into Cristina's suite and wait?"

"Do you need help?" she asked, feeling like an inadequate, ditzy female, a feeling she resisted wholeheartedly.

"No." There was a short pause. "But you can come with me, I guess. You shouldn't stand out here in the dark alone."

Great. She either sounded like a helpless ditz or like she was afraid of the dark. *Like it matters.* She shut the car door with a brisk bang. "Lead the way."

Did he hesitate for an instant? More than likely, he thought she'd just get in his way. He was probably right, but she didn't want to just stand there in the driveway like a useless idiot, anticipating the moment when he returned.

She followed him to a tucked-away, secluded entrance shrouded by trees and shrubs that she'd never before noticed on her arrivals for work. No one would ever find the door if they didn't realize it was there. He fleetly entered five numbers on a lit keypad and they entered.

"Wow," she breathed, staring around wide-eyed after they'd exited a long mudroom.

He'd led her to a garage that was the size of a warehouse. She counted twenty gleaming cars lined up, ten in two rows—everything from shining antiques to luxury, high-performance sports cars to sophisticated sedans to road hugging, fleet-looking racecars. There was a hydraulic mechanism for lifting the vehicles so they could be serviced. The car pulled to the front, a shiny black one that looked like it came from the 1920s, had its hood up, the engine exposed.

Montand turned.

"Oh—"

"What?" he asked sharply when she cut herself off, coming to a halt. He took a step toward her, eyes narrowing.

Emma shut her stupid, gaping mouth, but couldn't stop staring. She'd forgotten the impact of him. The cloak of darkness and the coveralls and his solicitous manner out there in the drive had made her forget. Somehow, the more casual clothing, oil-smudged hands, and a dark scruff on his lean jaw seemed even more devastating than the vision of him in a tux. He seemed more comfortable tonight. More *approachable*. And that was a dangerous thought to have about a man like Michael Montand.

"Nothing. You just look so . . . natural that way," she finished lamely, nodding at the coveralls. For a few charged seconds, he just continued to study her with that X ray stare.

"No reason I shouldn't. I'm more comfortable under the hood of the car or working on engines than I am in a boardroom," he said before he turned and walked toward the far side of the garage.

She followed him across the concrete floor, studying him curiously while he wasn't looking. He seemed younger today. Or maybe he didn't. It was difficult to categorize him.

His hair was worn more casually tonight, rippling back from his face in finger-combed negligence. In the front, a few long bangs had fallen forward, parenthesizing his striking eyes. The style, in combination with the dark scruff on his jaw, contributed to a sense of effortless sexiness. So did the easy, graceful saunter of his long, male body and the subtle glide of his hips. She hastily admired broad shoulders, a strong-looking back, and a trim waist. The coveralls were somewhat baggy, but even so, his butt looked just as good as everything else—

A metal clanging sound started her from her uncharacteristic lechery. He'd moved aside a tool on a table.

"This garage is huge. It's cut into the bluff?" she asked, mentally cursing the high-pitched sound of her voice. He had an unprecedented effect on her, one that she needed to try to minimize at all costs. She was way out of Michael Montand's league. He was megarich, powerful, world-weary . . . sexy as hell. He could have any woman he wanted. Emma wasn't sure she was even interested in *being* in his league.

He stood before a utility table and a wall hung with various tools, his back to her. "Yeah. A lot of the house is dug into the earth, but the garage most deeply. Keeps it nice and cool in the summers, warm in the winter. Good for working in here."

"So you like working on cars?" she asked, gazing back at the magnificent collection.

He nodded. "I like taking them apart and putting them back together, designing new parts. I have since I was kid. It's kind of hard not to know and like the ins and outs of cars in my family," he mumbled as he unceremoniously shoved aside more implements on the worktable and lifted some coiled jumper cables.

"You own a car company that makes racecars, isn't that right?"

He shook his head. "No. My company makes certain key parts for racecars and sports cars, not the cars themselves."

"But your father owned a French car company?"

He cast her a sharp sideways glance, and she realized how many questions she was asking him.

"To whom have you been talking about me?"

"Just some of the nursing staff."

"What else did they say?" he asked, turning toward her, looking mildly interested.

"Nothing much," she said, striving for an offhand manner. "Someone just mentioned in passing you and your father both were in the car business. Besides, almost everyone has seen Montand commercials. They're famous."

She squirmed a little while he studied her for a moment. Finally he nodded, and she disguised her exhale of relief.

"My father founded Automobiles Montand." Just the way he said the company name with such an effortless accent made her suspect he probably spoke French.

"Were you born here? In the States?"

"I've lived in Kenilworth my whole life, but I've spent a lot of time in France with my dad's family. My dad was born in Antibes and started his company there; my mom's family was from New York. I have a dual citizenship with the US and France."

"Are they both gone?" she asked softly.

His eyes flashed. For a few seconds, the aloof prince sitting at the end of that table last night had returned. Then his irritation seemed to fade to slight puzzlement as he stared at her. "Yes," he replied after a moment.

"Mine, too."

He blinked. "Really?"

"Well, not in the way you meant," she admitted. "My mom passed three years ago from breast cancer. When I say my father's gone, I mean he's nowhere I know of. He may be dead, for all we know. He left when I was five."

"He abandoned you?" Montand asked, his forehead crinkling into a scowl.

She nodded. "Gone for good. I don't recall much about him. You don't miss much what you never had," she said, following him.

"Lucky you," she thought she heard him mutter under his breath. What had he meant by that? Had he, too, been abandoned by someone in his life? "What about the rest of your family?" he asked.

"It's always been my mom, my sister, and me."

"Is your sister still around?" he asked, turning his head as he walked.

"Yes, we live together."

He stopped and turned abruptly. Emma started and pulled to a halt to prevent from running into him.

"So you're not married?"

She inhaled sharply. "No."

"What were you planning on doing out there?"

"Do? *When*?" Emma asked. It didn't help her bewilderment that she was looking him full in the face again, especially since this time she was closer to him. He was good-looking—*extremely*, the most effortlessly handsome man she'd seen in her life—but it wasn't his handsomeness that was setting her off balance. Or at least she didn't think so. She'd never been that shallow or giddy in the past around a good-looking guy. It was his eyes. She couldn't stop herself from looking straight into them even though doing it made her feel lightheaded, like the air pressure had just changed drastically. The light, iridescent color of them contrasted appealingly with arched, thick eyebrows, eyelashes, and short sideburns.

"Before I showed up," he explained. "Were you going to call someone for help with the car?"

She whipped her brain into focusing. "Oh . . . yeah," she said, realizing he must have seen her phone in her hand as she sat in the car earlier. "I was."

"Who?"

She stared, tongue-tied.

"Roadside assistance?" he prompted, leaning his head down slightly. On her anxious inhale, she thought she caught a scent of him—a subtle waft of spicy aftershave and the residue of peppermint chewing gum and . . . motor oil?

"Your sister? Your boyfriend?" he prodded pointedly.

"My boyfriend," Emma admitted in a croaking voice, stepping away from him. The word had never felt so hollow for her. She cleared her throat, struggling for her composure. Of course the word *boyfriend* wasn't meaningless. It meant Colin, a living, breathing, wonderful guy. "I was feeling guilty about it, actually, because Colin—that's his name—has been especially tired lately. New job and all. Hasn't gotten used to the schedule yet."

He didn't reply to her rambling. His angular, whiskered jaw worked in a subtle circular motion in the uncomfortable silence that followed. His thin goatee looked very sleek, the way it encircled his mouth distracting her. How could his lips look so hard and firm, and yet so soft and shapely at the same time?

He turned and walked away.

"Get in," he said gruffly, nodding toward a shiny little dark blue roadster that probably cost ten times as much as Emma made in a year. It was a convertible. A strange feeling fluttered in her stomach as she peered inside the dream car, seeing supple caramel-colored leather seats.

She got in. She glanced sideways as he got in on the driver's side, holding her breath for some reason. His large body fit into the small confines of the car like a puzzle piece sliding home. Had the space been made specifically for him?

He twisted his wrist, and the car hummed to life. She continued to hold her breath as the engine vibrated into her body, the feeling smooth and restrained, but undeniably powerful. He twisted the wheel hard. A thrill coursed through when they surged forward in the path between the two cars.

Montand must have touched some switch, because two large metal doors eased back, creating an opening in the bluff. They zoomed onto a dark drive. This road ran parallel from the one her car was parked on, Emma realized. They had to travel down it before it met up with the other road.

A minute later he deftly maneuvered the sports car next to her vehicle and applied the brake. He popped the hood and flipped open the car door in preparation to get out, at first not noticing her wide-eyed, stunned state in the passenger seat. His head turned when she didn't move. He did a double take.

"You *really* know how to drive," burst out of her throat. Her laugh rang out into the humid air. She couldn't help it, even when he gave her a slightly bewildered glance. He seemed to have no hint of how exciting even that short ride had been for her—the plunge into the dark night, the powerful car . . . his effortless handling of it. She hastened to explain her strange behavior. "I've never been inside a car like this. It's *amazing*. What kind is it?"

"A 750 XG."

"Is it a Montand car?"

He nodded.

"Did you have anything to do with designing it?" she asked, glancing around with admiration at the swift, badass little car.

"Yes." He leaned forward slightly, hands gripping the wheel, looking at her as if he'd never seen a female in his life. The overhead lights had come on when he'd opened his door, allowing her to see his lips curve slowly into a smile. It wasn't the grim one she'd seen on him in the past. This grin unsettled her even more than his former mirthless one had.

"Do you know much about cars?" he asked.

"Nothing, really," she managed to get out despite that deadly smile of his. "But you really don't have to know much to appreciate it, do you? You can feel it."

His smile faded. "What do you feel?"

She swallowed thickly, suddenly very aware of his stare on her face.

"It's like it's alive. It's like . . . riding a creature or something."

"It's true," he said soberly after a taut moment. "A car like this can be dangerous. The power of it can go straight to your head. If you don't watch it, you can find yourself doing something stupid."

Something flickered in her belly like a dozen moths trying to escape a rising flame.

"You sound like you're speaking from experience."

His sensual lips twisted slightly. "I've had some experience with fast cars."

Disappointment went through her when he pushed back his door. She blinked guiltily, hastening to follow him out of the car. What was wrong with her? She was here because her battery was dead, not to flirt in a sexy car with an even sexier, unattainable man.

Although her original intention had been to help him somehow, Emma knew better by that time than to get in the way of his easy mastery. The only thing she was required to do was turn the key in the ignition. It took him about three seconds flat to get her car purring with life again. She got out of the driver's side door.

"You could be one of those guys in the . . . what are they called? The pits? At car races?" she said with a grin as he disconnected the cables and slammed shut her hood.

She saw his mouth quirk in the headlights of her now-running car. "I have my share of experience in the pits, too."

"Really?"

His shrug looked a little weary. "I told you I was a gearhead."

She smiled. "Well I'm thankful for it. This is all my fault, really. The car's been due to be serviced forever, I just never have the—"

"Do you work tomorrow?" he interrupted.

"Yes," she said, watching as he recoiled the cables by clutching one end and looping them around his bent elbow. Every movement he made struck her as knowing. Masterful.

"What time?" he asked, dropping his arm, his hand gripping the recoiled cable.

"Three to eleven. That's my shift."

"If you leave your car unlocked and the keys under the front seat, I'll service it for you while you work."

She stared at him for a few seconds. Aloof billionaire Michael Montand was going to service her car instead of one of a dozen interchangeable mechanics down at the FastOil where she usually went? It seemed highly improbable, like the idea of the president volunteering to clean her bathroom.

"That's okay. Thank you for the offer, but you've already done enough. I'm sure you're busy with other things."

"I wouldn't want you not to show up for work because your car didn't start. Leave the keys."

Lightning lit up the night sky and thunder answered. A storm was about to break. She could feel it churning in the sky just behind her, just like her mind spun desperately to think of a way out of accepting his hospitality. She wasn't sure why, but the prospect intimidated her out of proportion to his offer. It thrilled her, too, which made her all that much more wary.

"Why are you so hesitant? What else have you heard about me besides the family business?" he demanded suddenly.

What had he read on her face?

"Nothing," she insisted.

The small, grim smile returned. "You're not a very good liar, Emma. What else did you hear?"

Her heart began to thump uncomfortably in her chest at the sound of him saying her name. To hide her discomposure, she rested her forearm on her open car door. His dark brows quirked slightly, his manner the cool, slightly impatient one of a prince being kept waiting.

"Okay. But you're the one who insisted," she said. "The rumor is that you're a cold, selfish bastard."

His expression remained masklike. A car passed on the country road in the distance, the sound striking her as lonely in the cloaking darkness. A puff of rain-scented wind swirled around them, rustling his thick hair.

"It's seems to me they're wrong," Emma added, her voice shaking a little.

"No. They're right," he said.

For some reason, her chin went up defiantly. Neither of them spoke for a stretched few seconds. His face looked like carved alabaster in the harsh white lights, his gaze fierce. Emma cleared her throat and looked away.

"Well, you certainly were kind to me tonight. Thank you again. Good night," she said, starting to get into her car.

"How far do you live?"

"Evanston. Not that far."

"That storm is about to break," he said, nodding to the western sky. "I'll follow to make sure you get home okay."

"*No*, that's all right."

He blinked at her adamancy. Did he think she didn't want him to follow her because she didn't want him to know where she lived? If anything, the opposite was the truth, and that's what had made her speak so harshly. An alarm in her head blared that she was approaching some seriously dangerous water, while the rational part of her insisted that the idea that Michael Montand was vaguely interested in *her* was ridiculous, so what was she worried about? He was idiosyncratic, that's all. Weren't rich people known to be odd and unpredictable? Didn't they live by different rules than someone like her? Besides, he'd just been warning her away from him by saying all the nasty rumors about him were true.

Hadn't he?

"I just meant that you've already done enough for me tonight. I'll be fine," she said.

He nodded, and for a few seconds, she thought he'd actually succumbed to her wishes. But then—

"I'll follow you," he repeated in a tone that didn't brook argument. He started toward the sleek sports car but paused and looked back at her. "And remember to leave your keys in the car tomorrow," he said pointedly. "You can put them under the front seat. I'll find them."

The decision to agree to that seemingly innocuous request felt like too weighty of a choice to make in that moment. She lowered into the driver's seat and shut her door.

She couldn't stop glancing at her rearview mirror on the trip home. Every time she saw those steady headlights behind her, something swelled tighter in her chest. He stayed a respectable distance behind her.

He might as well have been inside her head, she was so aware of him.

Chapter 5

A quarter of a mile from her home the sky unloaded. Thunder boomed threateningly as rain fell in torrents, pounding on her car. As she turned into her apartment's parking lot, she noticed Montand's distant headlights turn and disappear abruptly. He'd whipped the car around in a tight U-turn and accelerated in the other direction without a pause. She just made out the dark red rearview lights before he was swallowed by the rain and dark gray gloom.

A bitter flash of disappointment went through her, making her grit her teeth in self-disgust.

She opted for the rear entrance so that she could remove her now-soaking shoes on the tile floor of the utility room instead of the wood floor of the entryway. Afterward, she padded barefoot into the kitchen and picked up a dish towel, wiping off her wet arms. Exhaustion struck her all at once, the adrenaline high of the evening—of her unexpected encounter with Montand—running thin in her blood. In the distance, she heard the crashing of swords and the grunts of video game characters doing battle.

"Hi," she said wearily, rounding the corner into the dim living room. She came to an abrupt halt. Amanda and Colin sat on the couch, side by side. Two video controllers lay on the floor before their feet, forgotten. Amanda's body jerked at the sound of Emma's voice, but Colin continued kissing her, his hand running hungrily along the side of Amanda's tank top–clad torso and brushing a breast. Amanda made a wild, muffled sound and pushed at Colin. Emma caught a glimpse of her sister's frightened face around Colin's shoulder. The vision made a hot knife of sensation stab through her belly, forcing reality into her shocked haze.

Colin finally got a clue and turned. They both stared at Emma, pale faced and openmouthed.

The silence was horrible. Strangling. Emma couldn't think of anything to say. Her tongue had gone numb.

"Emma . . ." Amanda muttered, shock ringing in her tone. She flung herself off the couch and stood. She wore shorts, her long, lustrous dark blond hair falling down her back like a cloak. The skin of her bare legs and arms gleamed in the flashing light from the television, the only source of illumination in the cozy scenario except for occasional flashes of lightning from the storm.

You're the stupidest woman on the face of the earth. What kind of female left her boyfriend alone night after night with a stunning woman like Amanda? It'd never even occurred to Emma to be jealous.

Colin stood slowly.

"I thought you wanted to get to bed early tonight," Emma said to him, distantly surprised by how calm she sounded.

"I couldn't sleep," Colin said hollowly. He glanced uneasily from Emma to Amanda, and then back to Emma again. "We . . . I didn't hear you come in."

Emma nodded. "Yeah. Obviously. I came in the back door. The rain must have muffled the sound." She started toward the hallway, moving like a robot set on automatic. "Well personally, *all* I can think about is sleep. Good night."

"*Emma*," Colin called sharply at the same time Amanda cried out, "Emma, wait!" Her sister's voice rang with a mixture of anxiety, anguish, and disbelief. Emma didn't turn around or stop walking.

"Forget it," Colin said sharply when Amanda started to call out again, sounding panicked. "She's not going to listen to us. Not now. Let's go."

That made Emma whip around. She flew across the floor toward them so fast, Colin's eyes widened in alarm. He took a step back.

"*You* go," she grated out, her teeth clenched. "This is my sister's home. It's *mine*. She doesn't have to leave right now. *You* do."

Colin's mouth fell open in shock. She glared at him fiercely.

"You're right. I'll go. We can talk about this tomorrow," he said after a moment, glancing worriedly at both of them. Amanda just stood there, looking shattered.

Emma turned to resume her exit when Colin started for the front door.

"Emma, stop. We have to talk," Amanda entreated.

"I don't want to *talk* to you. You're the last person on earth I want to *look* at right now."

She didn't know what she was feeling aside from blindsided. Her brain and body vibrated with shock. Maybe she shouldn't have acted so holier-than-thou just now. Hadn't she just been lusting after another man? Hadn't she been having intensely erotic dreams, dreams she'd never associate with Colin and their sex life in a million years?

In her room, she locked the door and mechanically stripped, changed into some shorts and a tank top, turned out the light, and plunged into bed. When the knock came at the door a few seconds later, along with Amanda's pleas for her to open up and let her in, Emma reached for her headphones. She curled on her side and let the harsh, loud music crash into her, blocking everything out. Even though she clenched her eyelids shut, Emma knew for a fact she'd never sleep that night.

It'd been her secure relationship with Amanda she lost tonight, she realized numbly. The loss of a lackluster romance with Colin Atwater was *nothing* in comparison to that wound.

* * *

Death rarely followed a smooth downward decline. Emma was reminded of that the next day at work when Cristina joked with her tiredly when she woke up at around six in the evening, telling Emma she looked like something the cat had dragged in.

"Out partying last night with that boyfriend of yours, were you?" Cristina asked as Emma poured out her pain medication.

"No. I just couldn't sleep," Emma replied honestly. How could she rest with all the disturbing images she had swirling around her head? Colin's hand moving along the side of her sister's body, skimming her breast; the message in Montand's stare as he'd stood in the headlights of her car; the silent, somehow miserable climax of that man—Vanni.

Yes. Her voyeuristic incident was still bothering her deeply, and she was doing everything in her power to repress it. It felt like her whole world had been toppled over.

"I understand from Margie that you had a good appetite today," she said, changing the subject.

"A yogurt and half a supplement shake. *Good* if you're an anorexic or a dying woman, maybe," Cristina replied dryly. Neither of them spoke as Emma administered the medication and held up a glass with a straw while her patient laboriously drank a few mouthfuls of water.

"That was some storm last night," Cristina gasped as she resettled on her pillows. "Maybe that's what kept you awake?"

"Maybe it was the storm," Emma said dubiously, setting the water glass on the table. What did she know about what she was feeling, after all? She'd briefly told an equally bewildered, tearful Amanda that this morning when her sister finally confronted her in the kitchen.

"It only happened that one time, Emma. I want you to know that."

"Is that supposed to make me feel better, that it happened once?"

"No! God, what you must be thinking and feeling—"

"I don't know what I'm feeling, to be honest," Emma said honestly.

"What do you mean you don't know how you feel?" Amanda asked wildly. "You must be furious at me. At Colin, too."

"I don't care about Colin, Amanda," she seethed.

She'd only been telling the truth about her bewilderment, though. Nothing and no one felt certain to Emma anymore. Even she herself had become a mystery in this past week. One thing of which she was certain: she felt no flaming jealousy when she thought of Amanda and Colin together, which seemed pitiful more than anything. Mostly, she felt a scoring sense of loss. She didn't want to feel betrayed by her sister, given the fact that she now realized it'd been a mistake to stay with Colin.

But she did.

And she felt lonely, she realized. She'd never felt so alone in her life, even after her mother had died. It suddenly seemed that everyone was capable of entering a world of forbidden passion, while she herself was left behind, an outsider, too afraid to enter that complicated, bewildering place.

She'd been honest with Amanda about the lack of jealousy. It was Amanda she worried she'd lost, more than her safe relationship with Colin. Exactly what had gone through her sister's head when she came to the conclusion that being with Colin was more important than her relationship with Emma?

Things were still rattling around precariously in Emma's world later that evening as she spoke to Cristina.

"Would you like me to turn on the television?" she asked Cristina. She could use a little mindless distraction. Between lack of sleep and the most disturbing dreams when she finally had gone under for a meager few hours, she was feeling less than her sharp, feisty self.

"No. There's been something I've been meaning to speak with you about," Cristina said. "Remember when I asked you if you were going to preach to me about God and repentance and fire and brimstone?"

Emma grinned as she sat in the upholstered chair next to Cristina's bed.

"Well, I don't remember it precisely that way, but yeah . . . in general."

"And you said you never preached to people because you don't like to be preached to," Cristina recalled. Emma nodded. "You sidestepped the issue."

"What issue?"

"Of whether or not you believe in God. Are you religious?" Cristina inquired. Her thicker than usual accent informed Emma she was growing tired.

"I don't think so, not in the classic sense. I'm very spiritual, though."

"Why?" Cristina demanded.

"I've seen things. Experienced them."

"You've experienced a lot of death," Cristina filled in for her. "Because your mother was a nurse in that old folks' home and you used to spend a lot of time with all those—what's that charming word you Americans use—*geezers*," Cristina recalled what Emma had told her when they conversed a few days ago.

"They weren't just old people. Many were my friends."

Cristina shook her head on the pillow. "It wasn't right, for such a young girl to be exposed to so much disease and death. There's something twisted about it. It was wrong of your mother to allow it to happen."

"You say it was twisted because you're afraid," Emma said quietly.

Cristina glanced at her incredulously. "How can you sit there, a girl of twenty some odd years, fresh and dewy as a bud still on the rosebush, and say something like that to me?" she demanded hoarsely.

"I can say it because I know. There's nothing to fear, Cristina."

For a few seconds Cristina just stared at her in openmouthed awe. Emma saw the doubt slink back into her expression.

"Look at me," Cristina demanded bitterly, glancing at her frail body beneath the sheets. "I'm skin and bones and seeping sores. My insides are being eaten away by cancer. How can you say death isn't twisted and awful?"

"It is awful at times. Painful. Scary. But one never sees life more clearly than when death approaches. And maybe that's the biggest gift of death—life's final gift—if we can accept it."

A shudder went through Cristina. "You say you're not religious, but you certainly sound like you want me to repent of my sins before I go."

Emma smiled. "I don't know if I'd call them sins, necessarily, but if you have something you want to talk about, I'll listen."

"And not judge?" Cristina wondered skeptically.

"And not judge," Emma repeated calmly. "You brought this up, Cristina. There must be something you want to get off your chest."

Cristina stared at the closed curtains across the room, a faraway look in her eyes. "There are so many things," she whispered, sounding uncharacteristically sad. Wistful. After a moment, she focused on Emma again. She looked very tired. "But I still don't think it's right."

"What?" Emma asked, confused.

"For a young girl like you, so full of life, to surround herself with death. Maybe you're the one who is afraid."

"What do you mean?" Emma asked.

"Maybe you're such an expert on death because you're afraid to live," Cristina said in a thready whisper. Her eyelids closed. She didn't speak again for several seconds. Emma thought she slept, and grew lost in reflecting on Cristina's words.

"You really do believe it, don't you?" Cristina asked in a quavering voice after a minute. She opened her eyes. "That dying isn't frightening?"

"No," Emma said quietly. "I *know* it."

Cristina studied her searchingly for several seconds, and then closed her eyes again. Emma watched over her as she sunk into a comfortable sleep.

Was there any truth to what she'd said about her being afraid of life? Her relationship with Colin for the past two years had kept her comfortable. Safe. That seemed glaringly obvious now. She'd clung to the familiarity. She'd needed security after the death of her mother. Maybe Colin was tired of being her security blanket and longed for something more risky. More passionate.

Who could blame him?

"Emma."

She started from her thoughts and turned in her chair, surprised to be interrupted. Margie was already gone for the day. She and Cristina were usually alone on this floor of the house at night, and her patient was fast asleep. Mrs. Shaw stood just inside the threshold to the bedroom, perhaps rightfully aware she wouldn't be welcome by Cristina.

"I've come with a message," Mrs. Shaw said. "Mr. Montand says you forgot to leave your keys in your car, and so he can't service it. He asked if I could collect them from you now."

Emma stared, heat rushing into her cheeks. The decision of whether or not to leave her keys in her car this afternoon had taken on gargantuan significance in her head. She'd been a coward not to leave them. Wasn't she a coward, period? Now it felt as if her vulnerability and confusion had been put on display for Mrs. Shaw, a very undesirable audience.

"I'll get them," Emma said breathlessly, hurrying to her purse. She handed her keys to the housekeeper a moment later. "Thank you for doing this."

"He asked me to give you the entry code to the garage." Mrs. Shaw said the five numbers like she was uttering a malediction at Emma, before she turned and glided out of the suite.

* * *

It's not a big deal, Emma reminded herself later that night as she looked at her reflection in the bathroom mirror. Debbie was there for her shift and had been briefed. Emma was free to go. She was just going to the garage to pick up her car. There was absolutely no reason to be nervous.

If you're just going to claim your car and it's not a big deal, how come you put on perfume and eyeliner? she asked herself snidely. She'd tried to put on some powder, too, to conceal the hated, light sprinkling of freckles across the bridge of her nose, but eventually washed it off. Amanda could make them disappear when she applied Emma's makeup, but Emma herself always botched it.

Thinking of the familiar little makeup ritual with her sister made hurt and anger slice through her. She stifled it with effort.

Her brown eyes looked especially huge, whether from anxiety or the eyeliner or the contrast of her pale face and blond hair, she wasn't sure.

You look like a deer in headlights.

That's what she felt like, too.

Annoyed by her uncalled-for nervousness, she left the bathroom and said good night to Debbie. Cristina was still sleeping.

Unlike last night, she could see thousands of stars in the sky when she walked out the rear entrance. Her memory served her correctly. She easily found the hidden garage door behind the grove of trees and shrubs and used the passcode. Her footsteps sounded abnormally loud on the concrete floor of the mudroom. When she entered the huge space, she saw her car parked first in line on the row of vehicles on the right, along with a pair of long, coverall-covered legs and brown work boots sticking out from beneath it. Rock music was playing. Emma looked around for the source of the music but saw no radio. There must be built-in speakers somewhere.

"Hello?" she called out uncertainly.

Montand rolled out from beneath her car on a creeper, catching himself with practiced ease on the bumper with a gloved hand. Emma held her breath as she watched him sit up. He gripped a wrench in one hand. Unlike last night, he was clean-shaven. The goatee had disappeared, but he looked no less piratical. His hair was a mess of finger-combed, rich brown waves. There was a streak of oil on his jaw. His aquamarine-colored eyes lowered over her slowly.

"Hi," she repeated stupidly. She'd been wrong again.

He was clearly a *very* big deal.

He sprung up from the creeper and set down the wrench on a trolley filled with tools.

"She's all ready for you," he said, walking toward her. Emma unfastened her gaze from the vision of him removing the work gloves from large, well-shaped, very . . . *capable*-looking hands.

"How bad was it?" she asked.

"Not bad at all. Just needed someone to give it a little attention."

She grimaced. "That hasn't been me, unfortunately. So many things have been breaking down recently. I haven't had the energy to deal with something that wasn't broken. Yet," she added sheepishly.

"What else is broken?" he asked, studying her from beneath a lowered brow.

"What isn't?" she asked with a laugh. "I've put in about a hundred requests with my apartment owner for maintenance to come fix my backed-up kitchen sink, the hot-water heater, the icemaker . . . the list goes on, but there doesn't appear to be a lot of consequences for a landlord who just ignores a tenant's requests." She noticed his slanted brows and slight scowl and realized how whiny she probably sounded. "It's not a big deal. I have a friend who has a dad that's a cop in Cedar Bluff. He used to work for the Chicago Police Department. He said he'll walk me through how to file a formal complaint with the housing commission against our apartment owner. Apparently, the owner isn't the most upstanding citizen. Anyway, I can't thank you enough for fixing the one thing I *really* couldn't afford to have broken," she said, waving at her car. "A hospice nurse spends a lot of time driving."

"It's a nice little car."

Emma laughed. "Seriously? You were working way below your normal standards," she said, nodding toward the other superexpensive, rare, and luxurious vehicles lined up in the garage. "Like having to eat cornflakes when you're used to caviar."

"I hate caviar."

"Me, too." She realized she was grinning at him idiotically and looked away. "Even though I only had it once."

"You're not missing much," he said, flicking his gloves against the palm of his hand. Was he impatient to be gone?

"Well I can't thank you enough, both for this and last night." There didn't seem to be a good place anywhere to rest her gaze.

"Do you want to see some of my cars?"

"Okay," she said. Had he realized she was uncomfortable and tried to distract her from her embarrassment? That was nice, but somehow even more embarrassing. She fell into step beside him as he began to walk between the two rows of cars.

"You look pale," he said bluntly. "Is everything okay?" He sounded stiff asking. With a flash of insight, she realized he wasn't cold. Not really. He just wasn't used to being solicitous.

He'd slowed down next to a gorgeous, shining ivory-colored vintage car.

"I . . . kind of had a rough night, that's all," she said shrugging, stopping because he'd stopped.

His blue-green eyes raked over her face. "Fight with your boyfriend?"

She exhaled in disgusted disbelief. She was either the most transparent person in the world, or those eyes of his really were X rays. "As it turns out, I don't have a boyfriend anymore."

"What?"

To her horror, she felt emotion tighten her throat. Had it lain in wait this whole time, ready to spring up on her at the moment she least wanted to feel it? She laughed to hide her sudden discomposure and looked away from his intent expression.

"I walked in on my boyfriend with . . . someone else last night." She hadn't breathed a word of the truth to anyone, why Michael Montand, of all people? "We've been together for two years," she added lamely.

He muttered a muted, yet blistering curse.

"It's okay," she said, avoiding his stare. She feared she'd see pity on his bold features—or worse, impatience or bemusement at her personal admission to a near stranger. "I probably should have called things off between us a long time ago."

"Why didn't you?" Montand asked.

"Because he was a safety net? Because I'm a coward?" she asked, a bark of hysterical laughter popping out of her throat.

She couldn't stop herself from meeting his stare.

"You are *not* a coward," he said quietly. As in many things he said, it was a proclamation. He stepped toward her, and her heart leapt.

"Come here," he murmured.

Her feet moved as if of their own volition. His arms surrounded her. Her cheek pressed against the thick fabric of the cotton coveralls and his hard chest beneath them. The thought struck her that the sensation of the cloth against her cheek was familiar—his scent was—but then the dreaded emotion rose higher in her throat, and she turned all her resources into tamping it down.

She made a strangled sound and shuddered in humiliation. His arms tightened around her, the sensation divine and awful at once. She contained her misery, but just barely. Maybe it was the fact that she hadn't told him about what was really bothering her—about *who* she'd found her boyfriend with—that she managed to not break down. Or maybe it was that he felt so amazing next to her that was distracting her so much. He opened his hand at her back and made a soothing motion against her spine, his fingers curving around her waist. His body felt so solid . . . so *good.* She'd never been pressed against someone so hard. He seemed like the most solid of things in a world spinning off its axis. His hand cupped her hip. Her thoughts fractured and shot off in a million directions when she felt his body stir. Hers replied in kind.

"Emma?" he asked tensely.

She leaned her head back and met his stare. His hand rose to cup her face, his thumb feathering her jaw. He felt it, too. It was right there in his eyes. The shared knowledge of their mutual need seemed to throb in the air between them like some kind of naked, shared heart.

"Yes," she whispered her answer, parting her lips.

And his mouth was covering hers.

Week

TWO

Chapter 6

He didn't know why he'd done it. He'd ordered himself to steer clear of trouble. True, he'd been thinking about Emma Shore a lot. So much so, in fact, that he'd cautioned himself to stay away. She wasn't for him—something so fresh and unexpected for something so jaded and tired?

He didn't think so.

He wasn't denying his lechery toward her; it wasn't that. That was impossible to deny. His sleepless night had been haunted by her form. Her smile. Her eyes.

It was like being a teenager all over again, his mind obsessed with graphic, imagined sexual scenarios, his body burning like it hadn't in a decade. He'd masturbated repeatedly like a teenager, that much was certain. As unpleasant as unrequited lust was, it strangely felt like he was coming to life again. His body was prickly with sensation, primed with need.

But it hadn't been biting lust that had made him step forward and take Emma Shore into his arms. It had been instinct. Maybe it was the fact that her pale, delicate face and dark eyes held so much bewilderment and hurt. Or maybe it was seeing the way she fought like crazy to contain that pain. It'd wrecked him a little, that expression, like seeing the face of a good, strong child who had just been uncharacteristically backhanded by a loved one.

She didn't *feel* like a child. She felt good against him, slender and svelte, firm and supple beneath his stroking hand. Her head cuddled against his chest, the gesture striking him as natural. Sweet. He glanced down and saw that small spray of freckles across the bridge of her adorable nose. Those freckles epitomized the paradox in her that he found compelling: freshness and raw sensuality. He could smell the light, fruity smell of her golden hair and wanted to touch the soft waves. A shudder went through her, and he stroked the length of her spine, wanting to give comfort but feeling woefully inadequate to the task. He sensed all the emotion trapped inside her. It seemed to resonate into his hands until he felt like he held *it*—her confusion, her pain. He didn't like feeling it, but he hoped he lessened it for her by absorbing it, so he didn't let go.

A tightness grew in his chest, but he couldn't say why. It had something to do with how unexpected she was, or the sharp knowledge that a girl with a smile that could light up a room could ever be sad. Life really was a cruel, ruthless bitch if it could randomly lash out at someone like her, at something so fine and undeserving.

His fingers stretched, mapping the beautiful curves he'd admired in the past that led from her narrow waist to her hips. How incredible it would be to sink into the sweetness of her taut little body, to watch her troubled expression transformed by bliss.

His cock stiffened with unprecedented vigor.

Irritation spiked through him. How foul could he be to have the urge to fuck rise up in him like a striking snake in this situation? He despised the evidence that he was no better than his father, but didn't darkness and selfishness beget the same?

He knew she'd felt his cock harden. It was hard to disguise the evidence, as close as they stood. She stiffened against him, but almost immediately softened, pressing tighter to him, her hips pressing closer, as if she wanted to feel the contours of his arousal.

"Emma?" he asked warily, not fully trusting his senses, all too aware of the lust boiling just beneath his surface, straining to erupt.

Her whispered "yes" was so sweet, he couldn't resist leaning down to taste her acquiescence on his tongue.

It was like being abruptly plunged into a pool of boiling sensation. His mouth shaped her flesh to his, a firm, insistent master. His hands molded just as his lips did, pressing her flesh against his. He groaned and dipped his knees, aligning them. Emma cried out softly at the exquisite feeling of his groin fitting between the juncture of her thighs. As if he'd sensed the give in her flesh, he penetrated her mouth with his tongue at the same moment that he pressed his sex to hers. Emma flamed high at his stark possession. She grasped at his shoulders and strained closer, wanting more, tangling her tongue with his.

The sweet residue of a peppermint candy or gum lingered in his mouth, but beneath it, she tasted something else, something complex, intoxicating and new. He seemed just as fascinated by her taste. His sleek tongue explored her thoroughly, the primal edge to his hunger sending a thrill streaming through her veins. His hand opened at her middle back as he leaned down over her, his kiss seguing into a dark demand. She bowed her spine, answering his call, pressing her hips closer to his erection, circling slightly. His hand lowered to her ass, cupping her against him even more firmly. He groaned roughly, his teeth finding her lower lip and scraping it between them. A jolt of electrical arousal went through her at the evidence of his arousal. Somehow, his kiss was more exciting than any full-out sex she'd ever experienced.

His *kiss*. That's all. It was *all* of that: hot, mind-blowing, addictive to a degree that it should be considered illegal . . . so good, that she gasped in acute displeasure when he abruptly tore his mouth from hers.

"You should go," he said stiffly.

"I don't *want* to go," she replied breathlessly, staring at his mouth, her hunger awakened. Rabid.

"Only a selfish asshole would take advantage of you when you're this upset. I am selfish. But I don't *want* to be. Not with you," he bit out viciously.

Her well-kissed mouth hung open. "Don't stop," she whispered. "I think I need this."

"You'll regret it later."

"I'll regret stopping," she corrected without pause. She studied his rigid features. "Please don't tell me what I want or need. I'll decide for myself." Even though he'd stopped kissing her, he still held her fast. His heavy erection throbbed into her, his strength.

His vulnerability.

She put her hand at the back of his head, her fingers delving into his hair. It felt even more arousing than she'd imagined, to touch the thick waves. She pulled him to her. He came reluctantly.

But he came.

She kissed his slight frown, coaxing him. Softening him. She glanced into his eyes cautiously as she nibbled at his firm mouth. His gaze blazed down at her. His utter stillness made her wary, but excited her as well. She ran her tongue delicately along the inner lining of his lower lip, and felt the shudder in his body.

"Fuck it," he said, before he seized her mouth and sealed it to his.

His tongue plunged between her lips at the same moment that he turned her, urged her . . . taking control. Her ass and back thumped against the hard surface of a car. He pressed her to it tighter with his body. She burned for a moment between the two hard surfaces and beneath his voracious kiss. Distantly, she heard a metallic click. He lifted his head and stared down at her.

"Get in," he said. She looked around dazedly and saw that he held open the door to the backseat of the beautiful luxury sedan. It was a challenge he'd growled so softly.

It was a challenge she was more than willing to meet.

Her heart slamming against her breastbone, she pried herself away from his pinning body and walked around him. The only movement he made was the slight give in his body as he released her. She looked at him before she sat in the car. He watched her by moving only his eyes, holding his head immobile, his facial features pulled tight. Once she was inside the car, she scooted over on the seat, glancing around anxiously.

It was some kind of vintage luxury vehicle, the likes of which she'd never before seen. The name Bentley had come to mind earlier, but she didn't know if that was the correct name of the car or not. Her imagination supplied a vision of some 1950s, fur-draped movie star being driven by a chauffeur to a glamorous red-carpet event in a similar car. The seat was very long by today's car standards, and was made of decadently soft, ivory-colored leather. The dashboard looked like it was made of tortoiseshell.

She fleetingly noticed these details before his body blocked the light from the garage in the open door, and he was sliding onto the seat next to her. The door shut. She'd thought the interior of the car unusually large until he was in it with her. His presence made her feel as if she was secreted in a small, dim place with him . . . trapped, but excitingly so.

"Come here," he said grimly, reaching for her. She went into his arms, eager to be submerged in his heat again. He leaned down and met her kiss, immediately taking control of it. She whimpered softly into his mouth, melting. This is what he *did*, some befuddled part of her brain acknowledged. He turned women to goo. His seductions were as easy and practiced as his mechanical ability around cars. The realization didn't bother her at that moment. His expertise was what she required. What she *needed*.

Even though his kiss was a firm, hot delight, he'd reined himself in during the interim when she'd gotten into the car. She loved his mouth's making love to her with such consummate, toe-curling heat and skill, but she longed to feel the sharp edge of his desire again. She sealed their kiss and turned her head, brushing their mouths together experimentally, nibbling, learning his shape and texture.

His scent penetrated her awareness—clean skin, a remnant of his spicy cologne, a hint of motor oil. Familiar. Thrilling. Wonderful.

She plucked at his lips with curious ardor, but he remained utterly still. Chained. Her fingers sunk into his hair—thick, gorgeous man-hair. Need clawed at her insides, lust like she'd never experienced it. Her fingernails scraped his scalp forcefully.

His low, guttural groan sent another sharp thrill through her. His hands bracketing her waist, he leaned down over her, his tongue piercing her mouth. He pulled her against him roughly. Her back arched, her breasts crushing against him, yet he wasn't close enough. His tongue swept the depths of her mouth, as if claiming it as his territory. He applied a suction that she felt in the far reaches of her body—her nipples, her belly, the very core of her.

Fisting his thick hair, she pulled him closer with knuckles on his skull. He groaned in rough dissatisfaction, and she thought she knew why. They couldn't get any closer in their sitting position.

He pushed and she yielded, lying back on the supple leather seat. She made a muffled sound of protest when he sealed their torrid kiss momentarily. Hands on her waist, he slid her farther along the seat so that her head rested near the far door. She saw the glint of his eyes in the shadowed interior. She gave a little squeak of surprise when he scooped up her legs behind the knees and threaded them around his still-partially-upright body, his actions quick and precise. He let go and her legs fell between his back and the back cushion. Then he was coming down over her reclining body, his weight on top of her feeling heaven-sent. He grasped the side of her head, his fingers threading into her hair, her skull fitting into his palm. A wild quiver of anticipation went through her when she saw his lust-tight features.

He captured her mouth with his own, and the kiss resumed, hot and wet and deep. Her hands moved over his back, desperate to outline his shape and texture. She wanted—no, she *needed*—to feel his arousal pressed against her flesh, craved the evidence of his reciprocal desire. But he was still in a partial sitting position, his hip on the seat, his booted feet on the floor. She could lie out flat on the long seat of the luxurious car, but he was much too tall. She transferred one hand to his belly, wild to absorb him one way or another, pressing against fabric to feel the taut wall of muscle beneath it. Her hand lowered below his waist, reaching. He lifted his head. Gritting his teeth, he slid his hand down her arm, grasping her wrist. He did the same to the other, and before Emma knew what was happening, he'd pressed both her hands above her head.

He stared down at her, nostrils flared slightly, his breath coming as choppily as hers.

"Don't you dare tease me, Emma."

She blinked at his harshness. He was holding her tight. She couldn't move. Despite his biting words and the restraint that she sensed she couldn't break if she tried, she wasn't afraid of him. Her excitement only mounted. He closed his eyes briefly, and she sensed his regret.

"I'm not going to do this in the back of the car in a garage," he said more evenly after a pause. "I'm not a teenager anymore." His gaze lowered to her heaving chest. "Or an animal," he added, this time less certainly.

Emma swallowed back a protest. For a few seconds, she just lay there, trying to gather herself. It was hard, with his upper body pressed against her and his head hovering so close, inhaling the scent that did something unprecedented to her brain. She'd never wanted a man more. She'd never wanted *anything* so sharply that it cut her to the quick. Still, she heard what he was saying.

"I understand." She twisted slightly beneath him and pulled at her hands in his grip.

"No, you don't," he said with a flash of irritation, refusing to release her hands.

"What's not to understand?" she asked, exasperation tingeing her tone. "I'm not going to beg you. If you don't want to, fine."

He abruptly caught her right wrist and drew it downward, taking her by surprise. He pressed her hand between his thighs. She gaped up at him. He felt huge throbbing next to her palm, furiously erect. It'd been the evidence she craved, but now it left her speechless.

"That's how much I want to," he grated out between a rigid jaw, pressing her hand tighter to his swollen cock for an electrical second. He seemed to notice her stunned expression. He jerked her hand away, grimacing. He lowered his head, obscuring his face. For a few seconds, he remained like that, his chest moving in and out in silent pants.

He glanced up after a moment, that marblelike surface she often saw on his features back in place. His hand skimmed down over her belly. Her stomach muscles jumped at the caress. His fingers slid beneath the waistband of her jeans. Her eyes widened.

He flipped his wrist in a precise, expert motion, and the top button of her jeans came unfastened.

"You're confusing me," she said, her heart thumping in anxious, wild anticipation.

Long fingers moved over her fly, methodically releasing button after button. She bit her lip, finding his touch so near her sex almost unbearably exciting. He stared down at her steadily. "I'm trying to convince myself that I'm being noble. You've had a really crappy twenty-four hours. You need some time to absorb what it all means to you without having some asshole humping you in the backseat of a car. Still. You deserve some pleasure. That's what you're telling me you want. To forget what happened last night, if only for a little while. I can do that for you."

"Oh," she mumbled. Is that what she'd been telling him, not only with her mouth but also her body? She increasingly didn't care, as long as he kept touching her. With him touching her, all thoughts of Amanda's shattered expression in that living room last night vacated her brain.

His fingers burrowed beneath her jeans, skimming her labia through her underwear. Rubbing. Pressing. The whole time, he watched her expression tightly. When he struck her bull's-eye, she gasped at the ideal, direct pressure on her clit. Her core clenched tight.

She grimaced at the sharp pinch of need and pressed her hips up against him and whimpered uncontrollably.

He really knew his way around a woman's body.

Oh my God.

To say the least.

He lowered his head until his mouth was just a fraction of an inch from hers, his gaze holding hers fast the whole time.

"The thing of it is, though, I'm still just being selfish. I'm not going to rest until I feel you shake against me," he said, his tone a strange mixture of thick arousal and anger.

His fingers found the edge of her panties and slid beneath them. She whimpered shakily as the ridge of his forefinger burrowed between her lips, gliding in the well-lubricated valley. He'd mapped her out well in his little expedition above her panties. She shook as he played her. He grunted roughly against her mouth.

"So what do you say? Do you think you can grant me rest tonight, Emma?" he murmured, rubbing her clit and plucking and biting at her upturned lips in a way that made her burn in places she didn't realize she owned.

"Oh *yes*," she whispered.

"That's what I wanted to hear," he said hotly as both his finger and tongue plunged in unison.

Chapter 7

The thing of it is, though, I'm really just being selfish. I'm not going to rest until I feel you shake against me.

Despite his words, what he was doing to her felt far from selfish. She drowned in decadent, flooding pleasure. He moved in her outer sex, pressing and sliding, his hand every bit as skilled at this maneuver as it was the deft, precise handling of a car. He owned her mouth at the same time that he touched her. He may have expressed his doubts about making love to Emma in the backseat of a car in a garage on a night when she was so vulnerable, but his kiss was wholesale, deep and compelling, holding nothing back.

Emma found herself giving just as completely. Her fingers plunged into his hair. She loved the feeling of it in her hands.

His finger continued to agitate her, gliding and rubbing her clit in a way that made her core contract and her eyes roll back in her head. God, she was burning from the inside out. She was wet, very wet, she could tell by the easy glide of the stiff ridge of his forefinger, the slippery movement of his seeking fingertip. It felt so good—better than when she touched herself; more concise, more imperative. She could so easily lose herself to this feeling . . . to him.

"That's right," he murmured against her lips. "Just give in to it."

She moaned, the fever in her rising, the friction he wrought with his skillful hand mounting. He pierced her lips with his tongue, capturing her groan of ecstasy. She grew so hot, so excited, that the soles of her feet tingled and her nipples grew painfully hard against her bra. As if he could read her body with his mind, he abruptly broke their kiss. She gasped in excited surprise when he pressed his mouth to the upper curve of her right breast. His head moved, his lips charting the swell of the flesh.

"Oh God," she moaned in dazed arousal when he closed his lips around the nipple and sucked through her T-shirt and bra. Her hips pressed up more insistently against his hand between her thighs. He was playing her clit expertly, but she longed to have him penetrate her. Fill her. She could feel the heat of his mouth on her breast, the wetness penetrate the cloth, the delicious suction. The stimulation on her nipple and clit at once nearly brought her to climax. But then his hand moved, his dragging forefinger along her naked pelvis and lower belly leaving a wet trail of her juices.

"Oh . . . no," she protested, disoriented by the sudden absence of his magical touch. He lifted his head.

"Shh," he whispered, the hushing sound soothing, but also firm, authoritative, as if he was saying, *wait, your pleasure will come in due time*. She bit her lip to stifle her ragged breathing as she watched him lift her T-shirt, his actions deliberate and focused, as if he didn't want to rush this. He carefully arranged her T-shirt over her breasts, his stare so intent her clit pinched in anguished arousal. He whisked a fingertip over the top of her breast and inserted it inside the edge of her bra.

"Jesus. You're beautiful," he said quietly when he'd pushed back the fabric and exposed a nipple.

He looked up at her desperate whimper.

"Just a little longer, baby, keep still," he soothed and commanded at once.

He dipped another finger beneath the fabric of the other cup, holding her stare the whole time, his touch scalding her. He lifted the flesh over the edge and then pushed the bra down securely beneath her exposed breasts. She forced her hips not to rise on the seat. She needed pressure on her pussy so badly. Her gaze moved down with his. Emma gritted her teeth and moaned in agony when she saw the picture her breasts made, both of them standing up pertly over the bunched cups, her nipples dark pink and very hard with arousal.

A surge of liquid heat went through her when he groaned roughly. "Look at that, like tight little buds," he muttered, sounding awed as he plucked at one nipple, then another. The ache of desire inside her clamped so tight, it hurt. She had to shut her eyes, the vision was so erotic—his dark, masculine fingers against her pale skin, caressing and pinching her delicate nipples, an expression of rapt hunger on his handsome face.

She made a strangled sound in her throat. He paused in his illicit caresses, and she opened her eyes warily. Their gazes met for a heart-stopping second.

Then his head lowered and he sucked a captive nipple into his mouth, and his finger slid again beneath her panties. Twin bolts of pleasure pierced her, pinning her to the spot, forcing her to submit. She trembled in the face of a huge, intimidating wave of pleasure. It was going to crash down on her, steal her breath—

"Come. I've got you," he rasped next to her damp breast. Then he took her nipple into his wet, warm mouth again, sucking harder this time. She cried out sharply as heaven fell. Shudder after shudder wracked her. One of his hands found its way to her back. He lifted her slightly from the seat, her back arching against his hot, demanding mouth. Then he was pressing her against him tightly, his lips now on her neck and near her ear, his finger playing her clit relentlessly.

"That's right," he whispered roughly next to her ear as she shuddered yet again. "That's what I wanted to feel. I can't wait to be high and hard inside you and feel that squeezing my cock." Another harsh shudder went through her at his erotic description. "*Emma*," he groaned, absorbing her shocks of pleasure as she quaked against him, helpless in the clutches of bliss.

* * *

She sagged into the seat a moment later. He firmed his hold on her wrists and again pinned them above her head. A thrill penetrated her satiation when she saw his focused, feral stare. He captured her shaky moan with his mouth. It was a little difficult for her to return his forceful kiss at first as her lungs silently screamed for air. His rabid hunger awakened her own, however, their lips shaping, bodies straining, tongues delving, heads twisting, breaths mingling. The heat between them blasted her. Delicious.

Dangerous.

She pulled on her restrained wrists. She wanted so much to touch his face and hair, feel the hard strength of muscle. Instead of just releasing her, however, he heaved himself off her abruptly. The absence of his weight and heat left her feeling disoriented. Bereft. God, he'd been so hot on top of her. So hard.

He went to a seated position and lowered his head to his hand, his elbow on his knee. He sat there while his heavy breathing slowed, clearly trying to master himself.

"I just wanted to touch you," she whispered, thinking maybe he'd thought she was trying to escape him when she'd struggled in his hold just now.

He turned his head, peering at her in the dim light with his hand still pressed to his temple. His gaze lowered and his expression stiffened. Emma realized her breasts were still exposed, sticking out lewdly over the bunched up cups of her bra.

"I'm not suggesting it this time," he said thickly. "I'm *telling* you, Emma. *Go*."

She inhaled sharply at the steeliness of his tone. Feeling vulnerable, she hastily replaced the cups before shoving down her T-shirt. She sat up, swinging her legs out from behind him. It suddenly felt like there wasn't enough oxygen in the enclosed space of the luxury car. Maybe he thought so, too, because he abruptly flung open the door and got out, leaving the door open.

God. Had she really just been making out with Michael Montand in the back of a car, climaxing against him furiously? Her life was certainly throwing her some wild pitches lately.

She hurriedly fastened her jeans, feeling dazed, and followed him out of the car. She was a little surprised her legs still held her weight when she stood, that was how undone she felt from the thunderous climax and renewed arousal.

He met her stare across the space of the few feet that now separated them. The air seemed to crackle between them. She'd never experienced chemistry like this. She hadn't known it existed to this degree. Her clit twanged between her thighs. Without ever intending to, her gaze lowered over his body hungrily. The coveralls he wore were loose, but she could easily see the outline of his still-erect cock where it arrowed upward along his pelvis and hip at a diagonal angle, tenting the material next to it as the weight pulled the fabric down. She could tell he was beautiful there, just like he was everywhere else.

"*Don't,*" he bit out, giving her a burning glance of warning that froze the air in her lungs. He started to walk away.

"Wait. What are you doing? Where are you *going*?" she sputtered, her disorientation rising.

He turned around and glanced down at the significant bulge in the front of the coveralls. "What do you *think* I'm going to do?" he asked with blistering sarcasm.

His voice seemed to echo all around the garage and in her head in the silence that followed, harsh as a whip.

"Fuck you," she replied succinctly when the pain of that lash finally penetrated her confusion.

His lip curled and his eyes closed briefly. He cursed under his breath just as heatedly as she had, white teeth flashing in a snarl.

"I told you you'd end up regretting it. I told you I was selfish," he hissed in what appeared to be pure, distilled frustration. He raked his fingers through his hair anxiously, avoiding her stare.

"Your keys are in the ignition of your car. I'll open the garage doors for you," he said before he turned his back to her and walked away.

Emma had never looked forward to a weekend less.

When she returned home on Friday night following that earth-shaking experience in Montand's garage—she felt hollow and dazed, yet strangely alert, too. Raw.

Were anger, confusion, and unprecedented lust going to become her permanent emotional state? It felt as if that's all she'd experienced since climbing into that armoire last Tuesday. That damn armoire.

Her Pandora's Box.

It certainly didn't help things that Amanda was sitting at the kitchen when Emma arrived home, her cheeks damp with tears. A cup of tea sat in front of her on the oak table. She'd clearly been waiting anxiously for Emma's arrival. God, this was the last thing she needed at this moment.

"*Not* tonight, Amanda," she bit out.

"When, then?" Amanda asked. "We can't just go around acting like nothing happened. I've hurt you. I know that. I love you too much to just ignore this."

"But not enough to keep from fooling around with my boyfriend?"

Her harsh words seemed to vibrate in the air between them. Amanda looked like she'd been slapped and was holding her breath.

Emma set down her purse on the table with a loud thump. She knew she couldn't keep avoiding Amanda. She was her little sister, for God's sake, her lifetime companion, fellow latchkey child, the single surviving column of the structure that gave the shape to Emma's life since their mother had died. Never before had Amanda done something so hurtful. It wasn't in her nature. Emma believed that. Despite the bizarre circumstances, it'd been Amanda's shattered expression that had caused Emma's mother-bear instinct to flare to life with Colin last night.

Once there had been three—Mom, Amanda, and Emma—against the world. Then there were two.

Now there was still two, but Amanda was moving swiftly away from her, too far to be an anchor anymore. She dreaded the idea of not having Amanda there as a confidant . . . as her only family.

But look what she did behind your back!

Emma stilled the choking thought with effort.

"I'm not hurting in the way you're thinking," Emma said.

"I've betrayed you." Amanda said stiffly, as if she spoke toxic words that burned her throat and tongue.

She looked into her sister's beautiful, tear-stained face. "Changes come, whether you want them to or not."

"Please tell me I haven't ruined our relationship forever."

"You'll always be my sister, Amanda. I'll always love you. But things *have* changed. How am I supposed to trust you like I did before?"

Misery settled on Amanda's face, giving the quick impression she'd aged five years in an instant. "And to think," she whispered after a pause, "all because I couldn't control myself. All because I wanted something I didn't really need."

The memory of Montand's thick self-disgust for his lust flamed into Emma's awareness. "Who's to say you don't need it? If not Colin, then passion. Risk." Emma mumbled distractedly, the image of Montand clouding her consciousness.

"You're condoning me kissing your boyfriend in the name of taking a risk?" Amanda asked incredulously.

"No. I'm saying that some things are inevitable. Life is filled with the unexpected and irrationalities and change. You must have wanted Colin an awful lot to have acted on it, given the circumstances."

"Part of me still can't believe I let it happen."

"And the other part?" Emma asked wryly.

"I know you probably don't want to hear this, but I think . . . I think I've fallen in love with him."

"And Colin? Does he feel the same way about you?"

Amanda nodded, more tears filling her eyes. "I'm so sorry, Emma. *God*, this is so screwed up."

Emma sighed. She felt wrung out. Exhausted. Heartsore. "I should have broken things off with Colin a long time ago. I've been living in a dreamworld, acting like everything is fine, holding on to him because he was my own personal safety net. I was in the relationship for all the wrong reasons."

"Tell me what to do to make this right, Emma."

"I can't make everything better for you on your timetable, Amanda," she said, frustration entering her tone. "That's not fair to expect it."

Amanda swallowed. "You're right. I'm sorry. I just don't want to lose you, and I'm scared."

"I'm not going anywhere and neither are you. We'll eventually get past this. But right this second, I'm just . . . *really* tired. I'm going to bed."

Amanda nodded, tears leaking down her cheeks. Emma was usually her comforter. But there was nothing she could say to soothe her little sister at that moment. She was too confused herself, and her frothing emotions and thoughts had nothing to do with Colin.

Saturday morning, she finally sat down with Amanda to talk, knowing her sister wouldn't rest until she eradicated her guilty conscience. Given Amanda's red eyes and pale complexion, she had a feeling her sister had been up crying all night again. Besides, Emma couldn't help but be curious about the circumstances between her sister and Colin.

"So your feelings have been growing stronger ever since the two of you have been spending so much time together?" Emma asked after listening to Amanda's emotional confessions over morning tea.

"We have a lot in common. You know I'm interested in forensic medicine, and he's learning so many amazing things in his new job. Plus, we're so *comfortable* together."

"And that's what you want? *Comfortable*?" Emma asked dubiously.

"Well yeah. Who doesn't?" Amanda said, as if it were obvious. "But I *never* planned to act on the feelings I was getting for him, Emma. Please believe me. I never will again, if you say the word, despite the way I feel about him. The other night, it just . . . *happened*. You'll never know how terrible I felt, seeing you standing there, imagining what you were thinking of me." Emma had the rather random, uncharitable thought that Amanda looked absolutely gorgeous even with her face all red and splotchy and her long hair pulled back in a haphazard bun.

Emma sighed. "If you really like Colin, you shouldn't just give up on the whole thing because of me. It's like I told you yesterday, you'll always be my sister."

"But . . . but what about *you* and Colin?" Amanda asked in a quavering voice.

"It's over. It's like I said last night. We were comfortable together. There was no real romance. What happened last night just brought all that to the forefront. What are *you* going to do in regard to him?"

"I don't know. I'm so confused."

"Yeah? Join the club," Emma said under her breath.

"I'll be starting school in the fall. You know how hard the program is going to be. I don't have time for a relationship."

"This is one decision I can't help you with. You'll have to decide on your own. But don't *not* be with Colin because you're worried I'm still in love with him. I'm not," Emma said with finality, pushing back her chair.

"Do you think you can ever forgive me?" Amanda asked shakily.

Unbidden, a vision of her mother popped into her mind's eye, her face sad. Worried.

God, Mom would hate this.

"I'm going to work on it," Emma said honestly, briskly drying an errant tear with her thumb. "I'm going to try for Mom and for us. You're too important to me not to try. But forgiveness is a process, not a snap decision. Don't push it, Amanda."

Later, after Amanda had gone to wash up, Emma sat at the kitchen table with her computer in front of her, mindlessly checking e-mails and reading some articles on the Internet, trying to relax a little on her day off.

A few minutes later, she squinted at the computer screen, reading intently, certain phrases popping out at her more than others.

Automobiles Montand, French car company based in Antibes, France, that manufactures some of the most sought-after luxury sports cars and racecars in the world . . .

. . . Michael Montand (Sr.), French, founded the company in 1959 . . .

. . . Michael Montand (Jr.), American, sole owner and current chief executive officer of Automobiles Montand in addition to being founder and chief executive officer of Montand Motorworks, located in Deerfield, Illinois . . . exclusive maker of engines, intake manifolds, and carburetors for luxury sports cars and racecars . . . founder and backer of the world-class, experimental road race, The Montand French-American Grand Prix, to be held on the French Riviera . . .

She clicked on a link and a recent *Chicago Tribune* article popped up on the screen. Her gaze immediately stuck on the image of Montand at a podium, two gleaming stock cars on display behind him. He looked sober and compelling in a tuxedo, his hands braced on the podium, his posture suggesting the intensity and focus she'd come to expect from him.

Montand Motorworks Brings American Racing to the Côte d'Azur, the headline read.

She checked the date of the article. It was July 17, the date when he'd called her to him in the Breakers dining room, she realized, recognizing the tux in the photo. This was the publicity event he'd described, the one with the "vampires," as he'd called them. If he disliked high-profile events such as the premiere road-racing grand prix he'd organized on the French Riviera, he must be uncomfortable a lot of the time.

"Emma?"

Emma started, glancing around when Amanda said her name. She hadn't really been aware of her intention to Google Montand's name.

"Yeah?" she asked Amanda, shutting her computer lid guiltily, which was stupid. It was only natural that she was curious about him, after all. It wasn't every day she was set on fire by a gorgeous, aloof, cynical billionaire who kissed her like he thought she was his last meal on earth, and then rejected her like he'd realized she was poison.

"You're not going to believe who's here," Amanda said in a hushed tone, looking stunned.

Emma's heart lurched. Surely it wasn't—

"Toby Martin," Amanda whispered, glancing pointedly over her shoulder.

Emma's hopes plummeted back to earth with a crash. Did she honestly think Michael Montand would show up at her front door?

God, you're stupid sometimes.

Toby Martin was the name of their apartment maintenance man. He was the *only* maintenance man for more than two hundred apartments spread out over Evanston, Skokie, and northern Chicago. Their cheap-wad landlord refused to hire an adequate number of employees to service his units.

"He's here to do our repairs," Amanda hissed disbelievingly. "*All* of them."

"Well miracles *do* happen," Emma said after a stunned moment.

Colin had left at least a dozen messages on her phone since Thursday night along with another half dozen texts.

I know you're pissed, and you have every right to be, but please let me explain.

I know what it looked like, but it wasn't that . . . or it was, but not as bad as whatever you're probably thinking. Please just call me so we can meet and I can explain in person. Emma? PLEASE?

Look, I know things are over between us. But would you at least call and let me know you're okay? I'm getting worried.

Emma knew she couldn't keep putting him off. She had to get this over with. Besides, she felt a little guilty after hearing the desperate quality of his tone and messages. He imagined her betrayed, furious, and depressed. She *was* set off balance and angry, but it was strange to realize what had happened with Colin and Amanda was only a small part of her odd state. Colin had been part of the fabric of her life for years now, as much a part of her existence as Amanda. The fact that Colin and Amanda were interested in each other sexually and romantically definitely changed things, adding to that sense of shifting ground and a precarious future.

Their relationship needed to officially end. Colin needed to see she wasn't suicidal or something. She wasn't feeling sexually rejected by him, that much was certain. She'd been turned to quivering mush the other night in the backseat of a car by a gorgeous billionaire whom she couldn't stop thinking about despite all the drama surrounding her.

Not that she planned to confess that part to anyone. She was having trouble enough coming to terms with it herself.

What if you really are *upset and don't realize it, and are acting out in a self-defeating way with Montand because you're feeling rejected by Colin?*

One look at Colin's face when he answered his apartment door on Saturday evening, and she knew that wasn't the situation at all. She was ready to end it with him.

More than ready.

When he saw the carton she brought with all of the things he'd left at her place over the years, he looked sad and resigned. Even if it hadn't been for her unexpected experience with Montand, Emma knew she would have eventually realized this breakup was long overdue. Amanda and Colin making out had just hastened the inevitable.

Now all she had to do was deal with the poison fallout in regard to Amanda.

On Sunday, Emma decided impulsively to go shopping in downtown Chicago. When Emma returned home at around four thirty, she saw Colin and Amanda standing next to Colin's dark green sedan in the parking lot. They both stepped apart guiltily when they noticed her car. Feeling uncomfortable, Emma gathered her bags and headed toward her apartment.

She entered the still, empty apartment, closed the door, and pressed her back against it, her bags still clutched in her hands. What was she feeling? She tried to be honest with herself. *Was* it jealousy for seeing Amanda and Colin together?

No. That wasn't it. What she experienced was a gaping sense of uncertainty about her future. What she experienced, she realized with a sudden sense of clarity, was the precise reason she'd clung to Colin for so long, even when she knew they weren't right for each other.

The recognition fortified her. At least she'd put a name to what she'd been afraid of. She marched down the hallway, suddenly eager to look at her new purchases again.

Chapter 8

The following Tuesday when she went to work, the skies were gray and brooding. Maureen Sanderson, the nurse on the day shift, greeted her wearily when she entered the suite.

"What's wrong?" Emma asked.

"Cristina had a bad night," Maureen explained in a hushed tone, glancing toward the bedroom. "I thought she was gone at least half a dozen times. But she seems to be holding on for some reason. Her stepson is out of town. I know they have a rocky relationship, but maybe she's waiting to see him once more?"

"Montand is away?" Emma asked. No one had mentioned it during her shift yesterday, but she really hadn't conversed a lot with anyone but Cristina, and that only briefly.

Maureen nodded. "When she was doing so poorly earlier, I asked the maid to make sure he was aware that Cristina's time was probably soon, just in case he wanted to say good-bye. Alice told me he'd gone to France."

"When?" Emma asked, regretting her sharpness when she saw Maureen's bemused glance.

Maureen gathered her things. "I don't know. On Saturday, I think."

Emma nodded, striving to push down the hollow feeling that seemed to be expanding in her belly and pressing up on her chest cavity. What should it matter to her if he was gone? He was confusing and rude and it was better to be rid of him altogether.

It matters, a stubborn voice in her head said. She tried to ignore that, too.

She hastened to the bedroom, where she sunk into the upholstered chair next to Cristina's bed. She saw what Maureen meant. Cristina's color was terrible and she looked so tiny and shrunken lying there on the grand, luxurious bed.

"Cristina?" Emma called, seeing her patient's eyelids flicker. "It's me, Emma."

Cristina rolled her head on the pillow and regarded her with rheumy, crusted eyes.

"There you are," she mouthed, her voice barely above a whisper. "My confessor."

Emma smiled and stood. "Hold on to your confessions for a minute. I'm going to get a cloth for your eyes."

A moment later she washed Cristina's eyes with a warm cloth. Afterward, she gently applied one of Cristina's expensive creams to the dry skin of her face, rubbing gently. "Would you like a sip of water?" she asked when she was done. Cristina nodded. After she'd drank a few laborious sips, Emma set aside the cup and straw. "There, that's much better," Emma said. She pulled the chair closer and sat. She realized what she said was true. Cristina's gaze seemed sharper as she looked at Emma, a hint of her strong personality in evidence once again.

Maybe it's not the end for you yet, Cristina.

"What's this about me being your confessor?" Emma asked, her tone brisk and matter-of-fact.

"I don't like it when you're not here."

"I was just here yesterday. Do you think I should work 24-7?" she asked, touched despite her jocular tone. She knew Cristina was not the sentimental, touchy-feely type.

"No, you deserve the time off, but that doesn't mean I like it," Cristina gasped.

"Watch out, Cristina, or I'll think you actually like me."

Cristina scowled at her. "Look at you," she rasped after a moment, and Emma realized she was actually studying her appearance closely for the first time since last week.

Emma glanced down at herself dubiously. "What?"

"You're all dressed up. Or at least for you, you are. What's the occasion? Did you do your hair and put on a halfway-decent blouse because you thought you were coming to my funeral today?"

"I did no such thing," Emma said levelly, refusing to show her embarrassment over the fact that she'd spent some time on her hair the past two mornings and relished wearing her new clothes.

And he's not even here. He's halfway across the world.

She squirmed a little uncomfortably when Cristina's gaze narrowed on her.

"I know that look. You dressed up for a man. Well?"

"Well what?" Emma said, standing and straightening up the nightstand to hide her discomposure.

"Who's the man? It can't be that boyfriend you talk about. The impression I got of him is that he wouldn't inspire a blush, let alone that glow I see on your face right now."

"I must have rubbed your eyes too hard," Emma muttered.

"Have you met my stepson, by chance?" Emma's heart jumped when she took in Cristina's sharp stare. She felt so transparent. "Because . . . that might be a very good idea . . ." Cristina faded off musingly.

"Why? Does he need a nurse?" Emma hedged, rolling her eyes in a show of amused exasperation. Unfortunately, she wasn't the best of actresses. "You said you had something you wanted to say to me?" she asked, sinking into her chair again.

Something flickered across Cristina's pinched features. She stared at the curtained windows.

"Is my stepson here?" Cristina whispered.

"No. From what I understand, he's in France. Cristina, do you need to speak to him?"

Cristina's mouth pinched together in the silence that followed.

"No. Not yet," Emma thought she heard the older woman say.

Emma's shift seemed to drag by. Cristina slept through most of it. The silent mansion itself seemed to mock Emma, as if it knew about her stupid hopes in arriving there the past two days, had full knowledge of her naïve wish to run into Montand again. What did she imagine would happen? That he would seek her out, mad to be with her? That when she explained that she didn't mind his using her to assuage his lust, because she needed him to do the same for her, that he'd immediately give her what she needed? It would be a lie anyway, because she *did* mind. Or at least *at times* she found the idea of him making love to her with no other impulse but lust unbearable.

Her body was less worried about it.

She was thankful when the annoyingly slow hands of the gold and glass clock on Cristina's nightstand read ten thirty. Not too long now—

Her skin prickled when she heard a slight rustling sound out in the living room. She sat up straighter.

Someone is out there.

She hurried out of the bedroom, entering the living area in time to see Mrs. Shaw's stiff-backed form walking away quickly.

"Mrs. Shaw?" she called, shocked by her unusual presence so late and the fact that she was leaving without speaking. In the distance, Emma heard the muted sound of steps on the stairs. The housekeeper was gone. Had she been spying? Why?

Something caught her gaze on the coffee table in front of the couch. A dark blue, flat leather jewelry box sat there. It definitely hadn't been there before. Emma saw a white linen card lying beneath it. She hastened over to the table and picked up the card, reading the typewritten message.

Emma,

You are made of much finer stuff than me.
I'm sorry.

Her face slack with shock, she flipped open the lid on the box. Nestled in velvet was a delicate gold chain with an exquisitely filigreed and etched charm attached. She'd never seen anything like it. She fingered the object in awe. It was a butterfly; or was it a spritelike fairy creature? The necklace was strikingly lovely and unique.

She jumped when the phones in the suite rang. A tingling sensation rippled through her limbs, her fingers still touching the precious gold charm. Worried about waking Cristina, she sprung up to answer in order to halt the noise.

"Hello?" she said cautiously, her heart starting to pound in her ears in the silence that followed her greeting.

"Emma."

It wasn't a question. He'd known it was her, just as she'd known it was him somehow when she'd started at the sudden, sharp ring as she stared at the unique necklace.

"Yes?" she replied through a tight throat.

"It's Montand."

"I know," she breathed out quietly.

Again, that silence that sent the hairs on the back of her neck standing on end.

"How are you?" he asked, and she knew by the tone of his voice he was asking about what she'd impulsively confessed to him the other night about Colin, but also his reluctant, yet powerful seduction . . . his subsequent rejection. All of it.

"I'm fine," she assured.

"And Cristina?"

"Not well," she whispered very softly. "She asked about you earlier."

A short pause.

"What did she say?"

"Not much. She just asked if you were here. I think . . ."

"What?"

"I think she wants to say something to you. Before she goes."

"I'll be home tomorrow," he said.

Emma nodded as if he could see her.

"I'd like to see you tomorrow. After your shift," he said.

She gulped thickly. For some reason, she could almost picture him perfectly in her imagination, standing in the shadows and looking out an open glass door that looked out onto a grayish-pink dawn, his phone pressed to his ear, the familiar somber, intent expression on his face. The coolness of the chain looped around her fingers penetrated her awareness.

"Thank you," she blurted out. "For the necklace. It wasn't necessary."

"I disagree. You deserved an apology," he said stiffly. Neither of them spoke for a breathless few seconds. "Meet me in the garage tomorrow night. Do you remember the code?"

"Yes."

"All right. Good night."

"Good night," she whispered. She returned the receiver to the cradle very carefully, like she thought the instrument was as fragile as the moment had been.

Cristina had not rallied the next night, by any means, but she had plateaued. She was certainly no worse. Emma's shift was relatively uneventful. She saw no sign of Montand, and she was too self-conscious to ask Maureen or Cristina herself if they had news of him. She wasn't entirely sure he'd even returned.

By the time she left work that night, the formerly cloudy, humid day had cleared. A near-full moon and a star-strewn sky bathed the back drive in soft luminescence. She entered the code to the garage and took that increasingly familiar, heart-knocking trip across the mudroom. The garage was silent when she entered, the lights turned down too low for Montand to be working on his cars or engines.

"Hello?" she called out, her voice echoing off the walls in the wide-open space of the garage. She walked into the path between the two rows of cars. "Are you here?"

Silence. She'd tried to prepare herself for a variety of scenarios that might occur tonight, but hadn't considered this one. He wasn't here. Disappointment flooded her. Should she wait for a bit? Perhaps he'd run into a delay traveling back to Chicago?

A scuffling noise at the back of the garage distracted her. Her heart jumped. She heard a door click open and then shut and the sound of shoes on the concrete floor. She saw him coming toward her in the distance, emerging from the shadows at the back of the garage. He wasn't wearing coveralls this time. She'd been wrong about thinking he was gorgeous.

He was devastating.

"Hello," he said soberly, approaching her.

"Hi."

He wore a light blue and white button-down shirt and jeans, but it was what he did to the garments that left her tongue-tied. She could see his body more clearly when he wasn't sitting at a table or wearing the coveralls. His waist and abdomen were leaner than she'd thought, his shoulders and chest even more powerful looking. He wasn't like some of the guys she'd seen at the gym who lifted weights constantly with thick necks and muscles bulging all over the place. Instead, he was perfectly proportioned, his strength apparent in every line of his long, fit body. She recalled how hard he'd felt pressed against her, how solid.

He came to a halt several feet away from her.

You look . . ." She faded off, realizing she was about to make a fool of herself by blurting out how amazing he appeared. "You look taller without your coveralls," she finished lamely.

There was a scruff on his jaw tonight, but the goatee was still absent. The whiskers highlighted his mouth almost as well as the goatee had. Or maybe it was just that she couldn't stop looking at his lips and remembering what they'd felt like on her own. His thick hair was finger-combed back from his forehead. His eyes looked especially light in the shadows as they lowered over her.

"*You* look beautiful," he said. She blinked in surprise. He said what she'd been thinking about him so effortlessly. Plus, she wasn't used to his complimenting her. It packed a punch. He finished a perusal that left her feeling extra warm, and met her stare. "I like that color on you."

"Thanks," she murmured, glad she'd settled on the new blouse. It was a pinkish, apricot color and much more feminine than her usual clothes. Even she—who was normally very severe on her appearance—thought it did good things for her skin and eyes. A gleam of amusement and something else—was it pleasure?—entered his gaze.

"I like your tomboy look, but this suits you even better. You should dress up more often," he said.

"I'm not *dressed up*," she said, feeling a little prickly that everyone kept seeing through her so easily. Her heart started to thump erratically. His expression took on a bland cast and he nodded quickly as if to say, *of course not.*

"Are you *teasing* me?" she asked incredulously after a second, seeing the lingering trace of humor in his face. It seemed so uncharacteristic of him, she couldn't quite be sure.

His eyebrows went up. "Maybe we're both acting a little out of character tonight."

He grinned then, slow and sexy. His untainted smiles were so few and far between, she couldn't resist smiling back. His gaze settled on her neck. She touched the gold necklace at her throat.

"Thank you again for it," she said breathlessly. "I'm not sure I should take it, though. It looks very valuable."

"Of course you should take it," he said, his expression sobering. "I thought of the artist who makes them by hand almost immediately when I met you. It's a *petit ange*. Fitting for you."

"Really?" she asked, her tone flat with incredulity, fingering the charm at her throat. “What does *petit ange* mean? It’s so pretty, but I wasn’t sure what it was exactly. A fairy?” she wondered.

His gaze flickered over her wistful smile. “Little angel,” he said quietly.

“I’m no angel,” she assured wryly.

His smile left her flustered. She grasped for a safe topic. “Did you have a good trip?”

“Good enough. I was a little preoccupied.”

Emma nodded in understanding. “Cristina isn’t any better tonight, but not any worse, either,” she said softly.

They stared at each other. Against her will, the memory of being pressed against his length, of his possessive mouth covering hers, coaxing . . . demanding, of shaking against him as he played her flesh like a master, entered her awareness. She moved restlessly on her feet as the subsequent memory of his harsh, crude words sliced through her like an ice pick.

She wasn’t used to feeling this level of uncertainty and intense awareness with a man. It seemed to encapsulate them in some sort of airless bubble.

“Cristina and I are not the best of friends,” he said. “We never have been. It’s . . . complicated.”

“I understand,” Emma said quickly. “Every family has their history. Their stuff. I’m not trying to intrude or judge. That’s not part of my job, and it’s not a part of who I am, either. You’ve provided for Cristina extremely well, despite this obvious . . . rift between the two of you.”

“A rift implies we were once close. Trust me, that’s never been the case,” he said, and once again, she sensed a razor-sharp edge to his tone.

“But when I told you she asked about you, you seemed—”

“I’ve left my number with the night nurse, and Mrs. Shaw will inform the day nurse. If Cristina says she wants to speak with me, I’ll come. Now I’ve told you as well. But just so you know, I’m not holding my breath for anything,” he said pointedly. Emma nodded.

"There's something else I'd like to discuss with you. Would you like to go for a drive?" he asked, taking a step back.

She started and stared dubiously at the rows of cars. "I . . . *Yes.*"

"Which car do you want to take?"

"I get to pick?" she asked, a grin breaking free. She couldn't help it. An unexpected, giddy feeling of excitement rose in her.

His gaze caught on her smile. "Lady's choice," he assured quietly.

Chapter 9

She eyed another sports car, perhaps swept away by the uncustomary feeling of euphoria she'd experienced on that other brief ride with him. She pointed hopefully at a fierce, fast-looking, dark red car. His small smile and raised brows seemed to say "nice choice," which only enhanced her feeling of giddiness. The whole scenario took on the feeling of a waking dream when he opened the passenger door for her.

He slid into the seat next to her. The little car hummed to life, and as before, an unidentifiable thrill went through her. She had the strangest feeling when she was with him that anything could happen.

Anything *would*.

And that it could be heaven . . . or scary as hell.

He lowered the convertible top. Emma glanced cautiously sideways, admiring the virile, powerful image he made; the long, bent legs and strong, jean-covered thighs.

"How have you been doing?" he asked quietly once they had started down the dark drive. She thought he was referring to Colin.

"I'm fine," she assured. "I had a talk with Colin. It's over."

He gave her a flickering sideways glance. "So you didn't . . . I don't know," he shrugged. "Go ballistic on your boyfriend?"

She laughed and shook her head.

"Is that normal for you?" he asked. "To be so even-tempered?"

"No," Emma replied honestly. "Maybe that's how I know for certain that we weren't meant to be together. I'm not mad at him. I'm not jealous. I hate to admit it, but I'm actually relieved."

"You seem awfully certain."

"I am," she said. "About that, anyway."

She hadn't told him she'd found Colin with her sister. The inevitable shift in her relationship with Amanda was a source of vulnerability. She was too uncertain of Montand, unsure of his interest in her, to open up about that. She didn't completely understand her own motivations concerning him, either. It was as if part of her understood the unprecedented, intense attraction to him all too well. Another part of her seemed clueless in her motivations. No . . . not clueless, necessarily, but her intentions seemed murky. Clouded.

"Colin and I were just too comfortable with each other," she continued thoughtfully. "There was no . . ."

He paused at the turnoff to the country road. Her cheeks felt warm and she knew he looked at her.

". . . spark," she finished quietly. The word seemed to hang in the area between them for a second, vibrating, charging the atmosphere.

He swung the little car onto the road.

"What does he do for a living?" Montand asked gruffly after a moment.

"Colin? He's a computer programmer—a forensic science technician. He's very, very smart. Most of what he says goes right over my head. Between him, my sister, and me, I'm definitely considered the slow one. *Oh.*"

He'd accelerated. The wind whipped her short hair against her cheeks and swirled around her body, giving her a weightless sensation.

She'd worried a little he'd drive superfast on the dark country road. Wasn't he the scion of a car dynasty with roots in racing? Wasn't it inevitable he'd speed? She realized, however, that while he drove faster than the speed limit, it wasn't by a large amount. It was the sheer power of the car that had thrilled her. It couldn't have been more obvious that he had complete control.

"Faster?" he asked her quietly after a moment, and she realized he'd been accustoming her to the sensation of forceful, precise acceleration.

"Yes," she said, her voice vibrating with excitement.

The car accelerated smoothly. There was no sense of hurtling chaotically through space. Instead they glided. Zoomed. She felt like she flew along the road in a tight, fluid flight. The car responded to his slightest touch, as if all he had to do was to think a command and it followed his bidding, like machine and man were one. She realized after a moment that she was grinning broadly.

"Is it the car, or you . . . your driving, I mean?" she asked a few minutes later. *Which is it that's causing this feeling inside me?*

He kept his eyes trained on the road.

"The car," he replied shortly, but she wasn't sure she believed him. His mastery over the machine was singular. He downshifted and they rounded a curve. She saw the lights of the city on the horizon.

"Where did you grow up?" he asked.

"In the city," she said, nodding toward Chicago. "On the north side, the Rogers Park neighborhood. My mother was a nurse at an Edgewater nursing home."

"Is that how you got interested in nursing?"

"We spent a lot of time at the nursing home after school. My mom worked the evening shift, and it was really the only time we could see her while school was in session."

"They didn't care about having little kids there?" he asked, his brows bunching slightly in consternation as he stared at the road. "The managers or administrators of the nursing home?"

"No. We made ourselves useful. We played games with the residents. Read to them. Visited with them. It wasn't a wealthy nursing home," she explained, familiar with the fact that many people thought it odd that children spent so much time in such a facility. "The residents were mostly low-income people. A lot of the time, they didn't have family. None who visited, anyway."

"So you and your sister became their family," he stated rather than asked.

Emma shrugged. "For some of them."

"They must have lit up every time they saw you," he said thoughtfully after a pause. "It certainly sounds like a unique way to grow up."

"That's a pretty good way to describe it, yeah," she said with a laugh.

He glanced at her. She saw his small, grim smile in the glow of the dashboard lights. "I guess I shouldn't expect anything less."

"Why's that?" she asked.

"It had to be some unique circumstances. To make you," he added, his gaze trained on the road again.

It was like a precise, electrical caress in the darkness.

She was so giddy with speed, so caught up in the promise of being with him on that country road as the warm, fragrant summer air rushed around them and the little car ate up the asphalt, that she momentarily forgot their tense parting last Friday night. She was so fascinated by the vision of his hands on the leather wheel that it took her a moment to register they'd come to a halt. She turned to him. He wore a small smile as he watched her unsuccessfully trying to smooth her windblown hair out of her eyes and cheeks. *His* thick, waving hair looked artlessly sexy, like it'd been fashioned to be caressed and whipped by the wind.

"That was amazing," she told him. "You're an excellent driver. How did you get so good?"

He shrugged, his hands still loosely holding the wheel. "My dad loved cars almost as much as I do."

"Was he a mechanic as well?"

"Yes. And an engineer, although he was never formally trained as one. He put me behind the wheel when I was only six."

"Six?" she repeated, shocked.

His quick, flashing grin made something leap deep inside her. "He'd put me in his lap to prop me up."

They laughed. His low chuckle struck her as delicious in the warm, still air, his smile impossibly beautiful on such a typically aloof man. It was like a crack opened up on his cold surface and a bright light shone through. A tightness grew in her chest.

She realized she could see him because of several overhead lights. She blinked, recognizing the parking lot belatedly.

"Lookout Beach," she said, giving up on her mussed hair and looking around. "My mother used to bring Amanda and me here when we were little."

"Amanda? The sister you live with?"

Emma nodded.

"Is she a nurse, too?"

"No. She's going to be a doctor. She starts medical school this fall."

He studied her for a moment and then abruptly glanced toward the lake, the patrician, cool man returning. "Do you want to walk down? I want to talk to you about something."

She nodded, too anxious and anticipatory to speak.

A minute later they stood at the rocky bluff overlooking the lake, he to the left of her and several feet away. The sound of the waves rhythmically hitting the shore lulled her a little. They both watched the black lake rippling in the distance. He seemed so lost in his thoughts, so intent, she started a little when he finally spoke.

"How come you didn't go to medical school?" he asked.

"I didn't want to. I wanted to be a nurse."

"The kind of nurse that you are now?" he asked, perhaps a little delicately.

She glanced over at him and saw the slight puzzlement on his face. "*Yes.* A hospice nurse. That's what I wanted from the first. I didn't just fall into it by accident," she said amusedly.

He frowned. "I didn't mean to be offensive."

She broke into soft laughter. "No, it's not that. It's just I've seen that expression a time or two—or a hundred—when I tell people what I do for a living." She saw his slanting brows. "That puzzled expression you wore a second ago," she clarified. "When people understand I actually *chose* to be a hospice nurse, that I don't do it just because I couldn't get another nursing job, they seem confused. Trust me, it's a pretty good way to clear a room at a party, saying you're a hospice nurse."

"I know what that's like."

"You know what it's like to clear a room when you say what you do for a living?"

"No. To have people decide everything about you before they know you. But in your case, it's the idea of death that makes people prejudge you."

"Yeah. It does," she said quietly. "But just because death makes people uncomfortable doesn't mean that it *should* be uncomfortable."

"It's not uncomfortable for you?" he asked.

She sighed and looked out at the black water. "No. Not anymore. It can be sad at times. Poignant. Full of meaning. But no, not uncomfortable."

"I'm sorry. I can't agree with you. Death is random and cruel."

She blinked at the harsh finality of his tone.

"You've known a lot of it?" she asked softly.

"So much so that I wonder at times if life isn't playing some kind of sick joke on me," he said, his lip curling. He was trying to be funny, and failing.

"Death is a natural part of life." He gave her a burning, sardonic glance. "Sounds like an empty platitude to you, does it? It does for lots of people," she mused thoughtfully, looking at the lake, not at all put off because they didn't agree.

She looked around when he gave a dry laugh. "What?" she asked, her gaze caught by the flash of white teeth against tanned skin.

He shook his head while a breeze ruffled his hair. He peered at her as if he wanted to bring her into better focus.

"Why are you so confident talking about death?" he demanded.

She hesitated, but then shrugged. "I died before," she said simply.

She gave a small smile when she saw his blank expression segue into one of incredulity.

"*What?*"

She didn't know why she'd told him. Given people's reactions to such a declaration, she'd learned early on to avoid the topic at all costs. She sighed.

"I was born with a condition called alpha thalassemia. My body had a hard time making hemoglobin, so I was always mildly anemic as a kid. It wasn't bad enough to cause any severe symptoms except occasional fatigue, but when I was nine, something happened. My iron count plunged and my organs weren't getting enough oxygen. I had a heart attack." She noticed his stiff expression. "Don't look so worried. I hardly remember any of it. Long story short, when I recovered, I had a profound certainty that death was nothing to fear. Also . . ." She repressed a smile because she was sure he wouldn't believe her. "I was cured."

"You were cured," he repeated in flat disbelief, stepping closer.

She laughed, even though she was set off balance by his nearness. The streetlamps in the parking lot reflected in his eyes, making them gleam in his shadowed face as he studied her intently. She just nodded. "I'm very healthy. My cells now synthesize perfectly normal hemoglobin. The doctors ramble on about how maybe the crisis I went through somehow reset my cells, but technically speaking—"

"You're a medical miracle."

She shrugged, hearing the thread of disbelief and amusement in his tone. "I knew you wouldn't believe me. Very few people do, except for the staff at the hospital, my mother, my sister, and the physician who researched the case."

"And you."

"No. I don't believe. I *know*."

He shook his head slightly, looking puzzled and a little amazed. "I'd almost believe it of you. You're very . . . odd."

"I've heard that before," she muttered.

"That's not what I meant," he said, and even though he hadn't been sharp, exactly, her heartbeat began to thrum in her ears.

"You didn't mean that I'm a freak?" she clarified, trying to keep things light.

"No. I meant that you're rare. Different. Even a little otherworldly at times," he said quietly. He reached up and touched the charm where it rested at the base of her throat. Her pulse leapt just inches from his pressing fingers. So much for keeping things light. She stared up at him, her glib comment melting on her tongue.

"I know I was harsh last week in the garage," he said.

She swallowed thickly. What had occurred in the backseat of that car had become a hovering three-ton elephant for her, and yet he mentioned it so casually. She stared up at his face, spellbound. His fingertips moved, stroking her throat lightly, and then her jaw, holding her stare the whole time. Her flesh lit up beneath his touch, sending a cascade of sensation through her body, making the hair on her nape stand on end. She couldn't unglue her gaze from his mouth. It'd gotten closer somehow as she looked up at him, although she'd never seen him lean down. His fingers caressed her temple. When they sunk into her hair, it was with a greedier, more forceful gesture. She couldn't prevent shuddering at the sensation of his fingertips skimming her scalp.

"I wasn't preoccupied while I was in France because I was thinking about Cristina," he said, his mouth slanting into a frown as he stared down at her. "I was distracted from my business because I kept thinking about you."

"Oh," she said thickly.

"I'm not telling you that I was wrong the other night. Everything I said was true. I take what I want. I *am* selfish."

"Then why did you walk away that night?" Emma challenged quietly.

He fisted her hair. He looked quite fierce. "I'm not walking away now, so don't imagine that I'm something I'm not. And *never* be so stupid as to think I'm noble. Do you understand me?"

"I . . . I think so. You want to have an affair with me? Or a one-night stand, is that what you want?"

His gaze traveled over her face. She found herself wondering what he saw there.

"As much as I want you, it's going to take more than just one night," he stated grimly. "You've done something to me. I can't take it anymore. I can't sleep. I'm having trouble eating," he said, his gaze narrowing as her lips parted in wonder.

Michael Montand wanted her so much that he couldn't rest. It struck her as strange. Surreal.

"I'm aware that I'm not what you deserve," he continued. "But I don't do long-term relationships, Emma. I'm sorry for that, in your case, more than I ever have been in my life. But I don't want to lie to you. Plus, I have to travel a lot—lately nearly every week, with a big racing event I've sponsored happening very soon. Do you want me enough to take the risk, knowing all those things?"

"Yes, I think I do."

He studied her closely. "I'm not used to doing this. I know that you're young and vulnerable, though, so I'm trying."

"I'm not vulnerable. And I'm not that young."

"I disagree. But it doesn't matter anymore. If this keeps up . . ." he looked bewildered, even a little wild. "I don't know what'll happen. As long as I know you exist out there somewhere, I'll want you. The only possible thing that would stop me is if you told me no. Are you *sure* you want to agree to this?"

She nodded.

"Why?" he demanded, stepping closer to her. "*Why* are you sure?"

"Because you're beautiful," she said, trapped in a spell of honesty, ensnared by his eyes. "And because I can't stop thinking about you, either. And . . ."

"What?" he said, cradling her head in the palm of his hand, the gesture striking her as both tender and possessive. His head lowered toward hers.

"Because it's something I've never had before. The sparks," she whispered.

He swooped down and captured her mouth, the force and heat of him thrilling her. His other hand rose to her jaw, holding her in place. Her entire focus narrowed to the feeling of him. He parted her lips with his tongue, and her world became his taste. It wasn't a gentle kiss. It was a conquering one, a claiming without caution or apology. Yet the way he held her head and dipped his tongue between her lips made her feel precious somehow, like she was a treat he wanted to savor before he devoured her. He held her firmly, his clear, fixed intent to take his fill arousing her deeply. Her flesh softened in a way she'd never experienced, went warm and liquid and ready for him in seconds.

He lifted his head a moment later.

"As long as you understand," he said, taking her hand in his. "I see no reason to prolong this. I won't wait a minute longer."

Where are we going?" she asked in confusion when he led her down the stairs to the lake a moment later, her hand in his, the sound of waves hitting the beach growing louder in her ears.

"To the beach. You're flushed. You must be warm. You could use a swim," he said briskly.

"I wasn't flushed because of the heat," she muttered under her breath. She hadn't meant for him to hear her, but knew he had when he squeezed her hand. She heard his soft laugh. His amused understanding helped steady her in the face of what was to come.

A nearly full moon reflected off the white sand beach, lighting up the night to a surprising degree. He led her off the deserted public beach, however, toward the rocky shoreline to the north. Visibility was poorer here without the white expanse of sand, but her eyes had accustomed to the glowing moon and starlight. The lake was relatively calm tonight, the waves caressing the shore in a hushed, silken rhythm. She could make out the shape of piled rocks to the left and Montand's dark, compelling form walking next to her. Neither of them spoke, the sense of anticipation building to an almost smothering degree.

He paused next to a black pile of rock and moved behind her.

His dark, solid shadow lowered. She realized he'd sat down. She plopped down next to him when he pulled on her hand, a surprised laugh popping out of her throat. They sat on the relatively flat surface of a rock, facing the lake.

Her thigh and hip were pressed very tight against his solid length. His arm encircled her, pulling her even tighter. She looked up, all amusement vanished, knowing she'd find him in the darkness. His mouth closed over hers. She abandoned herself to the moment, to the rushing, cool wind and his hot kiss. She felt herself heating even more, softening against his solid length.

He broke the kiss, but she craned toward him, a bee to honey.

"How about a swim?" he asked her gruffly, nibbling and plucking at her mouth in a highly distracting manner.

"What?" she mumbled, her lips sliding against his, shaping them hungrily to her own. She couldn't get enough of his scent. His taste. His texture. Her fingers sunk into his hair, stroking and then fisting the thick waves greedily. Was this what people meant when they talked about a grand passion? No wonder they were known to do crazy things for love. Or lust, in her case. Under this mesmerizing influence, loved ones were sacrificed, kingdoms fell, pride and honor were forsaken. *Yes*, she could almost believe it while she was under the spell of his kiss. Having never experienced this dizzying rush of heat and need, Emma had always been a little skeptical it existed until now.

He stroked the skin of her bare arm, and she shivered.

It existed, all right. In spades.

"Do you want to take a swim?" he repeated patiently, his long fingers touching the edge of her blouse, and then burrowing beneath it, sliding against the skin of her shoulder. It was a relatively innocent caress, but the way he did it made her become even more warm and damp between her thighs.

"Um . . . okay," she replied breathlessly. She wasn't exactly sure what was expected of her. She'd never taken a midnight swim with a man like him before, a swim that was the prelude to sex. She'd never done something so impulsive and sexy, period.

He stood, pulling her up next to him. The side of his hand brushed her breast, and her breath caught. He began to unbutton her blouse. His hands moving against her skin as he deftly undressed her sent the swooping butterflies in her stomach into frantic mode. He paused just below her belly button as if he'd actually felt them fluttering frantically.

"Are you okay?" he asked, his warm breath brushing her hairline.

"Yes," she said hastily. He remained still. "I've just . . . never done this before."

She felt him stiffen. "Never done *what*?" he asked, and she heard tension harden his tone.

"Gone swimming in the lake naked?" The silence made her a little desperate. "With . . . with someone like you?"

"Someone like me?" His fingers resumed their journey downward, and she sighed in relief.

"Someone so . . ." She gulped when he swept back both sides of her blouse and the lake breeze hit her bare skin. "Wait . . . are you looking for a compliment?"

His low, rich laughter was delicious.

"Maybe. It might be nice, hearing one from you," he said.

"I complimented you up there. On the bluff," she reminded him distractedly. The warm fingers of one hand had slid beneath the back of her bra strap, making a ripple of pleasure go through her. Her nipples pulled tight. Her bra seemed to snap open as if by magic at his mere touch.

"You're very good at that," she said doubtfully, referring to his bra maneuvering.

"That wasn't the compliment I was aiming for. Besides, from your tone, it might have been an insult," he said as he drew the straps off her shoulders and down her arms, his light touch on her skin making her shiver. It took her a moment to register the wry humor in his tone.

"It wasn't an insult," she said as the cups of her bra evaporated into the darkness and the light breeze licked and swirled against her sensitive bare breasts. "But as for my tone, it sort of gets to the point."

His large hands settled on her bare shoulders, his touch warm and reassuring, and somehow forbidden and electrically exciting at once. "Speak English, Emma," he said, sounding less amused this time as his hands swept down her arms and back up again, as if he experimented with the feeling of her. She firmed her resolve, as difficult as it was to do with his warm, strong hands moving over her naked skin.

"I don't have all that much experience, and it seems like you do."

His hands paused in their exploration on her shoulder blades.

"Experience could mean a lot of different things," he finally said warily.

"I know. Just forget it. It's only . . . I wanted you to know I don't usually fool around with men I've known for a week. In fact, I've only ever been with . . . you know," she muttered, her cheeks starting to boil. Thank goodness for the darkness. She didn't want to say Colin's name out loud. She was already ruining the spontaneity of the moment as it was.

"And you were with Colin for two years," he said, understanding and something that sounded like relief seeping into his tone.

"And it was never sex on the beach," Emma admitted, wondering if he'd intuit the manifold meaning behind the words *sex on the beach.* It'd never been crazy or raunchy or a spur-of-the-moment impulse. Sex had never been extremely bad or mind-blowingly good for her. It'd been nice sometimes, a little trying others.

It'd never been scary or beautiful or heart-pounding-in-your-ears wild.

It'd never been *this.*

Why had she brought it up at all? Nerves. The bane of her existence when it came to sex. That's what Colin used to say, anyway. Maybe Montand would end up telling her the same thing—

His arms came around her, sending her thoughts scattering. Instinctively, she embraced him back, her arms looping around his waist. With one open hand, he caressed the side of her from hip to just under her upraised arm, his palm skimming the side of her bare breast. She trembled.

"Do you feel that?" he asked quietly, his mouth very close to her ear. His hand moved ever so slightly, and she shivered again.

"Yes," she breathed out against his chest.

His hand lowered and joined its mate just below her waist. He dipped his knees and aligned her against him. She felt him throbbing, full and vibrant, next to her lower belly.

"And that?" His dark tone sent another shudder of excitement through her.

"Yes," she whispered, her hands clutching at his taut waist. She strained against him, feeling his shape through their clothing. A lump formed in her throat. He felt so good. So exciting.

"That's all that matters. What happens when we're together. No one else. *Nothing* else," he rasped before he kissed her ear persuasively, and she shuddered in mounting excitement.

His hands cupped her ass. She suppressed a whimper when he pushed her against him, clearly as eager to feel her shape as she was to feel his.

"It doesn't matter how much experience either one of us has," he continued hoarsely as he kissed her temple. "All that matters is you and me, and what feels right. What feels good." His hands swept up over her naked back and sides again, his manner more forceful, kneading her muscles, his hunger clearly mounting. "The way you feel is new to me."

"It . . . it is?" she asked in amazement.

"You make me almost feel new, too. Almost . . ."

She suppressed a whimper, stunned, moved by the quiet intensity of his tone. She wanted to thank him for the unusual compliment, but his mouth covered hers. Her returned kiss spoke for her. Or at least she hoped it did.

Their hands moved while they tasted each other, unbuttoning, undressing, pausing every once in a while out of necessity to remove jeans and shoes and socks.

Finally Emma was completely naked, her bare feet sinking into the cool sand, her arms empty. He knelt before her, removing his final remnants of clothing, but then he rose, a large, solid mass in front of her. Her heart jumped against her breastbone when he spread his hand at her waist.

"Come here," he said gruffly. She went to him at that arousing, increasingly familiar bidding.

She closed her eyes, wonder and need sweeping through her when she felt his hard, naked body press against her in the darkness. He swept back her hair with one hand and cradled her head in that claiming manner that always made her breathless. His fingers fisting her hair, he pulled gently and her chin went back. He pressed his hot, open mouth to her pulse, tasting her, his lips moving sensually on her skin. She arched against a wall of solid, ridged muscle, her breasts crushing against his lower chest. His cock leapt against her lower belly and hip like a living thing, the size and weight of him thrilling. Intimidating.

But it was only pure disappointment she felt when he brushed his fingers down her arm, his hot mouth still against her neck, and took her hand in his. He stepped away.

"Let's get in," he said.

She followed his slow pace. "Careful," he directed as they made their way to the water, and she knew why he'd warned her. The sand from the city beach had blown here, but small rocks intermixed with it. His hold on her was steady, though, even when the surf swept across her feet and she started.

"Oh my God, it's so cold!" she blurted out.

He chuckled. "It's Lake Michigan. It's always cold. You'll get used to it."

His hand tightened around hers and she followed him unerringly. She could barely see anything. Her skin actually hurt from the goose bumps covering it, and there was an uncomfortable pressure growing in her stomach as her body protested against the rising cold and the eerie blackness in front of her. She instinctively followed him, however, trusting the feeling of his firm, warm grip even more than her body's primal urging for warmth and safety.

A wave lapped against her belly. She shrieked at the unpleasant jolting sensation, and then snorted with laughter. Impulsively she let go of his hand and plunged into the darkness. Cold encapsulated her, the tingling sensation in her flesh blending with her bubbling excitement. She swam blindly for a few moments, then surfaced.

"It feels fantastic!" she called out breathlessly. Her feet searched for the bottom. She'd swum out farther than she'd thought. She began to tread water automatically.

"Emma, come back here."

She blinked, her euphoria slightly dimmed by the tension in his deep voice. Maybe he was right. She was an okay swimmer, but nothing great—

"*Emma*?"

She swam toward the sound of his voice. "Here I am."

Her outstretched hands brushed against the round, dense muscles of his shoulders, and suddenly he was hauling her against him. He caught her around the waist and propelled them toward the shore with a powerful kick in the water. Her feet floundered for the bottom, but she still couldn't reach it.

"It's okay. I've got you," he said, and she realized he now stood, the water up around his neck, and was holding her above the waterline. She gave a nervous laugh. Her heart raced like mad. She didn't know why. Her skittishness about what was happening with him had made her imagine his sudden anxiety.

Her hands slid across slick, hard flesh as if of their own volition. He felt amazing. She felt the tension in his muscles yield slightly. Her fingers skimmed across the hair on his chest. The velvety head of his cock flicked next to her thigh. Arousal spiked through her, a hot needle through her chilled flesh. She gripped his shoulders and he brought her closer. His cock wasn't as erect as it had been when they stood on the beach, but it still felt formidable and beyond exciting feeling him pressed next to her skin.

"You're so warm," she said, seeking him out instinctively with every inch of her skin.

The contrast of his heat and the cold water was wonderful. His hand lowered to her ass, his fingers flexing in her upper thigh. She followed his nonverbal command without thought, understanding him even in the silent darkness. She raised her legs, gripping his hips with them. He lowered his other hand to her ass and lifted her higher against him, their skin sliding together in a sweet, frictionless glide, their faces coming closer.

"You're so soft," he murmured, his lips brushing against hers, his big hands moving on her ass.

"Is that a polite way of saying I need to get to the gym?" she joked, looping her arms around his neck and sinking her fingers into his damp hair.

"No. Are you fishing for compliments now?" he asked when she pulled gently on his hair and he tilted his face back for her kiss.

"No," she replied, nibbling at his damp mouth . . . such succulent, firm male lips. She could never get enough of them. "But it might be nice, hearing one from you right now," she said, echoing what he'd said earlier.

"Okay." He squeezed her ass cheeks into his palms gently before he stroked her thighs, and then cupped her bottom again. "When I look at you from the back, I lose all sense of reason, so I try not to as much as possible," he said, his quiet, deep voice pitched just above the sound of the surf in the distance. He swept one hand along the side of a buttock up her hip to her waist. "This curve? This one right here," he said thickly as he swept it back down to cup her ass again, "makes me lose all sense of logic."

Emma had stopped nipping playfully at his lips and gone still in his arms. A frisson of excitement had rippled through her at his honesty. "It does?" she asked weakly.

"I'm here, even though I know I shouldn't be. What more proof do you need?" he said with a low growl, his mouth closing briefly on hers. "Everything is just as bad from the front, mind you." He swept one hand along her sensitive side. She shivered at his warm touch in the cool water.

"Oh," she exhaled when his hand closed over her breast. He shaped her to him gently.

"So soft here," he said. His fingers caressed her nipple. "So hard here. Such pretty little breasts," he murmured thickly. He pinched lightly at the erect flesh. Emma gripped his waist tighter with her legs and pressed her sex against his hard midriff, desperate to alleviate the pressure growing there. He pushed against her with his hand on her ass, at once helping her find relief and mounting her excitement higher. "I wondered how responsive you'd be. When I found out the other night, that was the end of restful sleep. I can't remember how many times I jacked off over the weekend thinking about how your nipples felt against my tongue."

"*Oh God*," she exhaled raggedly and pressed her lips against his neck, intensely aroused by his sexual honesty. Her hands slicked across his muscular back, absorbing the sensation of his stark male strength.

He nuzzled the back of her head with his nose and chin, and then spoke gruffly near her ear. "But as much as I might lech over your gorgeous ass and perfect breasts and pretty face, it's not those things that make me the most crazy. It's your kindness. Your freshness. Your eyes—"

"*Don't* say that," she said, halting her feverish kisses. Men who offered nothing but a sexual affair shouldn't say things like that. Her fingernails dug into his back, her hips flexed against him hard. She didn't know why she suddenly felt so desperate. Shouldn't she have protested over his dirty talk rather than his sweetness? But it was the intensity of his tone just now that had felt so wonderful and unbearable at once.

"Shh," he soothed, as if he knew what was happening inside her, knew how wild she felt, how overwhelmed. But how could he? His mouth covered hers, and it was like he'd thrown a life preserver into a boiling sea. His kiss enflamed her as always, but it also steadied her somehow, his taste and mastery a familiar touchstone. He really knew how to use his mouth, she realized dazedly. Sensual and giving, yet so firm. So demanding. She experienced the slight suction he applied to her mouth at the very core of her body. It took her a moment or two to realize he walked toward shore. Only when gravity took hold as he lifted her out of the water did she start to sag against him, and their kiss broke.

"Hold on," he instructed.

She firmed her hold on his shoulders and gripped his waist as tightly as she could with her legs. His muscles tautened beneath her fingers as he took her full weight, both hands on her ass.

"You can put me down," she said shakily.

"Hold on," he repeated in that tone that didn't invite argument.

He carried her out of the water and onto the shore. He let go of her with one hand, the other keeping her in place, his supple strength and balance amazing her. She realized when he bent slightly that he was arranging some of their clothing on the flat rock. He turned so that her back faced the water.

"I'm sitting," he informed her, firming his hold on her with both hands.

A little puff of air flew past her hips when he sat, bringing her with him. She plopped into his lap, her ass falling back onto his hard thighs and the thick, engorged column of his cock.

"Oh my," flew out of her throat.

"Are you okay?" he demanded.

"Yes," she said quickly. He throbbed against her ass. His grip on her hips tightened. He flexed his arms, pulsing her against him. She gasped.

"That?" he asked, still referring to why she'd exclaimed so emphatically.

"Yes," she whispered, understanding him perfectly.

"I can feel you, too. You're warm and soft and wet. It's going to feel so fucking good inside you," he rasped, naked longing ringing in his hoarse voice. With her legs opened, her pussy pressed snuggly against his lower belly. "I can't wait anymore, Emma. I couldn't even wait for how long it'd take to drive back home and take you in my bed," he said, his lips fluttering against the pulse at her neck. "Are you ready for me?"

She arched her back and pressed the erect tips of her breasts against his chest, craving his hardness and heat.

"Yes," she whispered. "*Please.*"

Chapter 10

His mouth grew more voracious on her neck, his teeth lightly scraping her skin amplifying her already immense arousal. She dragged her nails against his scalp and turned her head, raining kisses on his temple, so hot. So ready.

"You'll have to scoot back for a moment," he grated out. Emma blinked, the realization hitting her that he was applying pressure on her hips with his hands, pushing her back . . . away from him.

"Why?"

"Condom," he said, and by the terseness of his tone, she knew he wasn't exactly pleased by the idea of unsealing their damp, naked bodies, either, even for a moment.

A *necessary* moment.

"Of course," she whispered, a little mortified. She was glad at least one of them maintained the ability for rational thought. She scooted back on his thighs, her bottom sliding against dense muscle and crinkly hair. He was cool on the very surface from the swim, but just beneath it, she felt his heat. It was too dark for her to see much of anything but the shadows of the towering rock behind him and just the outline of his form. Sometimes even his dim outline blended into the shadows so that he seemed to become invisible, the sensation of his hard, warm body her only guidepost. She thought she saw his arm move and heard clothing rustle, and knew he was retrieving a condom. She heard the ripping sound as he opened the package, the erotic vision of him applying the prophylactic springing vividly up in her imagination.

"I wish I could see you."

He made a hissing sound under his breath. Had he cursed?

"I told you I was no angel," she said softly.

He reached for her, his hands wrapping around her upper arms. "Come here," he said, and by the hastiness of his movements and the tension in his voice, she knew he liked what she'd said. He placed a hand at her lower back, pushing her close to him, the other beneath a buttock, the pressure urging her to rise over him. "Put your knees down next to me," he instructed. "I've got my clothes under us, but if your knees start to hurt, tell me."

Emma scurried to try to find a position that worked. She wanted this so much, to join with him. She settled on her knees and was poised over his lap.

"Raise up higher," he urged, one hand on her hip, guiding her. She felt the tip of his cock brush against her opening and gasped. He felt large and hard as steel. His fingertips were tender, though, as he gently parted her delicate tissues.

"Help me, Emma," he said, and her heart jumped in her chest at the desperation in his tone. She would have done much, much more than was required in that moment to relieve his anguish. She firmed her hold on his shoulders at the same time that she flexed her hips. Gritting her teeth, she pressed down on him. At first, her body seemed to resist him, but then she felt herself stretching around him . . . melting around his hardness.

"Ah, Jesus," he hissed. "You're so small. So warm. *Hot.*" Both of his hands cradled her hips now as he assisted her, guiding her, taking just enough of her weight to let her ease down on his cock without too much haste or force. Emma was glad he couldn't see her in the darkness. It wasn't painful, but it *was* uncomfortable at first, as her body grew accustomed to him. She bit her lip to restrain a moan, worried he would interpret her discomfort and stop what she wanted so much—

"Emma? Are you all right?" he asked sharply, and she realized that her absolute silence had been warning enough for him. He increased the pressure on her hips, holding her immobile, keeping her from flexing farther down on him. She paused with several inches of thick, tumescent flesh piercing her. She craved more.

"Yes," she said, air puffing out of her lungs. She'd been holding her breath, and now he knew it. "Please . . . don't stop," she begged brokenly.

He remained unmoving for a moment before he pushed down gently on her hips and another inch of him carved its way into her body. "As if I could," he muttered darkly, and he brought her closer yet.

He was filling her, the sensation overwhelming. Wonderful. She finally sat in his lap, his cock fully sheathed inside her. He held her tightly against him. Emma pressed her face into the crevice of his neck and shoulder and shuddered. They panted together, their ragged breaths and the sensation of his cock pulsing high and hard inside her becoming her entire world. Then he nudged her ear with his nose and said her name. She couldn't decide if those two syllables on his lips were a command or a plea, but it didn't matter. In that moment, there was only one way she could reply.

She lifted her hips several inches and sunk down on him again, gasping at the intensity of the pressure. His low, rough groan sounded like it might have been ripped out of the core of him. His fingers sunk into the flesh of her hips and buttocks as he began to assist her in the rise and fall of her body over him.

"Oh God," she moaned, because his driving cock was starting a fire in her flesh, the hard, relentless friction making nerves deep inside her burn. Her body ceased resisting him, beginning to crave his possession. Emma lost all sense of time and place as she rose and fell over him. His hands on her hips and ass tightened as he took away more control from her. She let him have it, trusting him.

She cried out as he thrust her down on him with force, and her buttocks slapped loudly against his thighs. He groaned gutturally, repeating the bull's-eye stroke again and again until both of them were frenzied. Her clutching hands moved on his shoulders down to his arms as he drove her down on his cock. His biceps were bulging and hard, as he took a good part of her body weight, lifting and plunging, until she longed for nothing else but ignition. Release. She sunk her nails into the dense muscle of his arms and cried out in wild desperation.

He slammed her down into his lap and pressed her down tightly to him at the same moment that he delved his fingers into her hair and palmed her head.

"Come here," he commanded harshly.

He kissed her forcefully—devoured her—while his cock throbbed deep inside her. The hand on her hip moved, his thumb stretching between her thighs. His fingertip found her clit, rubbing the slick, erect button, and Emma exploded. Waves of pleasure shook her, but he wouldn't release her from his relentless kiss. It was like being pummeled by two different storm fronts: pleasure and possession. She moaned helplessly into his mouth.

He ate up every cry.

He finally released Emma from his kiss when her sharp cries became whimpers and he'd worked every last shudder of pleasure from her sleek, sweet body. The fragrance of her climax perfumed the air, the scent of it mixed with their perspiration and the fresh lake breeze making him see red. He ran his hands over her naked body, his greed for her even sharper now that he was about to be appeased in his hunger.

For a short while, anyway.

His searching hands found her breasts, firm and thrusting from the plane of her chest, the skin exquisitely soft, the nipples small and hard, mouthwatering . . .

He took a beaded crest into his mouth, unable to resist, laving at the hard point with his tongue. He began to move her hips, riding her on his cock in tight little circles. It was like doling out tidbits to a beast, keeping it at bay for a few precious moments, knowing all the while it wouldn't last long . . .

He bit down very gently on her nipple and heard her cry out. He wasn't sure if it was in pleasure or pain, but then felt the flush of heat around his cock. He knew then. Everything went black for a moment. The next thing he knew, he held her wrists behind her back and she was crashing down over him. He experienced a moment of regret—he hadn't meant to become so controlling with her given her inexperience—but then it slowly hit his lust-drunk brain that she was riding him just as furiously as he drove her down on him.

"Arch your back, Emma," he grated out as he fucked her at a hard, fast pace. With the hand that held her wrists at the small of her back, he felt her follow his command. Her supple torso arched gracefully, her submission natural. Sublime. "That's right. Offer yourself to me."

She whimpered shakily. He latched onto a thrusting breast, sucking forcefully. Orgasm slammed into him at the sound of her sharp scream. He felt her convulse around his cock. His body pulsed with his pleasure. Hers. It all fused in the explosion.

After a final shudder of pleasure wracked him, he dropped his forehead against her chest, feeling the rise and fall of her breath and the rapid throb of her heart. He turned his face so that he could feel the precious pulse of life against his lips. He pulled her closer in his arms. She softly murmured something he couldn't quite make out, but which he understood, anyway.

He'd lost his virginity on this very beach when he was fourteen years old. It had nothing to do with why he was here tonight. He'd been to this beach dozens of times in his life. He'd come as a screwed-up teenager in a desperate search for fun. Forgetfulness. As an adult, he'd come many times for a solitary walk.

But the reason he distantly recalled losing his virginity on this beach during a drunken escapade with an equally drunk, bored socialite friend of his stepmother's had nothing at all to do with holding Emma right now while her heartbeat fluttered against his lips. He only thought of it because the two experiences were direct opposites of each other. Yeah, they both involved sex and a woman and pleasure. Lots of experiences from his life involved that, but comparing those incidents to *this*?

The truth was: it was like comparing dust to a diamond.

After that first time, they remained clasped together. Emma thought she might be projecting her own novicelike feelings onto Montand, but it seemed to her that there was a desperation to their tight embrace, as if they dreaded what might separate them, fighting for this ephemeral moment, staving off the reality that awaited them outside the protective bubble they'd created together.

Surely it was an illusion—wishful thinking—on her part. She was quite certain no such musings or flights of fancy were occurring to him, especially given his careful description of their relationship.

"I have to move. The condom," he said gruffly near her ear a moment later, and her last thought was confirmed. She was thankful that he was much more practical in these matters than she was—the nurse—who should have known better. At least she was on birth control following her relationship with Colin. Pregnancy was one worry she needn't have.

He helped her rise off him. He still felt very firm as he withdrew. The ensuing empty ache she experienced was highly unpleasant to her. She sat perched on his thighs, bracing herself on his shoulders, listening to him rustling in the darkness. Then his hands were on her hips again, guiding her toward him. She started when she felt the tip of his cock nudge her pussy.

"Again?" she whispered, amazed.

"I changed the condom. Is it all right?"

"Yes."

"I wasn't finished being inside you."

"No. I wasn't finished having you there," she said with a small laugh.

She winced at first as he entered her, still tender from their first time. From him, in general. It wasn't like being with Colin.

She settled in his lap again, his cock lodged deep inside her, and sighed in relief. Bliss. "*Yes*," she repeated breathlessly, her arms going around his neck, her breasts pressing to his chest. She contracted her muscles around him and he gave a rough groan, pulling her even tighter against him. Now that he was inside her again, it felt wonderful. The crisp hair on his hard chest felt so good against her swollen nipples. One of his hands swept along her sensitive sides and settled on the side of her breast. He cupped her, and for a minute, didn't move. His hand felt warm surrounding her, delicious. Possessive.

He began to mold the flesh softly to his palm, his fingertips brushing across the nipple. She sighed, and he jerked inside her, the moment sublime.

They stayed like that for as long as they could, stroking each other. He occasionally uttered rough praise into her ear as he touched her. He said she was beautiful again and again, and she felt it, there, in his arms. As time wore on, and he began to move her on his again-rigid cock, the anthem he whispered heatedly became more terse and dark and raw. It was no less beautiful to her, though, and exponentially more thrilling.

Emma still felt dazed and shaky and euphoric by the time he approached the Breakers' driveway at 2:45 a.m. It'd been the most incredible night of her life. Everything felt different, as if she'd been opened up to another world, had finally gained admission to that coveted, forbidden, dangerous place called passion. Everything *looked* different, too, the starlit, dark blue dome of the night sky miraculous. This world sparkled and shone, and seemed to throb with life. Her bare skin tingled with new awareness. Even the ache between her thighs was pleasant to her, a reminder of what had happened on that beach in his arms.

She'd recall the purely physical reasons for the affair later, but not now.

He grabbed her hand once he'd gotten the little car up to the zooming speed that he wanted, his gaze focused on the road. She'd held it back fast, stealing glances at his profile, halfway amused by her inability to control her amorous behavior, halfway uncaring. How many nights like this happened in a girl's life, anyway? Certainly only one in Emma's so far.

He had to release her hand as he downshifted when they reached the Breakers. Sadness spiked through her intoxicated state at the idea of returning. She'd rather spend the night with him in his arms.

She looked over at him after he'd pulled the sports car into the garage and parked with almost mechanical precision.

He turned to her. It was the first time in hours that she'd looked him full in the face in the light. His solemn male beauty struck her anew. She resisted a strong urge to touch his jaw . . . sink her fingers into his thick hair. The realization that she still felt uncertain around him given her agreement to a purely sexual affair and what had just occurred on the beach sobered her.

"Can you stay?" he asked simply.

She was glad she'd crashed to earth before he said it, or else she'd undoubtedly have agreed. His allure was alarmingly potent.

"No. It wouldn't be right. Not only because Amanda would worry, but because of work. It's already wrong enough, what I did tonight . . ." she trailed off.

He took the keys out of the ignition, but didn't move to get out of the car. He placed his wrists on the top of the wheel, his relaxed hands draping over it, his lean body slouching in that graceful, insouciant, but strangely *ready* manner that seemed so much a part of him. "It didn't feel wrong," he said after a pause.

"No. It didn't."

She saw his jaw working in the silence that followed. "We'll go someplace nice next time."

"You didn't think tonight was nice?"

She couldn't decide if his sideways glance at her was amused, disbelieving, or vaguely irritated.

"I did. Very. But you should expect more, Emma," he said in that flat, authoritative tone that confused her at times. "I should have picked someplace more appropriate for the first time." He shrugged. "I just couldn't wait."

"I'm a pretty good judge of deciding what I think is nice, and what I want and don't want. Thanks."

"I just meant you deserve something better."

"Than your selfishness?" she couldn't resist teasing him when he was so grave.

He glanced at her with hard incredulity. Despite her determination to lighten the moment, she resisted the urge to flinch at his stare. May as well face it, he was not a man used to being teased.

"I did exactly what I wanted to do tonight. Stop taking yourself so seriously," she said, reaching for her car door.

He reached out and caught her hand. She looked around in surprise. Her eyes widened when she saw his blazing expression. His hand moved to the back of her head, cupping her to his palm in an increasingly familiar gesture. He brought her to him, seizing her mouth. He kissed her furiously. She'd thought the volcano of their passion had quieted for the night, but she'd been wrong. She felt herself submerged in the heat all over again. Arousal expanded at her core, an undeniable ache. He abruptly tore his mouth from hers and spoke next to her parted lips.

"Do you want to teach me how to lighten up, Emma?" he growled softly.

She swallowed with difficulty, her body vibrating with reawakened arousal. "I think someone should," she managed.

"Fine. Then just be prepared for the darkness during the attempt."

Her mouth fell open, but she wasn't sure how to respond to his remark.

"I'll come and get you tomorrow after you finish your shift," he said.

She nodded. Then he was turning and getting out of the car. And Emma was cast right back into that churning sea of doubt and longing.

She slept in the next day until noon, only to awake to sunlight blazing through the miniblinds. It seemed to burn away the vestiges of her dreams—dark, erotic dreams that held her fast in its clutches, dreams that had nothing to do with the beauty of what had happened last night on that beach.

That was what she'd focus on, that indescribably moving experience. And she was going to see him again tonight . . .

She bounded out of bed and flipped open the blinds, staring out onto a gorgeous July day. *A day reserved for the young and healthy*, she recalled Cristina saying. Emma wasn't so sure about that, but it did feel like a wonderful moment to be alive. It was like everything was freshly minted, a golden sheen applied during the night. Amanda gave her a surprised look when Emma entered the kitchen humming cheerfully after her shower.

"What's got you in such a good mood?" Amanda asked as she rinsed out a cereal bowl. Emma belatedly recalled her breakup with Colin—and Amanda's part in it—and realized how odd her presentation must be to her sister.

"Nothing. It's a pretty day, that's all."

"You look great," Amanda said, her gaze skimming over another new outfit Emma had purchased over the weekend, this one a simple body-hugging black V-neck and a new pair of jeans that did especially good things for her legs and hips. She noticed Amanda's focus on the necklace he'd given her. Her sister's expression grew suspicious. "Are you not telling me something?"

"Can't a girl be in a good mood?" Emma asked as she poured some juice.

"Sure, I guess," Amanda said slowly. "Emma, have you *met* someone?"

Jeez, first Cristina, then Montand, now Amanda. She really needed to stop being so transparent. Amanda distractedly hit the switch for the garbage disposal. Emma lunged over to the sink, hoping Amanda would forget her question. They both watched in satisfaction as milk, water, and leftover cereal were sucked down the drain in an instant. They looked at each other and shared a grin. For a few seconds, it was like they were twelve and ten all over again and they'd never even heard the name Colin.

Reality hit Emma, and she turned away. She was trying to make peace with Amanda. It was just hard.

"I can't believe our apartment is fully functional now," Amanda said, attempting to smooth over the awkward moment.

"Yeah. I'm still in shock," Emma admitted.

Toby Martin had been true to his word and fixed everything in their unit, even though it'd taken him the better part of three whole days to do it. What confused Emma was his amiability and downright cheerfulness at doing all the work that had been postponed for so long.

"Emma . . . I've been meaning to speak to you about what happened on Sunday when you saw Colin and me in the parking lot. I wanted to explain."

"You don't need to," Emma said, sipping her juice to neutralize her sharp tone.

"He was really worried about . . . everything."

"He was worried about you," Emma said levelly. "Are you going to see him tonight?"

Amanda looked stunned.

"I know you've seen Colin every night since Sunday," Emma continued. "Just be honest, Amanda. Are you going to see Colin? Regularly?"

Amanda nodded uncomfortably. "I'll make sure he never comes over here," Amanda whispered.

Emma sighed and set her glass down on the counter. "No. That's not necessary. This is your home." She glanced around at Amanda. "Maybe try to do it when I'm not around, though? At least until I get used to things?"

"Maybe it's not a good idea to have him here at all," Amanda said miserably.

"Don't worry about me, Amanda," she said, getting sick of being perceived as the tragic victim in all this. "Believe it or not, part of me wishes things work out between you and Colin."

"*Really*?"

Emma met her sister's stare and nodded. "If you guys end up euphorically happy together, if it becomes obvious you two were *meant* to be together . . . then at least I'll be able to make sense of what you did," she said before she walked out of the kitchen.

The brilliant day and her glow about what had happened the previous night stood in direct contrast to the bleak mood hovering in Cristina's bedroom suite when she arrived that afternoon. Emma took one look at Maureen Sanderson's drawn face and knew her patient had reached the end of her days.

"Is she still with us?" Emma asked quietly when Maureen joined her in the living room of the suite.

"Only just," Maureen said.

"Did she ask to speak to Montand?"

"No. She wants to speak to you. I held off on giving her afternoon pain meds because she asked me not to. She seemed worried she'd go before you got here."

Emma nodded and promised to call Maureen if anything happened on her shift in regard to their patient. She took a deep breath to center herself and stepped into Cristina's bedroom. After taking one look at Cristina's bleary-eyed expression and hearing her wheezing breath, Emma knew neither Maureen or she would be returning for work at the Breakers tomorrow.

"Hi, you," Emma greeted Cristina warmly when she saw her eyes were open. "Let me prop you up a little bit," she said when she saw how Cristina had slumped on the pillows. "Are you comfortable, Cristina?" she asked a moment later. Cristina nodded. She seemed to want to speak, but was conserving her energy. Her lungs rattled with collected fluid as she laboriously gasped for air. Cristina nodded significantly toward the windows. Emma looked around at the draped wall of glass.

"The windows? Do you want me to open the curtains?" Emma interpreted.

Cristina nodded, her anxiety evident even in her waning state.

Emma immediately opened the drapes. Sunlight reflected brilliantly off the sealike stretch of water. She turned, only to see Cristina staring out at the lake and the sunshine, transfixed. A film of tears shone in her rheumy blue eyes. Emma sat in the chair near the bed when she saw Cristina start to speak.

"Such a beautiful place to die," Cristina whispered.

Emma's heart lurched. The phone in the bedroom suite began to ring shrilly, jarring her out of the poignancy of the moment. She recalled Montand's direction to keep the drapes closed. Cristina had specifically made the request for her to open the curtains, however, and Emma wasn't going to deny her dying wish because of his inexplicable demand.

She started to go answer the phone, but it stopped abruptly midring.

"Here . . ." Cristina beckoned with her outstretched hand. Emma sunk down in the chair next to her bed and took her hand.

"What is it?"

"I'm sorry," Cristina whispered between gurgling gasps.

Emma nodded. "I know you are," she assured, understanding that

Cristina wasn't apologizing for anything she'd done to Emma. She was trying to do what she'd hinted she wanted to do; she was repenting in the bright sunlight. For what, Emma didn't know. It was enough that she unburdened herself and Emma was there to bear witness.

"Tell him . . . I'm sorry . . . for not wanting them. For hating . . . them, at times," Cristina pleaded with great effort, every word appearing to take gargantuan effort.

"Tell who?" Emma asked. "Your stepson?"

"Vanni . . . I couldn't share the spotlight . . . Michael's love. Any of it. I was better suited to be a plaything. A mistress, not a wife. Not a mother."

Emma nodded, tears filling her eyes when she sensed the deep well of the older woman's regret. Her desperation. The resentment she had spoken of just now had blocked her from speaking until she was at the threshold, and knew there was no going back.

"I'll tell him," Emma assured.

"And . . . tell Vanni . . . to forgive himself. I *know* he thinks it's his fault. Maybe because I refused to—"

Cristina wretched. Emma sprung up to alter her position, but before she could assist, Cristina caught her breath and continued, and squeezed Emma's hand hard enough to make her wince.

". . . to accept the blame. No child should have been left to feel so much. No man forced to feel so little. But I couldn't help him. Not *me*." She met Emma's stare, her eyes wild. "I am what I am, and nothing more."

"Try to relax, Cristina. It's going to be okay. *Please* rest easy," Emma implored, sitting again so that Cristina could more easily see her face. "I'll *tell* him."

Cristina's gaze shifted over Emma's shoulder, her stricken expression making Emma's throat tighten painfully.

"Don't be afraid, Cristina. It's going to be all right. You'll see," Emma assured.

But Cristina was clearly lost in her painful memories, her focus elsewhere. "I never . . . meant to harm Adrian," she gasped, her blue eyes now haunted. "I was selfish . . . neglectful, but not malicious. Forgive me, Vanni . . . *please.*"

Emma opened her mouth to assure her that her last words were being heard, but someone else spoke.

"Ask for my mother's forgiveness. Ask for Adrian's."

Emma blinked in shock upon hearing the male voice behind her. She turned around and saw to whom Cristina spoke. He stood just behind Emma's chair, his face as hard and beautiful as sculpted marble.

"Your mother and Adrian would forgive me, Vanni. It's *you* who won't."

"Ask it," he bit out harshly.

"I do . . . ask it," Cristina sputtered, fighting for breath.

"If you ask for theirs, there's no need for mine. I survived," Montand said quietly, something indefinable leaping into his blue-green eyes.

"Did you?"

He pinned the dying woman with his stare. Emma turned back when Cristina inhaled with great effort, seemingly clawing for air. Emma was reminded again of a drowning person flailing for one last breath, one last chance.

It wasn't granted to Cristina. The hand that clutched Emma's went lax.

"*Cristina,*" Emma cried out shakily, but Cristina never exhaled. She had died on an unfinished breath.

Emma went into automatic mode, standing and checking for a pulse. When she found none, she noted the time on her watch, then checked for a pulse a second time. Then a third.

After a stretched moment, she gently closed Cristina's eyes and drew the sheet over her rigid face.

"She's gone?" he asked.

"Yes," Emma replied woodenly.

She faced him.

Vanni.

He wore a simple white T-shirt and jeans. The brilliant sunshine flooding the room made his short-sleeved T-shirt look superwhite against his tanned skin. It brought out golden streaks in his brown hair. She realized numbly that every time she'd seen him before, it had been in the subdued light of the enormous garage or beneath a night sky. She *had* seen those golden highlights in his hair, though—in the lamplight of his bedroom suite. The shirt was short-sleeved, allowing Emma to see the Asian-looking tattoo symbols on his muscular biceps.

A strange, unpleasant tingling sensation started at the base of her spine and ran the length of her backbone.

"Emma?" he asked, his gaze narrowed on her face. He reached out to touch her—steady her, perhaps, because dizziness had assailed her—but Emma backed away, clumsily running into the chair and tripping. She caught herself on the back of the chair.

"You're him? Vanni? That's *you*?" she asked in a strangled voice. Blood started to pound in her ears as she stared at the tattoo, unable to deny the truth with the evidence right there in front of her. He'd cut his hair since that night. Most of the sun-lightened streaks had been sheared away, leaving it much darker looking. When she'd been trapped in the armoire, it draped his face. She hadn't recognized him sitting there like an aloof, lonely prince at the end of that grand dining room table or when he'd tapped on her window and offered his assistance. She hadn't recognized him, as he'd made love so fiercely—so perfectly—to her in the darkness.

Had she?

His expression flattened. "I go by Vanni. Giovanni is my middle name. My father's name was Michael, too, so—"

It was as if her brain overloaded. She began to shake. She didn't *know* him. The thought kept thundering in her brain, the pounding force of it threatening to burst something vital.

He reached for her again, but his hand fell slowly when he saw her flinch back. The cold, detached expression she'd seen on his face as he spoke to Cristina settled on his features once again, the same expression he'd worn when Cristina had begged him for his forgiveness just now.

Forgiveness that he'd refused to grant.

A wave of nausea hit her as she recalled what she'd witnessed when she'd been trapped in that armoire, and then what had happened on that beach last night.

"You need to contact the funeral home," she told him as she hastened past him.

"Emma, what *is* it?"

She made a beeline to the bathroom. She shut the door and turned on the tap with trembling fingers, not wanting him to hear her being sick.

Week THREE

Chapter 11

Emma had been fooling herself. It shocked her beyond words that she had the ability to blind her own judgment, to delude herself into not seeing the obvious, like a magician with a sleight of hand.

When she exited the bathroom a few minutes later, she found Mrs. Shaw and Montand—*Vanni*—in the living room of the suite. His gaze landed on her when she entered the room, but he continued talking with subdued authority to someone on the phone. Ignoring Mrs. Shaw, she found Cristina's chart and began to make an entry in regard to the death.

"When are they coming to get the body?" Emma asked quietly when Vanni hung up the phone. Just thinking his name in her head caused a bitter taste at the back of her mouth. She continued staring at the page as she wrote methodically in the chart.

"They'll be here within the hour," he said. "Vera? Leave us, please."

Emma blinked in confusion. Who was Vera? Her question was answered when she glanced around and saw Mrs. Shaw hastening out of the room, even if her disapproval seemed to linger.

Her gaze leapt over to him, anxiety rising in her when she recognized they were alone. He stood next to a coffee table, his expression rigid. In his jeans, simple white T-shirt, and with the shadow of dark whiskers, he really might have been the familiar man she had begun to know . . . care about, even. She *thought* she'd begun to know him. It'd been an illusion—a spell—one she'd cast herself. She'd already thought him way out of her league. Her certainty was greater now that she knew he was that man who liked to tie up and whip women whom he cared nothing about.

It was too much to think about the details now that the elusive face from that night—from her dreams—was clear to her.

He studied her for a moment; the silence seemed to swell and billow around them.

"What is it?" he asked quietly. "Did Cristina's passing upset you that much?"

"No. Yes," she corrected. She closed her eyes briefly in frustration before she met his stare again. "You're not who I thought you were."

His eyebrows furrowed. "What's that supposed to mean?

"You cut your hair," she said starkly, lost in her ruminations. "If it'd been long, I might have recognized you."

Something flickered across his stark features. He took a step toward her, his eyes narrowing dangerously. Emma held her ground, but it took an effort.

"What did you say?" he asked.

Swallowing back an enormous lump in her throat, Emma turned and gathered up the hospice paperwork in preparation to leave. "It's nothing. It's not important. You haven't done anything wrong. It's me. I'll inform the hospice and contact the night nurse so that she won't come—"

"Don't walk away from me, Emma."

"I have to," she said miserably before she could stop herself.

"You're condemning me for what you saw in there without knowing anything about Cristina and me?" he demanded sharply, pointing to the bedroom. "I thought you were less judgmental than that. I'm disappointed."

You're disappointed?

She caught herself just in time from saying the words out loud. He didn't deserve her angst and agitation. Besides, it wasn't that. Not really. She wasn't *disappointed*. He hadn't done anything to hurt her on purpose. It was just that he was more than she'd bargained for. How could she explain to him? She couldn't. It was too humiliating. Too overwhelming. She'd agreed to this affair, but she hadn't agreed while knowing who he was.

While *acknowledging* the truth fully, anyway. Now the truth was inescapable, and all Emma wanted to do was hide from it again.

"You just . . . aren't who I thought you were," she repeated inadequately.

"Well I'm damn sorry for not being what you expected."

She turned and left the room, hating his quiet, snarling cynicism . . . despising her cowardice even more.

She only slept for a few hours a night for the rest of her workweek. When she did finally sleep on Sunday night, it was no relief, because she dreamed.

Again, she was blinded by night and was in Vanni's arms, his cock piercing her, her flesh quickening and thrilling around him. She was secure in the cocooning darkness, safe to move at her body's urging and at his command, free to take his intimate touches, glad to hear his hot, whispered words as he took control of their fierce joining.

"Arch your back, Emma. Offer yourself to me."

Her spine curved in supple acquiescence, thrusting forth her breasts as far as her restraints would allow. Restraints? Yes, she wasn't on the beach, after all. The dream had shifted. Her wrists were bound securely over her head. Her legs were spread wide, and his cock thrust high inside her, pounding her like a relentless wave. She couldn't move. She didn't want to.

"That's right," he murmured darkly in her ear as if he'd just heard her thought. "There's nowhere for you to go now. You can't escape."

He thrust so hard that a cry popped out of her throat. It hurt. No . . . it wasn't pain, it was a knot of pleasure so tight, it felt like a brutal cramp. But then the pressure unfurled, and she was climaxing.

"Look at me." She gasped, her body shuddering in sharp pleasure. "Open your eyes. *Look* at me," he shouted. Only then did she realize she couldn't see him because her eyelids were clamped tight.

She opened her eyes and saw him over her, naked and savage, bracing himself on muscular arms. She was on a bed, and the room was lit with golden light. His face was rigid and cold, but his eyes burned her. He thrust his hips and grunted gutturally, the symbols on dense, swelling biceps flashing in her dazed vision like they were lighted neon, not black ink. She felt his cock jerk and erupt inside her, his warm semen filling her.

"Don't you dare look away," he grated out, white teeth flashing.

Emma awoke with a start, Vanni's command still ringing in her ears. Without thinking, she plunged her hand beneath her shorts and underwear and moved it frantically, gasping as she finished climaxing powerfully.

A moment later, her hand fell against the bed, damp from her juices. She panted softly. She was in her bedroom, dawn peeking through the blinds. The dream was still with her, the memory palpable. She could still see his eyes, feel his cock swell inside her before he grunted in release, savage and beautiful.

There's nowhere for you to go now. Don't you dare look away.

She rose sluggishly from her mussed bed. This was reality, not a dream, and she needed to get ready for work. Her hospice had quickly reassigned her to a dozen households where she visited several times a week. It was both a comfort to go back to her usual schedule following her assignment at the Breakers, and yet also jarring somehow, as if she was trying to fit a new Emma into an old world.

On the way to the bathroom, she felt compelled to check her cell phone. Vanni had called again last night. She'd listened to the first message he'd left last Friday with a strange mixture of wariness and hunger.

“I need to speak with you. I think I might understand,” he’d said in that clipped, authoritative manner of his. “Call me at this number.”

How could he understand when she didn’t? She’d teased him about his insistence that he was selfish, not really believing because of what she’d seen of him, because of how much he gave her with his smallest touch. But he and that man with the voluptuous Astrid were one and the same. He *was* selfish, and he’d been *right* to warn her.

She was to blame. She’d only seen what she wanted to see. All her life, she’d made a habit of doing that. Her mother would fret and worry over lack of finances or Emma’s health. After Emma’s health crisis had resolved, circumstances had altered. Both Amanda and her mother had started to look to Emma for a sense of steady optimism, the go-to girl for a laugh and for seeing the glass half-full. She was her mother’s “miracle” child, a spot of sunshine when the fog of doubt settled. She was the stubborn one who refused to admit defeat, no matter the intimidating playing field. It was that quirk in her personality that had made her overlook what was happening with Colin and Amanda, what was probably obvious to everyone else.

It was that same fault in her character that had made her see only what she wanted to see with Vanni Montand. She’d wanted to experience a grand passion so much that she’d blinded herself, exposed herself to a situation where her naiveté and lack of experience would have undoubtedly wounded her in the end.

It already *had* wounded her. Thank God there wasn’t a chance for the knife to cut deeper.

She jumped slightly when her phone began to ring. It was Vanni again, she realized as a tingling sensation rippled down her limbs. She dropped the phone abruptly onto her dresser with a thud when she recognized how much she wanted to answer, how much she wanted to hear his voice again.

It suddenly struck her that her phone number was unlisted, and she’d never given it to him.

* * *

She was leaving her last home hospice visit that afternoon when she noticed a gleaming silver car whip into her patient's driveway and glide toward her with silent stealth. The hair on her nape and arms stood on end. She recognized the vehicle from Vanni's garage—a sleek, aerodynamically shaped four-door. Apparently, Automobiles Montand could make even a sedate sedan look as fierce and edgy as its sports cars. Her patient, Mrs. Slater, resided in a neat, working-class neighborhood in Evanston. The car couldn't have been more out of place.

A mingled sense of dread and excitement went through her when the driver's side door flung open.

The image of him uncoiling his long body and stepping onto the pavement burned her consciousness. Sunlight turned his hair into thick, burnished brown waves. He removed a pair of sunglasses and fixed her with his stare. Everything came to a temporary halt.

Her heartbeat. Her judgment. Time.

He wore a black suit, white shirt, and light silver tie. He looked impossibly handsome and . . . *foreign* somehow to her stunned brain. Exotic. She was reminded that he was the CEO and owner of a French car company and had extensive family roots in Europe. His tall, lean, muscular body might have been made to wear suits like that. He looked perfectly comfortable and natural in the expensive, fashionable clothing. He probably wore suits like that all the time. Most people were likely used to seeing him attired in such a way. She'd witnessed the exception, seeing him in gray mechanic's coveralls and jeans.

The realization that she'd peered into his private world and seen a part of him that the rest of the world hadn't made her feel heartsore, like she'd lost something.

Something you never had.

The thought galvanized her. Without saying a word to him, she hurried toward her car, digging in her purse for her keys.

"Emma," he said behind her. She gave him a reluctant sideways glance as he approached while she unlocked her car.

"How did you find me?" she asked, straining to keep her voice even.

He shrugged as if the question was unimportant. He was clean-shaven today. His cheeks looked a little hollowed out, but he didn't appear gaunt. If anything, he looked more handsome to her than he ever had.

So far out of her league.

In more ways than one.

The realization made her drop her gaze and reach for the door handle.

"Cristina's funeral is in an hour," he said. "It's a small one. Graveside. I'd like you to come."

A stabbing sensation of sadness went through her. She lowered her head, protecting herself instinctively.

"You really liked her, didn't you?" he asked quietly, and she knew he'd noticed her sudden sadness.

She nodded, reigning in her upsurge of emotion. "I *did* like Cristina. She was edgy and sharp, yes, but she had a forceful personality and she made me laugh."

"*Laugh?*"

"Laugh. She was an excellent observer of character. She saw straight to the heart of someone and read their faults," Emma said, staring unblinkingly at the top of her car.

Maybe you're the one who is afraid. Maybe you're such an expert on death because you're afraid to live.

"Everyone's faults but her own," Vanni stated dryly.

Emma recalled Cristina talking in her sleep during that nightmare. *You knew what I was capable of and what I wasn't.*

"She did see her faults," Emma said quietly. "She felt so guilty about them that it was hard for her to speak of them out loud. She dreamed of them, though. They haunted her."

His gaze narrowed on her. "Did she tell you anything significant about her life?"

"What do you mean?" Emma asked slowly. "Are you talking about what she said at the end?"

"No, I heard most of that. Anything about when she was young?" he prodded.

"She told me about that shop that she owned where all the women donated their designer clothes and things, and other women bought them. She used to talk about your father and the French Riviera, just little details."

He didn't respond. She glanced at him uneasily and was caught in his gleaming stare.

"I came to get you," he said simply.

She shook her head adamantly. "The hospice holds two funerals every year for all of our patients that have passed. Family can come, but it's primarily an opportunity for the staff to mourn," she explained, avoiding his steady stare by examining her hand on the door handle. "If I went to every patient's funeral, it'd—"

Finish me.

"Were you there? In my bedroom suite last Monday night? When I was with Astrid?" he asked suddenly.

Chapter 12

Her hand fell away from the metal handle. She stared up at him, dry-mouthed. Mute.

After a moment, he closed his eyes and lowered his head slightly. The breeze ruffled his thick hair in the taut silence that followed.

"You *were*," he said with an air of grim finality. He inhaled, a tried executive who had just realized his worst assessment of the situation had come to pass, and was grimly positioning himself for his next move. Her heart beat uncomfortably against her breastbone. "Why?" he asked simply, opening his eyes.

"I didn't want to *be* there. It was an accident," she said, unable to keep the misery from her tone. His arm jerked slightly, as if he wanted to touch her, but then it went still at his side. She recalled how she'd flinched away from him after Cristina had died. He'd thought she'd recoil again at his touch, she realized, her throat swelling. "The washer was broken in Cristina's suite and the repairman said he wouldn't have the part to fix it until the end of the week. We needed clean linens and towels."

"So you searched for a washer and ended up—"

"In your suite, yes, by accident," she said, the words tumbling out of her throat now as if the confession had been stored under pressure and the lid had just been released. "I heard you two coming, so I hid. I *know* it was stupid, but I thought I'd be in trouble for leaving Cristina's suite. I panicked," she admitted.

"You hid in the armoire," he said heavily.

She swallowed back the dread rising in her throat. "You knew I was in there?" she whispered.

"No," he said, staring off into the distance, his light eyes reflecting the low clouds and blue sky. "I just put it together this weekend. I thought I'd heard something rustling in there that night, but dismissed it. Later, I saw you walking up the steps. You carried a bag."

"That was the laundry," she said tremulously. Her pulse began to throb at her temple. Her head ached with all of her thoughts. He knew she'd watched him flog that woman. He knew she'd seen him screw her with such ruthless precision using that gliding rack that had clearly been designed for his selfish kink. The same man had made love to her with sweet, intense passion on that beach. What was she supposed to do with the paradox? Michael Montand Jr. *Vanni.* She rubbed her temple. She was going to have a headache later. "I never saw your face," she murmured, wanting to get this over with now that she'd started. "And like I said last Thursday, your hair was longer and lighter looking. When you cut it, a lot of the sun streaks disappeared. And she—Astrid—called you Vanni. I didn't know that was what you were called."

"So you didn't realize Vanni was me, am I right?" he asked, exhaling heavily, his tone making it clear that the pieces were falling into place for him. "Emma?" he prodded. He waited for her to answer.

"You didn't realize it was me until you heard Cristina call me Vanni. Do I have it right?" he pushed.

His gaze narrowed on her when she didn't reply.

"I wouldn't have wanted you to see that," he grated out. "I didn't *ask* you to watch. In fact, it'd be one of the last things I'd want *anyone* to witness," he said in a hard, quiet voice. "I'm well aware it wasn't my finest moment. But what you saw was consensual between Astrid and me. I'd never even *met* you. It was just a bad coincidence. It doesn't have anything to do with what happened between us."

"Of course it doesn't. For *you*."

"What's that supposed to mean?" he asked, anger entering his tone.

"Why didn't you just tell me your name was Vanni?"

"I don't know," he replied just as edgily. He paused, seeming to search for an explanation for her question. "Not everyone calls me Vanni. Besides, I don't recall you ever calling me *anything*. What did you mean when you said you watching me with Astrid doesn't mean anything to me, but it does you?"

She rolled her eyes. "I'm not going to stand in my patient's driveway and have this conversation," she said, once again reaching for her door handle.

"What was it that upset you the most?" he demanded, subduing his anger.

Her mouth sagged open with disbelief. She couldn't seem to inhale a full breath. She felt cornered by his direct question and piercing stare.

"I'd be hard-pressed to name something that *didn't*. It *all* disgusted me," she blurted out.

He caught her wrist when she reached for the door. She looked up at him, startled.

"You've been lying to yourself, Emma. You knew it was me. Or part of you did. You knew since that night I called you to the dining room." She gasped in shock at his calm, concise understanding of the private inner workings of her mind. His fingers moved slightly on her skin as if to soothe the sting of his words. He lowered his head and spoke near her ear, his warm breath making her shiver. "I'm not an animal. Don't label me depraved just because it makes things easier for you. Are you forgetting I've made love to you? You might be inexperienced, but you enjoyed giving control to me. There's nothing wrong with it. It was natural the way you responded to me. Beautiful," he said, his softly uttered words striking her as palpably intimate even in this unlikely setting. "Don't run from what you don't understand."

It was too much. His quiet voice, not entreating her exactly, but calling to her. Speaking to something deep inside her that he knew she heard.

Somehow.

I've told you what I can offer you. It's the same I can offer any woman. It isn't much, she recalled him telling Astrid so coldly. *I'm going to bind you onto the sliding track, then use the flogger on you.*

Something hot and volatile swelled in her chest. He was too complex for her, too dark. The last thing she needed was someone like Vanni Montand in her life. She couldn't handle it. She couldn't handle *him*.

He leaned down, his lips brushing her temple, and her fearful thoughts evaporated.

"Leave your keys under the seat," he directed in her ear. "I'll call someone and have them pick up your car and deliver it to your apartment. Come with me now. I want you at Cristina's funeral."

"Why?" she whispered numbly.

"Because she made you laugh." She turned her head and met his stare. "She deserves to have someone there who liked her, don't you think? But that's not the only reason. *I* need you there."

She stared at him, aghast at his harsh declaration of need.

"We'll talk more about what you saw later, after the funeral. You're not a coward, Emma," he said, his quiet words piercing her like hot knives. "You can't keep running from this."

She tugged again on her arm and this time he let her go.

His expression was impassive when she faced him after putting her keys beneath the driver's seat and slamming the car door. Even so, Emma didn't think it was her imagination that she saw stark relief flicker across his bold features ever so briefly.

After Vanni had opened the passenger door for her and she got inside, she looked down at what she was wearing.

"I can't go to Cristina's funeral like this," she said once he was seated next to her, anxiety overtaking her. "Can you take me to my apartment to change?"

His gaze swept down over her in a cool assessment, making her skin prickle in awareness. It was warm today, so she'd opted for a lightweight floral skirt, a pink T-shirt, and flats. It was better than jeans and high-tops, but it was still inappropriate for the funeral of Cristina Montand.

"You're fine," he said. "It's going to be a very simple ceremony. Only a few people will be there."

"But—"

"You're *fine*," he repeated quietly. *You're fine because I said you were fine.* He didn't say it, but it seemed like he did. She opened her mouth to protest.

"There isn't time for me to take you to your apartment. *Please*, don't concern yourself about what you're wearing. It's the last thing I'm worried about, Emma, and I told you. I need you there," he said quietly. Forcefully. Again, she was reminded of the brew of complex emotion she sensed boiling behind his cool façade.

"All right," she said in a choked voice.

He cleared his throat, and the charged atmosphere seemed to dissipate. He reached for a hands-free phone headset.

"I hope you don't mind. There are a few phone calls I need to make on the way. My company is sponsoring a big racing event in France this summer. It's the first time for it." He grimaced as he put on the headset. "I just hope it's not the last."

Emma exhaled, relief going through her at the realization they weren't going to plunge into anxiety-provoking topics like what she'd experienced in that armoire. "Is it that French-American grand prix road-racing event Montand Motorworks is sponsoring on the French Riviera?" He gave her a surprised glance. "I read about it in the *Chicago Tribune*," Emma explained.

He nodded. "It's experimental. I'm not sure how it'll go over. I'm tramping on European tradition a bit, attempting it."

She didn't really understand what he meant. She'd never been remotely interested in car racing. Him, she understood better. Or at least she experienced his unruffled manner and bone-deep confidence. "If anyone can do it, you can," she said.

She saw his blank expression of surprise. "Why would you say that so certainly?" he asked, dark brows furrowed in puzzlement.

"Because of your background and your knowledge of cars and everything. You're both American and French and you know all about racing and you have that . . . cachet."

He leaned forward slightly, hands on the wheel. "Cachet?"

"Sure," Emma said, hiding her blush by digging in her purse for her phone. "*The Aloof Automobile Prince Raised in America. Race-car Royalty Returns to His Roots*—"

She halted her rambling and looked around at the sound she heard. He laughed. *Really* laughed. The sound was deep and rich and uninhibited. His smile cut her to the quick. Somehow, he seemed *relieved.* Something twisted and pulled inside her at the vision of white, straight teeth and the look of stark amusement on his face. There was something else gleaming in his aquamarine eyes: genuine warmth as he stared at her. *This* was the same man whom she'd watched make love so coldly.

Knitting the two images together was going to be so hard. Wasn't it?

"You really are odd at times," he said, his gaze narrowed on her. She held her breath when he reached up and touched the angel at her throat. It suddenly struck her that she hadn't removed it, even while she slept, since she'd hurried out of the Breakers after Cristina's death. Surely that meant something.

"You're not so normal yourself," she muttered.

He smiled slightly and dropped his hand, and she immediately regretted her need to lighten the moment. His attention turned to driving and his phone calls, but Emma couldn't help but notice that although his smile had faded, his usually hard mouth looked a little softer. She really *had* provided him a moment of relief. The realization warmed her more than she liked to admit. It also made her wonder for the thousandth time about the unspoken tension that seemed to shroud him anytime Cristina was mentioned.

She was texting a message to her patient's daughter, explaining about her car being left in the driveway and someone coming to pick it up, when Vanni began to talk. He spoke to someone named Jake whom he asked to retrieve Emma's car. When it came time for him to say where to deliver the vehicle, Emma leaned forward, trying to get his attention to give him her address. He remained turned in profile to her, however, and crisply supplied her street address as if it were his own. She was a little mystified that he'd been able to see the address, given how dark and rainy it'd been that night he'd followed her home.

On his next call he began speaking in fluid French. She stared out the window as the urban landscape passed by her, her entire attention focusing on the sound of him. At first, she tried to see if she could pull out any words that she might comprehend. When she couldn't, she found herself relaxing to the sound of his voice: the rich resonance, the rhythmic cadence, the foreign words blending together into a sensual anthem that both lulled her and created a tickle of excitement along her skin and at her core.

She cast a sideways, covetous glance at him, wondering all the while what she'd gotten herself into. If she wasn't careful, she'd end up crashing and burning like a novice behind the wheel of a superfast, high-tech Montand car.

For the hundredth time, she repeated a mantra for caution inside her head.

She was so caught up in the sound of Vanni speaking French that she forgot to be nervous about where they were going. That all came to a halt when he turned the sedan onto the grounds of a cemetery. Her anxiety started to amplify as he finished his call and deftly maneuvered the sedan on the narrow road winding through lush trees and grounds. Neither of them spoke, a hushed somberness seemingly overtaking them both.

He drove directly to a lovely spot atop a small hill. There was a lagoon with swans floating serenely on it to the right of Emma. He parked behind a hearse, three other luxury sedans, and a Nissan. In the distance, Emma caught a glimpse of the coffin down the small hill to the left of them topped with a lush, colorful flower arrangement. Her anxiety ratcheted up several degrees when she saw the pinched expression of Mrs. Shaw as she ascended the slight rise to the road. A handsome older man with a mane of silver hair followed her along with a younger, dark-haired man.

Emma got out of the sedan and went around the back to join Vanni, feeling more and more out of place by the second.

"Where have you been?" Mrs. Shaw asked Vanni with barely subdued anxiety as she approached him.

"There was something I needed to take care of," Vanni replied coolly, hardly sparing her a glance. He shook hands with the silver-haired man and then the younger one with the Mediterranean good looks. The latter grasped him with both hands, a concerned look on his face.

"You okay?" the young man asked in a quiet, confidential tone. Here was a friend to him, Emma immediately realized. She was glad of it. Vanni struck her as so alone sometimes, like a secluded prince.

Vanni just nodded. He put out his hand toward Emma in a beckoning gesture. She saw Mrs. Shaw's face flatten in disbelief when she turned to see Emma approach their small group. "Niki, Uncle Dean, this is Emma Shore. She's the nurse who took care of Cristina during her last days. Emma, this is Dean Shaw, my mother's brother. He's also the chief financial officer of Montand Motorworks. He used to work for my father as well. And this is my good friend, Niki Dellis." Both men greeted her warmly and took her hand in greeting. Niki's expression was amiable, but sharp and curious. Emma decided Dean Shaw had a nice smile.

"And of course you've already met my aunt, Vera Shaw."

Well, here was some news, Emma thought, hiding her shock. She'd had no inkling Mrs. Shaw was his aunt. Vera Shaw was nowhere near as welcoming as her brother or Niki Dellis had been.

"We should begin," Vera told him tensely. Vanni nodded significantly down the hill. Vera and her brother started ahead of them, Emma following between Vanni and Niki. She glanced up at Vanni when he took her hand as they went down the slope. She didn't require him to steady her balance, but she did appreciate his touch. This was an extremely awkward situation for her.

One look into his impassive features and stormy eyes and Emma knew it was a thousand times worse for him. Her self-consciousness diminished almost to nothing upon seeing his carefully controlled emotional state.

There were only three other people attending the simple service besides her, Niki, Vanni, Vera, and Dean. Two extremely well-put-together, very thin women already stood on the far side of the casket. They looked like they might be in their early fifties, but Emma's instinct told her they were older and just well-preserved by plastic surgery and regular, opulent spa visits. Friends of Cristina's most likely, she assessed, although they certainly hadn't bothered to visit her when she'd been ill. A middle-aged man was there as well, and Emma realized he was the presiding minister when Vanni nodded at him, and he began to speak.

It was a short, simple ceremony, but the beautiful surroundings and the luminous summer afternoon seemed to bless it as special. Vanni's and her handclasp had broken when they reached the bottom of the hill, but Emma was highly aware of him standing next to her. She sensed his tension level like a storm silently building on the horizon.

As the minister spoke, Emma glanced curiously around. The paradox of Vanni's feelings for his stepmother was obvious here as well. The carved mahogany casket with gold fastenings was of the highest quality, and the flower arrangements were lush and stunning. Emma noticed that a large gravestone next to Cristina's gravesite was also decorated with fresh flowers, as were two others next to it. Did those graves belong to Vanni's father and mother?

Was it *usual* for a husband to be buried next to both his wives? Emma thought it odd, but didn't have enough experience to know. And to whom did the fourth grave belong?

The minister led them in a prayer, and Emma cast her gaze downward. At the word *forgive*, Vanni jerked ever so slightly next to her. Without thinking, Emma grasped his hand. She tilted her head up slightly and saw that his stare was on her, the message in his eyes weighty, but unreadable.

The realization slowly dawned on Emma that it wasn't just her who seemed awkward at the funeral. Everyone there seemed tense, as if there were a million unspoken words zooming around their bowed heads, words Emma herself couldn't comprehend any more than she had Vanni's French. It was odd that Vanni's maternal aunt and uncle attended his stepmother's burial, but perhaps they were just there to support Vanni? The two well-groomed ladies barely showed any emotion at all during the service, except perhaps shameless curiosity as they stared at Vanni, and occasionally at Emma and Niki.

Poor Cristina, to have her life memorialized in such a stilted, emotionless fashion.

As the small gathering began to dissipate at the end of the ceremony, Vanni reached in his pocket and withdrew a crisp handkerchief from his suit and handed it to Emma. She saw the *MGM* monogrammed on the edge of it. Emma looked at him in confusion, but then realized her cheeks were wet.

"Thank you," she said thickly a moment later, blotting her face.

"Someone should cry for her," he said simply. His eyes were dry and clear.

After she'd dried her face, he took her hand and started to lead her up the hill. He paused when Niki approached them.

"Niki, would you mind?" Vanni nodded down at Emma significantly. "I'm going to . . ." He faded off and gestured with his head toward the graves. Emma was confused, but Niki seemed to immediately understand Vanni's request. Niki took her hand with a smile. He asked her in a friendly manner about her work, and Emma answered distractedly. When they got to the top of the hill, Emma looked back. She saw Vanni kneeling in front of the third grave from Cristina's coffin, his strong profile rigid. Was it his mother's grave? After a few seconds, he stood and placed his hand on the gravestone. Emma could almost feel how cold and hard it felt against his fingers and palm before he broke the contact then turned and walked away.

"Where are we going?" she asked Vanni quietly twenty minutes later. He hadn't spoken since they'd left the cemetery. He seemed thoughtful, although his driving was as skillful and adroit as ever as he maneuvered through crowded suburban evening traffic. He'd finally turned onto a rural drive that paralleled the lakefront and flew down a country landscape, and that's when she'd asked the question.

"I'm taking you home . . . the long way," he said, staring out the front window fixedly.

"Good." She noticed his sharp sideways glance. "Because I'm not ready to make a decision yet . . . about it all." She didn't want to go to the Breakers. She didn't want to be seduced by him. Or she *did*, but she knew how important careful thought was in this situation with Vanni, with whom rational thought was most difficult.

He stared ahead at the unfurling road. Maybe he'd just take her home more quickly, if she wasn't willing to continue with their agreement tonight? She felt cast at sea, sometimes, trying to imagine what he was thinking. It was an odd paradox to how inexplicably connected she felt to him at other times.

"I told you we were going to talk. That's all right, isn't it?" he asked, his gaze never shifting from the road.

"Yes," she said, looking at his profile. He turned suddenly, his gaze sweeping over her.

"What are you thinking about?" he asked sharply. She swallowed thickly, both relieved and anxious that they'd approached the intimidating topic.

"Our agreement."

"Are you regretting agreeing to see me? Now that you know that I'm the same man you saw with Astrid?"

"I'm not sure that 'regret' is the right word," she said slowly, thinking. "I'm uncertain. Confused."

"I realize you're upset about what you saw that night. About what you *think* you saw," he added under his breath.

"I know what I saw," she said emphatically.

"Maybe you do," he said soberly, smoothly taking a bend in the country road around a bluff. "But you don't know what any of it means."

"Are you going to want to do those things to me?" she asked the question that had been burning at the back of her throat ever since she'd agreed to come with him this afternoon . . . ever since she'd fully understood who he was.

He glanced sideways, his expression going rigid when he saw her anxiety. "I'm the first person to admit I'm not an expert on kindness, but if you actually think for a second that I'd be *that* selfish and uninspired as what you witnessed, you've got this all wrong, Emma. Besides, I could do those exact same things with you, and it wouldn't be remotely the same," he added under his breath, his lips curled into a frown.

She stared at him, wide-eyed, still confused, but also a little amazed at his burst of honesty.

He stopped at a stop sign and looked at her. "Just remember this. I'm not going to ask you to do anything you don't want to do. If you don't want something, just say it."

Her mouth hung open. "It's that simple?"

"No," he said grimly, staring out the windshield. "But that part is as cut-and-dry as it comes."

He pulled the car onto a narrow, weed-covered road with crumbling pavement that no one would ever have seen if they weren't formerly familiar with it. A moment later, the vista of the great lake appeared. He put the car into park before a three-foot-tall wall that must serve as a dam during high water. Today, the waves struck rhythmically against a rocky beach a dozen feet below them. It appeared to be an old, forgotten lookout, Emma realized as she got out of the car and Vanni did the same, taking off his jacket and tossing it in the backseat. Weeds and grass were breaking through the pavement as nature reclaimed the area. She walked up to the wall and stared, the evening summer sun making the ruffled light blue blanket of water wink and sparkle at her. She knew immediately when he stepped up beside her, but for a moment, neither of them spoke.

"How did you ever discover this place?" she wondered, thinking of how remote the turnoff had been.

"Old high school and college drinking spot."

Emma considered him for a moment. "Did you have a Montand car? When you were a sixteen-year-old?" she couldn't stop herself from asking.

"Yeah," he said, his shoulders twitching slightly as if he'd thought the question inconsequential.

Emma glanced around the secluded area. It would be an *ideal* make-out spot. Not that Vanni probably ever just "made out" even as a hardened, gorgeous high school boy in a car that cost hundreds of thousands of dollars. The thought made her shift uncomfortably on her feet.

"What's wrong?" he asked, glancing over at her with a furrowed brow.

"I hadn't realized Mrs. Shaw was your aunt," she said quietly, sidestepping the issue.

He nodded and placed his hands on the top of the wall. "Yes. My mother's older sister. Mom was the youngest, Dean is the oldest."

"Was your mother . . . like Mrs. Shaw, I mean, *Vera*?" she asked, experimenting with the name.

Vanni shook his head, the lake breeze ruffling his thick hair. "Not at all. My mother was warm and full of life. I realize Vera isn't the most . . . approachable of women. She *is* an excellent house manager, and she and Janice, my administrative assistant, work well together to make sure I have what I need both at work and home. My mother and Vera look a little alike," Vanni mused after a pause, his gaze cast out at the lake. "Once in a great while." Emma's heart squeezed a little at something in his voice. She wondered if he kept Vera around because of that, looking for similarities in his aunt, hungry for reminders of his mother. "They were definitely alike in one thing," he added.

"What?" Emma asked, leaning her hip against the wall and watching his striking profile instead of the sun-gilded water.

"They were both crazy about my father," he said dryly.

"Really?" Emma asked, making a face. "Wasn't that a bit awkward for your mother?"

Vanni shrugged, the action bringing her gaze downward to his muscular chest covered in the crisp dress shirt. "My mother never knew about Vera's crush. Or I don't think she did. Who knows, really, what a wife suspects?" he said, the reflection off the lake making his eyes look more blue than green at the moment. "My mother likely suspected a lot of things she wouldn't have told me about, as young as I was." He glanced aside and noticed her puzzled expression. "My father was an inveterate womanizer. There's no way my mother didn't know about his infidelities," he stated grimly.

"Do you mean that Vera and your dad actually—"

"No," he interrupted, catching her drift. "At least I don't think so. Aunt Vera's infatuation was unrequited. I always felt a little sorry for her, existing in the shadow of her sister . . . and so many others."

Emma didn't reply, a feeling of sadness going through her at his matter-of-fact assessment of such a crucial aspect of his family life.

He turned to her suddenly, leaning his hip against the wall, and touched the angel at her throat.

Chapter 13

She looked up. The wariness in her large, dark eyes ate at him. Her wavy, golden hair fluttered around her delicate features. He gave in to a need he often had upon seeing her, palming the back of her skull and sinking his fingers into the soft tendrils of her hair. He'd never known a woman to have such a pretty, sexy *head*. Every time he saw her he wanted to cup it in his palm, delve his finger into threads of coiling, golden-blond silk.

The truth was, if a similarly impossible scenario as the one that had presented itself with Emma came up with another woman, Vanni wouldn't have bothered to explain. He would have just chalked it up to bad luck and moved on. He didn't invest in relationships. There were other women. Why should he have to make an effort to rationalize his actions or his nature?

But here he was with Emma, determined to try. What made it even more incredible, at least from where he was standing, was that he was embarrassed about what she'd seen. It wasn't because he'd dominated Astrid sexually on that night that shamed him; that was background noise to him, even though he understood it wasn't to Emma. No, it was his bored, lackluster performance, the evidence of how his black mood permeated even his sexual life of late. That was what shamed him more than anything.

His gaze lowered to her pink mouth. That's how he knew just how strongly he wanted Emma. He was willing to sacrifice a fair portion of his pride in order to have her. What's more, he wasn't exactly sure how to proceed. The circumstances were unprecedented. He didn't have a lot of experience explaining himself to women. Either they got him, or they didn't. Fitting himself into some preconceived idea of what a woman expected of him wasn't something he was remotely interested in doing.

He saw the anxiety flicker across her face and sighed, dropping his hand from her skull, cupping her shoulder instead. She'd *really* curled up in that armoire and listened while he selfishly took his pleasure with another woman. She *really* was undone by this whole thing.

Yet here she was, willingly choosing to be with him. He admired her courage.

Another feeling rose up in him, a surprising, slicing one: Jealousy.

He couldn't recall being as anxious as Emma looked in that moment. Not even for a majority of his childhood. His hide was too tough. He was the strong one, or so everyone said. He was the survivor. He was too bitter, too jaded to ever wear that expression again, to ever feel that vulnerable. There had to have been a time when he was that open, that unguarded to the world, though.

Hadn't there been?

He shut his eyes briefly, shielding himself from her luminous face. It would be so much easier just to forget about it all. He'd have to examine himself far too closely for comfort in order to have Emma. It would be messy and just . . . too much of an *effort*.

Way too much. He should take her home this instant.

"I'm just a man, Emma. I'm not so twisted that you can't see that, am I?" he asked quietly instead, opening his eyes.

"I see you," she whispered.

The hair on his nape stood on end as she studied him. He suddenly felt anxious.

"And you're not twisted," she said. "Not yet, anyway."

He exhaled, realizing he'd been waiting for her assessment like an irreversible, binding judgment, stupid and illogical as that was.

He looked into shining, velvety-soft eyes. Innocent. Enigmatic. Her lush, unadorned lips trembled slightly. He experienced an overwhelming urge to plunge his tongue into her mouth, to pierce her everywhere he could . . . *anything* to feel her as deeply as was humanly possible, to be so tight and high inside her that for a brief, mindless moment of bliss, he possessed her.

Christ. He was kidding himself if he thought *he* was the master of this situation. Did he *really* think he could ever defile her? Not even in his wildest depravity could he begin to span the depths of this wisp of a girl's eyes.

He inhaled sharply, gathering himself. He put his hands on her waist and lifted. She gave a little of cry of surprise when he set her on top of the brick wall in front of him. Her face was almost level with his now. He stepped between her parted thighs, keeping his hands on her narrow waist.

"Okay," he said, holding her startled stare. "What should we talk about first?"

Her mouth trembled with amusement. "It's come to my attention lately that I have a problematic habit of denying reality," she said. "I've been known to prefer my own comfortable version of the world. I think it's best I face the truth when it comes to you, don't you?"

His expression flattened. She really was unexpected.

"Absolutely," he said. "You were disturbed by what you saw that night. And in the aftermath, you convinced yourself that I wasn't the same man you'd seen."

Emma nodded.

"Is this the problematic habit you referred to? The one where you refuse to see certain things?"

"Yes."

"Why do you think you didn't want to allow yourself to know it was me?" he asked, taking a step closer to her and holding her stare.

* * *

She swallowed thickly at the sensation of his body brushing against her open thighs. His gaze bore straight down to the center of her.

"Because it was safer to assume you weren't the man who did those things," she said honestly. He didn't reply, seeming to sense there was more. She bit her lip and looked away. "And because I was disturbed by what I saw."

"Disturbed," he repeated.

"Yes."

"And disgusted."

She nodded.

"Were you aroused?"

The silence stretched, interrupted only by the sound of the gentle, soughing surf against the rocks below. Her pulse started to leap at her throat like it wanted to escape her skin. *Face reality.*

"Yes," she said softly, her cheeks burning. Her gaze leapt to his. "But I *was* upset. It seemed wrong, what you were doing. And I was mad at you."

"Mad?" he clarified, his fingers moving subtly on her waist, the sensation distracting her. "For flogging Astrid? For restraining her?"

"Yes," she hissed, frowning at him for his ease at broaching the most volatile of topics. "But not just for that."

"What then?" he asked intently. "Emma?" he prompted when she just sat there.

"For making me feel so much," she admitted in a rush. "For making me feel things I didn't even know existed. I *was* disgusted, and confused, and curious, and angry, and . . . aroused," she forced herself to say the word. "It was too much to consider, you being that man when I met you face-to-face the next night. Too much to *handle*. I didn't do it consciously. I just ignored the facts."

"What facts?"

"Lots of things," she mused, studying his tie. "Like why would a guest room have a monitor for Cristina in it, or worse yet, that . . . that apparatus, that thing you tied . . ."

She faded off, embarrassment overwhelming her.

"Yes, I see what you mean," he said. "Why would a guest room have that? What else did you ignore?"

She gave him an exasperated look. "Why does it matter?"

"It matters," he said quietly. "Unless I understand your state of mind, it's hard to know how to relieve your anxiety."

She lowered her head. "Lots of things," she murmured. "I told myself not only was your hair shorter than the man's I'd seen, the color was darker as well. But of course when you cut your hair, the highlights went, too, for the most part. Every other time I saw you afterward, it was in dim light, so it looked even darker." She inhaled through her nose slowly. "Your scent," she added in a whisper. "Sandalwood with just a hint of citrus and leather. My mother loved things like candles and potpourri. Her sense of smell was very sharp. She could tell what certain stews and soups needed just by smelling the broth. I got her nose. When I was in the armoire," she mumbled, "I could smell you, but there was something just a tad different mixing with your scent: motor oil. The garments I was sitting in when I was in the armoire—I couldn't see them, because it was dark—but they were your coveralls, weren't they? The ones you wear when you're working on cars?"

"Yes."

Her throat ached when she swallowed. "I knew it," she said softly. "Or part of me did. I recognized your scent and the texture of the fabric when you held me last week in the garage and you were wearing the coveralls."

He said nothing. She looked up at him uncertainly. Expectantly. His long bangs had fallen forward in the lake breeze, so that his gleaming eyes were shadowed.

"What do you imagine that I'm going to tell you now?" he asked.

"I don't know," she admitted. "I guess you're a person who likes BDSM, and that's your lifestyle choice? And that it may not be everyone's cup of tea, but it's your sexual preference? That it's consensual and no one gets hurt?"

"Very politically correct," he said, his small smile gentle despite his mild sarcasm.

"Well what would *you* say?"

His hands moved on her waist, stroking her in a seemingly distracted fashion while he thought. "I'm sorry," he said, perhaps noticing her impatience. "Believe it or not, I don't sit around thinking up excuses for why I want something, or why I want it a certain way. But I will tell you this. You were right to be disgusted that night."

"What?" she asked, taken aback. She hadn't expected him to agree with her.

"I did behave coldly. Selfishly. You believe that your disgust came from sexual practices you weren't familiar with, which is part of it. But I think the reason you were disgusted is that you caught me behaving badly," he stated starkly. He met her incredulous stare. "You caught me in the act, Emma, of depravity. It's one thing to prefer to dominate a woman and to care about her security and her pleasure, to want to claim it. There was nothing wrong technically in the things I did that night. It was consensual, and I would never harm a woman. But because I didn't really care, one way or the other about Astrid's pleasure—or even remotely about her—it was wrong," he admitted.

"She certainly didn't seem to find her pleasure lacking," Emma said dryly, resisting an urge to touch his tension-filled face.

"I would have been better off masturbating instead of being with her."

"She was using you as well," Emma said after she'd recovered from his bald statement.

"We all use each other to some degree," he said quietly. His long fingers stretched, gently kneading her back muscles. Her undeniable attraction to him, her need, swelled in her breast. She wanted very much to pull him closer to her, to press against him.

Instead, she forced herself to focus on what he was saying. "So you're saying that I probably would have been upset even if I'd witnessed you having sex with Astrid by more conventional means?" she asked carefully.

"I'm guessing that's what disgusted you the most, yes, although not being familiar with the particulars, you were shocked by them as well. You knew I didn't care, that I felt no sense of connection or even true desire for her. You sensed I was bored and cynical—"

"I thought you were behaving beneath yourself," she said abruptly, interrupting him. "And it pissed me off."

They faced off in the silence that followed. His face was a mask, but the heat in his eyes told her she might have angered him.

"It's not a pleasant thing for me to consider, either," he said. "Do you even realize that? I wouldn't have thought twice about that night if you hadn't intruded, aside from some passing self-disgust. Your eyes were an uninvited, extremely uncomfortable mirror," he bit out, "and yet here I look into them."

His voice rang and rattled in her head.

No, she hadn't considered how difficult it might be for him to think of her watching him in the midst of his bitterness. He'd been vulnerable while having sex that night, but not to Astrid.

To Emma.

She blinked and felt the burn in her eyes. She realized something else.

"I thought you were beautiful," she said. "Despite it all."

His features stiffened. His hands tightened at her waist.

"I have never wanted a woman the way I do you," he said. "Tell me what you need to make this right."

Her heart began to pound in her ears.

"There are so many things I don't understand," she admitted.

"Then ask."

"Okay," she said tremulously. "Who is Adrian?"

He blinked. He definitely hadn't expected her to ask *that* question.

Ask for Adrian's forgiveness, she recalled him saying in Cristina's last moments. Vanni had demanded that Cristina ask for his mother and Adrian's forgiveness, then denied her his own. Cristina had mentioned the name, too. Emma had been wildly curious since she'd heard the name. She knew from Googling the Montand name, and Vanni's explanation for his nickname, that Michael was the name of his father, so *he* wasn't Adrian. In her imagination, the name Adrian had taken on some kind of forbidden charge, a name that was thought but never said . . . one of the unspoken words hanging like a dense cloud at Cristina's burial.

She drew three shaky breaths in the silence that followed, her anxiety ratcheting up. His face looked rigid. For a few seconds, she thought he wouldn't answer. She shouldn't have asked.

"My brother. My twin brother. He's dead."

Her mouth sagged open. "You had a twin?" she asked, shocked. "How . . . how did he die?"

"He drowned, but Cristina killed him."

Emma gasped at the quiet, yet brutal, slicing quality of his tone.

Vanni exhaled and dropped his hands from her waist, placing them on the wall near her hips, his thumbs touching her skirt. He lowered his head so that she couldn't see his eyes.

"We were swimming in Lake Michigan. We were nine years old and shouldn't have been in the water that day at all, but if so, only under close supervision. That was what Cristina was supposed to be doing, but she was too busy with more important matters," Vanni said in a weary, bitter tone. "Cristina was kind enough to Adrian and me when my father was around, but when he wasn't, she could be vindictive and negligent. It was the latter that ended up being the most deadly of her sins, although I always felt there was a fair share of the former in the instance of Adrian's death. More likely, she hadn't thought things through much, if that was the case. It was *me* she hated the most, and I was always physically stronger than Adrian. It was that way ever since we were born—"

He broke off. Emma just sat there, wretched at having brought up the awful topic, miserable at the glimpse of his pain.

"There was a strong undertow that day," he continued in a flat tone that she hated. "Other beaches along the lakeshore had been closed, but that's not the kind of thing Cristina would have bothered to find out before she told two nine-year-olds to go swim and then attended to matters of real importance—her social schedule. We were caught by a strong undertow and pulled out toward the breakers. He hit them, and was wounded. Afterward he was weakened. He didn't have a chance of keeping his head up in the rough water with that undertow pulling at us."

"Oh my God," Emma whispered, horrified. "Vanni, I'm so sorry."

And he'd been there. He'd seen it all, as had Cristina, most likely. Vanni had survived, and his twin hadn't.

"Did it happen at the Breakers?" Emma whispered, a little frightened by the idea for Vanni's sake.

"It was there, but a different house. I had the Breakers built after my father died several years ago, on the site of my childhood home."

She just stared at him a moment, connecting dots, trying to make sense of it all and struggling. *Such a beautiful place to die*, she recalled Cristina saying on the day she'd passed. Emma had mistakenly thought she'd meant her own impending death. Now she understood that Cristina had meant Adrian's.

"You say that you blame Cristina," Emma said slowly, "but you insisted on the drapes being closed in her suite, blocking her from a vision that she would have undoubtedly found upsetting to endure, day in and day out. You say she was negligent, but *you* were very careful about keeping her well cared for and shielded from the site of Adrian's death." He remained unmoving, his head lowered. "And *you* were there when Adrian died, too," she whispered, a prickly feeling of dread rising in her. "Yet you built a house where you have no choice but to stare at the place where he died. You can never escape from it . . ." He straightened, his hands falling to his sides. She faded off when she saw that hard, glacial look enter his eyes. Once again, she'd dared to tread where she shouldn't.

Where she had no right.

She shook her head, trying to rid herself of the sudden feeling of intense sadness. "I'm so sorry, Vanni," she said sincerely. "To lose not only a brother, but a twin at that age."

"My other half," he said, as if to himself. A grim smile pulled at his lips. "My better half. Much better.

"Do we have to discuss this now?" he asked after a moment. "I thought we were going to talk about your uncertainties. Do you want to be with me or not, Emma?"

This time, she didn't stop herself from reaching up and touching his face.

"You know that I do."

"Do I? I'm not so certain. You have no idea what I see in your eyes, do you? Right this second?" he said, his mouth twisting slightly. "You're afraid of me."

"No," she said steadfastly. "If there is fear there, it's for myself. I'm worried about what could happen to me, being with you. Don't you think that's natural?"

He looked like he'd just eaten something bitter. "I think it's right that you should question it. Maybe it's for the best," he said, stepping back so that her hand fell from his jaw.

"I haven't decided yet, Vanni," Emma said starkly. He glanced up and she saw the surprise in his eyes, the flash of hope. The subsequent wariness.

"Give me some time to think about it, okay?" she asked more quietly. "I just want your word that if . . . if I agree—"

"I'll keep you safe, Emma. I wouldn't harm you. Ever. I only want to challenge you. I want to see you helpless with desire, just as helpless as you're making me. I want to look into your face and see nothing but pure need."

Her mouth dropped open. A rush of heat went through her, a fire set by his raw words and the spark in his gleaming eyes.

She nodded and stared at her knees. "Okay. Thank you for telling me," she said through a tight throat. "I'll think about it. I'm pretty busy with my schedule this week. Are you going to be here this weekend? I have Sunday and Monday off."

"I'm leaving on Monday for France," he said, and her heart plummeted.

"Sunday afternoon then?" she pressed hopefully.

He lifted her chin until she met his eyes. "I've given you the code to enter the house. I'll wait for you at the Breakers at around four o'clock on Sunday. And Emma?" he said more intently, his long forefinger brushing against her jaw.

"Yes?" she whispered.

"If you decide you don't want to be with me, don't come. It'll be easier for both of us that way."

Emma swallowed thickly and nodded.

Chapter 14

She kept herself busy all week with work, but at night, she thought about Vanni and what she wanted . . .

. . . What she dared.

She made her decision when she realized that all the dark, erotic dreams she'd been having lately were her own secret wishes, her own desires rising to the surface. It wasn't just about fulfilling Vanni's sexual demands. It was about fulfilling her own hunger to be with him . . . even for a short period of time.

By Saturday night, she knew what she was going to do, and she had a plan for how to give herself some measure of protection.

Sunday dawned hot and humid. She did some grocery shopping with Amanda. They were getting along fairly well, although Emma insisted on keeping things light and superficial between them. She could tell that her distance pained Amanda—and it pained Emma, too—but her sister had stopped trying to force serious topics, knowing how Emma would respond.

After they shopped, they stopped at a local sandwich shop, and Amanda asked her if she was feeling all right.

"Your cheeks are flushed, and you seem kind of out of it. You've seemed spacey all day, in fact," Amanda had said as they stood in line to order. The question had necessitated some nonchalant, airy acting on Emma's part.

At two thirty that afternoon, she showered and dressed carefully in a sundress and sandals, taking care with her makeup. Her hair reacted to the humidity by turning into a cap of loose, finger-combed curls and waves. She was glad Amanda was nowhere to be seen when Emma scurried through the kitchen and snuck out the back door.

It felt strange to be pulling up on the back drive of the Breakers, arriving there with such a different intent than she had before, with full knowledge of what she was doing. She was walking into Vanni's home—Vanni's world. If her eyes had been determinedly clamped shut before, they were wide-open now.

Her palms left damp spots on the wheel as she brought her car to a halt.

She thought the code Vanni had given her would work on any of the entrances to the house, but she took the one she was familiar with through the garage just in case. She knew there was an entrance to the Breakers at the back of the warehouselike underground structure, recalling how Vanni had come through it that night after he'd returned from France in order to meet her. Indeed, she found the door at the back of the garage, which was unlocked. A rush of cool, delightful air-conditioned air rushed over her heated skin as she shut the door behind her. She stood in a long, dim hallway.

The hallway she entered led past a large kitchen to the right, eventually ending on Cristina's suite's level through a door she swore she'd never seen while working there. She flew down the flight of stairs and peered around cautiously, listening. Everything was still and silent. There was no one in sight. Perhaps the day staff had Sundays off? She thought of how unpleasant it would be to run into Mrs. Shaw.

She hurried down the next two flights of stairs and saw the closed, carved wood door of his suite. Only then did she realize she'd dreamed of taking this path many times.

Her hand trembled slightly as she reached for the handle.

She saw him immediately when she entered. He sat behind his desk, wearing a dark red, short-sleeved T-shirt. He stood slowly, dropping the pen he'd been holding. Their gazes held as she shut the door behind her. She found herself holding her breath as he sauntered toward her, looking very sexy and just a tad dangerous. In some distant part of her brain she noticed he was dressed casually in jeans, and there was a shadow of whiskers on his angular jaw.

"You came," he said quietly, halting a few feet away.

"I came," she whispered.

"Was it difficult to?" he asked, his gaze running over her face and lowering, pausing on the angel at her throat. She was sure the little charm was throbbing in rhythm with her racing heart.

"It would have been more difficult to stay away."

His gaze darted to her face. She gave a little sigh of nervous relief when he stepped forward and took her into his arms, pulling her against him. With his scent tickling her nose, and the feeling of his long, hard body pressed against her, she knew the threshold had been crossed.

There was no going back.

"You remember what it was like in the garage, or on the beach?" he murmured, obviously sensing her anxiety. She placed her open hands on his chest and nodded. "It's not going to be that different, Emma. Just you and me."

She met his stare and nodded again. He studied her for a moment before he dropped his arms and took her hand in his. "Come here," he muttered. He led her over to a leather couch and sat, urging her down into his lap. It felt wonderful to sit there with his hard thighs beneath her, surrounded by his arms. For some reason, his somber gaze on her made her throat ache with emotion.

"I've thought about this a lot all week," he said. He opened his hands on her hips and circled her ever so subtly in his lap. Her eyes sprung wide when she felt the clear outline of his cock through his jeans. "*That* isn't the kind of thing that can be faked. It would be enough for me, if the kind of sex you preferred was what we've done so far. Say the word and we'll leave it at that. I prefer to be the dominant during sex, and I do like restraining a lover and administering light punishments, all with the purpose of amplifying pleasure and excitement, never to harm. But I'm not some kind of card-carrying BDSM master. I've always just acted on what feels right to me. When it comes to you, those are things that I could do without, though, if it feels like too much for you."

A tingling sensation of warmth went through her flesh. She couldn't believe he was saying this. She found herself at another crossroads. He was giving her an "out" she hadn't expected. She stared into his aquamarine eyes, experiencing the sharp focus and depth of his character.

"Are you forgetting that I admitted to being aroused, despite it all?"

"No," he said starkly. "And I'm no fool. I knew you were very responsive to being restrained. I consider myself a pretty good judge of this, and in my opinion, if you trusted enough, you would be a natural sexual submissive."

His eyebrows arched, and Emma realized she'd flinched at the last two words.

"It's not demeaning, Emma. I said *sexual* submissive. It's just a natural dynamic for some people during sex, not others. I'm just saying that I think you have the tendencies, if you trusted your lover enough. If you trusted yourself, you would reap a great deal of pleasure by letting go. From my experience of you so far, I'd hardly call you a submissive in any other aspect of life," he added with a raised brow.

She smiled at that.

"I don't know yet how you'll respond to more stringent measures, especially now that you've labeled it in your mind as a perversity." She made a sound of protest at the word. "Don't deny it. I saw the disgust on your face when you described to me what you saw that night. You definitely thought it perverse. But you're here, and it's your decision to explore whatever territory you prefer. Leave whatever you choose in the darkness. I'll respect whatever you decide."

* * *

Emma glanced around the office uneasily, finding it difficult to concentrate with his steady stare on her. It was necessary for her to steel herself, at least until she'd made herself clear to him. She realized she must have replayed the moments being trapped in his study so much that it actually looked familiar to her, despite the fact that it'd only been fleeting seconds that she stood there.

Or maybe she'd dreamed about it so much.

She swallowed thickly. "I choose not to prohibit anything . . . until I'm faced with the situation," she said. "You can . . . introduce me to whatever you like, but—"

"You have the right to say no. Always," he finished for her. He raised his dark eyebrows. "Are we in agreement then?"

"Yes. But there is one other thing."

"What?"

"I heard what you said to Astrid that night about having nothing to offer a woman but sex." He opened his mouth to speak, but she halted him this time by shaking her head. "I'm not upset about it. At least you're honest. I can appreciate that. But I'm different than you are, I think. I'm not sure I can have an affair indefinitely and not give away too much of myself."

His brow furrowed. "So what are you saying?"

"I need to know I control something, so I'll control the end. I'll give you four weeks. And then it's over. We both walk away, but on my terms."

Chapter 15

His expression darkened. "*Four weeks*?"

"Is that too long?" she asked anxiously.

He looked nonplussed. "No . . . maybe. *I* don't know. I've never had a woman put it quite that way before. I didn't expect *you*, of all people, to be so calculating."

She gave him an apologetic glance. "I'm just protecting myself. This will keep my expectations in check."

His brow knitted tighter together. "Does this have to do with what that asshole boyfriend of yours pulled on you?"

"No," she said honestly.

"Why did you pick *four weeks*?"

"I remember my mother saying once that it took all of five weeks for the fire to leave my father's eyes. I wouldn't want to be around to witness yours going out," she said simply.

"Jesus," he muttered, his jaw going hard. He looked at the wall behind his desk. She could almost hear his mind churning. "I'll be away a lot in the next few weeks. It won't be enough time. Give me eight," he finally said in a hard tone.

"No," she whispered. "I'd get lost with that much time."

He nostrils flared as he met her stare. "Six weeks then."

She felt the pull of his powerful personality. She wanted to give in. "Five," she bargained shakily. "Starting now. Today."

His handsome mouth curled slightly in dissatisfaction. "All right, five. *If* you agree to spend some of the time with me in the South of France."

"I don't think I can. I have work—"

"We can make it happen," he interrupted. Looking at his determined, rigid expression, she didn't want to argue. Not now. "Just say yes," he said.

"Yes," Emma agreed, trying to ignore her uncertainties. It seemed so improbable, her being with him in the glamorous, gilded playground of the French Riviera. At the moment, all she could think about was how tense he looked. Was he upset by her proposal? She couldn't tell for sure. She leaned down and kissed his lips, like she thought he was a statue she could magically bring to life. He became the aggressor, his hand sliding up to the back of her head, his mouth molding hers boldly. A thrill went through her at sensing all the frothing, repressed emotion in him, all the friction and heat.

He pulled her closer. It was wonderful to sink into the delight of his embrace, freeing somehow, now that they'd both spoken their minds.

Now that she'd set some parameters.

Five weeks, to touch him and luxuriate in his touch, to explore him . . . and herself.

"I want to do this. I want to take the risk," she whispered next to his mouth a moment later. She felt him quicken and harden beneath her. He scored her with his stare.

"I'm going to make it five weeks you'll never forget, starting now," he promised before he pulled her against him, and covered her mouth with his own.

His kiss deepened and Emma drowned in its decadence, letting the heat of it wash away her anxieties and insecurities. He touched her while he made free with her mouth, his large hands running along her arms and squeezing her shoulders lightly. She felt his cock lurch beneath her bottom when he molded her flesh to his. One hand played along her spine. The other fisted the hem of her dress. He drew it up her thighs.

Despite his matter-of-fact manner, she started slightly, breaking their kiss, at the feeling of cool air and his warm knuckles sliding against the skin of her naked thighs.

"It's all right," he said thickly. The way he stared at her mouth, heavy-lidded, and trailed his blunt fingertips along the tender skin of her inner thigh made her heart jump into overtime. "I'm just going to keep kissing you," he explained as he slipped his fingers beneath the elastic band of her panties. He tugged on them, and she lifted her bottom instinctively. He slipped the underwear down her thighs and over her knees. His hand returned, cupping her sex. She gasped.

"You've made out before, haven't you?" he asked, his deep, seductive tone and small smile melting her almost as much as his hand warmly cupping her pussy.

She nodded, speechless.

One hand returned to the back of her head. He pulled her to him until their breaths mingled. "That's all this is. Kissing. And I'm going to play with you a little. Just relax," he growled before he kissed her coaxingly and moved his hand, slipping a thick finger between her labia.

She moaned into his mouth. How could she possibly relax when he was pressing and sliding his finger along her clit and melting her with his kiss? She tensed in his arms.

"Relax your muscles, Emma," he ordered against her lips. "Let go. Just kissing. There's nothing to get all worked up about."

"Easy for you to say," she mumbled incoherently because he'd continued to play with her pussy while he spoke. Masterfully. His touch was shockingly deft. He lifted his finger and then slid back into the cleft between her labia, pressing and rubbing against her clit. She bit her lip to stop her sharp cry and flexed her hips against the divine pressure. He pressed his lap upward slightly at her wiggling. She felt his cock press tighter to her and moaned.

"Sweet little pussy. Sweet little mouth," he muttered thickly before he caught her lips again with his and began to devour her.

She couldn't have said how long they remained like that on the couch, his hand moving between her thighs, his cock throbbing against her ass, his mouth enflaming and taming her at once, soothing her when her flame grew too high. She felt herself turning molten beneath his touch, and knew she was growing very wet by the increasingly easy glide of his finger. The burn in her clit became delicious and untenable several times. She clutched his shoulders and tried desperately to return his forceful kiss while climax loomed, but somehow, it never crashed down. It took her arousal-dazed brain a while to realize he was cooling his strokes on her clit subtly every time she approached climax, keeping her riding just below the crest of release. His other hand made soothing motions on her back; it was almost unbearably unexciting.

She broke their kiss and pressed her forehead to his, breathing raggedly. A fever raged in her. Her clit burned. Her nipples ached. She wished he'd pinch them. Suck them. Just the idea made her moan feverishly.

"Why are you doing this to me?" she whispered on a soughing breath.

He lifted his hand from her outer sex. He grasped her hips with both hands and ground her down on his cock. She whimpered, her arousal peaking once again. She leaned back and saw the hard glint in his eyes as he moved her in a tight circle against his cock.

"Because I want to take you into my bedroom now and restrain you—just your arms—while I continue to touch you," he said. "And I didn't want to see anxiety on your face. Just excitement. Are you all right with that?"

She nodded, her breath sticking in her lungs.

"All right then." He pressed his lips to her warmly, and then sat forward, gathering her tightly into his arms. Emma made a little sound of surprise when he lurched up from the couch, bringing her with him.

The next thing she knew, he was carrying her across the threshold to his inner sanctum.

She had a flashing impression of a seating area surrounding a fireplace decorated with rich, luxurious fabrics in shades of muted red, dark brown, gold, and ivory. He set her down on her feet. When she turned to him, she realized he'd placed her at the foot of an enormous bed with a carved cherrywood headboard and four posters that must have been eight feet tall.

He walked to a mirrored door and opened it. When he disappeared, she craned to see him. He returned a moment later carrying a small box and . . . something that looked like cloth handcuffs attached to a black strap. The handcuffs were stitched very close together onto the length of tightly woven fabric.

"I'm going to tell you exactly what I plan to do, and if you choose not to participate in any part or all of it, just say so," he said, walking toward her. She realized he'd probably noticed the uncertainty on her face when she'd seen those cuffs. He set the box on the bed and held up the black strap. "Go ahead and touch it," he said quietly. She took the item and held it up to examine it while he unfastened the first two buttons of his dress shirt. "What do you think?" he asked.

"It's very lightweight," she said, trying to be objective even though her choppy breath betrayed her. She squeezed one of the cuffs. "And soft."

"Metal handcuffs can bruise," he said. "Especially in the heat of the moment. Your skin is pale and delicate. I'll have to take extra care."

She raised her brows and gave him an amused glance. He smiled and pointed at the tall bedpost. "I'm going to have you put your hands over your head, wrists together, and restrain you to the bedpost. Then I'm going touch you again. Any way I please, but for your pleasure."

Any way I please, but for your pleasure.

She swallowed as his voice replayed in her head.

"I don't understand," she confessed, despite the sexual charge that had gone through at his stated intent. "Why do you have to restrain me? Isn't touching me enough?"

"Oh, it's more than enough," he assured. "And if that's what you'd like, you know what I've told you. Just tell me. I won't be disappointed. Trust me. Do you believe me?"

She nodded.

"As for your question, maybe you should just find out for yourself why being restrained might have its advantages. For me, it's because I have you at my mercy. You have to accept what I give you. On the other hand, everything you experience, all the anticipation and the pleasure, are mine. Mine to give. Yours to receive." His eyes took on a feral glint.

"All right," she said. "You can do it."

"You haven't heard the rest yet," he said, his dark brows arching. "After you're restrained, I'm going to put this inside you," he said, lifting the box. He approached her and pointed at the photo on the box with his finger. "It's a dual vibrator, very compact. One end goes inside you and the other buzzes your clit. It does its job so that I can touch you at my leisure," he said, his deep voice dropping in volume and tickling her ear and nape. She nodded anxiously. She'd never used a vibrator before on her own, let alone with a man. It didn't look *too* intimidating, however.

"What's that?" she asked, pointing at an item featured on the box.

"Remote-control mechanism. I'm going to set the vibrator at a low level," he explained, opening the new package, "and you can hold the remote control."

"I get to hold it?"

He nodded, watching her face as he withdrew the vibrator. "I'd rather do it myself. I told you I was selfish, and I have a feeling I'm going to be over-the-top selfish when it comes to owning your pleasure." Something about the way he said it made her nipples pinch tight. What mysteries was she about to experience? "But I realize you need some control at first, and this is a way for you to have it. What do you think?"

She nodded. She was having extreme trouble controlling her breath. "And when I'm restrained, you're just going to touch me?"

"Yes. My hand against your skin. That's all. And you're going to come," he said bluntly. "Several times. Then I'm going to lay you on that bed and fuck the daylights out of you."

He watched her closely, the corner of his gorgeous mouth tilting when he saw her amazement. Without telling herself to, her gaze flickered down the length of his body. The bulge in his crotch area was glaringly obvious. As she looked, she saw the thick crown of his cock flick against the denim. She looked up into his face quickly and saw his knowing smile. "I think I'll take you in a straight-up missionary position, like Grandpa and Grandma did it," he murmured intimately, a thread of humor in his tone. He reached for the bottom of her T-shirt. "It's going to be fantastic. We'll reinvent a classic."

She laughed softly at that and had a glimpse of his grin widening. She appreciated his levity as both her anxiety and arousal escalated. His fingers moved along her back, and she realized he was unzipping her dress. It was strangely exciting, hearing him speak aloud what he planned to do to her. He moved so quickly and concisely that before she knew it, she stood before him wearing only a light pink bra-and-underwear set, her dress pooled around her feet.

She stepped out of her sandals and kicked them aside. She looked into his face as he reached around to unfasten her bra. His head was lowered and they stood close. She caught his male scent and resisted an urge to bury her nose in his cotton-covered chest. How could he smell and feel so *good*? Was it possible to become addicted to another human being?

The hook on her bra released, and he met her stare as he drew the straps over her shoulders and down her arms. Her clit pinched in acute arousal when she saw the heat in his blue-green eyes. When he slipped the straps over her hands and the bra fell to the floor, he caught her forearms and lifted both of them over her head.

"Stay like that," he instructed huskily. His gaze lowered over her. "It's the first time I've ever seen you in good light." He opened his hands on her ribs and swept them upward. With her arms above her head, her skin was pulled tight. She shivered at the sensation of his whisking hands. He cupped her breasts from below and held them up for his inspection. It was lewd. Arousing.

She held her breath as he ate her up with his stare.

"So beautiful," he murmured, running his large thumbs over the peaking crests. "I'm not going to get enough of these nipples. Look how tight they get, just from a touch. And the skin is so soft," he said, his fingers moving ever so slightly on the mounds.

Heat rushed through her core. It wasn't just his touch that burned her, it was his intent, focused lust.

She whimpered and he glanced up. Much to her disappointment, he dropped his warm hands. He turned to the bed and picked up the black strap and cuffs and held them up, a question in his eyes. She lowered her wrists, looking at his face for signs of what she should do.

"Like this," he said, briefly putting his inner wrists together. She copied the movement, and he fastened the cuffs around her wrists. She fisted her hands and pulled experimentally at the restraints, freezing when arousal spiked through her unexpectedly. Vanni was in the process of tying off a loop at the top of the strap and paused when he sensed her stiffen.

"Are you okay?" he asked, brows pinched.

"Yes," she said hastily, hoping he wouldn't notice the pulse leaping at her throat.

He studied her face closely before resuming his task. "Come here," he said quietly, pointing at the corner of the bed. She faced the post. "Arms straight and over your head." She followed his instructions, lifting her arms and bound wrists. The position made her feel even more vulnerable than usual, pulling the skin tight along her ribs, leaving the sensitive sides of her torso exposed. He reached, tossing the small loop at the end of the strap around the top of the post. It came to rest several feet down the poster at the top of an especially fat newel in the carving. Looking up, Emma pulled. She was bound securely. She wasn't even close to being tall enough to flip the loop off the post. Her heart suddenly beat so furiously, she felt as if there wasn't room in her chest cavity both for it and her franticly working lungs.

"Shh, it's okay. Easy," Vanni soothed. He'd clearly noticed her sudden rush of anxiety. He stood close, his hands stroking her hips and her belly. The front of his pants barely brushed the skin of her hip, but the sensation distracted her completely. He was aroused—very—and that knowledge somehow evened the playing field. He was clearly turned on by the proceedings. That aroused her, in turn. She was vulnerable, yes, but his need was evident. He couldn't remain aloof in this situation.

Slowly, she became focused on his caressing hands, absorbing how good it felt to have him enliven her skin and mold her curves gently. Her choppy breathing began to even under the spell of his touch. "Better? Or do you want me to unfasten you?" he asked after a moment. He was behind and to the side of her, his long legs lightly bracketing one hip, his head lowered so that his nose grazed against the shell of her ear. She turned her head, and suddenly his mouth brushed against hers. Shivers roughened her flesh. He charted them with his fingertips.

"No," she whispered, brushing her lips against his. "I want to continue."

She felt his smile on her lips, and then he was kissing her deeply, his hands sliding over her hips and belly and ribs. Her anxiety evaporated from the rising heat. By the time he touched her nipples with questing fingertips and cupped her breasts in his hands, Emma wouldn't have been surprised if she was steaming.

He broke their kiss and moved behind her. This time, her anxiety at not seeing him seemed to spice her arousal instead of interfere with it. He stood behind her and cupped her breasts from below, massaging and shaping them.

"Oh," she cried out sharply when he pinched both nipples at once lightly, but firmly. Arousal tore through her, stabbing at her clit. She flinched inward slightly at the sensation, squeezing her thighs and buttocks together to contain the ache.

"Do you like that?" he asked from behind her, continuing to pinch her nipples with finesse.

"It hurts," she said in a strangled voice. His fingers stopped their plucking.

"On your nipples?"

"No," she gasped. "Between my legs."

He cursed harshly and reached for her panties, drawing them down her thighs.

Chapter 16

He couldn't get over how responsive her body was. Everywhere. She was like a taut, vibrating cord. It was such a pleasure to play her. It was like she'd been given twice the number of nerves as most people.

He drew her panties off her feet and stood, gnashing his teeth as lust stabbed at his cock, making it swell and jerk. He'd never seen her naked from the back until now. It was a cruel sight for a man intent on patience. He thought her perfect, some strange combination of graceful feminine beauty and lush sexuality. Her elegant back, narrow waist, curving hips, and plump ass made him want to bend her over and take her then and there in a savage fury. But he also couldn't wait to see all her anxiety disappear as she sacrificed it to surrender.

He saw her craning around to see him, her delicate features drawn tight, her eyes wide.

"I'm right here," he assured, stepping forward and touching her shoulders. He lowered his hands down the beautiful sweep of her back, relishing satiny skin. He kissed her neck. "I was just admiring you. You're exquisite," he said, molding her hips to his palms.

She laughed raggedly. "Hardly exquisite. But thank you."

"I'm not flattering. I'm stating the truth," he said in an unflinching tone. She clearly had been lulled by the rest of the mediocrity-satisfied world into believing she, too, was middling-pretty when in fact, she was a gem of the highest quality. "I'll buy you some dresses to show off this beautiful back and gorgeous ass." She gasped and moaned softly when he took both firm ass cheeks into his palms and squeezed. His hands skimmed up her belly and along her ribs, thrilling to the subtle vibration of her trembling. He took her breasts into his hands. "A dress that molds these perfect, pert breasts," he said near her ear.

"Small breasts," she said, a whisper of embarrassment and apology in her voice.

"You need to learn about the difference between quality and quantity," he said, pinching lightly at her nipples as he molded her flesh to his. Jesus, that's all she thought of her breasts? That they were "small"? They belonged to a goddess. They were the type of breasts that drove a man mad with a need to touch . . . to devour.

He regrettably let go of them now. Playing with them, feeling how tight and hard the little buds grew beneath his fingers, was making the ache of his cock take over his brain.

"I'm going to put a finger inside you now," he told her. She was clamping her thighs closed to alleviate her arousal, which pleased him. But he wanted access to her. Full access. "Spread your thighs, Emma. I will usually want you to keep your thighs open for me. Do you understand?"

"Yes," she replied, opening her legs.

"That's right," he murmured, sweeping his hand between her firm thighs from behind. He immediately slipped his fingertip into her sheath. He grunted at finding her warm and very wet. She moaned shakily as he thrust his finger high into her. He gritted his teeth. One thing was for certain, he hadn't been kidding himself by remembering how tight and sweet she was. Heat rushed around his finger.

"I think you like being restrained and touched," he said, thrusting his finger in and out of her.

"By you, I do," she muttered through a constricted throat.

He said nothing to that, because an image popped into his head of Emma being restrained like this while some faceless, unlikeable male dipped his finger into her snug, soft pussy. He may be the first man to initiate her into the pleasures of submission, but perhaps he wouldn't be the last.

A snarl shaped his mouth at the intrusive, unpleasant thought.

"Bend over a little," he said, pushing gently on her shoulders. "Lean into the restraint. It will hold you."

She did as he'd instructed. The strap went taut as she bent slightly at the waist, giving him better access. He plunged into her more forcefully, his middle finger seeking her outer sex. Her pubic hair was soft and growing damp with her arousal. He slid a finger against her clit. She bit off a shaky moan. He felt her lithe body tense. She began to bob her hips against his hand as her fever rose. He knew she liked it—a lot—but aside from some sexy, soughing gasps, she didn't cry out. He longed to hear her lose control.

"I want to feel you come this first time," he said. He felt her stiffen even more, and then her vagina tightened around him. God, he couldn't wait to feel that sensation clamping his cock. "Emma?" he prodded when she didn't respond as he continued to finger-fuck her and stroke her clit. "Do you want to come?"

"Yes, so much," she said, her voice quaking. He'd primed her out there on the couch. His stimulation now was added fuel on a steady, high burn.

"Then come against my hand," he demanded.

Her slender body jerked slightly and she made a choking, sobbing sound. He drew closer, kissing her warm nape and inhaling her scent. He felt the muscular walls convulsing around his plunging fingers and the rush of heat.

"That's right. Give in to it," he ordered thickly. "That's so good," he praised as she came, her soft, muted whimpers killing him a little.

When her shuddering had ceased, he withdrew his finger, anxious to continue, his brain and body fevered, to get inside her. His finger was glossy with her abundant, warm juices. Glancing up to make sure she wasn't looking, he slid it into his mouth and sucked it clean.

Maybe on some level, he knew it was dangerous to reveal how greedy he was for her.

He couldn't help making a sound of intense satisfaction as her taste spread on his tongue. He withdrew his finger when she started to look over her shoulder, then he stepped toward the bed.

"Do you use one of these?" he asked her as he forced himself to attend to the mundane task of removing the vibrator from the packaging.

"A vibrator? No," she said between soft pants.

He made the mistake of looking up. He was caught by the beguiling image she made, naked with her hands restrained above her head; her flawless pale skin; the slope of her spine; the lush curve of her ass; firm, high breasts thrusting forth from her rib cage as she panted, recovering from her orgasm. He could see the light golden brown, downy hair between her slender thighs and experienced an intense urge to have her spread on the bed before him, bound and ready for ravishment.

He shut his eyes, trying to erase the potent image. Another time, he would have her that way. For now, he had to stick to his plan or risk losing her trust.

She watched him with those big, haunting eyes as he held up the sex toy. It was shaped like an arch, with a vibrator at each end.

"We'll get you used to it, quick enough. It's not complicated. It's meant for your pleasure, nothing more. Certainly nothing less," he said, stepping behind her. "I'm just going to put it inside you. You're plenty wet enough," he rasped, reaching between her thighs. He found her slit and slid one end of the arch inside her pussy. "That's it," he soothed when she gasped. He lodged the other end of the vibrator next to her clit. "Is it comfortable?"

"I think so," she mumbled, and he could tell by the tone of her voice it felt unusual to her.

He picked up the small remote-control device. "I'm going to turn it on a low setting."

He saw her muscles jerk slightly as the mechanism began to vibrate her channel and clit at once. "Feel good?" he asked quietly, enjoying watching her as pleasure and friction tightened her muscles yet again.

"Oh God. *Yes*," she said, stunned.

It felt so good having the vibrator buzz her sensitive flesh, both from the inside and out; it left her rigid with arousal and amazement for a moment as the new sensation unfurled in her consciousness.

"It has a heating mechanism," Vanni said, stepping next to her. "It will start to warm inside you." She looked at him, her mouth hanging open.

"It feels very good," she said, repressing a little gasp.

He studied her closely, and then raised a hand to brush back her hair. He stroked her cheek with his long thumb. Her heart fluttered in her chest at the expression in his eyes when he did it.

"You *do* like it, don't you? Not all vibrators are suited to everyone. I got lucky the first time around," he said, fluttering the tip of his thumb across her earlobe. "I'll use this one on you the first time I punish you. Not now. Another time."

She stiffened at that. "You mean . . . whip me?"

"*Whip* you? Of course not." Understanding hit him. "Oh, you mean what you saw," he said quietly. "That was a flogging, not a whipping. And the case was entirely different, like I told you before. Astrid has far more experience than you. And she tends to like it . . ."

"Rough?" Emma asked shakily, licking away some sweat gathering on her upper lip. The vibrator was warming. Between the heating mechanism and the vibrations, it was charging her pussy with more incendiary energy than she'd ever experienced. How was it that she'd never treated herself before to this experience? Probably because she hadn't realized it could ever feel this good. Besides, Vanni's heated stare and stroking hand was perhaps the most active ingredient to her pleasure.

He frowned. "She believes she does. She doesn't realize that I'm actually careful to give her a sense of what she wants while never harming her."

Her mouth trembled. His brow quirked. She looked at him helplessly. She'd forgotten what they were talking about while under the influence of the buzzing vibrator. He seemed to guess her dilemma.

"It's okay," he muttered. "None of that will happen now. Only what I told you. Now straighten up," he said, stepping closer and putting his hand on her bottom, urging her to stand upright again. He reached up toward her bound hands. "Here is the controller. You control the amount of power you want like this." He put his fingers on top of hers and manipulated them to push the buttons. "That's down, and that's up."

She gasped at the increased stimulation. "Oh my God," she exclaimed, her head falling forward. His hands dropped away.

"You have the control. For now you do," he reminded her, a dark edge to his tone. He encircled her waist with his arms, his big hands stroking her sides. She shuddered uncontrollably, her clit going from a simmer to a burn in a matter of seconds. She punched blindly with the buttons and the direct, focused stimulation eased to a delicious buzz, sending tingling sensations up her spine.

"Better?" he murmured, kissing her neck.

"Yes," she whispered. She turned her head, suddenly wild to feel him. He accepted the invitation of her proffered lips, capturing her mouth with his and pulling her closer into his embrace. It all was so new to her. So heady and powerful. She felt herself swimming in a sea of desire. His hands moved over her hip, waist, belly, and thighs, his focused, eager caresses leading her to believe he was as hungry as she was. He pressed to the side of her, the fly of his pants against the curve of her hip. The round, firm shaft of his erection pressing against her skin, the sensation taunting her. She'd never held him naked in her hand. She'd never held him naked in her arms. The realization was suddenly unbearable. The vibrator only amplified her burning, boiling want.

How was it that he made her desire for him so acute? Was it because she couldn't touch him while he touched her wherever and however he chose? He'd made her the focused object of his desire, but in the process, he made her want him with a slashing, single-minded sexual intent she'd never known.

He broke their kiss. "What is it?" he asked, caressing her ass with one large hand.

Emma blinked. She realized she'd been moaning into his mouth as her fever rose. She gritted her teeth and clamped her vaginal muscles around the vibrator.

"I want to touch you," she whispered.

"That's good," he said, nipping at her sensitive lips. His long fingers slid down the crack of her ass and continued. He pushed lightly against the end of the vibrator inserted into her vagina, pressing it like a button, in and out, in and out. She gasped, her entire body beginning to tremble, on the verge of explosion. Oh God, what was happening to her?

"It's *not* good," she said desperately. "Because you won't let me touch you."

"It's good because your desire will make your pleasure sharper," he explained, removing his hand and stepping behind her. She bowed her head, clamping her eyes shut, disappointed that she couldn't even see his handsome face anymore, let alone touch him. She could only feel, and she'd never done it more in her life. He'd made everything sharper. More imperative. He bracketed her hips in his hold and he stepped forward, his fly brushing against the upper part of her buttocks. His hand dipped between their bodies and she felt him readjusting his cock. Her eyes popped open at the sensation of his long, heavy erection pressing against her ass and lower spine. He squeezed her buttocks and flexed subtly against her. She cried out in excitement.

"Anyone can come, Emma. I want you to burn. I want you to have the memory of your pleasure stamped in your consciousness forever."

"I am burning," she said, her pleasure and need a sweet agony. "I *will* remember." She backed against him, circling her hips, craving the sensation of his hard body and cock. God, she was writhing against him like a cat in heat, but she didn't care. For a moment, he firmed his hold and ground her ass against his erection. He groaned gutturally.

"What a sweet little ass," he muttered thickly. "God, the things I want to do to you . . ."

Emma gyrated more forcefully against him, aroused instead of intimidated by the edge to this tone. It felt so good, so hot, so delicious. He popped the side of her buttock with his palm. She halted her mindless writhing, shocked at the sensation.

"Just a little reminder," he said. His hands swept up her belly. He took her breasts into his palms and began to squeeze them, this time more lewdly than last.

"A little reminder of what?" she asked in a choked voice. His cock was still pressed to her backside, but he no longer was grinding against her. The sheer weight of his arousal next to her skin drove her mad, but he'd spanked her for crushing herself against him.

"That you hold the controls," he rasped, massaging her breasts, his actions bold and lascivious. It felt good, naughty. Exciting. "Do you want to come?"

"Yes."

"Then *do* it," he bit out, pinching her nipples lightly between thumb and forefinger while he moved his hands up and down, bouncing her breasts. Emma squealed, punching the button several times. The pulsation escalated to a breathtaking pace. Her body ignited. He stepped forward abruptly, encircling her in his arms, capturing her first shudder of climax.

"Oh yeah. That's good," he said thickly in her ear as she came almost violently. It took her a moment to decode what his hot mutterings meant, bliss shook her so hard. "That's right. Keep it coming," he demanded, and another wave of pleasure hit her, and another.

At some point, he reached up and turned off the vibrator. He must have realized her body was too busy short-circuiting to stop it. She heaved a sigh and sagged against him, panting . . . undone. He stroked her arms and shoulders. He throbbed against her backside, heavy with need, but still lingering over his task of pressing his lips against the skin of her nape. He tasted her sweat with the tip of his tongue and she felt his hunger.

Never had she imagined feeling so exquisitely desired.

"Do you think you might begin to understand the advantages of being restrained?" he asked before he kissed the opening of her ear. She shivered against him and turned her chin. He leaned over and she saw the hint of humor and the hard gleam of desire in his aquamarine eyes.

She smiled and shook her head, still panting. "I understand."

"A little, maybe. There's more. Much more," he said, breaking contact with her. She missed his warm, solid length. He reached for her cuffs and unbound her. She lowered her arms with a sigh of relief. "But right now, you'll have to deal with me."

"Deal with you?" she asked, pausing in the action of rubbing her wrists.

"That's right," he said in a hard tone, taking her hand and leading her toward the great bed. He drew her around and she sat at the edge. He whipped off his T-shirt, muscles flexing beneath smooth, golden-brown skin. She saw the hard tilt to his mouth, and recognized the full extent of his arousal. "You were more than I was expecting," he said.

He fleetly began to unfasten the button fly of his jeans, holding her stare the whole time. "Now you'll have to accept the consequences."

Week
FOUR

Chapter 17

Vanni jerked down his jeans and a snowy pair of boxer briefs at once. His cock sprung free. The shaft was straight and long, the cap succulent and fat. It hung suspended from his body, heavy, flagrantly virile . . . ripe, forbidden fruit.

"*Oh God*," she whispered, staring up at his face, wide-eyed, awe and wariness tingeing her tone. Had she really taken *that* inside her in the darkness on the beach that night? Or was he perhaps especially swollen and needy tonight with suspended gratification? She stilled when he smiled, her core clenching tight.

He kicked off shoes and removed his socks hastily, his jeans and underwear disappearing down long, tanned legs dusted with dark brown hair. Sensing his arousal, she wasn't entirely surprised when he placed his hands around her waist and heaved her back on the bed, ready for business.

"Lie back," he ordered tersely. She scurried back on the soft duvet, eager to have all that naked, gilded, rigid muscle and sheer maleness pressed against her at last. Her head fell against an assortment of pillows. Tearing his gaze from her, he opened the top drawer of the bedside table and withdrew a condom. He ripped open the package. She watched, spellbound, air stuck in her lungs when he rolled it on his swollen, ruddy cock with expert haste.

He came onto the bed on his hands and knees. Emma's heart began to pound frantically in her ears as he prowled toward her.

"Open your thighs like I told you," he said, his voice a low growl. "I want you to keep them spread unless I tell you otherwise." He positioned himself over her. She couldn't breathe. Hadn't he joked that they'd have sex in the missionary position, making it sound like it'd be a walk in the park after the challenge of being restrained? She anxiously eyed his heavy cock hanging between his legs. Missionary sex with Vanni suddenly seemed as erotic and challenging as the most advanced positions in the Kama Sutra.

"Don't look at me like that, Emma," he chided as he placed his hands on her inner thighs and matter-of-factly spread her even wider. He stared at her exposed pussy for a moment, gritting his teeth. "You wouldn't deny me this moment of pleasure after you've had yours, would you?" he asked, pressing back her thighs so that her hips rolled back on the bed.

"No, of course not," she managed as she watched, wide-eyed as he used his hand to place the fat, fleshy crown of his cock at her entrance. It wasn't a lie. The idea of having him inside her again excited her so much, it was like an achy knot at her core. It's just that he overwhelmed her as well.

She moaned at the pressure of the hard, swollen head of his sex pressing into her. She was extremely aroused, and very wet, but her channel resisted his girth at first.

He thrust, holding her hips steady. She gasped loudly. Her tissues stretched around him, finally submitting to the relentless pressure.

"No. You're much too sweet to deny me this, aren't you?" he grated out, coming down over her and seizing her mouth in a furious, possessive kiss. He flexed his hips. She screamed as he filled her, his mouth muffling her surge of excitement and crashing, ruthless sensation.

* * *

Sinking into Emma was like piercing heaven . . . or a particularly salacious part of hell.

He should have been satisfied with the feeling of her squeezing his cock into the sweet lock of her body, but he wanted more.

Always more.

Falling down over her, he braced himself on his forearms. His tongue plunged between her lips.

He sunk deeper into her pussy and she screamed into his mouth. He lifted his head reluctantly, nipping at her lush lips. His cock throbbed furiously in her clasp, demanding more. He resisted with a Herculean effort.

"Shh," he soothed roughly. He waited until he felt her kissing him back excitedly, her soft whimpers driving him crazy. Her hands moved anxiously on his back, her fingertips sinking into muscle. He groaned and penetrated her to the hilt. He grimaced, his eyes clamped shut.

"*Fuck*, you're a trial," he said.

He blinked his eyes open, realizing belatedly he'd spoken the blistering thought out loud. He focused on her lovely face, her delicate features pulled tight with arousal. Glancing down, he saw her small, firm breasts rising and falling rapidly. His cock lurched in her clasping channel.

"I'm sorry," he said, regretting her slight wince.

"Don't be," she whispered. "You feel so good."

His nostrils flared as he stared down at her. "If you had any idea of what I want to do to you right now, you might not say that."

Her lips fell open, the vision of the wet, red depths of her mouth like a lancing spear to his restraint.

"Just the missionary position, remember?" she gasped softly.

He stilled, his skin roughening. "Are you *teasing* me?" he asked disbelievingly.

"No. Tempting you."

"You fresh little witch," he bit out before he drew his cock out of her and plunged it back in to the hilt. Air popped out of her throat at the hard thrust. Her legs jolted slightly. "Spread your legs again," he ordered tensely. She widened her thighs, raising her bent knees higher. "That's right," he muttered before he began to fuck her.

He stared at her face as he took her, enraptured by the wild, helpless expression on her face. He thrust harder, smacking into her taut body. God, he was hungry, and she was a feast unlike any other.

She gripped at his shoulders, her expression growing frantic. Her nails sunk into muscle. His cock swelled and pounded.

"Put your hands above your head," he grated out, never ceasing in his thrusts. "*Do it*, Emma," he said sharply when she just stared at him with dazed, doelike eyes. He drove into her, their skin slapping together.

Her eyes would be the death of him.

She finally seemed to understand him. Her hands fell over her head, her elbows bent, the pale, tender underside of her arms exposed. Her hands were open on the pillows, the palms upward, her fingers curling slightly inward. It was a striking image of beauty. Of submission. She'd done it so naturally, never realizing the effect it had on him.

He cursed, arousal biting at him, goading him onward. He fucked her harder. Her pink-tipped breasts strained upward, bouncing slightly every time he plunged into her. She bit her lip as his cock drove faster. Her pussy was warm and liquid, her nipples erect. Her expression was rigid, her eyes glazed with desire.

"Why don't you scream for me?" he bit out, angry at the blatant evidence of her arousal and subsequent silence, for some reason. He despised porn-star theatrics in bed. He was disgustingly *used* to porn-star theatrics in bed, so it was a strange thing for him to demand Emma to scream her need.

She blinked. "Do you want me to?"

"Fuck *yes*," he snarled. He sunk his cock and ground his pelvis against her outer sex. He circled his hips, stimulating her clit.

Her perspiration-glazed face rippled with tension. A cry popped out of her throat. She clamped her eyes shut and stifled a moan. He felt the walls of her pussy convulse. Her whimpers broke free. They fell on his ears like the sweetest of blessings.

"That's right," he muttered viciously. He pushed her knees back onto the mattress, opening her body to him further. He came up on his toes, his feet digging into the bed and finding traction. He fucked her climaxing pussy with wild abandon. The sound of the bed creaking at his forceful thrusts melded with that of her frantic cries and his own pounding heart.

God it was *good*.

He hadn't meant to take her so ruthlessly, but something had snapped in him when she'd climaxed. He'd been scorched and snagged by the fiery whip of pure lust.

His roar as he came was triumphant. Savage. His sinews seized as pleasure crashed into him.

He fell over her a moment later, his lips instinctively finding the sweetness of her neck. He panted wildly for breath, swallowing the fragrance of her skin and her arousal, filling his lungs with it. His nerves buzzed and crackled in the electrical aftershock.

The stupid, yet compelling thought hit him that Emma had reanimated him, somehow.

Cristina had died more than a week ago while he stood looking on with Emma. He'd initiated Emma into the world of challenge and passion.

But Emma, that innocent, unlikely fey creature that stood at the gateway between life and death, had tempted him.

She'd done the unexpected, Vanni realized. She'd jerked him, raw and exposed, into the bright, blinding light of the living.

Emma stared up at the ceiling, trying desperately to calm her body and then her mind. She understood now, or at least she understood *better,* what she'd seen that night in the armoire. When she was restrained to that bedpost, and just now in this bed, she'd been the single, focused point of Vanni's desire. She hadn't comprehended him earlier entirely when he'd said that he deserved her judgment for making love to Astrid so callously, but she did now. If such methods were to be used, it should only be used in situations of caring and trust.

But this—what she'd glimpsed of herself beneath Vanni's hands and cock and focused desire—had amazed her.

He had.

She lowered her hands and caressed his shoulders and back, wondrous anew at the sensation of thick, smooth skin gloving lean, rippling muscle. Warmth swept through her when she felt him nuzzle her neck and then press his lips to her still-leaping pulse.

"How do you get so *hard*?" she asked, amazement spicing her tone as she ran her hands along his sides.

"Exercise," he said next to her skin. "It helps me to relax. Reduce tension."

If he needed to exercise as much as his hard body suggested, he must carry a mountain-load of tension in him. There was exercise like she practiced it—four or five hours a week at the local gym—and then there was exercise like *this*, she realized as she touched a rock-hard, curving biceps. She looked down at what she stroked in her hand, focusing on the tattoo.

"What does it mean?' she asked, her fingers brushing over the Asian characters.

"Twins," he said hoarsely after a moment. "It's Chinese for twins."

Her fingers stilled and then resumed tracing the intricate markings.

"What was he like? Your brother?" she wondered cautiously. He had told her on the day of Cristina's funeral that he didn't want to talk more about Adrian, but that unknown little boy seemed so present at times. Or was that Emma's overactive imagination?

He exhaled heavily. She waited, but she didn't feel the tension leap back into his muscles that she'd half expected.

"He was dreamy. Sweet," Vanni added after a pause, not lifting his head from her neck. "We looked alike, but Adrian was slighter.

He was fragile. Physically. You've never seen two more different kids on the surface. I was fire and force. I didn't walk anywhere, I ran. I could take apart an engine and put it back together by the time I was seven. Adrian wasn't interested in cars or engines, but his brain was just as methodical once he focused on something. He'd get distracted by a hundred different things crossing the length of the yard. He'd stop and watch a bunch of ants or some other animal, and then draw them in amazing detail. If there were such a thing as fairies, Adrian would have seen them." Emma felt his small smile against her skin. "He *was* strong, just in a different way than me. That was one thing my father never understood. He never realized how much I respected Adrian, or how much Adrian respected me. We were different, but we understood each other perfectly. We even had our own language," he said with a dry laugh. "Nobody else could understand us."

"Two sides of a whole," Emma whispered, a sharp, cutting feeling rising in her chest, making drawing air difficult. What would it be like, to feel so connected to another human being, to even feel like part of oneself resided in another, only to have that elemental part cut away? Her hands caressed his biceps carefully. She sensed that those things that characterized Adrian were inside Vanni, too. They always had been. Adrian had just been the embodiment of them, that part of Vanni made flesh. Vanni had been Adrian's strength and fiery focus.

Now Vanni remained, believing himself to be only a part of what he was, existing in a severed state.

No child should have been left to feel so much. No man forced to feel so little.

Cristina's remembered voice rose into her consciousness. The ache in her chest swelled. Cristina had been talking about Vanni—about his life since Adrian died.

He rose suddenly and flipped onto his back, effortlessly scooping her into his arms. Her head rolled onto his chest, her cheek pressing to a wall of dense muscle and springy hair. She pressed her lips to his warm flesh, trying to calm the upsweep of emotion she'd experienced.

His open hand swept up her spine, making her shiver. He cradled her head in his hand, his fingertips rubbing her scalp.

"Vanni," she said, her lips brushing his skin. "How much exactly did you hear Cristina say on the day she died?"

"Enough," he said.

"But there was something she said—"

"I don't want to discuss it. I told you. I heard enough," he said, and she could tell by the cool, clipped finality of his tone that it wasn't a topic they'd be broaching anytime soon.

He felt her tense slightly in his arms and frowned. He hadn't meant to sound so sharp. She had no inkling of how raw he felt. How exposed. He needed distance.

He required it.

Yet he couldn't bear to part from her at that moment.

"I told you that the next time we were together, I'd take you someplace nice," he said, his fingertip running down the ridge of her pretty nose, caressing the sprinkle of freckles.

"That's okay," she murmured. "You don't have to."

"I know I don't have to." He leaned down and kissed her. He'd meant it to be a brisk kiss, but he caught her flavor and scent, and lingered. She smelled like lemons and honey. Even the taste of her sweat was sweet. "I want to," he said a moment later, looking into her sex-flushed face. His gaze ran down the length of her appreciatively. Unable to stop himself, he caressed a pale breast and delicate pink nipple. Desire flickered in him when he felt her bead beneath his touch. Five weeks? Would it be enough? he wondered idly. When she set the limit, it had initially annoyed him until he realized she'd given him a convenient out. Wasn't she making it all easy for him, and for her as well? That was important in her case. He didn't want to hurt her.

Emma made *everything* so easy. Certainly his desire had never been this sharp, ready to rear up and clutch at him with just a glance or a touch.

"Why are you frowning?" she asked softly, touching his furrowed forehead and splintering his thoughts.

"I took you very hard. I hadn't intended to. Waiting all week for your answer . . . it made things very trying . . ." He faded off. "Are you all right?"

She gave him a half-shy, half-mischievous glance. "Yes. It was incredible."

"It was," he agreed. He smoothed her hair back from her forehead distractedly. "Come on, I'll take you into the city for dinner." She opened her mouth but he preempted her. "Don't worry, we'll stop by your apartment and pick up what you might need until tomorrow morning."

"Tomorrow morning?" she asked, clearly surprised

He turned, rolling off the bed. "We'll stay the night at my place in the city. I'm not flying to Nice until late tomorrow.

"You have a place in the city?"

He nodded. "My plant is in Deerfield, but I have a business office in the city. I need a place there for when I work late."

He felt her eyes on him as he walked around the bed toward the bathroom. He was starting to think he'd feel her eyes on him even in his sleep.

Chapter 18

Her mind was preoccupied almost exclusively with one—admittedly stupid—thought all the way home. *Should I ask him inside my apartment, or would he prefer just to wait in the car?* Asking Vanni inside seemed *intimate*. Somehow it didn't seem to match up with the purely sexual affair she'd agreed to with him for a circumscribed period of time. She suspected *he* felt that way, at any rate, and so she wanted to act accordingly.

Earlier in his suite, he'd asked her politely if she'd like to shower there or at her home, to which she'd answered the latter. Then there'd been nothing left for her to do but sit in a chair in the sitting area and watch in mounting fascination the tail end of his grooming/dressing ritual.

He'd quickly showered after they'd made love, and then changed into a suit. It was a dark gray, with which he wore a white shirt, a slim black tie with two white stripes, silver cuff links, and a crisp white pocket square.

He'd donned his clothing in a methodical fashion, as efficient as a knight putting on his armor. He'd put on the pants, shirt, socks, and shoes in a large dressing closet, where she couldn't see him. When he'd stepped out, she stared at him with a mixture of fascination and lust. He looked beautiful with the shirt unbuttoned, his ridged abdomen and powerful chest showing through the two-inch gap between the plackets. He hadn't shaved, and an attractive dark scruff was on his jaw and upper lip. She watched, spellbound as he fastened his shirt and crisply tied his tie in the mirror over his dresser. His hair had still been a little damp around the collar by the time he snapped on his platinum watch and turned his gaze to her where she sat on a chair in the seating area, blinking at her expression of bemused fascination. She'd been a little undone viewing the Vanni Montand dressing ceremony, that ritual of blatant male sexuality and precision.

Now he sat there in the driver's seat, smelling delicious from his shower and looking impossibly gorgeous. The idea of him inside her apartment seemed . . . just *odd*. Unlikely. Surely he'd rather wait in the car.

"I'll just hop in the shower and change for dinner. It won't take me more than ten minutes," she said awkwardly when the car came to a stop in her apartment parking lot.

He didn't reply. She studied his profile in the soft summer evening light.

"Um . . . do you want to come in?"

Much to her surprise, he nodded once and twisted the keys out of the ignition. Her heart jumped when he reached for his car door.

Oh my God, how is Amanda going to react? I haven't even told her I was seeing anyone, let alone someone *like Vanni Montand.*

"I'm on the third floor. It's a walk-up," she mumbled apologetically a few seconds later as they approached her building. Again, she experienced that dazed, dreamlike sensation watching Vanni rise up the starkly mundane wooden staircase that led to her third-floor apartment. They passed an overlook to the parking lot below on the second floor. Emma's feet halted when she saw Colin's car in the parking lot. She'd been so preoccupied sitting in the car with Vanni and inhaling his subtle, addictive scent that she'd hadn't noticed it before.

"Emma?" She blinked and looked at Vanni where he stood on the first step to the third floor, an expectant look on his face. Her brain whirred and then stalled. What excuse could she make? She couldn't think of anything else to do but continue.

"Sorry," she breathed, following him up the steps.

She led him to her door and fumbled the key in the lock. Suddenly, his hand was on hers. She looked up in surprise. His blue-green eyes seemed to glow in the shadows as he regarded her calmly. Soberly.

"I don't care if your house is a mess, if that's what you're worried about," he said.

Her house a mess? She almost laughed. It was a mess, but not in the way he meant it.

His hand turned the key in the lock. The door swung open.

Emma led him through the small foyer and into her modest but comfortable living room, a lump swelling in her throat. She paused abruptly on the threshold.

In some ways, the situation echoed the other night when she'd caught Amanda and Colin together. The pair sat close together on the couch and looked startled by her appearance. At least they weren't kissing, though, Emma thought numbly.

In actuality, it was drastically different. Vanni came to a halt beside her, and Colin and Amanda might have been a mile away. His presence altered the dynamics of the situation almost beyond recognition. How could she worry too much over Colin and Amanda's new relationship with *him* standing right next to her?

"Hi," Emma said in a high-pitched voice.

"Hi," Amanda replied. She gaped at Vanni. So did Colin. For a few seconds, no one spoke.

"Hi. I'm Vanni Montand."

Emma blinked in rising horror when she saw Vanni crossing the room. He held out his hand to Amanda. He'd had to introduce himself, because he was the only one in the room not tongue-tied. Emma forced herself to move.

"I'm sorry. Vanni, this is my sister, Amanda." Amanda stood to shake hands, still staring at Vanni dazedly. Vanni nodded cordially at her and turned to Colin.

"And this is Colin Atwater," Emma introduced through a dry throat.

The small, warm smile Vanni had given Amanda flickered and faded. His dark brows slanted dangerously. He glanced at Emma and she read the sharp questions in his eyes. *The* Colin? Your *old boyfriend* Colin?

She gave him a wild look. Colin had stood in the meantime. He looked younger than usual, studying Vanni uncertainly. Colin started to put out his hand, but Vanni gave him a burning scowl and he let it drop. Vanni grabbed Emma's hand instead.

"Excuse us," he said coolly, drawing her away. "We have a dinner reservation to make. Emma needs to dress."

"Why didn't you tell me?" he demanded immediately after she'd pointed to her room and he'd followed her in, closing the door behind him. His voice was quiet, but his gaze shouted all kinds of things.

Emma glanced around nervously. If it'd been strange to think of Vanni in her apartment, it was downright bizarre to see him in her bedroom. He shrunk the size of it just by standing in it. His abundant good looks and the careless way he wore the expensive suit seemed to make her carefully chosen bedroom set and accessories appear shabby by comparison.

"I don't know. I didn't think it was important," she hedged.

He took a step closer, his gaze boring down into her. She had to force herself not to step back. "You walked in on your boyfriend fooling around with your *sister*? And you didn't think that was an important detail?"

"All right," she said, anger rising in her. Why was he acting like *she* had done something wrong? She turned and dropped her purse on her bed, then immediately wished she hadn't. Now she had nothing to do with her hands. "I didn't want to tell you because I knew you'd . . ."

"What?" he prodded when she faded off.

"Feel sorry for me," she shot defiantly over her shoulder.

He put his hands on her shoulders and spun her around. She glared up at him. "Don't you think compassion would have been appropriate in that situation?" he breathed out ominously through a stiff jaw.

"No, because even though no one believes me, I'm honestly not all that upset about what happened. Colin and I weren't meant to be together."

"You and your sister are."

She inhaled sharply. Hurt tightened her face.

Regret flickered across his stark features.

"Dammit, Emma, you should have said something. And what the hell are they doing out there together? This is your *home*, for Christ's sake. Don't they have any decency, parading around in front of you?" he seethed.

"I told Amanda she could bring him here. This is her home, too. *I'm* not upset by it. Why should it matter to you?" she mumbled, looking down at the floor. Tears had prickled in her eyes when he'd said that thing about her and Amanda being meant to be together, and she didn't want him to notice them. She was distantly gratified by his anger on her behalf, but she was mostly embarrassed. No matter how you looked at it, it wasn't an admirable position to be in, to have a man pass over you for your gorgeous sister, no matter that you didn't *want* the man.

Or to have your only family member sacrifice you for a man.

She slumped as pain swept through her at the thought. His hands slid down her shoulders to her upper arms. He palmed the muscles.

"So you're not upset," he said dryly.

"*No*," she replied furiously, stubbornly meeting his stare despite her tears.

He just studied her soberly for a few seconds. "It was bad enough that I pounced on you in the garage after you'd told me you broke up with your boyfriend. I knew you were upset, I just didn't guess the full extent of why."

"So you're saying you wouldn't have made out with me or proposed a strictly sexual affair if you'd known it was Amanda I caught Colin with?" she asked, her voice dripping with sarcasm. His eyes went frigid.

"No. You're right. I would have gotten there eventually, no matter what."

"Well then what are you worried about? You can't be both selfish and outraged on behalf of my feelings at once, Vanni."

He dropped his hands abruptly. Even though she was irritated at him—at the world, at that moment—she missed his touch.

"You *do* realize that makes me even more of a jerk than Colin, don't you? I just told you I would have seduced you even if I'd known why you're so vulnerable."

Anger swelled up in her, nearly choking her for a moment. "For the last time, I am *not* vulnerable. And I'll decide who I think is a jerk or not."

He shook his head, his mouth twisting slightly. "You're very naïve, Emma."

"Yeah? Well you're very full of yourself. Not everything is about you and your supposedly horrible, selfish self. I'm *not* a victim, Vanni. Did you ever consider I'm doing exactly what I want to be doing? Maybe *I'm* the selfish one," she snapped before she walked over to her closet, stiff-backed. She jerked open a sliding door and stared blindly at her wardrobe. "And I haven't got anything to wear to whatever . . . stupid, uppity restaurant you picked," she added angrily.

He didn't reply for several seconds. She just listened to her own escalated breathing in the billowing silence, her back to him. She was so sure the evening was ruined. Suddenly his hands were on her shoulders. Exhaling choppily, she felt his lips move on her nape. She closed her eyes and shuddered. Relief swept through her. So did liquid warmth, the strength of her arousal in this situation shocking her to the core. He turned her to face him.

"You're the opposite of selfish. But maybe it wouldn't be such a bad thing if you were a little more cynical sometimes."

"Really?"

He studied her face and frowned. "No," he sighed. "Do you really *forgive* them for what they did?"

"You say *forgive* like it's a dirty word," she said. He just continued to pin her with his stare, waiting for an answer. "*No*, I haven't *forgiven* Amanda yet. I'm *working* on it. It's a process. For both of us. It's not a black-and-white thing! How do you think forgiveness works, precisely?"

"I wouldn't know," he said blandly. "Certainly not in a similar situation."

"She's my only *family*. What do you expect me to do, throw her out on the streets? As for Colin, I don't think he needs my forgiveness. He's not going to be a major part of my life anymore."

He didn't respond immediately, but he didn't move. *You're very naïve, Emma.*

He didn't say it, but his remembered words hung in the air at that moment. Suddenly he kissed her temple very tenderly, taking her by surprise and sending a cascade of shivers through her and raising goose bumps along her arms.

"Go and shower. I'll pick something out for you to wear."

"You *will*?" she asked, amazed. Then she looked at the clothes hanging haphazardly in her closet and thought of his expensive, immaculately organized wardrobe.

"No, that's all right." She saw his small smile before he brushed his firm lips against her warm cheeks.

"I wish you'd stop getting embarrassed," he said.

"Well it's not something I can stop that easily," she fired.

"I just mean," he said in a low, patient tone, despite the sardonic arch of his eyebrows, "that I wish you wouldn't, because there's absolutely no reason in the world for you to be embarrassed. *Ever*," he repeated succinctly. One glance into his hard gaze, and she knew he didn't mean her lame wardrobe, but the embarrassment she'd experienced facing Colin and Amanda with him standing at her side.

She appreciated that.

Eying him warily, she went on tiptoe and slid her mouth against his. He smiled that smile she rarely saw before he bent down to take what she offered in deep earnest. Then he was turning her in the direction of the bathroom, and Emma tried to remember what she was supposed to be doing, so befuddled was she by his kiss.

"I won't profess to being an expert at this, but I'll figure something out. Go on," he said. She glanced over her shoulder as she walked to the bathroom. He was scowling darkly at her closet like it was an unexpected but worthy challenge.

There was nothing he couldn't do, she thought fifteen minutes later as he opened her bedroom door for her. He'd chosen a dark teal blue, sleeveless cotton dress and paired it with a thick, dark purple belt that went with another outfit. Emma wouldn't have ever thought to put the two together but it worked fantastically. She took the two items from him, dubious at first, and went into the bathroom to finish getting ready.

The dress, which she had long ago forgotten about, looked brand-new with the belt to freshen it. The braided collar encircled her neck and left most of her shoulders and arms bare. She hadn't spent a lot of time in the sun so far this year, but her skin still gleamed next to the teal of the dress. Then she added a long, gold necklace with a medallion at the end of it. It served to not only accessorize her outfit, but to accentuate the shape of her breasts in the draping fabric. Her hair was behaving tonight and waved softly around her face. She applied a little more eye makeup than was usual and a natural shade of lipstick.

The male heat in Vanni's eyes when she exited the bathroom,

along with a slightly smug smile, told her she was beautiful to him. She *felt* like she was pretty.

"I missed my calling," he said, his mouth tilting as he opened the door for her.

"Something tells me you're much more of an expert at undressing women than dressing them," she told him under her breath as she passed.

"I'll happily do both for you." It was shameless flirtation, but Emma couldn't resist. She'd like to meet the straight woman who professed she could resist Vanni when his blue-green eyes went heavy-lidded and hot. She paused and brushed her fingers across his angular, whiskered jaw and went on her tiptoes.

"Thank you," she whispered before she kissed his mouth. He placed his hands on her shoulder and drew her closer, leaning his head down. Then he was kissing her deeply. Emma gave a muted moan, her body going soft and heated. He was like a Montand car, taking her from zero to a hundred in record-fast time.

"Emma?"

Emma started and broke the kiss, flustered. She turned, self-consciously wiping her lipstick-smeared mouth with the back of her hand.

"We're just stepping out for a bit," Amanda said uncertainly from the other end of the dim hallway. "We'll talk when you get back from dinner?"

Emma opened her mouth to answer but Vanni took her hand and led her down the hallway. "Don't wait up for Emma. She's staying with me in the city tonight," he said as they approached Amanda.

"I'll call you tomorrow," Emma told Amanda as they passed her.

Instead of taking the route that Emma would have—through the kitchen—Vanni led her through the living room. Colin stood there in his jeans and old college T-shirt, looking sideswiped. She had no doubt he'd heard what Vanni had said.

Which Vanni had intended, of course.

"See you," Emma called to Colin as she hurried to keep up with Vanni's long-legged stride.

Did she take any satisfaction from Amanda and Colin's stunned expressions as they witnessed her in all her finery walking hand in hand with a gorgeous, powerful man who was light-years out of her league?

Maybe a little.

She was only human, after all.

She thought they'd go straight to dinner, but Vanni had something else in store. He parked in a newly built high-rise just across from the Art Institute.

"Where are we going?" she asked, staring around at the surrounding city once they'd taken an elevator down to the ground level and stepped out onto Michigan Avenue. It was a warm summer night. The glass-sided skyscrapers gleamed in the light of the setting sun. It was thrilling for her, not just to be in the midst of the city—which was uncommon enough for her, despite the fact that she was a native Chicagoan—but there with Vanni. There was a thread of unreality to the whole thing.

"I thought we'd catch the last half of *My Fair Lady*, if you're up for it. I have season theater tickets, but rarely get to use them myself," Vanni said as they walked across Monroe at the light, her hand in his.

"I'd *love* that," she said, grinning. "I've never been to a show before."

He gave her a sideways glance. "Never?"

"Do you ever look at the price of the tickets, or just have your secretary buy them for you?" she shot back. His eyebrows arched in a wry expression and she laughed. "I thought so. The theater definitely isn't in a nurse's budget, or at least so far it hasn't been. But I've always wanted to go."

"Well you're here now," Vanni said, opening a golden and glass door open for her to enter at the Shubert Theatre. "I only wish I'd known. I'd have insisted on making the first half." She gave him a doubtful look, thinking about what they'd been doing instead of rushing to make the beginning of the show. His mouth quirked. "You're right," he said under his breath. "It was well worth it to miss the first half."

She smiled, feeling so excited, she thought she might be glowing.

They had just enough time for Vanni to get them two glasses of champagne before the crowd started streaming out into the lobby for intermission. Her wonderment grew when he led her to a small, ornate balcony that looked down directly on the stage. They would have an amazing overview of the stage, but were still up front enough that they'd easily see the actors' faces. There were eight velvet chairs in the space, but Emma saw no seat numbers.

"How do we know which ones to sit in?" she asked him.

"Pick whichever ones you want. It's a private box."

"And no one else is coming?"

Vanni just shook his head. She sat, staring down over the balustrade. She could see straight down in the orchestra box before the stage. He came down next to her, and she beamed at him.

"This is amazing," she told him, not even trying to guard her excitement.

His eyebrows rose. "Is it?" he asked, taking a sip of champagne.

She gave the luxurious, empty box a sweeping glance and then looked pointedly at the ornate, gilded theater.

"Open your eyes," she said, laughing.

Open your eyes.

Her joyful admonishment kept ringing in his ears as the play resumed a few minutes later. One thing was certain, he realized as he glanced sideways at Emma's radiant expression as she watched the play.

He couldn't take his eyes off her.

If she hadn't confessed to this being her first theater visit, he would have touched her. *And* if that damn thing hadn't happened at her apartment. He grimaced and looked away from her shining face, guilt swooping through him for his lascivious thoughts as the memory interceded.

He *might* have very well done more than touch her in the privacy of the box if he hadn't seen that pinched, anxious expression on her face when she'd introduced him to that traitorous sister and bottom-feeder boyfriend of hers.

Ex-boyfriend, he reminded himself with a spike of vicious triumph.

He knew Emma said she didn't mind, but he was furious that her sister invited Colin over to Emma's home, and what was worse—the asshole actually *came*.

His gaze roved back to her. Her gleaming shoulders and arms beckoned him, just as the alluring shape of her breasts outlined by the draping fabric of her dress did. Yes. If it hadn't been for the fact that she'd confessed this was her first time at the theater, or that teeth-grinding incident at her apartment, he would have traced that elegant line of her jaw with his fingers, and then his lips. He'd have inhaled the sweet, clean smell of her neck. He might have taken her to the shadow-filled rear of the box and touched her until he'd felt her quake against him.

His cock stirred. Yes, he was that selfish.

He took the last swallow of the chilled champagne and set it aside. He stared at the movement and color on the stage, not really taking much of it in. His gaze flickered back to Emma's rapt profile as Eliza sang "Just You Wait." He followed the shape of her cheek, jaw, neck, and thrusting breasts. For a moment, he just stared, enthralled, watching the delicate rise and fall of her breasts, his body hardening. The number came to a crescendo and she turned to him, her smile like a lance.

Her smile froze and faded when she saw him staring at her. What had she seen on his face? he wondered. Hunger, no doubt. Blatant lust. Her lips trembled. She swayed slightly toward him. He jerked suddenly, his fingers delving into her wavy, soft hair, cupping her skull. He put his head next to hers and inhaled her scent.

"Enjoy the play, Emma," he whispered near her ear. His cock swelled and tingled when he felt her shiver. "Because later on, I'm going to have my fill of you," he added darkly into her ear before he raised his other hand, and gently turned her chin so that she once again faced the stage.

He leaned back in his seat, teeth clamped tight, arm draped on the back of the empty chair next to him, lest he do something else with it. It was his fault. He could have just kept her in bed and had his fill of her. *Tried* to get his fill of her, he amended grimly. He'd hungered for her all week, the edge of anxiety about whether or not she'd come only amplifying his lust. He needn't have insisted upon taking her out. It was just this prickling paradox he experienced around her, a desire for rational distance, an overwhelming need to draw her close . . . to witness that smile . . .

To be pounding high and hard inside her.

She turned her chin ever so slightly, regarding him with a mixture of wariness, excitement . . . and just a whisper of a challenge. His body tightened.

How was it that her dark, shining eyes were so soft, and yet they cut straight to the core of him?

For Emma, there was magic in the summer night when they exited the theater. Vanni hailed a cab, which whisked them through the South Loop to the restaurant. She recognized that she was wide-eyed with awe when Vanni led her to the entrance of the renowned restaurant, but she couldn't repress her excitement. Even when she recalled Vanni calling her naïve earlier, it didn't diminish her happiness. Yes, she would likely think herself a fool at one point five weeks in the future when she had to say good-bye, but that moment wasn't now. Now she would relish these nights she had with him, stamp them firmly in her brain. Some day, her memories would be all she had of this affair.

The maître d' led them to a secluded table in the elegant restaurant, which gave them a stunning view from the fortieth floor down onto the glittering city. They talked about the play, and then his plans for the pioneering Montand French-American Grand Prix in the South of France. All the while, she sipped a dry white wine that seemed to open her senses even further, making the four-course meal beyond delectable. Or maybe it was just the man who sat across from her that honed her nerves. He made everything seem so sharp and sensual. She'd never tasted anything so delicious as the food served to her.

When she wavered in choosing from the dessert menu—everything looked so fantastic—Vanni grabbed her menu and handed it to the waiter.

"Bring her one of each," he said dryly, and the waiter hastened to fulfill his demand. A flash of mortification went through her—her appetite had been embarrassingly good tonight—but then she saw the glint of humor in Vanni's light eyes, and she laughed.

"I don't understand why you are so worried the race you're sponsoring will be a failure," she said a moment later as the waiter served coffee. "You said you've sponsored dozens of racing events here in the States and that Montand Motorworks has its own racing team and cars. You seem experienced in the matter."

"Formula One racing dominates in Europe, with very few exceptions."

"What are Formula One cars like?"

"Like the ones you see in the Indianapolis 500." She formed a mental picture in her mind of occasional glimpses of the race over the years and nodded. He continued. "Americans have become avid fans of stock cars, though," he said, stirring his coffee thoughtfully. "My company sponsors stock car racing here in the States, and F1 racing in Europe, but this is the first time we've tried to do a stock car road race in France. You've heard of the Monaco Grand Prix? My race won't be covering that specific route, but we'll still be on very hallowed F1 racing ground."

"And you're worried the French will give your American cars the cold shoulder?" she asked, taking a sip of coffee.

"And the drivers, yes. Although I've managed to convince some very big names in European racing to enter, including some major Formula One drivers."

"And they all will drive stock cars?"

"That's the agreement." Something about his wry expression suggested to her that he'd wrestled and bargained considerably to get that agreement from the Formula One racecar drivers. He noticed her raised brows. "It helped having Niki as the Montand Formula One driver. He agreed to it, and then dozens of drivers signed on, if only for the chance to beat him at a game where he might show a weakness."

"Niki Dellis is a racecar driver?" Emma asked, recalling the handsome, charming man at Cristina's funeral.

"The best," Vanni said simply. "He's driven a Montand car almost since the beginning of his career."

"Is Niki French as well?"

"Greek. Although he has relations in Italy, Monaco, and France. He comes from a very old family." He seemed distracted for a moment, his long, blunt-tipped fingers caressing the handle of his coffee cup. Warmth infused her. It was a strangely erotic sight, his masculine fingers idly stroking the delicate china. "In fact, Niki is distantly related to Cristina." Emma blinked in surprise. "Cristina and her sister were both renowned Italian socialites. Her sister is Maria Carboni."

"The actress?" Emma asked, vaguely familiar with the curvy, tempestuous film actress who had transferred her success to Hollywood in the 1960s and '70s.

Vanni nodded. "Maria is Niki's grandmother, an older sister of Cristina's. I try not to hold his relationship with Cristina against him," he said with dark amusement. "But that's how we met. He came and visited us in the States when he was ten, and we've been friends since."

"When did your father marry Cristina?"

"When I was eight. Nine months after my mother died."

He appeared entirely impassive saying it, but something struck her. She set down her coffee cup with a clatter she hadn't intended. "Your mother passed away the year before Adrian did?" she asked weakly.

He nodded once. "I suppose someone like you would say it was a blessing."

"*What*?" she asked, stunned and more than a little confused. "What do you mean *someone like me*?"

"Someone who believes that there's meaning in something random like death," he said. He noticed her stung expression. "Since my mother died young of leukemia, she never had to see one of her children die. That would have killed her on its own. You probably see that as a blessing. Meaningful. That's all I meant. Of course, Adrian would never have died if she hadn't died first, and if my father hadn't felt the need to run off and find someone else to fill his bed and play mother to us. Someone entirely incompetent, at the latter task, anyway," he added cynically under his breath.

She sat forward slightly. "Is that what you think?" she asked quietly. "That I don't realize how hard it is, how sad, to lose someone you love, just because I told you about my experience with dying? That's not fair, Vanni." He blinked at the cold steel in her tone. "I still grieve my mother. I miss her every day of my life. Do you want to know the real reason I haven't gone all self-righteous over this whole thing with Amanda and Colin?"

"I assumed it was a combination of the facts that you were ready for the relationship to end and that you're a kinder, more forgiving and a much, *much* better person than I could ever be," he said dryly.

Her expression fell a little at that. "It's not that I'm *kind* or better than anyone. It's just I . . ."

"What?" he asked, leaning forward, his elbows on the table,

when she faded off. She suddenly felt very vulnerable and stupid, sitting in the midst of this glamorous, fairy-tale setting with a gorgeous, sophisticated man, exposing her heart. Surely her confessions were neither appropriate nor wanted.

"Emma?" he pressed, his gaze on her fierce.

She swallowed. He didn't look like he wanted her to shut up. Just the opposite, in fact. Besides, she couldn't be someone different than she was just to fit into his world.

"It's just that I keep picturing how sad Mom would be if she knew Amanda and I had a falling out over something as insignificant, in the grand scheme of things, as a boy."

He listened, then shook his head slightly, his mouth tight. "What they did to you was inexcusable."

"Yes. But not unforgivable. At least that's what I'm trying to do . . . get past it. It's like I told you, it's a process. At least it is in my case. With Amanda. You'd do the same, if you loved someone the way I do my sister. You don't know her. She doesn't go around doing stuff like this as a matter of course. She's never done anything like this before, so I can't help but feel that this thing with her and Colin is something major."

Something flickered across his stony expression. He reached across the table and took her hand. "You're wrong, Emma," he said gruffly. "You really are a much better person than me."

The distant sounds of china clinking and murmuring voices faded to a distant hum. Their gazes held, and she saw the warmth in his eyes. He may not agree with her choice of action when it came to Colin and Amanda, but he understood now. *Better*, anyway. They both knew what it was to lose someone and have an irreparable hole torn into your life. You behaved differently, at times, with the imagined ghost of that loved one looking on.

She was vaguely aware of someone passing the table. Vanni leaned back slightly and dragged his gaze off her.

"Excuse me," he said. The waiter who had been passing paused. "We'll take that dessert to go. And the check please."

"You don't want to eat it here?" she asked, dazed after the waiter hastened to follow his instruction.

"No," he said, leaning back and dropping his napkin negligently on the table. "I want to give it to you."

Her core clenched tight, his words taking on a distinctly charged, erotic meaning after the intimate moment they'd just shared. She placed her napkin on the table, her pulse flickering at her throat.

He clearly was intent on giving her something, and she had the thrilling feeling that it wasn't just the dessert.

Chapter 19

The cab dropped them off at the same building where he'd parked the car. They returned to his sedan to retrieve his leather portfolio and the canvas bag in which she'd packed a change of clothing for tomorrow and a few other necessary items. After they'd left the car, he led her to a different elevator than the one they'd taken from the street.

"Is your apartment in this building?" she asked him when they left the elevator and entered a sedately opulent lobby situated just off Michigan Avenue.

"Yes," he said, nodding to the doorman who greeted him by name and hurried to open the door for them. "My offices are just a block away from here."

She was having a little trouble keeping up with his long-legged stride. When they got onto the residential elevator, he pushed the button for the fifty-sixth floor. Emma leaned against the brass railing and panted softly.

"Are you all right?" he wondered, dark brows slanting in concern.

"Yes. You were walking kind of fast," she said, grinning.

He stepped forward and palmed her jaw. Her panting breath froze in her lungs when she noticed his intent expression.

"You are certain you're well, aren't you?"

"What?" she asked, surprised.

"I know that you said you were . . ." he hesitated. "*Cured* of that childhood ailment, but are you certain?"

Her mouth fell open. "Of course I'm sure. I just was at my doctor's last month. I've been perfectly healthy since it happened when I was a kid." A horrible thought occurred to her as the elevator lifted them silently. "You're not afraid you'll *catch* something from me, are you?"

He stiffened. "What? Of course not. Don't be ridiculous."

"Then why . . . *oh*," she said, realization dawning. "You thought maybe I was carrying my eternal optimism too far. You think I'm fooling myself into believing in the miracle cure." She couldn't help but smile. "I'm not that much of a Pollyanna. I'm a nurse, too, you know. I can be *very* practical."

He seemed to relax a little. The elevator dinged and the door opened. He took her hand and led her into a hallway.

"I'm sorry," he said. "And I'm sorry for rushing just now, too. I'm impatient."

"For dessert?" she asked cautiously, stopping when he did in front of a door. He paused with a key in the lock, leaned down and brushed his lips against hers. An electrical tingle went through her, a hint of what was to come.

"For dessert," he agreed before he pushed open the condominium door. Emma entered, staring in openmouthed awe. He didn't switch on a light, but he didn't need to. She hardly noticed the sumptuous living room as she walked through it. Her attention was snagged by the stunning view of Millennium and Grant parks, the Art Institute, and the brightly lit tiny ribbon of cars far below them that was Michigan Avenue. She sensed Vanni step up next to her as she gazed out at the splendid sight.

"Which view do you like better? The one at the Breakers or the one here?" she asked wistfully.

He didn't immediately reply. A shock of regret went through her when she realized that the view at the Breakers was the site of his twin brother's untimely and tragic death.

"Vanni . . . I'm sorry, that was an insensitive thing to ask."

His face looked compelling and unreadable in the dim light provided by the city far below them. He didn't appear offended, however, so she couldn't stop herself from speaking her pressing thought out loud.

"Why did you do it?" she whispered. "Why did you build a house where you're constantly forced to look out at the place where Adrian died?"

The silence stretched. He reached for her with the hand that wasn't holding the desserts and his briefcase.

"Because there are more things in that view than the place where Adrian died. There are also places in it where he lived."

If only you *could live there as well. Truly live.*

Not only his words, but her thought echoed in her brain. She wasn't sure if he'd given her an answer full of meaning, or if he'd sidestepped her question altogether. She did know this in that moment: Vanni Montand had been leading half a life.

"I don't want to talk about depressing things, Emma," he said with quiet finality. Maybe he was right. She nodded in agreement. "Can I get you anything to drink?"

She shook her head. "When will you return from France?" she asked.

"I'm due back the following Monday."

"I'd imagine things are really heating up in France, with the race coming up."

He nodded, his stare on her unflinching. "I regret having to be away so much now. We'll talk more about you coming with me for the last trip, during the race itself. But not now." He tilted his head toward the hallway. "Come. Let's go finish our dinner."

She followed him, sensing his focused intent, her heart beginning to pound out a warning, yet thrilling, drumbeat.

He turned on a bedside lamp, using a control panel on the wall near the door, and then dimmed it to a cozy, golden glow. The bed here was more streamlined and modern than the one at the Breakers, but it was just as large and sumptuously dressed in austere, masculine luxury with muted grays, dark browns, and creamy beige tones. The curtains were drawn, giving the room a hushed, secluded ambience. He set the bag he was carrying on a bedside chest of drawers. He removed his jacket and tossed it on the back of a deep upholstered chair, then set down his leather portfolio. She stood there, admiring his form and easy, athletic grace. Did his masculine confidence and beauty strike such a deep, compelling chord of longing and lust in every woman he seduced? Or was it singular in Emma's case? Her heart sunk when she realized she was too inexperienced to know. She wasn't even sure what the feeling *was*, let alone whether or not it was common. She watched, curious but also increasingly anxious, as he reached into his briefcase.

He withdrew a velvet drawstring bag and slid something out of it. He turned, holding the vibrator he'd used on her earlier today in his hand. Her eyes widened.

"Come here," he said quietly when he saw she still stood just inside the threshold of the bedroom.

She walked toward him, unable to look away from his eyes.

"What . . . what are you going to do?" she asked when she came to a stop a few feet away.

His eyebrows arched. "The anxiety is back, I see. I thought it might make an unwelcome return. That's why I brought the desserts. It's hard to be nervous when you're playing a game . . . and eating sweets, don't you think?"

"Playing a game?" she asked uncertainly.

He held her stare and nodded. His aquamarine eyes looked softer than usual in the ambient light. "Take off all your clothes except for your underwear, and I'll explain," he said.

She swallowed thickly and set down her purse on the chair. She didn't know why his request struck her as so intimidating. One had to take off their clothes to have sex, didn't they? But he didn't undress, she realized as she slid off her high-heeled sandals and unbelted her dress. He just watched her steadily, obviously interested, all the while holding that damn little instrument in his large hand. Both his hand and that vibrator had made her climax so efficiently earlier today that she'd nearly blacked out both times. Her core turned molten at the incendiary thought, but her skin pebbled when she lifted her dress over her head, exposing her bare skin to the cool air-conditioning and Vanni's hot stare. She hesitated as she reached for the clasp on her bra, but then she met his gaze. Maybe it was just the lighting, but that atypical softness remained in his gaze alongside the heat of desire. It was like a reassuring caress. There was no logical reason why he should, given his apparent impenetrable confidence, but he felt compassion for her anxiety. He *knew* this wasn't easy for her. The realization steadied her.

She dropped her bra in the chair on top of her dress and stood before him, naked save her panties.

"Now. What's your game, Speed Racer?" she teased him warily.

His flashing smile was like a swift punch to the gut. She could really get used to seeing his unguarded, warm smiles. They were so rare and beautiful in comparison to his grim, cynical ones.

She could get *dangerously* used to them.

"It's pretty simple," he said, picking up the bag of desserts and walking over to a dresser. He opened a drawer and removed a long black scarf. He took all the items over to the bed and sat on the edge. Setting down the bag and the vibrator, he beckoned her closer. "You may have noticed that the desserts featured some kind of seasonal fruit in addition to other things, like chocolate, cake, pastry?"

"Yeah, I think so," she said, even though she was struggling to remember precisely what was on the menu. She drew near him, stopping near his long, bent legs.

He held up the scarf. "I'm going to blindfold you and feed you the desserts, and all you have to do is guess the fruit correctly."

"That's all?" she asked warily.

"No," he conceded, his shapely mouth tilting. He loosened his tie, holding her stare, and slid it from around his neck. The hissing sound of silk against cotton inexplicably made her sex contract and her nipples tighten. His gaze flickered downward to her chest, and she inhaled sharply.

He'd noticed.

"I'm going to bind your wrists in front of you," he said, holding up his tie. "And I'm going to blindfold you, so you can't see the dessert."

Her eyes widened.

"It's only fair. You'll get them all correct, most likely, if you can see them."

"Is that all?"

Her clit pinched tight when he slowly shook his head. He reached for the vibrator. "I'm going to put this in you," he said, his voice a low, sultry threat.

Her eyebrows arched higher.

"There are four desserts in here. If you guess the fruit correctly, you get another bite." The devilish gleam that entered his eyes made her heartbeat start to race. She'd never seen him look so playful . . . or so sexy. She couldn't help but grin.

"And if I get it wrong?"

"You don't get another bite," he said, shrugging. "You'll have to take a consequence, and we'll continue."

"A consequence," she repeated dryly.

"You could take a spanking. Five swats for each time you're wrong."

"A spanking? Using your hand, you mean?" she asked, straining to keep her voice even.

He nodded. "My hand against your bare ass."

She swallowed thickly. Her heartbeat pounded in her ears and pulsed erotically in her sex. How hard could it be, really? How many types of fruit were there? Surely she wouldn't miss, and if she did . . . well, five swats wouldn't be that bad . . .

. . . and they might be very good.

"Well? Do you want to play?" he asked quietly, the glint of a challenge in his eyes.

"Yes," she replied honestly. "Just tell me one thing first."

He nodded.

"Have you played this game before?"

He blinked and she knew she'd taken him by surprise with her question. His grin slowly faded. She held her breath. He shook his head slowly.

"It's not a game. Not really. It's just *playing*, something to ease your anxiety. I'm making it up as I go along, because I don't usually *play* in the bedroom. Not until you, and only *for* you. Do you understand?" She nodded, though stunned by his admission. "Then come here," he said, holding out his hand.

He spread his thighs and she walked between them.

Vanni held up the vibrator that had buzzed her with such wicked precision this afternoon.

"I'm going to put this in, but first I'm going to touch you, just to see if you need some lubrication on the vibrator before I insert it."

She stared at him, shocked a little, but also strangely aroused by his matter-of-fact language. Holding her stare, he slipped his finger beneath the top band of her panties. Heat flooded her sex and her face. *Oh God, how embarrassing.*

"Spread your thighs," he urged as his long finger slid deeper. She did what he instructed, holding her breath. It escaped on a little gasp when his fingertip touched her entrance, then penetrated her just a half an inch or so. He grunted softly, and her cheeks turned from hot to scalding.

"Why are you blushing?" he murmured, studying her face as he slowly pushed a finger into her another half an inch. "It's a wonderful thing, to find you so warm and slick."

Her lips fell open as he gently sawed the top of his finger in and out of her for a moment. She still was embarrassed at being found wet even without any prior prolonged stimulation. He had kissed her several times this evening, but never for longer than a fraction of a minute or so. It'd been the experience of just *being* with him all night that had so well prepared her for this moment.

He withdrew his hand, and her underwear slipped back into place. Despite her embarrassment, she missed his touch. He picked up the vibrator from the bed. "Now this," he said simply before he pushed down the elastic band of her underwear again. Holding one end of the U-shaped, slender vibrator, he pushed it between her thighs. Again, he watched her face as he inserted the tip into her channel, penetrating her several inches until the bottom of the U was pressed flush against her sex, the other tip lodged next to her clit. The vibrator remained in place.

"Okay?" he asked.

"Yes," she said, feeling sweat pop out against her upper lip.

"Good." He picked up his discarded tie. "Put your hands in front of you. I'm going to bind them."

She followed his instructions, her heart chugging away in her chest. He looped the silk tie around her wrists and bound her with quick, expert precision. How many times had he bound a woman before? Was she crazy for allowing this? Her anxious thoughts evaporated when he picked up the black scarf.

"Just lower your head a little, and I'll blindfold you," he said gently.

Even though he sat, and she stood, he was so tall that their heights weren't that disparate. The last vision she had before he placed the silk scarf over her eyes, blinding her, was of his hot, gleaming eyes. Even though she could no longer see them a moment later as she straightened, the vision of them was burned into her mind's eye.

"I'm going to switch on the vibrator now."

She tensed and inhaled sharply as the instrument began to buzz, doing its job, stimulating both her clit and vagina. Her skin roughened at the illicit, mechanical caresses. Her nipples tightened.

"You're exceptionally sensitive." His quiet, resonant voice rushed over her in the darkness. Her ears tuned in to the sound, made hyperalert by her blind state. "I'm going to turn it down a little."

Had he noticed the effect the vibrator had on her? He didn't miss much of anything, she realized, feeling even more naked and vulnerable than she had before.

And even more aroused.

She heaved a sigh of mixed relief and deprivation when the vibrations diminished to a pleasant, tickling hum.

"Now for the fun part," he said, and she heard the bag rustling as he removed the package of mixed desserts. She turned her head, breathless to hear any clue of what was occurring. She heard a scraping sound—the carton being opened?—and then the crinkling of plastic. Perhaps he was removing some disposable utensils?

"Okay. Challenge number one," she heard him say. "Open your mouth."

The tingle in her clit segued to a simmer. She opened her lips, exposing her tongue. Ready. Waiting.

Breathless.

A fork slid across her tongue. She instinctively closed on the morsel of food he'd inserted. He withdrew the fork slowly as her tongue began to absorb the sweet decadence. Her mouth closed, exploring a soft, creamy texture and a thin shell of crispiness.

"Hmmm," she hummed appreciatively. She smiled. This one was easy.

"Well?" he said, sounding warm and amused.

She took her time before she swallowed. "Banana . . . and chocolate and the richest, yummiest cream I've ever eaten in my life."

Actually, it'd been the most delicious bite of any food she'd had in her life, period. Maybe it was the exquisitely prepared dessert, or maybe it was how primed Vanni had made her senses with his game, but that was the simple truth.

"Very good. But just so you know, I gave you the easiest one first."

"But I got it right. I get another bite." He didn't immediately respond. She felt her nipples prickle in the silence that followed and wondered wildly if he stared at her.

"Yes. You do," he said after a pause. "Open your mouth."

Knowing what it was that was coming didn't diminish her pleasure. She closed her mouth, and again, he slowly withdrew the fork. He must have noticed her relish the mouthwatering dessert, because she heard his low laughter. It only piqued her sensual feast.

"It's a banana crème brûlée with chocolate. Okay, you won that one. Are you ready for the next?"

She swallowed and nodded, anticipation and excitement building in her.

"Open your mouth," he murmured.

She parted her lips, her mouth watering, and waited. Her body tensed in excitement at the first touch of the fork against her flesh. She closed around a remarkably dense and rich cake. A divine, sweet flavor filled her mouth. She chewed carefully, absorbing the flavors with every ounce of attention she possessed. This one was harder. The fruit taste was there, but as more of an accent. The buttery, creamy taste of the cake was at the forefront.

"Well?" Vanni said, after she'd swallowed. She heard amusement in his tone. He was enjoying this. "What fruit?"

"It was definitely a berry. Strawberry?" she asked shakily.

"Close. But no. It's a raspberry Kugelhopf, a kind of Alsatian cake. Strike one."

Her pulse leapt at her throat. She heard something rustle on the bed. She suddenly wanted to close her thighs to put a clamp on the pressure mounting at her sex.

"You don't have to sound so happy about it," she said breathlessly. Her heart lurched when she felt his hands on her hips.

"I'll try to keep my happiness to myself," he replied drolly. He caught the top of her underwear with his fingers and deliberately pulled them down over her ass. He drew them to her thighs and dropped his hands, leaving them stretched between her legs. The skin on her bottom tingled at being exposed to the cool air. The anticipation was killing her. Her lungs burned.

So did her clit.

She jumped when he put his hands on her waist.

"Shh," he soothed as he pushed her toward him. His long thighs pressed lightly to her outer thighs. "Bend forward slightly," he instructed.

One of his hands dropped away when she did what he'd said.

"Oh!" she cried out. He'd turned up the vibrator. Her hips twitched slightly at the arousing sensation.

Smack.

She gasped. The sound of skin against skin, the tingle and the burn on her ass left her stunned. A hot spike of arousal drove through her. Her sex clamped tight against the vibrator.

"I thought it was best just to get it over with and end the suspense," Vanni said thickly before he spanked her again, this time on the other cheek.

Chapter 20

It was a brisk, precise pop of his cupped hand against skin. This time, she kept her mouth closed over the cry that jumped out of her throat, muting the sound to a whimper. It didn't hurt terribly. It *did* burn. The prickle of nerves amplified the simmer of her clit. He kept his hand on her, massaging the stinging skin and muscle. That made her moan and her pelvis strain forward slightly. She wished like hell she could press her pussy against something solid.

"Speak to me," he said gruffly. "Do you want me to stop?"

Keeping her mouth shut tight, she shook her head.

"Emma?" he grated out.

"No, I don't want you to stop," she said emphatically, irritated that he'd made her put it into words and just . . . turned on. Her nipples ached. Her cheeks were on fire.

"That's all I wanted to hear. Three more."

His hand rose. Her heart stopped and then leapt against her breastbone when he landed another spank on the cheek he'd smacked first. It wasn't any harder than the first or second swats, but it stung more for having been previously punished. She bit her lip to stifle a sound. He caressed the prickling cheek, soothing the madly firing nerves. It aroused her, his big hand palming almost her entire ass cheek, massaging the warmed flesh.

"You have a very spankable ass," he said, and she took heart from the heat in his tone. "Tight and round and ripe," he added distractedly as he continued to massage her. Then he was palming her other cheek, now using both hands, his actions unapologetically greedy and lewd. Emma bit harder on her lip to prevent crying out.

"Bend over again," he directed, and she realized she'd straightened slightly as she tried to get friction on her sex.

He palmed one cheek from below, squeezing it, and applied two firm, succinct spanks on the captive flesh. Emma started and couldn't stop herself from crying out softly. He rubbed both of her cheeks at once.

"There. It's all done. Your first spanking. How was it?"

"Okay," she managed.

"Okay? Or better than okay?" he asked, continuing to squeeze and massage her ass.

Shyness suddenly fell on her, a strange, unwanted feeling that mixed oddly with her intense arousal.

"Better than okay. Much," she whispered the last.

His massaging hands stilled. "You're so sweet."

She just stood there, speechless at something she heard in his voice.

"I told myself I could wait for dessert, but I've never had to wait for something like you," he said, his warm breath ghosting her breast. Then his hands were on her upper arms and he was pulling her closer.

His warm mouth closed around an aching nipple.

"*Vanni*," she said shakily, her hands pulling on the restraint at her wrists. It wasn't that she wanted to escape. It was just that his warm, wet mouth and laving tongue on her nipple were unbearably pleasurable. She panted, her body strained tight, feeling deliciously trapped as he resumed massaging her ass as he sucked on her nipple, and all the while, the damn vibrator continued on its merry way. Oh God, she couldn't take it anymore—

His finger was suddenly on the end of the vibrator on her clit, pressing lightly, tapping out an electrical code in her flesh. An electrical *command*. Her eyes sprung wide beneath the blindfold. Her muscles jerked tight.

She ignited. She cried out as orgasm shuddered through her. As soon as she began to quake, he slipped his finger beneath the vibrating tip and rubbed her manually.

He was better than the vibrator.

Much better.

Her cry escalated to a scream that she tried her best to contain. After a pleasure-hazed moment, she realized that he'd stopped sucking on her nipple and was holding her sandwiched between both hands, one spread on her ass, palming a buttock, the other open along her belly, his reaching thumb still stroking her burning clit between her lubricated labia while she gasped and shivered.

"You're beautiful when you come," she heard him say.

He'd been watching her while she lost control. His thumb strummed her clit, and another shiver went through her. "Amazing," he rasped, stroking her again ever so lightly. She rippled with pleasure and whimpered.

She felt his lips press to her belly, and his thumb moved again. It struck her that he was feeling her body tremble with his mouth. The caress felt deeply intimate, poignant . . . sacred, even.

But suddenly, his mouth and deft finger were gone and he was pushing her back gently. The vibrator was back in place, but he must have adjusted the controls. The instrument still buzzed her overly sensitive clit warmly, but with a weaker pulse.

She just stood there, breathing heavily, nerves she hadn't even known existed throbbing and aching and tingling all over her body.

"It's back to the game then?" she asked raggedly, striving for some levity in the midst of almost strangling sexual excitement and intimacy. She hadn't been prepared for the latter. The patch of skin where he'd kissed her belly still burned.

She heard his rough laugh, then a slight scraping on the bed, and she knew he'd picked up the desserts again. "Yes. Back to playing. Let's see if your little punishment increases or decreases your sense of taste."

"What do you mean?" she asked through pants, puzzling out his words in her head. "Do you think I'll miss because of anxiety over being . . . spanked?" she said, hesitating over that last volatile word.

"No. After watching the way you just lit up, I think you might miss because you want to be spanked again," he growled softly. "Now open your mouth, Emma."

She opened her mouth to protest what he'd said—she'd never been the type of person to lose at a game on purpose—but then the fork was slipping between her lips. She closed around it instinctively and moaned. The taste of a light, sweet cream filled her mouth.

It was delicious.

"This one is more complicated," he said. "There are two fruit flavors you have to name, one obvious, one more subtle." She had a sudden, vivid picture of him sitting on the bed, watching her with a narrow-eyed stare. Did he hope she would miss so that he could spank her again? Had he enjoyed it?

As much as she had?

She forced her attention off her graphic imagination and the mind-hazing buzz on her supersensitive clit. She focused on her mouth. Her tongue felt the round berries, her crushing teeth bursting the fresh, vibrant flavor onto her tongue.

"Blueberries," she said before she continued to experiment with the flavors on her tongue.

"There's another fruit. In the cream," he prodded.

She nodded, straining to taste. The need to swallow overcame her.

"Can I have another taste?" she asked.

"No."

She frowned at his calm, steadfast reply.

"Well then, it's either lemon or orange."

"Which one?"

"Lemon," she said more confidently than she felt.

Her skin tingled as she waited. She realized her skin was damp in several places: at her inner thighs, between her breasts, and the nipple he'd sucked on so abruptly, setting her body alight. She was going to end up a pile of ashes if he kept *playing* with her.

"Well? Was I right?" she asked desperately. "Why are you so quiet?"

"Because you were right," he said after a short pause. "And I was considering telling you that you weren't."

She laughed softly. "You're not as selfish as you make yourself out to be."

"Oh yes I am," he growled softly. "And just to prove it, if you miss on this last one, I'm going to spank you over my lap. And then I'm going to bend you over this bed, and no more playing. Understood?"

"And if I don't miss?" she couldn't resist asking.

"You'll just have to wait until another time to discover what you really missed out on, won't you? Now . . . open your mouth again, Emma."

He saw her pulse leap faster at her throat when he said that, could almost hear her mind churning over his response. She looked sublimely beautiful in that instant, the striking paradox of innocence and flagrant sexuality. A light sheen of perspiration had appeared between her thrusting breasts, and all he could think about was sweeping his tongue along that sweet valley. Watching her mouth move so sensually while she tasted the desserts, staring at her flushed, pink, bow-shaped lips, inhaling the perfume of her arousal; all of it had sharpened his hunger until it cut at him. He craved her sweat on his tongue.

The fantasy of tasting her pussy plagued him.

She parted her lips, waiting. Doing his best to ignore the stab of arousal at his cock, he lifted the apricot *fromage blanc* to her mouth. When she closed around it, he pictured those pink lips clamping around his cock. She chewed slowly—agonizingly, as far as he was concerned—and then swallowed. He waited on a bed of nails.

"Peaches," she whispered.

He leaned forward and whisked the blindfold off her head. She blinked several times, dazed by the light. He held up the carton.

"Apricot. I'm sorry," he said, setting aside the desserts.

"No, you're not."

"No," he admitted honestly. "I'm not. Did you guess wrong on purpose?"

Her back stiffened, making her breasts thrust forward. "No!"

"Okay. I was just asking. You're going to get spanked, one way or another." Her dark eyes widened at his frank response. He leaned closer to her. "Close your legs a little." She followed his instructions quickly enough, despite her show of pique. He pushed her panties down past her knees where they fell to her ankles. He reached between her thighs.

"Fuck," he rasped under his breath. He'd just meant to quickly remove the vibrator, but her juices were everywhere, and she was *so* blessed warm and soft. He closed his eyes briefly, steeling his will. She whimpered when he slid the vibrator out of her. He tossed it onto the bedside table, gritting his teeth all the while because his fingertips and knuckles were now coated in her sweetness.

He put his hands on the taut curve of her hips. "Lie down on the bed, across my lap. I'll help you," he added, knowing her wrists were restrained. He guided her as she knelt on the bed next to him, holding her body weight until she came down over him and her elbows hit the mattress. "Settle down," he told her, his voice patient even if his cock was roaring in protest at being kept waiting. It grew even testier at the sensation of her weight pressing down against it experimentally. Emma tensed, and he knew she'd felt his cock lurch at the contact.

"Let your ass curve across my thigh. Put your breasts on the outside of the other one," he instructed, closing his legs slightly to fit her measurements. He swept a hand along her smooth thigh and palmed a buttock, subtly guiding her precisely where he wanted her. "Let your weight go, Emma," he said sternly when he realized she was holding herself slightly off him with her elbows and knees, like she thought his cock was a red-hot poker or something. "Extend your arms above your head."

She followed his instructions with a muffled whimper. Without her elbows to support her, she sagged onto his lap. He grunted at the impact. He grasped her shoulder with one hand and then swept the other over her naked length, relishing the feeling of her silky skin, glorying in having her naked in his lap, helpless to resist his touch. She flowed beneath him as he whisked his hand along her thighs and over her ass and along her elegant back. Still, he could feel her rising anxiety.

"Why are you so tense?" he murmured. "It didn't hurt that bad before, did it?"

"No," he heard her muffled reply. Her forehead was pressed against the bedding.

"Why then?"

He saw her shake her head as he palmed a round ass cheek.

"I just wish you'd get it over with," she mumbled.

"All right. Open your legs some."

Her thighs parted. He let go of the smooth, firm globe. She was a little pink from her previous spanking and his forceful massaging of her ass. Nowhere near as pink as he'd like to see her. He landed a brisk slap against the tempting curve at the bottom of a buttock. His cock lurched at the feeling of firm, taut flesh stinging his palm. She jumped slightly in his lap, making him grimace at the stimulation.

"Stay still," he ordered, landing another spank on the lower curve of the other buttock. Her whimper transfixed him. His hand lingered, caressing warmed, smooth skin. His fingers stretched as if of their own volition. He couldn't resist. He thrust his forefinger into her slit.

God, she was drenched. He saw red for an instant as he plunged in and out of her snug sex. He blinked when she wriggled in his lap and moaned.

"I said to stay still," he reminded her thickly, firming his hold on her shoulder and removing his finger in order to grip her ass.

She stilled, her muscles straining tight. She made a soughing, choked sound, as if it'd taken effort to force herself to stop writhing. Her attempt at restraint pleased him, but strangely displeased him, too. He found himself wishing she'd lose all sense of control, lying there in his lap.

"That's so good, baby," he soothed, aware that clawing lust had made him sound sharp before. "Just a few more." He lifted his hand and cracked off two in quick succession. She muffled a cry. His cock swelled dangerously. He rubbed his stinging hand against her hot flesh, trying to soothe her as well as restrain his mounting lust. It didn't really work. He found himself releasing his hold on her shoulder and pressing down on her back, pushing her against his cock. She gave a frantic, muffled moan as he lifted his hips slightly, grinding their flesh together. It felt so good, his awareness hazed. "I'm going to fuck your juicy little pussy so hard in a few seconds, Emma, and I want to hear you scream to the high heavens. I'm tired of you holding it in. Do you hear me?"

"Yes," he heard her say in a cracking voice. She sounded every bit as dazed and rabid as he felt.

"One more now," he said, straining to keep his voice even as he rubbed her bottom. "You're doing well. Your ass is getting nice and hot. For the last one, I want you to raise it a little for my hand." He heard her breath soughing in the tense silence that followed. He waited, triumph slashing through him when she tensed, sliding her knees up the bed, raising her ass off his thigh. He'd like to drown in her sweetness. Still, he was selfish.

As always.

"Now ask for your spanking," he said roughly. When she hesitated, he was ruthless. He plunged his forefinger into her slit. She gasped loudly. He finger-fucked for a moment, grinding his teeth together at the wet, sucking sound it made. "Ask for it, Emma."

"Spank me. Please . . . *give* me the last one."

Chapter 21

She sounded wild. He drew his finger out of her channel and popped her raised ass, this time a little more forcefully. She yelped. No sooner had he done it than he was gathering her in his arms, lifting her as he stood.

"Playtime is over," he growled, turning and placing her hastily, but gently, on the bed. "On your hands and knees," he directed, too strangled by lust to be polite. He waited while she steadied herself with her bound hands. He started to move away to find a condom, but she looked over her shoulder. He halted. It would have been easy to say she'd stopped him in his tracks because of the vision she made, naked on her hands and knees, the light pink blush on her ass a beautiful contrast to her flawless pale skin.

The hard thing to admit was that while all that was true, what had jerked him to a stop in the midst of frantic lust was the expression in her dark eyes.

He hardened his resolve and took a long stride to the bedside table, where he extricated a condom from a drawer. When he returned, she still was watching him over an elegant, sloping shoulder.

He began to unfasten his belt, holding her stare. "I was going to taste you first," he bit out. "But then you had to go and look at me."

He saw one eyebrow go up at that. He realized why. He'd sounded almost angry at her . . . and he was, in a way. He was about to burst with uncontrollable, boiling lust, and he wasn't so sure he liked this feeling of another human being controlling him. "Now I'm just going to have to wait to taste you, and I don't like to be made to wait," he said pointedly as he jerked down his pants and slid his hand along the underside of his cock, snarling at the resulting shiver. He was stretched so tight, even the slightest touch was almost unbearable. He rolled on the condom and looked up. Instead of being miffed or offended by his words, she was staring at his cock, her flushed lips parted.

"Jesus, face that wall," he grated out, pointing at the wall opposite from him. He moved behind her and she turned her head slowly. He became uncomfortably aware that he was panting, and that she could probably hear him. Still, he couldn't slow. Not with heaven within his reach. His hands on her ass, he pulled her to him, positioning her. He parted her buttocks wide, salivating at the view. She was a glossy, vivid pink that acted on his brain like the stimulant of the red flag to the bull.

"Lower your breasts to the bed," he insisted, lifting his cock with his hand to her slit. He instinctively felt the ideal give in her flesh when she took the position and thrust. She gave a little yelp, and he tried to soothe her with his touch. He couldn't stop, though. He thought he might be grinding a layer of enamel off his teeth as she enclosed him, squeezed him like an exquisitely tight, soft suck. Gripping her ass, he watched himself sink into paradise.

She was just a woman, like so many before. He knew this.

So why did it all feel so different?

His shaved balls bumped against her damp outer sex, and the frothing boil of lust overtook his brain. He lost all ability to think. Instinct took over. He firmed his hold on her and began rocking her ass back and forth, driving his hips in a counterrhythm. Her soft moans and surprised little gasps and whimpers when he thrust with more force intoxicated him. He'd like to fuck her forever.

He needn't have controlled her hip movements so greatly, because he could feel her moving against him with a strength and mounting excitement. Even so, his arm muscles tightened as he crashed into her. Crashed her into him. He didn't know which. His pelvis was smacking against her ass faster and faster, a little cry erupting out of her throat when he popped against her outer sex and drove deep.

"You feel so fucking good," he ground out, sounding crazed to his own ears. She was driving him over the edge. He couldn't get enough. He lifted her hips, holding her against him, taking her lower body weight. Her knees slipped off the edge of the bed. His arms flexed hard, serving her pussy to his cock, pounding into her high and hard. Her cries rained down on him, whetting his appetite even more. He was feasting, gorging himself . . . but he wanted more.

"Scream for me, Emma," he grated out. He drove into her, a raging male animal intent on one thing. "*Scream.*"

He kept fucking her, hanging by a thread. Then it came, a high keen that grew louder like an oncoming train the more he pounded into her clasping body. He felt her muscular walls convulse around him. He let the savage loose. Placing her knees back on the bed, he fell down over her, bracing himself with his arms. He drove straight and hard into the hot, molten core of her, grunting. He lit up like a roman candle, popping and firing at first, aching and straining for full detonation. He heard Emma scream louder, her channel gripping him, and it happened.

He exploded into a million pieces.

She came back to herself, knowing she was still the practical, dependable Emma Shore she'd always been, and yet somehow knowing at the same time that she'd never be that girl again.

She absorbed the sound of their twining, panting breaths. It was a nice sensation. It lulled her. His weight was partially on her, pressing her down into the mattress, and it, too, was delicious: a heavy, solid comfort. She wished he'd press her down even more firmly. The idea of fusing with Vanni Montand even more securely and deeply created a sweet, swelling sensation of longing in her breast.

The feeling of him sliding out of her tender body was jarring and highly unwelcome. She must have made a sound of protest, because he kissed her ear and spoke in a sex-roughened, low tone that raised goose bumps along her damp nape.

"Here. Get under the covers. I'll come and join you in a minute."

She felt the edge of the sheet and duvet brushed against her naked hip and realized he'd pulled back the bedding. At the urging of his hands on her waist, she rolled over and swung her body so that her head sunk against a decadence of pillows and her feet slid between cool, exquisitely soft sheets. She blinked woozily, staring up at the striking image of him as he stood next to the bed and pulled the sheet and fluffy comforter over her. She curled onto her side, her cheek pressing against the silk of the pillow sham. Her gaze dropped over him and she swallowed thickly. He was still dressed in his crisp white dress shirt. He'd jerked up his pants as he stood, but his cock still protruded from the opening of his fly. The condom clung to his relaxed, but still-formidable sex. Her muzzy, sexually satiated state partially evaporated when she recalled how he hadn't removed all of his clothing with that woman—Astrid—either.

He turned, and she saw him in profile, and the intrusive thought scattered. He was so beautiful. It didn't matter what she knew about his lack of interest in intimacy with women or his challenging sexual practices. It didn't matter that he would get his fill of her soon, she realized as she watched him walk to the adjoining bathroom and open the door.

Her hunger for him wasn't something to be picked apart and tested rationally. It just *was*, and all she could do was pray she'd survive relatively unscarred after he'd gone.

When he opened the bathroom door a minute or two later, her eyelids were drifting closed. She immediately perked up upon seeing Vanni walking toward her wearing a pair of low-hanging black pajama bottoms that left very little to the imagination. Once again, she was struck by the golden-brown smoothness of his skin. His naked torso was a living sculpture of lean, well-developed muscles, his abdomen so taut she could have easily bounced a quarter off his flat stomach. Ridged, oblique muscles slanted like an arrow to his crotch, seeming to defy her not to look in the downward direction. He stalked toward her and the bed. Despite her acute awareness of his gaze on her, Emma couldn't tear her gaze off the image of his cock pressing lightly against soft cotton and hanging between his strong thighs: the very picture of temptation.

"Emma."

He stopped next to the bed. She looked up at his face sluggishly. His aquamarine eyes were narrowed and his angular jaw was hard.

"Yes?" she rasped.

"Don't look at me like that."

She had a vivid memory of him saying something similar when he'd bidden her to him that first time in the Breakers' dining room, and how intimidated she'd been.

Why are you looking at me like that? he'd demanded.

For the first time, she realized he'd seen naked desire in her eyes even back then, and had recognized it when she hadn't. Understanding that, her former confusion melted away. She continued to stare up at him, sliding her gaze over his torso and lingering on the small, brown disks of his nipples. Her lips parted in wonderment when she saw them roughen and tighten. Slowly, she met his gaze.

"I can't help it," she said softly.

His eyes seemed to spark. Her heart jumped with excitement but she forced herself to remain still when he abruptly reached for the corner of the bedding and flipped it back, exposing her naked body. His gaze traveled over her, hot and possessive.

"Why shouldn't I look at you, when you look at me like that?" she whispered, her skin prickling and her nipples tightening under his stare.

"Because your eyes make me want to do things I shouldn't," he said, his gaze fixed between her thighs, his stare hungry. Her clit pinched tight. She had an almost overwhelming urge to touch herself to ease the friction. He came onto the bed next to her, and her excitement only amplified. He took her into his arms and drew her against him. A small shudder went through her at the delight of pressing to his hard male length, the tips of her breasts crushing against warm, smooth skin. Their close contact was momentarily broken when he twisted, turning out the bedside lamp.

Then he was gathering her into his arms in the darkness. Emma exhaled shakily, her cheek pressed against a dense pectoral muscle. Her thigh was wedged beneath his legs. She could feel the outline of his cock. He was growing erect again. He felt sublime. Her curiosity goaded her.

"Why shouldn't you do those things to me?" she whispered. His cock swelled against her thigh. For a moment, he didn't speak, and her entire awareness focused on the feeling of his penis throbbing next to her skin.

"Because I rode you hard earlier, and I took you like an animal just now. You will be tender."

Emma shifted slightly against him, focusing her attention to the sensation between her thighs. He was right. She *was* slightly sore. With her amplified awareness of him, however, her sex also felt tingly with excitement. She swept her hand along the smooth, taut skin that covered his ribs, a spike of excitement going through her when she felt him shiver and his cock lurch.

"I feel fine," she whispered. She started slightly when he captured her wrist and pinned it next to her outer thigh.

"Don't try me more than you already have," he said.

She blinked in the darkness at his hard tone.

He exhaled heavily, and she sensed his frustration and regret. "I want to talk to you about something else," he said, his voice calmer and hushed. "Are you on birth control?"

"Yes," she whispered. "The pill."

"I would like it very much if you saw my personal physician tomorrow before we return to the suburbs. I'll see him as well."

"Why?" she asked numbly.

"So that we can both have exams in order to determine if we're safe. Sexually."

She didn't respond, her mind whirring.

"Would that be all right? We can sign releases so that we can see each other's results."

She leaned away from him, cool air filling in the space between their pressing skin.

"You really do think that I'm still sick in some way, don't you?"

"*No*," he said emphatically, his hand curling around her shoulder and bringing her back against him. "That's not it at all. I just want to be inside you."

"You mean . . . without a condom?"

"Yes. If you're on birth control and we're both healthy, I don't see what's preventing it."

She sagged against him. He brushed his fingers through her hair, causing prickles of sensation along her neck and ear.

"What are you thinking?" he demanded.

"Well . . . it's just . . . how do you know I won't sleep with someone else while you're away one of these times?" she fumbled.

His stroking fingers paused. "Do you plan to?"

"No!"

"So what you're really asking is, how do you know that *I'm* not sleeping with someone else when we're not together, is that right?"

"Yes. I guess so."

He resumed stroking her hair. She could almost hear him thinking in the silence that followed. "Vanni?" she prompted after a moment, her anxiety getting the best of her.

"I was just thinking of how to respond to reassure you," he said quietly. "The only thing I can think to do is be honest. It's up to you whether or not you believe me. I'd understand if you didn't. Do you recall me telling you at the beach after I returned from France that I was having trouble sleeping and eating because I couldn't stop thinking about you?"

"Yes," she whispered, entranced not only by his words, but also by the deep rumble of his voice vibrating against her skin and ear.

"I tried to be with another woman." She stiffened in his arms. "I'm sorry to be so blunt, but I thought, considering the circumstances, maybe it was called for."

"What happened?" Emma whispered warily.

"I started out with the single-minded intention of getting you out of my head," he said thoughtfully, his fingers curling in her hair, his palm cupping her head, his fingertips rubbing her scalp. Despite her anxiety over the topic, she found her eyelids drooping at his touch. "But it didn't work. I didn't want her."

"How do you know there won't be another that *does* make you forget me?" she whispered.

Her head dipped as he exhaled deeply. "I just know. You have my word. I know I've told you I'm selfish, but I'm also honest." One finger caressed the shell of her ear, making all the tiny hairs there stand on end. "I've never asked this of a woman before. I'd prefer to have the boundary there, to be honest. Both in the literal and figurative sense," he added dryly. "But you're very rare," he continued slowly, his voice low and gravelly. She had a distinct mental image of him staring up into the darkness, his expression thoughtful. "I dislike myself enough at times. I couldn't bear to make it any worse by . . . *spoiling* you in any way . . . something so fresh." Her heart paused in her chest when he faded off. "It's something I just couldn't do," he resumed more firmly. "So in short, the only thing I can give you is my word. Maybe that's not enough for you. I can tell you this, though. When I was in high school and college, I was a walking, talking lit fuse. I was determined to travel fast and furious all the way to hell without even a brief stop. Nothing made sense to me. Nothing mattered. It's a wonder I made it to adulthood alive. Then something happened that brought me to my senses, something that made me realize the one thing that did matter, the one thing I could control, was my word. I couldn't control anything else but that. It became my anchor. If I said a thing was going to happen, it happened. Too much else in the world didn't make a bit of sense, but *that*, I could control. I've fought to make that my reality ever since then."

She exhaled shakily and touched her lips to the crinkly hair on his chest. It felt like fingers clutched at her throat hearing him say those poignant words.

"Emma?" he prompted after a moment.

"Yes," she whispered.

His fingers moved on her scalp. "If I'm only going to have you for a limited period of time, I want you completely, and on my terms. Will you see Dr. Parodas tomorrow?"

She should say no. She was crazy to be considering it. It was a level of intimacy far beyond their agreed-upon relationship. But the mental image she had of him staring up at the ceiling, believing himself to be protected by the darkness, plagued her.

He was so alone, even here, while she was pressed so tightly to him, skin to skin. She wasn't his savior. She wasn't much of anything but a very average young woman. And yet, there was that connection she felt to him, a connection she couldn't entirely explain away by naïve imagination.

"Yes," she whispered, forcing the word out of her constricted throat. "I'll do it."

He fell asleep before she did. Emma lay there, feeling the subtle rise and fall of his chest beneath her cheek, entranced by the sensation, lulled by his clean, spicy scent mixing with the subtle perfume of sex, the fragrance heady and delicious. Being in Vanni's arms cast a spell around her. The last thought she had before drifting off to sleep was that perhaps her entrancement was why she'd agreed to sacrifice so much of herself, when he was offering so little in return.

She awoke in a warm cocoon to the sensation of her sex being cupped in a possessive gesture while a large hand stroked the curve of her hip lazily. Emma realized she lay on her side, facing the windows while Vanni lay behind her, his long, hard body curling against her backside. His cock pressed against her ass, the only thing separating her from his stiff, pulsing erection a thin layer of cotton. Morning light filtered around the luxurious drapes. His fingers moved slightly on her sex and she purred sleepily.

"I haven't slept that well since I was a kid," he said near her ear, the deep, raspy sound making the skin of her neck roughen. "But even so, all night I dreamed about this." His fingers moved again subtly on her pussy. "Are you tender?"

She bit her lip. "I'm fine," she whispered. In fact, her sex ached with a dull throb. She wasn't used to having as much sex as she'd had yesterday, nor was she accustomed to Vanni's forceful, all-consuming manner of lovemaking. His hand stilled between her thighs. She felt his warm breath on her neck when he exhaled heavily.

"You're lying, Emma," he said, sweeping the hand that had been cupping her sex up her belly. Emma swallowed thickly when she felt the warm dampness on his fingers. His cock flicked against her backside. She tried to turn to put her arms around him, to assure him that she was fine, but he stopped her with a firm hand on her shoulder. "Trust me," he said near her ear, his voice a dark, seductive threat, "you don't want to test me. I felt you flinch just now. I'm going to go jump in the shower."

"No, Vanni," she protested when he moved away from her. She turned over and reached for him, but he was already standing by the bed. He looked down at her, his face rigid, his blue-green eyes glittering.

"You'll have to have an exam in less than an hour with Dr. Parodas. Do you really think it's advisable?" he asked, his handsome mouth quirking, one eyebrow shooting up and giving him a devilish demeanor.

"Maybe you're right," she said slowly, but her gaze sunk down his ridged, sun-bronzed abdomen to the vision of his erection tenting his pajama bottoms. "There's something I should probably confess to, since you were being so honest last night," she mused, stretching luxuriously so that the sheet slid below her nipples. His gaze darted downward hungrily.

"What?" he asked warily.

"I knew it was apricots."

When he didn't respond immediately, her gaze slid up to his face. He wore a storm cloud expression.

"Dammit, Emma, you're going to pay for that," he grated out, pointing a condemning finger. He came down on the bed next to her, his mouth set in a grim line, and her heart began to race. She tried to reach for his cock, but he caught her wrists and pressed them to the pillows. She couldn't help laughing softly, even though he looked so fierce. "Don't you *dare* look so smug," he breathed out, and her laughter faded even though her smile lingered. "And don't say I didn't warn you, either."

He dipped his head, immediately spearing her lips with his agile tongue, sinking into her, taking his fill. Her flesh turned to warm, sweet syrup beneath Vanni's angry, wild kiss, and she remained completely unrepentant.

Week

FIVE

Chapter 22

The weather was par for the course in southern France when his pilot, Marco, landed. Vanni stared out the window onto a sun-drenched, luminous Mediterranean afternoon. They'd left Chicago in the middle of the night. He'd continued working on the flight, but also slept for almost four hours, which pleased him. Insomnia had become his constant demon as of late. Plus, he'd gotten an unheard-of seven hours of rest the night before, deep, peaceful sleep . . .

. . . with Emma in his arms.

How she could infuse him with energy, make him horny as a teenager, and yet promote a solid night's sleep at the same time was yet another mystery when it came to Emma.

As they taxied in the private plane at the Nice Côte d'Azur Airport, he fleetly checked the dozens of messages that he'd acquired on the transatlantic flight. When he noticed that Neil Parodas had called recently, he immediately hit redial.

"Neil, I hope I'm not calling too early," Vanni said when the physician answered on the second ring.

"No, I'm up and about. I was half expecting a call, after seeing you yesterday. We only had a little time to talk in private. That was certainly an unusual visit for you."

Vanni zipped up his briefcase. Through the window, he saw that Marco was approaching their usual spot for deplaning.

"Well, there's a first time for everything," Vanni said, referring to the fact that he'd never brought a woman to his personal physician with a request for blood tests and exams with sexual safety in mind. Of course he and Meredith had gone to him for their premarital blood tests, but this was different. He'd known Neil for almost ten years now. As his private physician, Neil was privy to quite a few personal and intimate details about Vanni. He was one of a handful of people that had earned a place of trust and respect in Vanni's life.

"I think it's wonderful," Neil was saying in his characteristic deep, warm voice that invited trust and confidence. "Ms. Shore is a beautiful young woman. Smart, too. What is it that you wanted to speak with me about?"

"Did Emma happen to mention during her exam yesterday anything about what happened to her when she was a child?" Vanni asked. The plane came to a halt, but he remained unmoving in his seat, staring intently out his window onto the luminous summer day.

"I'm not sure that I know what you mean," Neil said cautiously. Vanni sensed his unease in talking about another patient.

"Emma and I both signed release forms so that you could discuss our medical conditions to each other."

"Technically speaking, Van, those forms clear me to talk about the results from the exams and blood draws I did," Neil said dryly.

"Well this relates to the test results and exam," Vanni assured. "When Emma was young, she was diagnosed with alpha thalassemia. When she was nine, she had a heart attack because her organs weren't getting enough oxygen."

"Emma didn't mention anything about that," Neil said, sounding concerned. "Her vitals during the exam were excellent. She's the picture of health. Are you sure about this?"

"That's why I'm bringing it all up. Emma is convinced she's cured of the disorder."

"That's impossible," Neil said unequivocally. "There must be a misunderstanding. Thalassemia is a genetic condition. It's not a curable disease."

"I understand that. I looked it up myself. That's why I'm asking you to check her blood work for indications of the condition, in addition to the other tests we talked about. Like I said, Emma is convinced she doesn't have the disorder anymore."

"All right," Neil said slowly. "I'm confused, though. I spoke to her quite a bit during her exam. Emma seems bright, and she's very knowledgeable as a nurse. She should know thalassemia is a genetic disorder. It's not something that can be cured by a pill or something. Why wouldn't she have mentioned any of this to me?"

"I think she's learned not to speak of it," Vanni said, holding his phone to his ear with his shoulder so that he could straighten his tie. "People don't believe her."

"That's not surprising," Neil said. Vanni paused in jerking his tie when he heard the concern in Neil's voice.

"Neil? What is it? What's wrong?"

"I'll order the test, Vanni, if you think it's important. It's just . . ."

"What?" Vanni demanded, his skin prickling with wariness.

"I don't know that it's a good sign one way or another, for you to be so anxious about this girl's health."

A prolonged silence fell. Vanni dropped his hand and stared blankly out the window.

"You think I'm being paranoid about Emma? Because she's the first woman I've shown any real interest in since Meredith?" Vanni asked, knowing precisely what Neil was hinting at.

"The thought did cross my mind, yes. It's not every day you bring a lovely young woman like that to my office."

Vanni closed his eyes and waited for the upsurge of emotion that usually occurred when the topic of his dead wife arose—when the topic of death in general came up. Neil was one of the few people on the planet who knew how death seemed to have singled out Vanni to plague him, always taking and taking those he loved, always leaving him to suffer the barren landscape of life alone.

But no stabbing pain came this time as he thought of the short time he'd shared with Meredith. He inhaled a full breath of air. The only thing he experienced was a genuine wish to find out if Emma was well.

"This situation has nothing to do with Meredith or the reason I brought Meredith to you. This has to do with Emma, and Emma alone. She'll be the first to admit she's an eternal optimist. She believes wholeheartedly that she had this disease and was cured of it miraculously. I just want to check on the facts, that's all. I want to make sure she's well."

"And if she's not?" Neil asked. Vanni heard the worry in his tone.

"We'll cross that bridge when we come to it. I'd rather she know than not know, wouldn't you?"

"Are you sure it's not *your* knowledge of whether or not she has a life-threatening condition that you're concerned about, Vanni?" Neil asked.

"I just want to know. Period," Vanni replied flatly.

He heard the physician exhale. "Then you will. I'll let you know as soon as I get the results."

After he'd hung up with Neil, he stood from his seat and looked up another number on his phone.

"New Horizon Hospice, how may I help you?" a friendly female asked.

"I'd like to speak with the nurse supervisor, Mrs. Ring?" Vanni said, lifting his briefcase. A moment later, Mrs. Ring came on the line and greeted him warmly.

"I'm calling about one of your nurses, Emma Shore," he said, nodding at Marco as he passed him on the way out of the plane. "I've been very impressed by her work ethic and was wondering if I might be able to borrow her from you for a few weeks in the near future?"

* * *

That Saturday, Emma left the premises of the electronic repair shop situated in the charming downtown of Cedar Bluff. Ever since Vanni had given her that last toe-curling kiss in his car on Monday morning before he'd dropped her off and left for France, she'd been obsessed with checking things off her to-do list. She'd told herself it was just time to get her life in order, but privately, she knew her recent obsession with organization was a coping skill. She was filling the days of Vanni's absence, marking time until she could see him again next week. He'd said he'd call her Monday evening when he arrived in Chicago. That promise was like a huge red exclamation mark on her mental calendar.

Ever since he'd left her, she'd managed to drop off all her dry cleaning, pay all the bills, finish her grocery shopping for two weeks, drop off three large bags of old clothes she'd been planning to take to the Salvation Army, and now take her long-broken stereo in to have it fixed.

All of that, and she still missed him so much it was like a hard knot had been tied off in her chest.

To make matters worse, he clearly didn't miss her at all. He hadn't called once since he'd dropped her off after their extremely passionate, emotion-ridden time together. Or at least it'd been emotion-ridden for her.

He hadn't *said* he would call until he returned.

Still . . . she'd hoped he would. Stupidly. Now that the week of his absence was drawing to a close, she no longer hoped.

But she still ached.

She could have called him as well, she acknowledged fairly as she walked down the street, fingering the angel at her throat. She had his number. Somehow, however, the idea of speaking to him on the phone while he was so many thousands of miles away only made her ache even more.

"Emma!" a woman called.

Emma spun around, peering down the block. She broke into a grin at the sight of a familiar face. She gave the young woman who rushed toward her an enthusiastic hug.

"Hi! I didn't realize you were coming this weekend," Emma greeted her friend, Jamie Forrester. She'd gone to nursing school with Jamie. Jamie had gotten married last year and moved to Green Bay with her new husband, although Jamie and she still stayed in touch.

"Scott has a meeting in the city Monday morning, so we just came down for a few nights," Jamie explained, tucking an errant brown curl behind her ear. "Besides," Jamie continued in a more confidential tone, "my dad had a medical scare last week. They took him to the emergency room with chest pains. They thought it was a heart attack, but it turned out it was just indigestion. Still, it scared Mom and me. I just wanted to see for myself that he's okay."

"That's understandable," Emma said, concern tightening her features. She'd met Jamie's parents several times and liked the warm, friendly couple very much. "Please give Mort my best and tell your mother hello. Are you sure he's all right? He works too hard."

"Once a cop, always a cop," Jamie said, grinning. "But why don't you come and say hello yourself. I'm meeting my dad over at Joe's," she said, pointing at the coffee shop just yards away. "He'd love to see you. He was just asking about you last night. We'll catch up over a cup of coffee."

"I'd love that," Emma agreed.

They found Mort Forrester sitting at a booth in the coffee shop, with a laptop and cup of coffee in front of him. Emma couldn't help but smile at his likeable appearance—a man with the girth of a linebacker and a graying blond crew cut peering through a pair of nerdy-cool tortoiseshell Poindexter-style glasses while he punched away at his keyboard with thick, round fingers.

"You promised Mom you weren't going to work this weekend," Jamie scolded her father. "Look who I found out on the street."

Mort did a double take upon seeing Emma, grinned broadly, and stood to give her a big hug.

The three of them talked for a while, Emma sitting across from Mort and Jamie, three cups of hot coffee on the table between them. Jamie and she eventually veered off on a girlfriend tangent of conversation while Mort distractedly plucked at his keyboard.

"I can't believe you and Colin broke up," Jamie said, sagging back in the booth after Emma had broken the news. Mort looked up from his computer, his daughter's exclamation snagging his attention. "I thought you two would be together forever."

"Really?" Emma asked doubtfully as she took a sip of coffee.

"You thought so, too. Once," Jamie said with a pointed glance.

Emma shrugged, aware of Mort's shrewd observance. Mort may be a small-town cop nowadays, but he'd served in Chicago Police Department for years and he was a sharp observer of character. "It just wasn't meant to be. I'm fine about the whole thing."

"Well, that's good I guess," Jamie said. Emma understood her friend's disquietude. She and Emma used to talk a lot about their love lives while they were in nursing school, and she and Colin had been on a number of dates with Jamie and her husband, Scott. It was always uncomfortable when a familiar couple broke up.

"You really do seem fine with it," Jamie added after a reflective pause. "When I first saw you out there on the sidewalk, I thought wow . . . what vitamins is she taking? You look fantastic."

Emma blushed. She'd noticed a special glow to her reflection in the mirror all week as well. It was as if Vanni's uncommon brand of lovemaking had released some miracle chemical in her body. She felt like a blooming flower. It both embarrassed and pleased her to know that other people could see the results of her transformation.

"Is there someone else?"

Emma blinked at Mort's unexpected, quietly uttered question.

"No," Emma said automatically. Vanni didn't count as some kind of alternative to Colin, who had been a dependable, reliable "boyfriend," the likes of which Mort and Jamie would approve. She saw

Mort's shaggy eyebrows go up at her emphatic reply. "I mean . . . yes, I did meet someone. But it's not a serious thing," Emma assured when she saw Jamie's expression perk up with interest.

"I didn't forget about your problem with your landlord, by the way," Mort said, seeming to intuit her discomfort with the "new guy" topic he'd begun and trying to change it.

"Oh, thank you so much, but everything has gotten better," Emma enthused, leaning forward with a smile. Mort had promised to guide her through making a formal complaint with the housing commission in regard to her irresponsible and unresponsive landlord. "One day the maintenance man came over and said he was going to take care of every single item on our list," Emma explained. "Amanda and I were shocked. He did it, too, even though he had to buy quite a few replacement items. I have no idea what came over our owner."

"He decided to sell, that's what came over him," Mort said, nodding at his laptop.

"What?" Emma asked, taken aback.

"Yeah. I was checking out the title to the property while you girls chatted in order to get his name. I thought we could draft a complaint letter for the housing commission while you were here," Mort said to Emma. He swung around his laptop so that Emma could see the screen. "The title to your apartment complex changed hands several weeks ago. According to the county records, your new landlord is a very wealthy man. From what I know about Michael Montand, he's got deep enough pockets to get things taken care of at your apartment. I suppose you know who Montand is? Emma?"

Emma heard Mort's question through what seemed like thick insulation. She stared openmouthed at the property sale document, her gaze glued to the black print. *Buyer: Michael G. Montand of 3637 Lakefront Road, Kenilworth, IL.* A strange tingling sensation sunk down her tailbone.

"Yes," she said through a constricted throat, suddenly conscious that Mort was looking at her expectantly. "I have heard of Montand."

"Michael Montand, the guy who makes those hot, super-expensive sports cars?" Jamie asked.

Mort nodded, taking his computer back when Emma pushed it toward him on the Formica tabletop with numb fingers. She'd seen enough. There was no mistake. The address was familiar. The name certainly was. There was no doubt about it.

Vanni had purchased her home just recently . . . since she'd first met him.

Why had he done it?

"Yep, that's the guy. Montand cars are some of the best engineered in the world," Mort was saying. "Montand inherited the company from his father, although he started his own company here in Deerfield. From what I understand, it's even more lucrative than his luxury car business. He got his father's brains not only for business, but engineering. Michael Senior could put an engine back together blindfolded and come up with revolutionary mechanical advances in his sleep. I understand his son is even more of a mechanical genius."

"You say it like you knew Michael Montand Senior," Emma said, curiosity making her find her voice.

"I did, a little," Mort said, glancing up at her with sharp blue eyes. "We were both members of the local Lions Club. Montand didn't come around that much—I imagine he joined to be polite when someone asked him. But I met him a few times. Knew of his reputation and business. Knew about his son, too," Mort said dryly.

"What do you know about the son?" Emma asked, her pulse beginning to leap at her throat.

"Just rumors, mostly, although I did have a few real-life run-ins with him when he was a teenager," Mort said in his easygoing manner as he shut down his computer and closed the lid.

"You've actually met him?" Emma asked.

Mort nodded. "I'd just become the sheriff here in Cedar Bluff when Montand Junior was finishing high school. He tested the police staff of a few towns along the North Shore when he was young."

"He was wild, huh?" Jamie asked, taking a sip of her coffee.

"He was troubled, that much is certain," Mort said reflectively, taking off his glasses and rubbing his eyes. "His dad and his stepmom had their hands full with him. Some of these rich North Shore kids are spoiled rotten, but Montand had more reasons than some for dabbling in juvenile delinquency, I suppose. He never struck me as a bad kid, just mad at the world. He lost his mother really young, from what I understand, and never got along well with his stepmother."

"He lost a twin brother, too," Emma said quietly. Jamie looked over at her in surprise. "I'm familiar with him through a patient," Emma sidestepped.

Mort nodded thoughtfully. "A twin brother, huh? Well, that makes sense. We brought Montand in one night for underage drinking and getting in a fight with some South Side jerk who boxed part-time. Montand was only sixteen or so at the time. The guy he was fighting was a monster and years older than Montand, but Montand had held his own. In fact, he'd gone ballistic on the guy in the parking lot of some Cedar Bluff dive that's not open anymore." Mort shook his head in memory. "That kid had a death wish. He was like a lit firecracker, burning at both ends and inside out to boot. Once he cooled down, though, he was nice enough. He even fixed our busted police radio for us before his dad came in to post bail." Mort shook his head distractedly. "A twin brother, huh?" he repeated. "I'd never heard anyone say that. I *did* hear he married young to a girl he met in college. Montand Senior was dead set against the relationship, and was furious when his son brought the girl home and presented her as his wife. Senior tried to get the marriage annulled, but Junior was having none of it. At least that was what the gossip was. And then he lost her, too."

"What?" Emma asked, praying she'd misunderstood the last detail of Mort's rambling reflection.

"Yeah," Mort said, meeting her gaze and nodding sadly. "I don't remember what the wife died of, but I think she was sickly from the get-go. They couldn't have been married for much more than a year before she got ill, and then she was gone by the time their graduation date arrived."

His words pounded in Emma's stunned brain with the pulse of her blood. "Just goes to show you, I guess. Someone might look at Montand and think he's got it all—money, good looks, success, glamorous businesses and yet—"

"It's like life is playing some kind of sick joke on him," Emma finished dully, recalling Vanni saying similar words that night on Lookout Beach when they'd differed on the topic of death.

"Yeah," Mort said, taking a sip of coffee. "There's no fortune big enough that could ever tempt me into that young man's shoes."

"Amen," Jamie agreed fervently.

Mort blinked, seeming to come to himself. He gave his daughter a fond glance and patted her hand that sat on the table. "It was just a much too spicy cheeseburger," he reassured her under his breath. Jamie grinned up at him wryly and Mort winked.

"So that's the man who now owns your apartment complex, Emma," Mort said, dropping his hand. "I hadn't heard he'd ventured into real estate, but with money like his, I suppose it's smart to diversify. I'm glad he's taken care of things so quickly at your place. That bodes well. Maybe Montand has overcome all his adversities and become a decent man. I'd like to think so, anyway. I've heard good things about his business dealings. And I liked him as a kid."

"Emma?" Jamie asked, a strange expression on her face. She set down her cup and placed her hand on top of Emma's frozen one where it rested on the table. "Are you okay? That glow I was talking about earlier seems to have made a run for it. Your fingers are freezing," she said, concern etching her face as she chafed Emma's hand with her own.

Emma forced a smile. "I'm fine," she lied. "It's just the air-conditioning." She squeezed her friend's hand to reassure her and changed the subject to a safer one. In her head, however, she never left the topic of what Mort had revealed about Vanni. Her attention kept going back to it like it would a sharp wound.

* * *

That afternoon when she got home, she received a call from Dr. Parodas's office. Neil Parodas himself was on the other line, calling to give her the test results from Vanni's and her exam. He gave the information in such a friendly, amiable manner, it was difficult to be uncomfortable about his knowing the reason for the tests. He proclaimed both of them to be in excellent health. She hung up the phone and stood in her empty kitchen.

Another barrier of intimacy between Vanni and her had been removed. She'd agreed to have sex with him without protection.

She recalled what Mort had told her today about Vanni's young wife dying. Surely the sympathetic pain she experienced at the information was beyond what it should have been, given how long she'd known him . . . given their agreement? It worried her, that sharp ache when she considered his suffering. His loneliness.

She stared out the window over her kitchen sink and also remembered the other shocking information Mort had given her. *Vanni* was the one responsible for making sure every item on her punch list was completed with the highest efficiency. He owned her home. He didn't own her, though. Not if she could help it.

Surely she was a fool for not grasping at every little tidbit of protection she could get in this affair with Vanni Montand?

Chapter 23

Vanni spoke to Niki using a hands-free headset during his very swift drive between his villa near Saint-Jeannet and the airport on Sunday morning. An emergency had called him away from a planned meeting with some top officials in regard to the race in two weeks' time.

At least if felt like an emergency to Vanni. Others might disagree.

"Just smooth things over for me, won't you? Make something up. You're good at that," Vanni was saying as he took a hairpin mountain turn with the ease of long practice.

"I resent that," Niki told him, his unconcerned, mild tone at odds with his words.

"Only because you assumed I meant making up stories to your various women," Vanni said with a distracted smile. "In fact, I meant you're a natural diplomat. It's in your genes."

"We are talking about smoothing *royal* feathers here. That'll cost you double for the favor," Niki replied, referring to one member of the Montand French-American Grand Prix planning committee who was a relation to the neighboring state's monarchial family.

"You can do it. You're part of their family, after all."

"I'm a tacked-on leaf of a very disreputable branch," Niki replied dryly. "And I can think of one *non*-royal bird who is going to be extremely ruffled by your absence. No amount of Dellis diplomacy is going to smooth that over."

"I have complete faith you'll make her forget I even exist," Vanni said drolly as he plunged down the mountain, the sun-infused Mediterranean sparkling like liquid turquoise beneath a sky as smooth and blue as a robin's egg. The particular committee member Niki was referring to was a very beautiful, married socialite who had been vying for Vanni's attention since he was first introduced to her at her own wedding six years ago.

"You must give Estelle credit," Niki mused, and Vanni could almost see the glimmer of humor in his friend's black eyes. "She remains convinced after all these years she can change your mind about taking a married woman as a lover. I myself was always a little confused by this American fastidiousness of yours."

"You know it's got nothing to do with being American. It's got everything to do with being Michael Montand's son."

He didn't recognize how bitter he'd sounded until he noticed the silence on the other line. He'd seen firsthand what his father's frequent infidelities—what the ultimate betrayal—had done to his mother. No, Vanni was selfish, but he wasn't cruel like Michael Montand.

"What is this emergency, Van?" Niki asked, his Greek accent almost disappearing with his sudden, focused concern. "Does it have to do with that lovely nurse you brought to Cristina's funeral? I recognized what she was wearing around her neck. How did you manage to get Prisatti to give her one? Or did you mislead him somehow as to the identity of the receiver?"

"Do you think Angelo Prisatti thought it was for *me*?" Vanni asked sardonically.

"No, not a chance," Niki chuckled. "I'm just desperate to know what in the world you told him in order to get him to part with it. That'd be excellent knowledge for any single man."

"Only you would use a Prisatti angel to get a woman into bed."

"I don't need to. But isn't that why you used it?" Niki challenged glibly.

"Why don't you mind your own business?"

"You sort of are my business, unfortunately. Are you sure you're not more . . . *unsettled* by Aunt Cristina's death than you're letting on?" Niki asked.

"It has nothing to do with Cristina," Vanni said in a hard tone. "As for the reason I'm leaving, it relates to the fact that I can't sleep, and leave it at that," Vanni said, rounding a mountain pass.

"You never can sleep," Niki said with an air of stating the obvious.

"Now it's for a different reason, though."

He was telling the truth. He'd hardly had a moment's rest since landing in France. Memories of making love to Emma would pop up at the most inopportune moments—on a walking tour with the rest of the grand prix committee of the race circuit, at a luncheon hosted in Cannes for the press, at an exclusive dinner he'd hosted at La Mer for the drivers that had started to dribble in from all over the world.

He'd think of her incessantly in his empty bed at night.

Her dark eyes haunted his dreams when he did catch a few hours. His sense of restlessness and hunger had mounted as the days passed. All he could seem to focus on were memories and fantasies of touching her, of breathing her unique scent, of holding her while she shook in climax . . .

Yesterday, Neil Parodas had called and informed him that Emma had been one hundred percent correct in saying she was completely healthy.

I'm not saying she experienced a miracle cure, of course, Neil had cautioned. *There must have been some mistake if she was ever diagnosed with thalassemia. The most important thing, though, is that without a doubt, that girl is as healthy as they come.*

A strange sensation had gone through Vanni at the news. It was like someone had mainlined adrenaline into his blood. The world took on a lucid, vibrant cast that hadn't been there before, the brilliant colors of the flowers on the terrace of his villa, La Mer, the bright blue sea below the cliffs shocking his brain. If he didn't know himself better, he would have sworn that swooping feeling had been pure relief . . . euphoric joy?

The rush of feeling had been so sharp and overwhelming, and so unfamiliar that Vanni wasn't sure he trusted it. That didn't diminish the emotion any, however.

"Can you do me a favor?" he asked Niki presently as he turned onto the road to the airport.

"Of course," Niki replied.

"Call Vera and let her know I'm returning a day early. Have her send a car over to the airport. I've tried to reach her several times and failed."

"What car do you want delivered?"

"A fast one," Vanni replied grimly before he signed off.

On Sunday morning, Emma almost ran down Amanda on the way out the door. The meeting was unexpected. Both of them were startled and flustered, given their new, strained relationship and sudden close proximity, laughing and trying to get around each other. She noticed Amanda's heavy backpack slung over her shoulder

She had to give her sister credit; Amanda had been incredibly dedicated to her schoolwork so far. Emma had been a little worried this new thing with Colin would distract her just when she needed to focus the most as she started medical school. It had pleased her to see that didn't appear to be the case. Amanda had been up at dawn to go to the library to study since she had to work the evening shift at her waitress job tonight.

"Where are you off to?" Amanda asked breathlessly, leaving the front door open for Emma.

"I thought I'd go downtown and do a little shopping."

"You've certainly grown uncharacteristically interested in clothes lately," Amanda said, her expression friendly and amused, but curious as well. "It's nice. I could never get you interested," she laughed. She focused on the angel at Emma's throat. "I suppose it all relates to Vanni?"

Emma shrugged. Several times this week, Amanda had tried to broach the topic of Vanni Montand, but Emma hadn't been willing to share much except to say that she'd met him on her last work assignment and that they'd begun seeing each other on a casual basis. Given everything that had happened recently with Amanda and Colin, she felt hesitant sharing intimacies with Amanda. It was a fact that she hated, but that didn't make it any less true. She prayed for the prickly, uncomfortable atmosphere to ease between Amanda and her, but it certainly hadn't yet.

Besides, since discovering that Vanni had inexplicably bought her apartment complex, Emma was especially agitated on the topic of him. She wasn't sure what to make of the fact that the man who made love to her with such ruthless precision and yet made it clear he didn't "do" long-term relationships now owned her home. The whole scenario had left her bewildered and anxious. Talking about it with Amanda in the past would have probably helped her to clarify. All of that had changed, though.

What *had* Vanni intended by it all? It certainly left her in debt to him . . . not in debt, but *responsible* to him, somehow. He could drop her and forget her anytime he chose, but she couldn't remove *him* from *her* life so easily. Not when he owned the very rooms where she walked, ate, and slept.

Besides the issue with her apartment, she was still very heartsore over the news about his young wife dying. She'd tried to find more information about his marriage and the identity of his former wife, but there hadn't been anything online. Had Michael Montand Sr. used his influence, perhaps, to silence the news of his heir's unapproved marriage and his wife's untimely death?

"It would be hard to see a man like him and not want to look good," Amanda said, interrupting her chaotic thoughts. "I still can't believe it. Vanni Montand. You always did have all the family luck."

Emma blinked. "*I* did?"

"Sure," Amanda said, giving her a slightly startled glance before she set her backpack down on the entryway bench.

Emma gave a short laugh. "You're the gorgeous one. You're the brilliant doctor-to-be." *You're the one who my ex-boyfriend preferred.*

Amanda's smile faded as she took a step toward her. "Do you ever really see yourself in the mirror, Emma?" Emma just stared back at her. "You're beautiful. And what's more, you don't even have to *try* and you are. It doesn't surprise me in the slightest that you snagged Montand's attention."

"Thanks," Emma muttered, avoiding her sister's stare.

"And you know you're every bit as smart as me. You took that incredible load in nursing school and still aced all your classes and clinicals. And *lucky*?" Amanda shook her head incredulously. "You beat death, for God's sake. Mom used to call you her little miracle."

"I didn't beat anything," Emma said. "It just . . . happened."

"You walk in grace." Amanda shrugged when Emma gave her an incredulous glance. "Colin said it—after all this stuff with you finding us . . . you know. Together. And it's true, Em. No one would have handled this situation as gracefully as you. You've been so reasonable about the whole thing. I have a feeling you're being so patient because you're thinking of what Mom would have wanted. But no matter what the reason, I know it took a very big person to react the way you have. And I appreciate it. I just . . . wanted you to know."

"Thanks, but I think you're both being a bit too generous with the praise," Emma said shortly, taking a step toward the door.

She glanced back when Amanda grabbed her hand. "I'm not being too generous," Amanda said steadfastly, her lower lip trembling slightly. "Emma . . . I'm so, so sorry."

"For falling in love with Colin?"

"No. For falling in love in this way. It's the last thing on earth I wanted."

It was Amanda who stepped forward and hugged her. Emma stood stiff in the embrace at first. Something in her gave. She returned the hug every bit as warmly as her sister gave it. She shut her eyes and squeezed tight as emotion flooded her.

Abruptly, she backed away and reached for the door.

She'd missed Amanda *so* much.

It was going on two o'clock by the time she got off the subway and took the stairs up to State Street. She paused in the lobby of Macy's when a woman offered to spritz her with a brand of perfume that she knew she liked, but couldn't afford. She was in the process of rubbing her wrist on her neck, when her phone began to ring in her purse. Plucking out her phone in a distracted, unhurried fashion, she noticed the number.

"Hello?" she asked quickly, worried she'd taken too long and he'd hung up.

"It's me," Vanni said. "Where are you?"

"Downtown," she said, her voice ringing with amazement not only at hearing his voice, but also at his brisk question. "I'm at Macy's."

"I know," he said. "But *where*?"

"How did you know I was at Macy's?"

"Emma? *Where*?" he growled softly.

"Okay," she said, hearing the amused warning in his tone. She looked around the setting of the vintage, huge department store. "I'm in the perfume section on the first floor. Why?"

She glanced up, noticing that the salesgirl who had sprayed Emma's wrist was staring in wide-eyed fascination over Emma's shoulder.

"Because I'm looking for you," Vanni said.

Emma's mouth fell open in shock. She'd heard *him* speak in

addition to hearing his voice on the phone. She looked over her shoulder.

He was hanging up his phone and slipping it into his back pocket.

"There you are," he said briskly, blue-green eyes lowering over her in a satisfied manner. It was as if it were the most natural thing in the world for him to approach her in the middle of a bustling department store. "I was worried I'd have trouble finding you."

Emma spun around all the way, sure for several seconds she was hallucinating. But no, he didn't disappear. He looked very vivid to her stunned eyes, not to mention indecently gorgeous in a sexy, light blue T-shirt that sexily skimmed his lean, muscular form, and a pair of jeans. His tan had grown deeper since she'd last seen him. The color of his shirt, the sun-gilded skin, and the dark brows and lashes all combined to make his aquamarine eyes even more striking looking than usual.

"Vanni . . . what are you doing here?" she mumbled, her brain vibrating with shock—shock and something else even more powerful and primal. A thrill of pure excitement had gone through her at the vision of him, leaving her body tingling.

"I came back from France early." He stated the obvious. He looked behind her, quirking his dark brows, and Emma glanced over her shoulder. The salesgirl was still staring at him with that goofy grin. She seemed to come to herself at Vanni's glance and muttered an apology before she walked away, silly smile still in place. Emma rolled her eyes at the show of female weakness he inspired.

"But how did you know I'd be *here*?" she asked.

"I stopped by your place. Amanda told me you'd gone shopping here." His gaze flickered over her face and landed on her lips. He glanced aside distractedly when a woman with several large bags bumped into him. "Is this what you came shopping for? Perfume?"

"No," Emma said, still staring at him. She still couldn't believe he was here. She had an almost uncontrollable urge to touch him. Memories of sleeping in his arms when they were last together flooded her consciousness. She'd lain against his solid chest all night and stroked him whenever she chose, which was often. She'd allowed him to tie her up and spank her. They'd made love with savage abandonment.

Now he stood here so unexpectedly, and it was all so *unbelievable*. Her longing for him was still there—in fact it felt doubled. But the idea of touching him suddenly made her shy.

Idiot.

His eyebrows arched. His head lowered and she realized he was waiting for her to speak. "What are you shopping for then?" he prodded quietly as a group of shoppers rushed past them.

"Oh . . . you know. Just looking," she managed. "A dress, maybe. Possibly a swimsuit."

His steady stare seemed to swallow her whole.

"Dammit," he said suddenly under his breath. He stepped forward and his arms encircled her. "When are you going to stop going shy around me?" he asked, his mouth slanted in amusement.

"I'm not—"

His mouth cut her off. All her awkwardness and uncertainty evaporated in a second beneath his kiss. She forgot where she was as he pierced her lips with his tongue and his taste flooded her consciousness.

"God you smell good," he mumbled a stretched, delicious moment later, nuzzling her ear and neck. Emma shuddered in pleasure. "Is that the perfume you just put on?"

"Yes," she whispered.

"Did Dr. Parodas contact you about our test results?" he asked, his nose in her hair, his lips brushing against her ear and making all the hairs stand on end along her neck.

"Yes," Emma managed, finding his kiss and the topic both highly intimate in these mundane surrounding.

He looked at her, his expression shifting ever so slightly. If Emma had to guess, she'd say he was very satisfied by her answer.

"I have an idea," he said.

"What?" Emma asked. He might have suggested they jump naked

off the Willis Tower together, and she would have done it she was so momentarily enthralled by his eyes and deep, quiet voice.

"I'll take you to a place where we can shop for a few items you'll need. Then I'll take you to bed and keep you there until we're too weak to get out of it."

A lightning flash of arousal went through her.

"A few items I'll need for what?" she asked, choosing to focus on the safer topic.

"For your trip." He arched his dark brows significantly. "To the Côte d'Azur?" he prompted as if he was gently reminding her of something she'd forgotten because she was so clearly befuddled by his kiss and nearness.

"To the French Riviera?" she asked skeptically.

He smiled, slow and brilliant. She felt that smile at the very pit of her being.

"Now you're getting it. We leave on Tuesday."

"I don't know what you're talking about," she said bemusedly as he took her hand.

"It's simple. I have to be back in France soon for the buildup to the race and the race itself. We'll go back in a few days, but when I go, you do. I want you there with me."

"You do?" Emma asked. She blinked and glanced around at the familiar surroundings of the department store, trying to ground herself. She'd been flying around in his eyes for a moment. "I can't. I have work."

"You'll take a vacation," he said, pulling on her hand. She fell into step beside him. "You can call the office tomorrow, ask for time off."

"Maybe, but it might be kind of tricky getting it on short notice," she said, scurrying to keep up with his long-legged stride, her heart starting to pound with excitement in her chest despite the craziness of his proposal.

"It'll be fine. You need a vacation. You'll love the Côte d'Azur . . . and my house there." He gave her a gleaming sideways glance.

"*Maybe*," she hesitated, swept away by the sheer force of him. "It's *possible* I could figure out something for work . . . but what about—"

He shook his head and pulled her in front of him as they neared the revolving doors. "I'm not going to this damn race without you," he stated flatly. "Now . . . let's go finish your shopping so that I have you to myself," he said with grim determination, nodding toward the door.

Chapter 24

It was easy to be swept away by the power of his personality . . . by his intense attractiveness. By the time she sat in the passenger seat of a fierce-looking, ebony Montand convertible, reality hit her.

"I have a bone to pick with you," she told him, smoothing her ruffled hair out of her face as he zoomed out of the parking garage. She'd never known a person to make such tight hairpin turns so effortlessly.

"What about?" he asked unconcernedly.

"I found out about you buying my apartment complex."

He brought the car to an abrupt halt in the garage.

"How did you find out about that?" he demanded, eyebrows slanting.

"That friend's father who I told you about? The cop who was going to help me with my deadbeat landlord?" she clarified hotly, all of her confusion and irritation over the discovery blazing high in her suddenly. "Why did you do that? And why didn't you tell me?"

He shrugged slightly. "Because I thought you might react like this."

"Of course I would. And will you answer my question? *Why*?"

He began driving again. "I didn't intend to originally. When you told me about your trouble with your landlord, I had someone at my office look into it, just to see if I could nudge your owner into fixing all the stuff at your place."

"You shouldn't have done that. I could have taken care of it myself," she said, scowling. He continued like she hadn't spoken.

"The person I had working on it reported to me that Arthur Tamborg, the owner of your apartment complex, was in some seriously dire personal and financial straits and wasn't responding to most phone calls. I had a look at his financials and decided the apartments he owned weren't a bad investment. It was his lame management that was tanking things. So I decided to take the properties off his hands. I promoted somebody in order to manage, made a decent personal investment," he paused while he paid the parking attendant, "and you got everything fixed on your list," he said a moment later. He gave her a swift sideways glance before he pulled onto Wabash Avenue. "Why is that such a terrible thing?"

"So your decision to buy the apartments had nothing to do with me personally?"

"It related because I originally looked into Tamborg and the properties because of you, but after that, it was strictly business. It was a good investment. I wouldn't have done it if I didn't think so," he said, his gaze trained on the road.

"And it's not going to make any difference whatsoever that you're my landlord after we . . . after our time together is over?"

"Do you really think I'd try to hurt you somehow through your lease?" he asked, eyes flashing.

"No," she admitted.

"I'm not your landlord. I won't be even remotely involved in the day-to-day management of the apartments. That'd be the responsibility of the new property manager I hired."

"I guess I don't have any control over who buys or sells the place one way or another," she conceded. "It just seems odd, that's all. That you own my home."

"Would you rather Arthur Tamborg was back?" he asked levelly as he crossed the bridge over the river on Michigan Avenue. Emma noticed several pedestrians doing a double take and staring at Vanni in the sleek, badass convertible.

"No," she stated, frowning in memory of her dealings with the unresponsive landlord.

"Then there you have it. This way, if any other problems should arise at your apartment, you'll get immediate results."

"Just like everyone else who calls in with a problem," she clarified.

"Of course," he said smoothly as he pulled onto a side street. Emma studied him suspiciously, but she couldn't locate a crack in his armor.

"Are we good?" Vanni asked her a few minutes later after they'd parked the car and walked down the sidewalk of a quiet, tree-lined street.

Emma looked at his profile. He caught her stare, and she couldn't help but smile. It was hard to be miffed at him when her heart was doing cartwheels over seeing him again. He looked so tall next to her, so male . . . so beautiful.

"Just don't do me any special favors," she warned, forcing the smile off her face and replacing it with what she hoped was a forbidding glance.

He halted her by grabbing her hand and stopping. "What if I want to?"

Her fierce look faded at his sudden intensity and quiet question. "I meant in regard to owning my apartment complex. I don't want any tenant favoritism."

He gave a small smile and stepped forward. Her breath stuck on an inhale when he put his hands on her waist and the fronts of their bodies brushed together ever so slightly. "For now, you're mine, Emma. I won't have you struggling in any way if I can stop it. I'll show you all the favoritism I want to," he said before his mouth covered hers. She softened and heated beneath his kiss, his words ringing in her head.

For now, you're mine.

By the time he lifted his head and stared down at her a moment later, she'd completely forgotten why she'd been irritated with him, or even that she stood on a city street lined with brownstones interspersed with shops and businesses. His sleek, demanding tongue and addictive taste had *made* her forget. He lightly caressed the shell of her ear, and her sex tightened with desire.

"It's kind of hard to not show you any favoritism," he murmured and Emma swayed forward, entranced by the heat in his eyes and his singular scent. "Are you going to complain more if I take you into that store right there and spoil you a little?" he nodded down the block. Emma turned to see where he indicated, her expression freezing when she saw the renowned department store on the corner. It was so exclusive and expensive that Emma had never even dreamed of stepping over the threshold, let alone shopping there.

"I don't really need to go shopping, Vanni," she said, backpedaling from what she'd said at Macy's. "I was just passing the time when you found me."

He began to walk down the street and she followed, her hand in his. "Trust me, if we didn't need to do this, I wouldn't be here right now. I'd have you at the Breakers in bed."

"But I can't—"

"You said you needed a dress and swimsuit," he reminded her. "You'll definitely need some new things for the trip."

Emma sighed in exasperation as they entered the crosswalk.

"What?" he asked.

"I haven't even spoken to Mrs. Ring yet about taking time off. Just because you act like something is going to happen doesn't mean it *will*," she said chuckling, both irritated and amazed by his absolute confidence.

"You'll speak to Mrs. Ring tomorrow, and we'll fly out on Tuesday," he told her patiently. "You'll see. It'll be fine. And once we're in France," he nodded toward the department store, "you're definitely going to want a new dress or two. Or three. This is more than just a race, it's a social event that lasts almost a week."

Emma glanced at the famous glass entrance to the department store. "But I can't afford to buy things *here*, Vanni."

"That's all right," Vanni said, reaching for the door and opening it for her. He met her stare steadily. "You're with me."

She shook her head, refusing to enter. He frowned.

"It's a very simple thing, Emma. Do you want to come with me to the race?"

"Yes . . . if I can get off, that is," she said fervently, dreading the idea of missing another week of their time together.

"If you think you'll feel comfortable attending some of these events with me without any new dresses, then I'm fine with it. I was thinking of you in offering this."

"Vanni," she muttered under her breath, moved by his thoughtfulness and generosity, but torn. She glanced again anxiously at the name of the department store over the gilded entryway. If Mrs. Ring *did* grant her the time off and she indeed ended up going with him to France, he was correct. She'd look horribly out of place standing next to him in the extravagant European playground of the French Riviera. She didn't want to embarrass him.

And they only had so much time together, after all . . .

He put out his hand.

"Come on. Just a couple of dresses, and then we'll have some time to ourselves."

"Okay," she conceded, taking his hand.

The dressing room in the store was the size of her bedroom, featuring a lounging area with a sofa, coffee table, two armchairs, and an enormous, movable triple mirror. The friendly, chic middle-aged saleswoman, whose name was Sophia, escorted her into the changing lounge while asking her questions about fabric preferences and sizes. When Sophia asked her the names of her favorite designers, Emma gave her a wry grin.

"I doubt you'd find any labels from my closet here."

Sophia's smooth expression didn't falter. "Not a problem. We'll just introduce you to some new ones then."

A younger associate peeked her head into the door and asked Emma what she'd like to drink.

"Nothing, thank you," she told the young blond woman, a little flustered at the unexpected question.

"Bring her a tea service, please, and me as well," Vanni instructed. Emma turned in surprise. He'd followed them into the women's dressing lounge. Was there any place he wouldn't tread with complete confidence?

"I'll wait for you out there," he told Emma, pointing to the lavish sitting area that was part of the lounge. They'd passed it on the way in, so she knew to what he referred. He directed his attention to Sophia. "Please bring her out so that I can see the ones that are worthwhile."

"Of course, Mr. Montand. I'll be right back with some selections for you to start on," Sophia told Emma. "Just have a seat and relax."

The young blond salesgirl returned first, carrying not a cup of tea, but an entire service including a pot of tea, a tiered tray of small sandwiches, fruit, scones, jam and cream, and a glass of champagne. Despite Emma's awkwardness in the surroundings, she realized she was hungry and sampled one of the sandwiches and then a strawberry. A few minutes later, she sat on the couch with the teacup in her hand and a scone melting on her tongue, watching wide-eyed as Sophia breezed in with an armful of dresses.

"What about this one first?" she asked Emma, holding up a stunning mauve strapless gown. Sophia waved the dress over a sort of pedestal. Much to Emma's amazement, a video popped up on the mirror of a gorgeous, slinky model strutting down the runway wearing the precise dress Emma was about to try on. She gasped.

"Is there a chip in the dress?" she asked Sophia, standing.

Sophia grinned. "Yes, a tiny one on a tag. Our customers like to see the outfits we sell professionally modeled."

And the store likes to see their merchandise purchased, Emma thought amusedly as she began to shuck off her clothes. It was a brilliant sales maneuver. How many customers actually pictured themselves in the gorgeous model's shoes when they donned the dress?

She suddenly wished she'd put on a fancier bra and underwear set when she'd set out on what she thought would be a solitary, run-of-the-mill trip downtown this morning. Little had she guessed her solo trip to Macy's would end up like *this*.

"Oh my *goodness*," Sophia said, eyes going wide as she turned from hanging some dresses on a rack. At the woman's exclamation, Emma cringed where she stood in her bra and underwear. Were her undergarments *that* bad? Then she realized where the woman stared and her hand flew to her throat. "Is that a Prisatti angel?" Sophia asked, her tone hushed and thick with awe.

"I . . . I don't know. It's a *petit ange*. It was a gift," Emma said, letting her hand fall.

Sophia met her stare, a smile starting on her mouth. "From *him*?" she asked, glancing sideways in the direction of the sitting room where Vanni waited.

"Yes."

Sophia gave her a *lucky you* smile. "It's a Prisatti angel. They're extremely rare, handmade by a man named Angelo Prisatti, an Italian jeweler who lives in France. He only makes a few a year, the metalwork and etching is exquisitely detailed, even under a microscope. Prisatti insists on approving of the wearer himself. Their spirit has to match the essence of the piece he makes . . . match up to his standards, in other words. Otherwise, you'd see every spoiled rich girl in the world wearing one."

"*I've* never met him," Emma said. "Maybe it's not a Prisatti angel, after all."

"He must have altered his expectations for Montand," Sophia said with a knowing smile. "Because that's *definitely* a Prisatti angel."

Emma absorbed this amazing bit of news. It didn't surprise her that it was an extremely valuable necklace—she could have guessed that just by its unique, delicate beauty. What bewildered her was why Vanni would have taken pains to acquire such a rare piece for her.

As the rack in the huge, ornate dressing room began to fill with not just dozens of dresses, but resort wear, hats, shoes, belts, and accessories, Emma's confusion about Vanni's gift had to be moved to the back burner.

"I really just need a dress and maybe a swimsuit," Emma told Sophia uncomfortably.

"These are the items Mr. Montand indicated," the woman overrode her with pleasant politeness. "Here, let me help you with that," she said, moving behind Emma to zip up the gorgeous creation she'd just put on—a stunning green halter dress that came with a short jacket. When Sophia had zipped her in, she stared at her reflection in awe. The dress did amazing things for her figure. It made the gold of her hair look especially rich and vibrant and her skin gleam. She looked . . .

. . . *fantastic* in it.

"Oh my," Sophia said, stepping back and grinning. "This is definitely one to show Mr. Montand, don't you think?" She set down a sinfully sexy pair of strappy sandals in front of her. "Leave the jacket," the saleswoman directed when Emma reached for it after she'd buckled the sandals around her ankles. Emma saw the sparkle in Sophia's brown eyes. "He's not going to want it on you. Trust me."

Emma's cheeks went hot, but she followed a beaming Sophia out of the dressing room. Vanni was sitting in a Louis the XIV–style armchair, reading a newspaper, his tea service set out next to him on a circular table. Despite his T-shirt and jeans, he looked every bit the insouciant, confident prince of the palace.

"Well? Stunning, isn't she?" Sophia said.

Vanni glanced up as Emma came to a stop. His expression didn't change that much as he looked at her, but something in his eyes made the burn in her cheeks amplify.

"Well?" Emma asked when he didn't say anything.

"That one. Definitely that one," he said, his mouth set in a rigid line as he went back to his reading.

Sophia looked ebullient as she gave Emma a wink. With a sinking feeling, Emma thought she knew why. Emma had cringed upon seeing the price tag on the dress.

She would have thought she'd blush less each time Sophia indicated the outfit was worthy for Vanni to see. Instead, the heat in her cheeks only seemed to mount every time he glanced up and considered her with a stare that was both cool and assessing and scorching hot at once. She was embarrassed to admit it but she was actually becoming aroused by those dispassionate-seeming perusals that really didn't *feel* remotely aloof at all.

She walked toward him wearing a fantastic ivory cocktail dress that gave the illusion of transparency without actually being sheer, along with several ropes of pearls and matching pumps. Emma especially loved this one. It was an updated, sexier version of something a glamorous 1920s flapper heiress might wear on a jaunt across Europe. Vanni looked up and froze in the action of folding his paper.

"That's it," he told Sophia briskly, his mouth hard. "We'll take them."

"Which ones, Mr. Montand?" Sophia asked eagerly.

"All of the ones I've seen."

"Vanni—" Emma started to protest.

"Did you bring her swimwear and lingerie?" Vanni asked Sophia, cutting her off.

"Yes, sir."

"Choose several weeks' worth of items for her. We'll take one of the swimsuits now, but have the rest delivered to this address," he said, handing Sophia a business card and what appeared to be a credit card.

Emma gave him a helpless, annoyed glance over her shoulder as Sophia bustled her back to the dressing lounge. The sales associate was all smiles as she helped Emma undress. Three other associates entered, each of them leaving with armfuls of garments and teasing

Emma about how lucky she was. She had a feeling they were referring to the man sitting out in the sitting area more than they were the dream wardrobe he'd just bought her without a second thought. Sophia followed them a moment later carrying the final load. Emma picked up her bra—she'd had to remove it to do several of the dresses justice. She'd speak to Vanni about this privately. They'd agree to one dress, *two* if he said it was required given the events at the race, but—

In the reflection of the mirrors she saw the door open. Vanni walked in and shut the door behind him. Emma turned around, instinctively covering her bare breasts.

"Vanni?" she asked, her confusion mounting when she saw the single-minded intent gleaming in his light eyes.

He twisted the lock on the door.

"What are you doing?" she asked incredulous when he stalked toward her.

"It's all right," he assured, his nostrils flaring slightly as he glanced down over her. He reached for her hands and lowered them deliberately. Her nipples prickled and pinched tight beneath his stare. "Please don't ever cover yourself from me," he said.

"But . . . but what about Sophia and the others?" she asked numbly.

"They won't be coming back for a while."

"How do you know that?" she asked.

His gaze flicked from her breasts to her face. "Because I made sure of it."

There. Just like that. Whether she liked it or not, Sophia and her band of sales associates were definitely going to remain absent, and they'd keep anyone else from wandering into this dressing suite, too. Why? Because Vanni Montand had proclaimed it to be his desire.

Emma didn't speak when he reached up and put his hands on her shoulders, skimming his hands over her skin. She trembled as that familiar heavy pressure settled in her lower belly and sex. It felt *so* good.

"Do you know why I'm back early from my trip?" he asked her, his hands rubbing the back of her shoulders before they swept down her back. He pulled her against him. She moaned helplessly at the delicious sensation of pressing against his length, her erect nipples crushing against a soft shirt covering dense muscle.

"No," she whispered, reaching up to grab his shoulders. She suddenly felt very weak.

His hands slid beneath her panties. He cupped her buttocks and massaged them. Emma felt moisture surge at her core. He nuzzled the hair near her ear and she couldn't stop herself from shuddering in excitement.

"Because I couldn't stop thinking about you," he breathed out. "You're haunting me, Emma."

"You never even called," she said, pressing her cheek to his chest. God he smelled so good. He *felt* so good. What he was telling her made the sweet, hot pressure in her sex mount.

"I thought calling would make it worse," he said, lowering her panties over her ass to her thighs. His hands made a lascivious journey across her hips and bottom. "Why didn't you call me?" he growled softly before he kissed the opening of her ear. Emma gasped and tilted her head back to meet his stare.

"I thought calling would make it worse," she repeated breathlessly.

His handsome mouth curled into a small snarl. "I don't appreciate being tortured. That's just what it was, too, having you paraded in front of me like that." He pushed her tighter to him and dipped his knees. Emma's breath caught when he pressed his cock to the juncture of her thighs.

"It was your idea, Vanni," she reminded him dryly.

"That didn't make it any less of a torture session," he hissed, his mouth opening on her neck and then taking a tender bite out of her shoulder. Emma shivered. Hunger and heat seemed to radiate from him. How could he have looked so impassive and cool out there in the sitting room? "God you're beautiful. Every time I see you it's like being punched all over again," he grated out, sounding almost angry.

"You know that you're mine, don't you? For these few weeks, for these inadequate, skimpy little days and hours?"

She stared up at him. She was his whenever or however he wanted her. "Yes," she whispered.

He nodded grimly before he bent and pushed her panties the rest of the way off her.

"Then come here," he said firmly, leading her over to the couch.

Emma trailed after him, now completely naked. For a split second as he urged her to sit on the couch, she had a moment of clarity. She was in a store, for God's sake, a public place.

But then Vanni sunk to his knees before where she sat. She saw the hard glint of desire in his eyes and delved her fingers into his thick hair, everything else, *everyone* else, disappearing. His hands opened on her waist and skimmed her hips, his gaze trailing hotly over her breasts and belly and landing at the juncture of her thighs.

"It seems like I'm always waiting for you, like you're just out of my reach," he said under his breath, almost as if he didn't realize he spoke aloud. "I've waited too damn long to taste you."

Emma bit her lip, but a whimper of stark arousal escaped her throat, anyway. He put his hands on the backs of her thighs and pushed up so that her head fell back on the soft cushions of the couch and her hips rolled back. He urged with his touch, and she let her thighs fall open further.

"Hold your legs back," he instructed, and she reached for her knees, keeping her hips in place. She was spread wide for him . . . positioned to take whatever he offered her.

"Vanni," she said in a strangled voice when she saw the expression on his face as he stared fixedly between her thighs. His head lowered and her clit pinched in painful anticipation. It felt unbearably exciting. His face just inches from her sex, he inhaled and turned his head slightly.

"Jesus," he said thickly, his lips brushing the tender skin on her inner thigh. "So soft." He parted her labia with his fingers.

Then his mouth was on her sex, and Emma couldn't stop a muted cry. His tongue burrowed between her labia and laved her clit. It felt warm, firm . . . deliciously decadent and forbidden. She suppressed a moan of pleasure. His mouth closed on her while his tongue continued to stir her clit, his upper lip pressing down firmly on her sensitive tissues. The slight suction he applied made her toes curl and her muscles clench tight.

He groaned, deep and guttural, the vibrations resonating into her sex. He pushed again at the backs of her thighs until her knees were nearly parallel with her face. The soles of her feet began to burn in sympathy with her clit as he ate her. Nerves everywhere seemed to sizzle, eager to ignite. His tongue stabbed and pressed, slid and rubbed until a haze of lust and sensuality encompassed her like a dense, warm cloud. She had a fleeting glimpse of her face in the huge mirror across from her and hardly recognized herself, naked and wanton, her lips and cheeks floridly pink, her fingers clutching onto Vanni's head as if for dear life.

One large hand cupped her ass from below, right along the crack. He lifted slightly, blue-green eyes flickering up to meet her stare. A long finger reached, plunging into her pussy.

"Ohhh," she exclaimed shakily, unable to unglue her gaze from the vision he made, palming her ass like he might a lush fruit while he sank his finger and tongue into the sweetness. It was an incredibly lewd vision, but an intensely beautiful one as well.

He applied an eye-crossing suction and moved his head slightly, a growl emanating from his throat. Emma's eyes sprung wide at the acute stimulation. Then his tongue was back, a brutally precise, firm master.

"Oh God, Vanni . . ." she faded off, drowning in delight as climax loomed. He pushed back on her shins, forcing her knees into the couch near her ears. A helpless keen vibrated her throat. It felt incredible. Unstoppable. He laved her clit ruthlessly.

She broke in climax at the hard pressure, a cry escaping her throat. She bit her lip hard to restrain it, but couldn't stop whimpering as she shuddered in pleasure. He didn't let up on her a bit, agitating her clit with his stiffened tongue while she came, demanding every last shudder and shiver of pleasure she had to give him.

Emma checked out of reality for a moment.

She came back to herself when the warm pressure of his mouth disappeared. She opened her eyelids sluggishly, panting. A light sweat sheened her skin. He stood before her, looking down at her with a blazing gaze as he ripped open his button fly. A stab of rearousal went through her at the vision of his chin, mouth, and upper lip glistening with her juices. He made a hasty jerking motion with his hands and Emma glanced downward. He'd freed his cock. It poked out from beneath the edge of his T-shirt, the smooth, delectable-looking crown bobbing slightly in the air from his brisk movements.

She licked her abraded lower lip—she'd bitten on it forcefully to keep from screaming—watching in stunned arousal as his cock jumped slightly in the air. His eyes narrowed on her.

"Dammit," he growled. "Come here," he said tensely, putting out his hand. She reached for him, and he pulled her off the couch to stand before him. She felt a little dizzy and steadied herself by clutching his waist. With no prelude, he immediately cupped the back of her head, palmed her jaw, and swooped down to kiss her. It wasn't an angry kiss, necessarily, but it felt a little like it was. It was hard and wild and relentless. She was becoming used to his unleashed fierceness during lovemaking . . . or as used to it as a woman could be.

The sensation of his naked, swollen cock against her belly taunted her. She reached up and cupped his erection. The growl he made sounded dangerous. She moaned at the erotic heaviness of him, the smooth, warm skin gloving his arousal so tautly. He kissed her deeper. She tasted herself for the first time in her life, experienced the heady chemistry of her desire twining with his. He drank from her furiously, spearing her with his tongue again and again until Emma felt herself spinning from his dominant possession.

He eventually broke the scalding kiss with a rough groan. "There aren't enough minutes in the day to do all the things I want to do to you," he breathed out, white teeth bared. "There isn't enough time, period." His thumb pushed against her lower lip, separating it from the upper one. She stared up at him, helpless in her arousal, as he looked down at her mouth, his thumb moving in a tight little circle, his expression hungry as a wolf about to feed.

"You're going to make me wait again, Emma," he said, his soft tone highly at odds with his expression.

"For what?" she whispered, confused . . . overwhelmed by his raw, unguarded passion.

"For your mouth. I'm going to have to punish you for making me wait for what I want so much."

"I'm not making you," she defended, sliding her fist up and down his hard, pulsing shaft. A muscle leapt in his cheek.

"Oh yes you are," he said grimly, breaking their close contact and forcing her hand off his cock. "You're making me want you so much, all I can think about is taking you by storm."

He could feel his pulse throbbing in his cock, the resulting ache making him feel a little crazed. Her taste lingered on his tongue, fueling his rabid need. He led her over to the chair, his cock flicking in the air at the vision she made, completely nude, her cheeks and mouth as vividly pink as her pussy had been, her high breasts rising and falling with her erratic breath, her nipples tight and hard. He took both of her wrists and slid her beneath his arm so that she stood before him, her back to his front.

He placed her hand on the back of the armchair gently. It was so bizarre, the way he wanted to touch her with the tenderness of something most cherished, but at the same time, fuck her like an animal. He'd never experienced the paradox before. The sharpness of the resulting friction of his clashing desires clawed at him from the inside. Tempted by the elegant slope of her shoulders and graceful neck, he planted a hot kiss at the juncture of them.

"It's going to feel so good, being raw inside you," he lifted his head and met her stare. "I'm going to come in you, and it's going to feel so blessed good. Do you understand?"

"Yes," she whispered, twisting her chin to face him, her pink lips forming the single word scoring his consciousness. Her dark eyes shone with undisguised arousal. He stepped closer, wincing slightly at the sensation of his cock bumping and sliding across the smooth skin of her lower back.

"Bend over then," he said, his hands sliding down her ribs, waist, and hips, the sensation of those lush, feminine curves making him grind his teeth together in restraint. Too aroused to speak, he merely opened his hand on the warm, silken skin of her inner thigh. She parted wider for him at his signal. He moved closer behind her, his hands on her ass. He molded her firm flesh into his palms, opening her to him, hearing her whimper. His cock lurched at seeing such a temptation spread before him. He flexed, pushing his leaping cock against her damp, feminine warmth. She gave a surprised squeak and he spread her buttocks wider, his cock unerringly burrowing and finding home. He pierced her with just the tip and groaned.

God it was going to be so fucking good.

He flexed. Despite his almost rabid ardor and her obvious arousal, he felt her tight channel resist him. She made a choking sound, and he soothed her by caressing her silken hip.

"Shhh, try to relax," he soothed, his hand lowering to cup the underside of his cock. He pressed with his hips, guiding the first several inches of his flesh into her tightly clasping sheath. He felt a flush of heat around him. "There we go, that's so sweet," he managed, still trying to comfort even though he was about to explode with lust. He firmed his hold on her ass and began to rock in and out of her, working past the resistance, loving the hot, tight glide into heaven. She moaned. "Better?" he asked her.

"Yes," she said shakily. Her head was bowed. Her lithesome arms, the cap of golden waves, the elegant sweep of her naked back . . . the lush, round ass, all of it drove him mad. He didn't just want to sink into her.

He wanted to sink her into *him*. He wanted to consume her whole.

Giving in to the gnashing jaws of need, he tightened his hold on her hips and sunk his cock to the hilt. There was no pausing then. Being inside Emma raw was an all-or-nothing circumstance. Without pausing to experience the sublime sensation of her tight, soft, gloving flesh, he began to plunge into nirvana. He couldn't control himself. He couldn't diminish the force of his driving hips, couldn't muffle the slaps of his pelvis and thighs against her ass, and certainly couldn't stop staring with a feral focus at the image of his naked cock plunging into the sweetness of her again and again.

All he could do was give in to this orgy of sensation.

He noticed a flash of color from the corner of his eye. He glanced aside as he thrust and saw that her head was turned. She'd been watching him as he stared at himself fucking her. It'd been the vivid color of her lips and cheeks that had caught his attention. Her eyes looked enormous as she watched him take her like a madman in the ornate triple mirror.

Damn her eyes for always seeing so much.

He ground his teeth together, holding her gaze as he pounded into her, her body bobbing back and forth slightly as he drove into her with the force of a typhoon.

"God it's good, baby. You've got such a sweet little pussy," he told her, still holding her stare in the mirror. "Look at you . . . so beautiful," he said roughly, running his hand along her ass and hip up to her waist. She bit her lip and moaned, using her hold on the chair to push back against his cock. The way she followed his seeking hand in the mirror as he palmed a pert little breast from below drove him crazy. She whimpered, teeth tightening on her lip as he squeezed gently on both her breast and a buttock, using his hold to thrust her back and forth on his cock. For some reason, the image of her holding back infuriated him, even though he knew why she was doing it. They were fucking in a department store, what did he expect?

"You'll scream later on for me, won't you," he stated more than asked.

Her facial muscles tightened. So did her pussy around his pistoning cock.

"Answer me," he said harshly, his hips flexing fast and forcefully so that he drove nearly the full length of his cock into her with every stroke.

"Yes," she squeezed out between her teeth, grimacing. Heat rushed around him, her vaginal walls convulsing around his cock.

"Oh yeah, *give* me that," he grated out.

Both his hands on her hips, he sunk into her, their skin smacking together loudly. He clamped his eyes together, his body coiling tight.

He detonated. His eyes sprung open in surprise at the breathtaking flood of pleasure. When that first powerful wave passed, he lowered his head and moved, fucking her in short, hard thrusts while he ejaculated, popping her ass with his pelvis in a harsh, staccato rhythm. He knew then and there he must be an animal, to take so much primal satisfaction in leaving part of himself so high and deep inside her.

He held her to him tightly, gasping.

Please let that saleswoman hold true to her promise to keep everyone away from the large space of the private sitting room and attached fitting room.

He'd never intended to embarrass Emma.

He just couldn't get this grinding, feral need for her in check.

Chapter 25

As they left the locked-off dressing room suite later, Vanni must have noticed her discomfort.

"What is it?" he asked quietly, pausing next to the door.

Emma gave him an exasperated glance. "It's just so embarrassing. They all must know what we were doing in here."

"They can imagine whatever they want. They don't know anything. And it's not remotely their business either way."

Something struck her and she gasped, horrified. "Oh my God, what if there were surveillance cameras for security. Some places have those—"

"*Not here*," he said firmly, giving her a pointed glance. "Trust me. I checked into it. I wouldn't expose either of us like that. Okay?" he said with absolute certitude. She nodded.

His lips tilted as he lifted her hand to his mouth. Maybe he'd noticed her dazed expression. His lips felt warm when he brushed them across her knuckles. Immediately, the memory of what his mouth had felt like on her sex flamed vividly in her consciousness.

He exhaled and shook his head, an amused, fond expression on his face. "You're blushing bright red again. I'm just going to go and pick up a few items from Sophia. Go on down to the first floor by the doors and try to cool off. I'll meet you there."

She was thankful she wouldn't have to face Sophia or some of the younger sales associates again. She'd cringe in the presence of their knowing glances and smirks.

Once they were in the car and on Lake Shore Drive, Emma noticed something in the bag he'd set in the backseat. She reached behind her and withdrew the signature box of the perfume she'd been trying on in Macy's, the one she loved but could never afford.

"The perfume!" she exclaimed, grinning. "You asked Sophia to get it?" He was wearing sunglasses, so she couldn't see his eyes when he glanced at what she held.

"You smelled like straight-up sex when I found you at Macy's earlier. It might have been partially responsible for what happened back there in the dressing room," he stated wryly, staring at the road again.

"Really?" she said, letting the box fall back into the bag. "I thought it was really fresh and light, not . . . you know, musky or anything."

"It was you that smelled like sex, Emma. The perfume was just a nice sideshow."

At Vanni's insistence, she called Amanda's cell phone and left a message, saying not to expect her home that night. As they neared the Breakers, her excitement about spending the night with him mounted, but so did a niggling doubt.

"Will anyone be there, when we arrive?" she asked him delicately.

He shook his head as he drove down the country road. "No, I called Vera while you were in the dressing room and told her to let the staff go early, and for her to take off as well."

Emma exhaled with relief. He gave her a swift glance. "Why?" he asked.

"She doesn't like me. Your aunt. It would have just been . . . awkward to run into her in your house."

“Has she said something to you?” Vanni asked, scowling darkly as he pulled down the lane that led to his lakefront property.

“She doesn’t *have* to say anything, Vanni,” Emma said with a short laugh. “She practically oozes loathing every time she looks at me.”

His mouth clamped together as they approached the garage. “I doubt that. But if she makes you uncomfortable, just ignore her. I told you, she can be a bit territorial at times.”

“So she hated other women you’ve seen in the past?” Emma asked as they approached the garage.

Vanni shook his head. “Not that I’m aware of, no,” he said, frowning slightly. “I did notice she seemed especially irritated when I brought you to Cristina’s funeral. I just thought she was set off balance because I was late. Vera is a real stickler for schedules. I unfortunately challenge her desire for order way too often.”

“Well it’s nice to know that I’m the only one who brings out the worst in her,” Emma said lightly, determined not to let Vera Shaw—or anything, for that matter—dampen her mood on this promising, stolen night alone with Vanni.

It turned out that Vanni had asked Sophia to bag a swimsuit to go because he planned an evening swim. He led her to a luxurious shower and changing room on the workout facility floor—not the same one she’d briefly walked into that night when she searched for a washer; this one was apparently just for women. He instructed her how to get to the swimming pool from there, and then told her he’d meet her in a few minutes.

Inside the bag he’d left her she found not only the perfume he’d bought her, but a darling sky-blue bikini, a cute sheer tunic to be used as a beach cover-up, and a pair of flip-flops.

Once Vanni had left, Emma took a quick shower. She was still very wet from what had happened in the dressing room. She washed herself carefully, realizing with a rush of arousal she was rinsing away Vanni’s essence as well as her own. She’d never had a man come inside her. She and Colin had used a condom even though she was on birth control. Emma wasn’t sure why, except to say they’d started out having sex with a condom and hadn't altered their behavior. She heard so much about safe sex, especially as a nurse. Colin had probably thought her fussy, but he hadn't complained.

She really was crazy for allowing this level of intimacy with Vanni. As she rinsed away some of his semen from her fingers, however, she admitted to herself that she didn't regret it.

How could she regret anything in association with him? And it wasn't as if they hadn't taken measures to ensure safety.

She got out and dried off. In the shower area, she discovered a vanity with several grooming supplies stored beneath it. She opened a small bottle of mouthwash and used it and applied some deodorant. Knowing it was stupid, because it would only be washed away in the pool, she opened Vanni's gift of the perfume and applied some behind her ears and at her pulse, smiling when she caught the scent. It felt sensual and indulgent, having a bottle of the coveted fragrance all for herself.

A minute later, she self-consciously examined herself in the mirror, wearing only the bikini and sandals. There hadn't been much opportunity for her to be in the sun yet this year. She looked far too pale, although her cheeks, lips, and chest were still pink . . . sex-flushed, she realized.

She slipped on the beach cover-up, glad Sophia had the sense to include it.

It was a beautiful summer evening when she stepped out of the changing room door. The sun glinted off the gemlike spread of water, blinding her momentarily. It hadn't cooled off much since the worst heat of the day, but the breeze from Lake Michigan was refreshing. Clutching a small bottle of sunscreen that she always kept in her purse, Emma descended the outdoor flight of steps that led to the pool level. When she got there, she saw that Vanni was already in the water. He was swimming laps, knifing through the water, his muscled back flashing and gleaming in the bright sun. Emma shed the tunic and flip-flops and sat at the edge of the pool, dangling her legs into the cool water. She smoothed on the sunscreen, distracted by the spectacle of Vanni swimming with such effortless ease. She was rubbing some of the lotion onto her thigh, when he paused at the edge of the pool, swiping his wet hair from his face. He swam over to her in a more casual crawl.

"Don't let me interrupt you if you wanted to get more exercise," she said, feeling a little self-conscious in her new swimsuit beneath the hot sun and Vanni's stare. He grabbed ahold of the side of the pool with one hand, his forearm just an inch from her thigh. Her skin looked shockingly white next to his gilded glory.

"I'm fine. Here," he said, holding out his other hand. She realized he wanted her to hand him the sunscreen bottle. She gave it to him. His narrowed aquamarine eyes seemed to glow in his burnished face as he studied the label.

"It's a high enough SPF," he said approvingly. "You're very pale."

She blushed at his matter-of-fact assessment.

He handed the bottle back to her, placed his hands on the side of the pool, and heaved himself out of the water with a fascinating flex of muscle. A small amount of water sprayed her, but mostly she was spellbound by his show of effortless strength and male beauty. He wore a pair of black trunks. They hung very low at his hips, highlighting the full, glorious spread of his Adonis-like torso. She unglued her gaze from the image of his ridged, taut abdomen sheened by moisture moving subtly in and out as he breathed.

"I keep a bottle in my purse," she said holding up the sunscreen. Her fingers loosened in surprise when he reached for the bottle again. "I have to be prepared at all times, or else . . ."

"You burn?" Vanni filled in when she faded off. She watched him as he unscrewed the cap and squeezed a large dollop of the white liquid into his open hand.

"Yeah, but it's these I worry about," she pointed at her nose, "I really have to watch out for them getting worse," she admitted wryly.

His teeth flashed in his sun-darkened face. She tightened at her core. Vanni's smiles were like mainlining a sex stimulant.

"Your freckles, you mean?" He dipped his forefinger into the lotion and touched it to her nose. "I love these things," he said, rubbing the sunscreen into her skin carefully. Emma's eyes almost crossed as she watched him.

"You do?"

He nodded, his smile fading as he continued to smooth in the lotion." Very sexy," he said gruffly.

Her mouth fell open. His brows quirked.

"What? You don't believe me?" he asked.

"I *guess* so," Emma said, hiding her surprise. "It's just kind of hard to imagine, I've hated them for so long." He dropped his hand, apparently satisfied with that part of his task. He rubbed his hands together, spreading the lotion onto both palms. It was a very distracting sight.

"They're as adorable and fresh as the rest of you. Twist around a little so I can do your back and shoulders."

She did it quickly, glad for an excuse to hide her blush. He'd tease her about that, too.

"Is this stuff waterproof?" he asked from behind her as he spread the lotion onto her shoulders and the backs of her arms, kneading the muscles gently with strong fingers. The summer sun warmed the liquid. It felt wonderful.

"Yes," she murmured, feeling a little drugged by his massaging hands. He transferred them to her back. His fingers slid beneath the strap of her bikini. Her eyes sprung open when the clasp released. In one quick motion, he drew the top over her head and tossed it aside.

"*Vanni*," she said, stunned, her nipples prickling when a cool breeze swirled around them.

"What? There's no one around," he said unconcernedly, rubbing the lotion down her lower back.

"Oh. Okay."

His low chuckle near her ear made the hair on her neck stand on end. "You're blushing, aren't you?"

"No," she said, careful not to face him.

"If this makes you blush," he said, ignoring her denial. "You're going to be permanently red in the South of France."

It took her a second to figure out what he meant. "Oh . . . because they sunbathe topless there?"

"Don't worry, Emma," he said. She heard the smile in his voice and realized he'd probably heard the thread of her anxiety. "It's not like it's a law or something. You'll do whatever you're comfortable doing. Come here," he said quietly, his hands just above her waist. He hauled her into his lap. She squeaked in surprise, not only because she hadn't expected it, but also because he was wet and she wasn't.

As she settled, however, she realized he was warm beneath the cool moisture, and hard and . . . very nice.

"It's easier to get at all of you this way," he said, and she heard the sound of the bottle squeezing. She started to luxuriate at the sensation of sitting in his lap beneath a hot summer sun. She straightened in surprise, however, when instead of rubbing lotion onto her back, like she expected, he reached under her arms and cupped her breasts.

"Relax," he urged from behind her. It was a little hard to do, though, because his cock had twitched under her ass at the moment he touched her breasts. Plus, it felt decadent, having her breasts massaged by Vanni's lubricated, warm hands. He rubbed his whiskers gently against the back of her shoulder and she moaned. The slight abrasion in contrast with his squeezing, sliding hands sent a jolt of excitement through her. "You don't think I'd let these beauties burn, do you?" he asked next to her shoulder, his deep, rough voice a rich seduction. "They're even paler than the rest of you."

Emma swallowed thickly. The dancing blue water sparkled in her eyes, entrancing her. She couldn't think of what to say. She couldn't think of anything.

"Emma?" he said, and his sharp voice cut through her dazed arousal.

"Yes?"

"You're holding yourself off me. Stop it."

She blinked, coming to herself at his hard tone. She realized she'd placed her hands on the outside of his thighs and that her arms were tense.

"Oh," she said. It wasn't as if she'd literally been suspended over him, but she had been resisting giving him all her weight. She relaxed her arms, letting herself sink fully against his hard thighs and cock.

"That's better," he said, his hands still massaging her breasts. "Why do you always act like my cock is going to burn you or something?"

She heard the focused puzzlement in his tone. It both amazed and aroused her, the way he always spoke of sexual things without a trace of self-consciousness.

"I guess because it does," she admitted honestly. His massaging hands slowed. She felt him swell beneath her ass. "Not literally, obviously." She rolled her eyes in frustration at her lame explanation. "I just mean you overwhelm me," she said, closing her eyes, glad he couldn't see her scrunched-up face.

"And that's a bad or good thing?" he asked warily.

Her eyelids sprung open. Had he actually sounded worried? Vanni Montand?

"It's a very, very good thing," she assured. "I'm just not used to so much . . . potency."

He resumed massaging her breasts. She could almost hear him thinking behind her. He rubbed her nipples with his thumb and forefinger, the sensation delicious with the lubrication. She flexed her hips into his cock and whimpered.

The moment felt very ripe with sensuality—the hot sun beating down on them, his cock growing erect beneath her ass, his big, warm hands massaging her bare breasts; but there was a tenderness to the unfolding seconds as well, a breathless fragility. She'd sensed a crack in his golden, rigid armor and realized that despite all his effortless confidence, he wasn't all that different from her.

"Vanni?" she asked quietly, not looking around, but hyperaware of his face just behind her right shoulder.

"Yes?"

"Have you ever . . . done what we did . . . in the dressing room today?"

"Had sex in a department store?"

She laughed uncomfortably. "No . . . had sex without protection. I'm only asking because I haven't," she said quickly, anxious when he didn't immediately respond.

"You haven't?" he asked, his hands sweeping over her ribs and sides, spreading the lotion there. She shivered in pleasure and shook her head.

"Even though you were on birth control? Wasn't your relationship with Colin monogamous?"

"Yes. Or I thought it was," she said, thinking of Amanda and frowning.

"Why did you still use protection then?" Vanni asked behind her.

"It was my choice. And I don't know why," she said quietly, studying the rippling pool in front of her. "I was just thinking about that while I was showering before I came down."

A silence ensued as he rubbed some lotion along the tender strip of skin above her bikini bottoms. That thick, heavy pressure in her sex amplified. She suddenly felt hot. *Very* hot.

"Just once. With one woman, I mean . . . a long time ago," he said. She forced her attention back to the topic she'd broached. He was speaking of his wife, she knew by the tone of his voice. She wished she could ask him about her, but knew that had to be something he brought up. She couldn't force him to talk about it. His finger glided along that sensitive patch of skin. Her clit prickled with excitement at his nearness. "But otherwise, no," he mumbled. "Never."

"What?" she asked, her attention diverted once again by his magical hands.

"I haven't been with a woman like that in almost a decade. And there have been a lot of women, Emma."

His brutally honest words seemed to hang in the air around them.

"Is that because of what you told Astrid that night?" she asked shakily, continuing to avoid his gaze. It seemed safer somehow, talking to the shimmering pool. "About having little to offer a woman? Is it because you don't want to get too close to begin with?"

She sensed his tension at the question, but also his intent focus. Was he as caught up in the fragile moment as she was?

"Yes," he said quietly, still rubbing that strip of skin so close to her pussy.

"Do you not want to get too close because you're afraid of caring?"

His rubbing finger stilled. Emma couldn't expand her lungs in the silence that followed.

"Because you've lost so many people," she said on a gasp, already regretting her words, but knowing it was too late to turn back. *Typical me, always having to fall face-first into the graves I dig.* "I just thought maybe that was why you'd prefer not to get too close. This way, you don't have to lose anything else."

He still didn't say anything, although his hand remained frozen on her pelvis.

She rolled her eyes, disgusted with herself for having brought it up. She pushed off his thighs forcefully. The next second, she was dropping, cool water rushing around her overheated sex and cheeks.

If only she could stay underwater forever.

She felt his legs swoosh against her belly as she rose, and then his hands were on her upper arms, lifting them both in the water. She broke the surface with a gasp, laughing a little when she saw his wet, scowling face. He pushed his hair out of his eyes.

"Why'd you do that?" he demanded.

"I thought you might be getting tired of my questions," she said honestly, treading water. A rush of ebullience went through her at the delicious feeling of being in the cold pool in such a stunning setting. She spun in the water, looking around the landscaped terrace.

"It's so beautiful here," she said softly.

"Yeah . . . it's okay," he said, glancing around as if he hadn't seen it in a while. His gaze seemed to clear when he looked at her face again. "It's not La Mer, though."

"La Mer?"

"My villa near Saint-Jeannet. It's nestled on the cliff, but you can take a long staircase down the mountain to the Mediterranean. It was my father's family's home. Saint-Jeannet itself is this picturesque little medieval village. I can't wait to show it to you."

Emma blinked. He looked like a different man at that moment—relaxed and unguarded.

"It agrees with you," she said.

"What does?" he asked, brows quirked.

"La Mer," she murmured, studying his face. "You look happy when you talk about it."

"Do I?" he said, looking vaguely surprised.

She nodded. "Why don't you live there full-time?"

"Because my company is here. One of them, anyway. And because the Breakers is where I belong."

She hated the shadow that fell across his face. She found the Breakers to be sublimely beautiful, but she had a feeling Vanni felt trapped there, somehow. Not by physical barriers, but mental ones. Spiritual ones. She sighed, knowing she couldn't bring up such a weighty topic with him. But maybe she could lighten his mood, even in the midst of his shadows?

She splashed him full in the face. Emma couldn't help but laugh, seeing the aloof prince sputtering and blinking water out of his eyes, an incredulous expression dawning. Laughing, she splashed him again. His eyes flashed dangerously when he got the water out of them. She gave a little yelp, guessing his next move, and plunged back in the water. She swam for all she was worth, unable to contain her laughter despite the water that splashed into her eyes and mouth. She'd just reached the far side of the pool, when he grabbed her ankle and yanked.

"Where do you think you're going?" he growled, hauling her back against him.

She snorted with laughter, squirming in his firm hold. Things got worse when his fingers dug into her sides, tickling her.

"Oh no," she gasped, laughing. "*Stop*. I hate to be tickled."

"Well I hate having water splashed in my face," he replied dryly.

"You do?" she asked, her eyebrows pinching in concern despite her inability to stop laughing and writhing around in his hold. He sobered and his tickling abruptly halted. He grabbed on to the side of the pool, steadying them.

"*No*," he said, pulling her tighter against him so that her bare breasts crushed against the hard plane of his chest. His gaze traveled over her face hungrily. "I don't."

Then he was kissing her, deep and hard, his mouth hot in comparison to the cool water. Emma clutched his shoulders and forgot everything but the sensation of him.

"You give yourself so completely," he said quietly against her lips a moment later.

"What?" she asked, her lust-impaired brain having trouble decoding his words.

"Just now. When I make love to you. You give yourself completely every time I touch you," he said, his gaze traveling over her face with a tight focus. "I can feel it, Emma. I'm not sure it's a healthy thing for you."

"No?" she whispered.

He shook his head, a steely look overcoming his face as he stared at her lips. "No. But I'm becoming addicted to it, nevertheless."

Suddenly he was moving along the pool wall, pulling her with him. When he reached the shallow end of the pool, he transferred her, carrying her with one arm at her back, the other below her knees. He took the steps out of the water and walked onto the terrace, moving very quickly.

"Where are we going?" she asked him as he stormed toward the house, his gaze fixed on the entrance.

"To bed," he replied grimly.

* * *

He carried her all the way to his bedroom suite, closing the door behind them with a slam. Emma looked around curiously when they entered the bathroom. It was a wonderland, featuring warm, mahogany paneling on the walls, streamlined but beautiful white marble sinks, and a bidet. A small lounging area with two deep taupe armchairs and a table was arranged before a huge, deep, white marble tub. He set her in front of a stainless steel and glass shower. He opened the door and twisted the handle. Immediately water started to spout out from various directions and steam began to build.

"Get in," he urged, sinking his thumbs into his trunks. He pulled the waistband forward in order to release his cock and then bent to jerk them down his thighs. He stood.

"Emma?" he said in a hard tone.

Her gaze skipped up to his face. She'd been staring at his full, flagrant erection. It bobbed in the air, jutting out from his taut, toned body. He nodded at her bikini bottoms.

"Oh yeah," she mumbled, removing the last remnant of her clothing. He followed her into the shower and shut the door. "It feels so good," she moaned. Her wet skin had pebbled when he'd carried her swiftly through the air-conditioned house. The heat felt decadent on her overly sensitive skin. He stepped closer to her, chafing her arms. Emma went still at the sensation of the smooth, hard head of his penis against her belly. She looked up at him slowly. He was watching her, his gaze smoldering.

"Warm enough?" he murmured, still chafing her arms.

She nodded.

"Good," he said, his head lowering. He brushed his wet, firm lips against hers. "Your mouth is killing me," he said as he nibbled at her lips. "I'm going to have it now."

The sexual heat haze that had cocooned her popped. She stiffened. "I'm . . . I'm not very good at it," she said against his plucking lips.

He raised his head and looked down at her.

"Who says?"

"Me," she said honestly. Colin had never complained. It was just that Emma didn't like giving him oral sex. She found it uncomfortable and trying and . . . frustrating.

He frowned and reached to turn off the shower. He opened the door and steam billowed out.

"You're anxious again," he said, pulling her behind him into the palatial bathroom. He picked up a cushy white towel from a nearby rack and unrolled it.

"I can't help it," she said, a hint of misery in her tone. She hated to disappoint him, but—

He palmed her jaw and tilted her face up, halting her in midsentence. "I know. It's okay," he said simply. Her mouth sagged open. "You just haven't been introduced to it properly."

"There's a proper . . . introduction?" she asked awkwardly. He opened the enormous towel and started to dry her briskly.

"I suspect there is," he said wryly, chafing her back and ass with the towel.

"You mean you don't know?"

He bent his neck and pressed his forehead against hers. "We'll just play around a little bit. Nothing serious. Like we did with the desserts?" he reminded her gruffly.

"Oh," she said, a little amazed. And excited. "Okay."

She saw the glint in his eyes before he looked down to dry himself off hastily.

"It's like I told you before. I'm just making this up as I go along, Emma."

"How to be with a novice, you mean?"

"No," he said, taking her hand and leading her out of the bathroom. "How to be with you."

Chapter 26

They approached the great bed, where he dropped her hand and threw back the comforter and sheets and tossed aside a couple of decorative pillows. "Get in," he said, nodding at the bed. She clambered onto the mattress, sighing when he pulled the sheet and cover over her. It was a soft, cozy cocoon, but—

"Why aren't you getting in?" she asked him, propping herself up on a pillow with her elbow.

"I'm thinking," he said, looking distracted. "Do you mind telling me precisely what you didn't care for?"

She gave him a blank look.

"With oral sex?" he prompted.

"Oh," she said, her cheeks heating. "Well, you know, it's just . . ."

"What?" Vanni demanded when she faded off. Her gaze flicked over him. It was very difficult having this conversation with him naked. His beautiful body made things difficult. His erection was like some kind of neon sign flashing, blinding her, one that he didn't even seem to notice. She swallowed and looked away.

"I didn't hate it or anything, Vanni. I'm just no expert. And . . . it seems nicer for men than women, that's all," she mumbled. "I mean, that's what I used to think."

"You don't anymore?" he asked, taking a step toward her. She found herself staring at his cock again. It was only inches away from her face.

"No," she whispered. "I want to touch you very much. I want to please you, like you did me in that dressing room."

"You're not interested in figuring out a sure way to make that happen?" he asked, and she heard the humor in his voice. She looked up into his face and smiled.

"Of course I am. I'm just not sure how."

"You're not going to fail. Trust me. Right now, for instance, your eyes are doing a damn good job of turning me on . . . as usual."

She quirked her brows in confusion.

"Never mind," he mumbled. "Just touch me."

Her hand was already on the way. She wrapped her fingers around the shaft of his cock. He was heavy and hard and warm. She felt the subtle pulse of his heartbeat in the veins. His sharp inhale at her touch pleased her very much. She skimmed her hand upward over the defined rim beneath the crown, biting her lip in arousal at the sensation of the smooth skin covering dense flesh. Made bolder by her excitement, she ran her fist from balls to tip several times, holding up the shaft slightly so that she could stare at the virile vision of his round, heavy testicles. Her mouth watered.

"You're so beautifully shaped," she observed distractedly, running her hand up and down the shaft again. The crown especially excited her, smooth and defined, like the fat, tapered cap of a mushroom. "So hard." She flicked her fingers against the rim with extra force and heard him grunt softly. Before she could second-guess herself, she gave in to desire and leaned forward, inserting the large head between her lips. It excited her, how dense his flesh was, how warm, and yet the skin was velvety soft. She pushed slightly with her head and felt him parting her lips wide.

"Enough," he said roughly, and he stepped away. One second, she'd had the hard pressure straining against her lips, and the next it was gone, leaving her a little bereft . . . hungry.

She watched him in profile as he opened the bedside table, his cock jutting out between his strong thighs. Her eyes widened when he extracted the arch-shaped vibrator and remote control.

"I'm just going to slip this inside you while I get something," he said. "Do you need lubrication?"

Emma cleared her throat and averted her gaze. "I don't think so," she admitted. Things felt very warm and tingly at her sex. She'd practically melted into hot goo when she'd been sitting in his lap while he played with her breasts beneath a hot sun. That much arousal wasn't so easily rinsed away. Besides, she'd felt that familiar tickle and rush of heat with his fat cockhead pressed between her lips right now.

She saw his small smile as he turned to flip back the sheet. "I've told you, that's a good thing. There's no reason to be embarrassed."

"I know. I'm *not*," she insisted. His eyebrows arched expectantly.

"You know what to do," he prompted, his low voice making the prickling sensation at her clit amplify. "Anytime you see this in my hand, just open your thighs."

Licking her lip anxiously, she lay back on the bed and did what he said.

"That's right," he said, placing one knee on the mattress. He put the tip of his finger at her entrance, his jaw going hard. "You're right. You don't need anything. You're nice and warm and wet," he said gruffly. She bit her lip as he slid one side of the arch into her channel. She whimpered when he found her clit with his thumb, rubbing it once in a hard, tight circle, before he placed the other end of the arch on top of it.

He stood again, flipping the covers over her. "I'll be right back," he told her before he punched a button on the remote control. Emma started slightly as the vibrator buzzed to life, stimulating her. She stared covetously at the rear view of Vanni as he stalked out of the room to the walk-in closet, utterly insouciant and confident in his nudity.

He disappeared behind the door. She thought about what he wanted her to do. Her anxieties were free to surface. She recalled hiding in that armoire and hearing the subdued yet lewd sounds of Astrid giving him what sounded like strenuous, enthusiastic oral sex. She'd sounded quite expert.

He'd probably been with some of the most accomplished lovers in the world.

The sensation of the buzzing vibrator fractured her anxious ruminations. The instrument was starting to warm. Or she was. It wouldn't be so bad, would it? She certainly coveted Vanni's cock a lot more than she had Colin's. It was so beautiful, just like the rest of him, long and straight and thick. His testicles were the image of male virility, round and full, the sac gloving them tightly. The crown made her mouth water, so fat and luscious looking. She recalled how that thick, delineated rim felt beneath her lips. He hadn't let her feel it with her tongue just now, but he would give it to her . . . soon.

She moved restlessly on the bed, becoming aroused by the vibrator and her thoughts. If she became turned on enough, maybe her anxiety wouldn't get in the way and she wouldn't disappoint him?

A rustling resounded from the depths of the closet. He was preoccupied for the moment. She hastily picked up the remote control and turned it to a higher speed. She moaned softly at the increase in stimulation. It felt so good. She set down the remote and shoved a hand beneath the covers. She pressed quickly on the end of the vibrator next to her clit, sighing in pleasure.

The stimulation suddenly eased and she opened her eyes.

Vanni stood next to the bed, his finger on the remote. His expression looked hard, but his eyes were alight.

He flipped back the sheet, and she moved her hand away from her pussy hastily.

"Enjoying yourself?" he asked amusedly, sitting at the edge of the bed, his hip brushing against hers. His gaze moved over her, striking her, as usual, as cool and assessing and yet hot and scorching at once. His stare lingered on her breasts. Her nipples were very tight. "Never mind," he said dryly. "I have my answer."

"I didn't think you'd mind."

"I don't. This time." He met her stare. "I know that I let you have the controls the first time I used this vibrator on you, but I usually won't. I want you to let me be the one to control it. You said you wanted to please me before. *That* will. I want to know I'm responsible for your pleasure. Do you understand?"

Her channel clamped around the vibrator. She shifted her hips at the stab of arousal that went through her.

"Yes," she said honestly. He wanted to control her pleasure, the strength of it, the rate of it . . . the moment of detonation. *That* was what would please him. She was beginning to realize it would please her, too. Very much.

A smile flickered across his lips.

"Good. Now switch places with me," he instructed.

She rolled over, and he shifted to where she'd been, propping several pillows behind his back. For the first time, she saw that he held a small, clear bottle in one hand. He leaned back, his long legs bent and spread before him. "Come here." He gestured between his legs. "Kneel in front of me."

"Like this?" she asked a moment later, her knees bent, her bottom resting on her calves, her body upright.

"Yes. Put your hands on your thighs and arch your back," he added, eyeing her.

His gaze flickered over her breasts and belly when she took the position. She would have felt self-conscious about sitting there like that naked, her hands in her lap, her breasts thrust forward. It was a submissive pose, there was no doubt about it. But the vibrator was buzzing at her sensitive flesh, and Vanni was like a visual feast in front of her—an entire spread of gilded skin, hard muscle, and tumescent sex. And besides, she saw the way his gaze heated as he inspected her. He was pleased.

And so was she.

"You're very beautiful." She smiled because she heard the note of awed sincerity in his gruff voice.

"Did the vibrator stay in place?" he asked.

"Right on target."

His lips tilted at her quick response.

His hand opened, and he set the bottle of what she assumed was lubricant on the mattress. What was he going to do with that? He reached for his cock.

Her eyes widened when he looped something around the tip—a sort of thin black lasso. He pushed the flexible lasso down several inches of his cock. She blinked in amazement and looked up at him.

"Is that like a cock ring?" she asked hesitantly. She knew about cock rings. She was a nurse, after all, and had done training in an emergency room. It wasn't every day that a man presented with a cock ring ER nightmare, but they happened, and she'd been a witness to two, and heard tales of others.

"Why do you have that worried look on your face?" he asked.

"I'm a nurse," she said, shrugging. "Those things have been known to cause a man a real nightmare when the blood gets constricted and they get . . . stuck."

She blinked at his brilliant smile. "It's not a cock ring. And that's *not* what I'm using it for."

"Good," she said, relieved. "Because you don't have any problems with . . . you know. Being hard." *And beautiful and . . . delicious looking.*

"It's loose. See?" He wiggled the lasso slightly, proving his point. "I'm not using it to constrict anything. It's just a limit."

"A limit?"

He nodded, holding her stare. "You're only allowed to suck down to the limit. This time."

Her eyes widened as comprehension dawned. Relief rushed through her. She'd been worried about his size and girth, and he'd realized it. But she could handle this, couldn't she?

"Come here," he said, waving his hand in a beckoning gesture toward his cock. She bent and lowered her face over his lap, catching his male scent. Her mouth watered and she swallowed thickly. He picked up the lubricant from the mattress and opened it.

"I'm going to put this on the lower part of the shaft," he explained, his low, gruff voice causing the hair to prickle along her neck. He poured some of the lubricant on his hand. "I'll see to this, and you're responsible for the part above the limit," he explained. "But just watch for a moment, learn a little about what feels good to me."

She watched from her up-close position, her lungs burning in excited anticipation as he rubbed the shiny liquid up and down on his lower cock. Desire sluiced through her, sharp and breathtaking, at the vision of his big, male hand fisting his cock. He could encircle the girth completely, something she hadn't been able to do with her own hand. He pumped matter-of-factly, his actions quite forceful, shocking her a little. Every once in a while, he included his balls in his vigorous massage.

The smell of strawberries reached her nose and she inhaled. "It's scented and flavored," he said from above her, obviously noticing her appreciative sniff. "I have it specially made with a tincture of fruit extract. Unfortunately for you, tonight you only get the unflavored tip," he added, and she heard the smile in his voice. "Are you ready to suck?" he asked quietly as he continued to pump his cock.

She nodded fervently. Watching him jack himself was doing strange things to her. She suddenly felt single-minded. The stimulation on her pussy only seemed to amplify her hyperfocus on his cock. Given where he'd put the limit of the lasso, he got more of himself than she did.

She was jealous.

He lifted his left hand while he continued to pump his shaft with the other. He cupped the back of her head and brought her to him. She craned to take him, but he flexed his fingers into her hair, tugging back slightly.

"I'll instruct you," he said. She heard the sharp edge to his tone and tilted her head up to see his face. "I'm sorry," he said, obviously seeing her startled expression. "I want to make sure this isn't unpleasant for you, or it won't bode well for the future. But it will also turn me on, to tell you what to do. To tell you what I like. Okay?" he asked more gently.

"Yes," she agreed, giving him a small smile. If he instructed her, there was less of a chance she'd fail. He was setting up the scenario, in fact, so that she was guaranteed to succeed. A rush of gratitude and warmth for him went through her.

He stared down at her with a rigid focus. "Slip the head into your mouth. Lips nice and firm, hold me like a vice," he said. "I want to *feel* that hunger I always see in your eyes firsthand. If you want to show me what I see there right now, you can't be shy. *Suck*, Emma."

I want to feel *that hunger I always see in your eyes firsthand.*

Her lips strained around the head. She tongued him, curious and hungry, pressing to feel his shape. She wetted him, feeling that rim, laving it with a hard pressure . . . loving it. Finding the slit, she pressed, the salty taste of pre-ejaculate spreading on her tongue. He groaned and his pumping hand went faster.

"That's good. You have a strong little mouth. You're showing me, aren't you? How much you want to please me?" he murmured. She slipped her lips up and down on the head, clamping him, affirming her hunger. Her eyes sprung wide when she felt the buzz on her pussy amplify. He'd increased the power on the vibe. A moment later, he pulled gently on her hair, and his cock popped out of her mouth. She moaned feverishly at the deprivation.

"Wet it down to the limit with your tongue," he instructed gruffly, his hand still moving up and down on the shaft forcefully. She stared at his pumping fist as she licked his cock, tracing a distended vein, bumping against the thin silicone of the lasso—that limit to her hunger. Increasingly, she disliked that limit. She pushed at the thin silicone with the tip of her tongue. He was right; it wasn't tight. She nudged it farther down his cock, the flavor of strawberries spreading on her tongue . . . sweet, forbidden fruit.

"Emma," he grunted in warning, pulling back on her head. She looked up at him, her tongue still bathing his cock. His face went tight.

"Fuck," he muttered, his fist moving faster. He tugged gently on her head and pointed his cock toward her mouth, inserting it between her parted lips. "Show me," he demanded in a hard tone.

She knew what he meant. He wanted her to demonstrate her desire for him. The realization hit her that fellatio was the perfect way for a woman to do that for a man, if she truly felt it. It was a true surrender, a total abandonment for the pleasure of another . . . a finding of personal gratification in return for giving it. Emma yielded, giving herself to the feeling. Placing her hands on his thighs to give her balance, she sucked him into her mouth, giving her hunger free rein. Her lips bumped against the thin silicone lasso again and again as she squeezed him into her mouth. He filled her, even with the limit, the tip of his cock sliding along the length of her pressing tongue. When she sucked hard, her cheeks brushed against his flesh.

"Aw, yeah, that's good," he said in a choked voice. For a moment, his hand was gone from her head. The vibrator buzzed more strenuously, and his hand was back. She moaned in rising arousal and pumped him faster. It felt so good, the pressure on her lips, filling her mouth with his hard, pulsing flesh, the vibrator heating her . . . rewarding her hunger. In a frenzy of arousal, she pushed down harder, bumping her lips against the limit of the lasso, pushing it down slightly, wetting her lips with the lubricant, tasting strawberries on her tongue, gaining a half inch before he pulled back gently but firmly, with his fingers in her hair.

"You're getting greedy for it, aren't you, baby?" she heard him say, his voice thick with arousal.

She moaned an affirmative as she thrust her amount of allotted flesh in and out of her mouth, faster and faster.

"Here," he said, removing his pumping fist from his cock. He reached for her hand and put it where his had been. Instinctively, she tightened it. "You take over then. I like it hard, Emma. Grip me tight. Yeah, that's right. That's good." She squeezed him, both with hand and mouth, pumping him between her lips, the fever in her growing. Her eyelids flickered open when she felt liquid sprinkle against her knuckles. He'd poured additional lubricant on his cock. She gripped him tighter, appreciating the increased ease of the glide. So did he, if his rough moan was any indication. She loved that evidence of pleasing him.

She could grow addicted to it.

She lost herself to the rhythm, sucking and jacking him. Her hunger amplified. Again, her lips pushed at the limit, and the taste of strawberries spread on her tongue. For the rest of her life, she'd associate that taste with pure, rabid sexual hunger.

Vanni tightened his hold on her head, and for a split second, she felt him pushing, goading her on, encouraging her to swallow more of him.

Then he was pulling back. She cried out sharply when his cock popped out of her mouth. He put his hand on her wrist and jerked it off his cock. His cock fell to his taut belly, bouncing slightly.

"Sit up," Vanni grated out. She blinked, taking a few seconds to comprehend what he'd said, she was so aroused. "Scoot your knees closer to me. Now rise up on your knees."

She lifted her bottom off her lower legs and knelt before him, panting. His gaze lowered over her, scoring her face and breasts and belly. "Look at you," he said, his nostrils flaring. "Your cheeks are bright red, and your breasts . . ."

He faded off, his mouth shaping into a snarl. He opened one hand along her left hip, his thumb stretching beneath the vibrator. "You liked it, didn't you?"

"Yes," Emma gasped as he began to circle his thumb on her well-lubricated clit. Her buttocks clamped tight. She trembled. The soles of her feet began to burn. She was going to come.

"Tell me what you want," she heard Vanni say as if through a long tunnel. She bit her lip. She was about to explode. It felt *so* good.

"I want you to let me suck you again," she moaned miserably.

"Jesus," he hissed, putting the tip of the vibrator back against her clit "You're so fucking sweet." Then he was holding his cock up off his body, pushing her to him again. She took him into her mouth with a wild yet single-minded focus, squeezing him with her lips, sucking him until her cheeks hollowed out, ravenous. He groaned gutturally. Had he turned up the vibrator? She wasn't sure; all she knew was that the feeling of his cock swelling in her mouth was making her frenzied. Her head moved so fast, gobbling him forcefully, but it seemed like she ignited in slow motion.

Suddenly, climax hit her full force. She screamed onto his cock as her body shuddered. His fingers tightened in her hair, and he was jerking her off him. She continued to shake in orgasm, blinking her eyes open, disoriented. He pumped his cock, growling as he began to come. Semen jetted against her lips and she tasted him for the first time.

Ignoring his hold on her and the sting of her scalp, she leaned forward and took him into her mouth. His growl escalated to a roar as she sucked and he came on her tongue. He pulsed between her clamped lips, giving himself to her, and she craved—no, she *cherished*—every last drop.

A tense moment later, his fingers loosened in her hair. Emma released his cock from her mouth and fell forward slightly, her hot cheek falling above his hip bone. She still trembled from the onslaught of pleasure. She panted for air. His hand returned to the back of her head, his fingers rubbing her scalp. He shifted slightly and the vibrator stopped abruptly. She exhaled in relief. She hadn't realized until that moment how tense the continued stimulation on her post-climactic sex was making her.

"I don't think you have anything to worry about."

She lifted her head slowly, curious about the dazed, rough sound of his voice. Her eyes widened when she saw that he did, indeed, look a little undone, sprawling there on the pillows. He also looked indecently gorgeous.

"What?" she asked.

"You have a gift," he said, glancing down drolly at his damp, still-firm cock where it rested on his belly.

A smile flickered across her lips. They were sore from squeezing him so hard, but she found the sensation a pleasant reminder of her eagerness in showing him her desire . . . of his lesson in liberating it.

"No," she whispered, coming up on her knees and then lowering on top of him. She brushed her swollen lips against his mouth and felt him open his hand at her back. "You're the one with the gift, Vanni. Thank you," she murmured before he drew her closer to him with both hands, and kissed her in earnest.

After a delicious moment, she came up for air and settled her cheek on his chest, panting slightly. A feeling of lassitude and comfort overcame her when he rubbed her scalp with his fingers.

"Tell me more about your villa in France. La Mer," she said, her tongue lingering over the exotic-sounding words.

"You're going to see it soon."

"I know. But I want to hear you talk about it. What does it look like?" she prodded languorously.

"It's old," he began after a moment, sounding thoughtful. "La Mer was built in the late seventeen hundreds, but it's been renovated and added to many times. It's built in the Italian Renaissance style. I think there are secrets to it even Adrian and I—who explored it with single-minded intent for treasure and secret passageways as a kid—never discovered. But I like it that way . . . with a few secrets intact," he murmured, and she heard that faraway note in his voice, that wistful one that she'd seen on his face when he spoke of La Mer earlier. "It sits on the edge of cliffs, perched hundreds of feet above the sea. At night, with the windows open wide, you can hear the waves hitting the shore. It gets pitch-dark there, and it's always peaceful . . ."

Emma felt her eyelids growing heavy, listening to him talk. She fought sleep desperately, though, prizing the rare, wonderful experience of Vanni Montand sounding relaxed and content.

Week

SIX

Chapter 27

She fell asleep to the sound of his deep voice describing La Mer and his sweet, funny stories about Adrian and his childhood adventures there, fishing in the sea or playing knights in the surrounding countryside. She awoke to the sensation of his mouth blazing a trail of sensation across her neck, chest, and breasts, his upper body rearing over her, his hands holding her wrists above her head.

Later, she'd allowed him to bind her to the bed. He'd sensed her disquietude at being completely restrained—arms and legs both. He'd owned her anxiety, taking pains and expending patience to ease it, building her pleasure until he'd turned her uncertainty to dust from a conflagration of pure need. At one point after she'd surrendered to climax several times, he'd entered her, and she'd closed her eyes at the almost unbearable fullness of her desire.

Look at me, he'd demanded during those ecstatic moments as he pounded into her, taking her by storm.

With her eyelids clamped tight and his voice in her ears, she'd realized she was living a dream she'd had before. With a strange thrill, she'd pried open her eyes and saw him over her, naked and savage, bracing himself on muscular arms, his beautiful, ridged abdomen sheened with perspiration, his face rigid, his eyes burning straight through her. He thrust his hips and grunted gutturally, his muscular arms bulging huge, the twin tattoo flashing in her dazed eyes. She felt his cock jerk and swell. Then he was erupting inside her, his warm semen filling her.

"Don't you dare ever look away," he grated out fiercely as he came.

The next morning, they'd lingered in bed, stroking one another, talking of both serious matters and trivial ones. In a moment of mutual laughter, Emma had seen the warmth in his eyes and felt their bond tighten. Never again would she feel shy or self-conscious or disconnected from him.

At least that's what she'd thought at the time.

In the dark corners of her mind and spirit, however, that swelling feeling in her chest worried her. Had she given him too many days and weeks? If she felt like this now, how would she be weeks in the future?

It was like her present-day self—the woman who nestled skin to skin with Vanni, laughing and touching and making love, was sacrificing her future self, building up memories that one day would harm her, recollections that would pierce instead of warm. But it was so hard to acknowledge that looking into his face and seeing the heat in his eyes and his precious, small smiles . . . and every so often those bright, brilliant ones that made her heart squeeze in her chest.

There were moments when she thought she might sacrifice almost anything to see him happy, just once.

It was nearly impossible to focus on her future pain when she was in the intoxicating clutches of falling in love.

Finally, they'd arisen at around eleven and showered. It looked hot and sunny out when Vanni drew the curtains. He suggested they go for a swim, and then left her in the bedroom to retrieve the bikini top, sandals, and cover-up that he'd left poolside yesterday. When they went down together later, a table between two lounge chairs had been arranged with flowers, juice, coffee, fruit, and a covered basket of luscious-looking buns and rolls.

"Are there people in the house?" Emma asked after they'd swum and were eating their breakfast in the hot summer sun. She'd been curious about who had prepared the tray.

"Yes, Vera asked the cook for it and brought it out when I told her you were here," Vanni said as he paged through messages on his phone, looking every bit like a distracted bronzed god wearing nothing but his low-riding swim trunks.

"You told her I was here?" Emma asked, setting down her coffee. Vanni glanced up, doing a double take when he saw her expression.

"Vera? Yes. She'd already found your suit and things by the pool and brought them in, so she already knew someone was here. Why do you look like that?"

It was a little mortifying, thinking of Mrs. Shaw discovering clothing Emma'd removed during a sybaritic moment with Vanni. "I told you, she doesn't like me."

His eyebrows quirked at that. "It's what *I* think that matters." Emma rolled her eyes at his cockiness. His lips tilted and he handed her his phone. He clearly thought the topic of Vera was too inconsequential to pursue.

"Call Mrs. Ring. Let her know you'll be leaving tomorrow and won't return for two weeks."

She gave a heavy sigh. He was right. If she was going to do this, she'd better get it over with. "All right," she said, "but don't expect any miracles. I have the vacation days, I'm just not certain they'll be able to cover for me. It's not protocol for requesting a vacation, and it's such short notice."

"Just call," Vanni said, opening a newspaper that had been placed on the tray.

She realized he'd already found the number for her. She gave him a "here goes nothing" glance and called the hospice.

"It's not a problem. Maureen can cover for you," Mrs. Ring said a moment later after Emma had explained about needing time off for an unexpected situation that had occurred.

"That's incredible, I'm so relieved," Emma said. She glanced over at Vanni, barely containing her excitement. He gave her a small smile and resumed reading his paper.

I'm really going with him. Me—Emma Shore—*in the French Riviera with Vanni Montand. Incredible.*

"You're an excellent employee, Emma. You often cover for others when we've needed you with no complaint. We appreciate that here. Besides, no one should have to pass up an opportunity to go to the South of France. I'm quite envious," Mrs. Ring was saying. Emma blinked, her gaze fixing blindly on the sparkling pool.

"I never said where I was going, did I?" Emma asked her supervisor dubiously.

"Isn't that where you plan to go?" Mrs. Ring asked.

"Well, yes, but . . ." She turned her head and stared at Vanni, her mouth hanging open. His eyebrows furrowed and he briskly folded up his paper.

"You'd called Mrs. Ring *already*?" Emma asked in a hushed, incredulous tone a moment later after she'd hung up the phone.

He lifted his eyebrows and gave a small, almost imperceptible nod. "I wanted to make sure you had the time off."

"You wanted to make sure you got your *way*," she said, stung. "I can't believe you did that, Vanni," she said, anger entering her tone. She swung her legs off the lounger, placing her feet on the hot slate terrace. She suddenly felt like she couldn't look at him, she was so pissed off.

"Why is it a problem that I smoothed things over for you with your work?"

"That's what you'd call what you did? *Smoothing things over*? That's my *job*, Vanni," she exclaimed heatedly. "Maybe you think it's some kind of unimportant sideshow—I'm not a *doctor*, after all," she said, remembering how he'd asked her why she hadn't gone to medical school when Amanda was going. His eyes flashed. "But my job is important to *me*. You had no right to barge in and demand I get time off!"

His expression stiffened in rising anger. She couldn't believe he didn't understand how heavy-handed and domineering he'd behaved. He was overtaking her mind and her body and her life, and he couldn't seem to understand how much emptier that would make her when he was gone.

"You've already bought my home! Now you have to buy off my employer as well?" she demanded, standing abruptly.

"I didn't buy anybody off," he said through a hard mouth. "I simply put in a phone call to Mrs. Ring to explain the situation."

"To explain what *you* wanted the situation to be," Emma corrected as she picked up her cover-up. "And of course she was all too eager to make that happen. Don't try to tell me that you didn't make a huge charitable donation to the hospice. I suspected it ever since they assigned us to Cristina around the clock. That's not normal operating procedure for us."

"What if I did?" Vanni asked. How could he look so hot and sun-gilded reclining there, while his tone and eyes were frigid? "It's a good cause. And I wanted special care for Cristina."

"And you don't think all the money you sent Mrs. Ring's way had any effect whatsoever on her decision to give me a vacation on the spur of the moment when you requested it personally?" Emma asked sarcastically, trying to put on her cover-up and twisting it hopelessly because of her angry, jerky motions.

"I have no idea if it did or not," he said.

"Give me a break," Emma said disgustedly, jamming her foot into a flip-flop.

"Where are you going?" he asked sharply when she started to walk toward the house and the dressing room. Her clothing was still in there.

"Home. You know, that apartment *you* own?" she asked scathingly over her shoulder.

"Emma, stop."

She halted instinctively at his tone, but her immobility seemed to make the fury in her chest froth even higher. He touched her upper arm and she turned to see him standing there, his blue-green eyes seeming to glow in his tanned, shadowed face.

"I'm sorry if you think it was intrusive of me," he said stiffly. "I did it because I wanted to make things easier for you. Don't make more of this than it is."

Her eyes burned. "But it *is* more, Vanni."

"What do you mean?"

"I mean that you've offered me a limited affair, and I've accepted. You've agreed to give little of yourself, besides what you offer in bed," she said, her voice shaking with emotion. "You can't do that and then try to control the private parts of my life as well . . . my home, my clothing, my job. It's not *fair*."

"Emma, listen to—"

"No," she cut him off. Everything seemed to fall down on her all at once, crushing her, making breathing difficult. The whole situation with Mrs. Ring had flipped the lid off her anxiety . . . her fear that she was going to be hurt by him . . . her growing certainty. "Please send back all the clothing you bought for me yesterday."

His expression went flat. "What about our trip?"

"I'm not going," she said before she broke his hold on her arm and walked toward the house.

Wednesday evening, Emma heard a knock on her bedroom door. She quickly grabbed a tissue from her bedside table and wiped her cheeks and eyes.

"Come in," she called.

Amanda poked her head into the crack of the partially open door.

"I made grilled salmon and a big casserole of Mom's macaroni and cheese," she said, her gaze running over Emma's face concernedly. Emma gave her a tired, knowing smile. It'd been their favorite meal when they were kids. Amanda was trying to cheer her up, her worry mounting ever since Emma returned home on Monday afternoon, pale and upset. Emma had provided her sister with the skeleton of an explanation for her emotional state, saying she and Vanni had fought, and that she had canceled a trip to attend the Montand French-American Grand Prix with him. Amanda had been amazed by the news, but tried to be supportive and not ask too many questions.

After their confrontation, Vanni had finally agreed to take her home, but he'd been tight-lipped and fuming for the whole drive.

"You *do* realize that I have to leave tomorrow, whether you come or not?" he'd demanded when he parked the Montand sedan in her apartment parking lot.

"I know it," Emma had said, staring out the window because it was too difficult to look at him.

"And you're still going to continue with this . . . this *tantrum*?" he'd asked.

That'd poured fuel on her simmering anger. She flared like a flash fire. "Just the fact that you're calling this a *tantrum* proves my whole point. I'm not a child! What you did wasn't a small thing to me, Vanni," she'd grated out, reaching behind her neck to unfasten the Prisatti angel. She was choking with fear over her realization that she was falling for him, and that he would leave her. Soon. The angel was a constant reminder—

"Don't you *dare* take that thing off," Vanni had seethed, his low voice vibrating with emotion.

Her gaze had flown to his face. She flinched at the blazing fury and wild helplessness in his stare. Repressing a groan of misery, she clambered out of the car and slammed the door.

Since then, he'd called several times, but Emma had stubbornly refused to speak to him. She tried to return to work—the distraction would have done her good—but thanks to Vanni's interference, all the shifts were covered. There was nothing for her to return *to* until she supposedly returned from France in two weeks' time. She'd kept to herself for days, avoiding her sister and Vanni's calls.

Avoiding the truth, and failing.

"You really are brilliant," Emma said presently to Amanda, tossing aside the crumpled tissue onto her bedside table. "You figured that if anything could get me out of this funk, it's carbohydrates."

"I figured it couldn't hurt to try," Amanda said with a hopeful smile, stepping into the room. She came and sat at the foot of Emma's bed. "Are you okay?"

Emma nodded.

"Liar," Amanda said ruefully.

"What is it?" Emma asked, noticing her sister's hesitance.

"Vanni called me. Just now," Amanda admitted.

"What?" Emma asked, stunned.

Amanda nodded. "He said you were refusing to talk to him, but he wanted to leave an important message. He said that his pilot was flying back to the States as we speak. The message was that he has everything arranged for you to fly to meet him at his villa in the South of France. He said . . ."

"What?" Emma demanded when Amanda faded off reluctantly, hungry for the rest of the message despite her uncertainty . . . desperate for news of *him*.

"He said all you need to do is get on the plane. He has everything you'll need already there. His pilot, Marco, knows where to take you when you arrive. And he said . . . he expected you to come," Amanda said delicately.

"*Expected*?" Emma asked, her spine stiffening in rising anger.

Amanda nodded, studying her with sober blue eyes. "He said you'd agreed to spend the time with him, and that you weren't the type to go back on your promise."

Amazement broke through her anger. He really *did* have balls, sending a message like that. She once again sensed Amanda's hesitation.

"What else did he say?" she asked slowly.

"He said to remind you that you'd agreed to 'whom these days and hours belong.' And he said to say that you aren't a coward. What did he *mean* by that?"

Blood started to pound in her ears in the taut silence that ensued. She shook her head, her throat too thick to answer Amanda's question.

"Emma, I'm trying not to butt in, because I can tell you don't want to talk about this thing with Vanni," Amanda said quietly. "But I can tell you really like him. Are you worried you like him too much?"

"I'm worried I more than like him, Amanda. Much more," she said in a choked voice.

Amanda's eyes widened. "Oh. I see. No wonder you're worried about going to France."

Emma just nodded.

"It's just . . ." Amanda hesitated, clearly torn between speaking or not.

"What?" Emma asked.

"Well, you were the one who told me after Colin and I . . ." She faded off, but then rallied. "You were the one who said it was worth it to take a risk for passion. And I happen to agree with Vanni about one thing for certain."

Emma gave her a querying glance.

"You're not a coward, Emma. You never were," Amanda repeated. "He told me to give you this. He said as soon as you called, this man would arrange everything." Emma glanced briefly at the piece of paper with the name Marco Hagan and a phone number with an international prefix on it.

She remained unmoving, watching her sister leave the room.

Chapter 28

Emma was feeling some strange combination of nervousness, ebullience, and exhaustion when the sleek plane landed at the Nice Côte d'Azur Airport early on Friday morning. She hadn't slept much on the transatlantic flight, too awed by the luxury of the private plane Vanni had sent for her and excited about the prospect of seeing the French Riviera for the first time . . .

. . . Too overrun with anticipation at the thought of seeing Vanni again.

She still didn't appreciate his heavy-handedness in regard to her job and so many other things, but she did know one thing. She'd sent him away Monday because she was overwhelmed by what was happening between them. Vanni had known that. His message to Amanda was meant to prick her pride. But it'd been more than that.

I need you there.

She recalled him saying those words before Cristina's funeral. And whether she was a fool or not, she somehow had heard a similar, secret message in the one he'd given Amanda. Like before, she hadn't been able to refuse.

As Marco taxied the plane along the tarmac, she stared out the window onto a glorious Mediterranean summer day. The air itself seemed saturated with golden sunlight. As they'd landed, she'd seen the picturesque orange, pink, green, and white roofs of luxury residences and hotels that cascaded down the mountainside to the brilliant azure sea. The sea itself was dotted with thousands of tiny white boats and yachts. It was a scene right out of a glamorous Montand car commercial. Her excitement was huge, but she suddenly regretted not flying there with Vanni. She already felt out of place as things stood, an outsider who didn't know what to expect. Arriving there alone, she didn't have Vanni's epic confidence to ease her anxiety.

"Vanni isn't coming?" she asked Marco tentatively after they'd passed through customs and headed to a parking garage. Marco rolled an enormous trunklike suitcase behind him but still insisted upon carrying Emma's duffel bag.

"He couldn't. Time trials for the race were held this morning, so he's been busy with that," Vanni's pilot explained. He was a stocky, friendly American in his forties with reddish-blond, thinning hair and fair skin that looked as if might be perpetually sunburned. He'd acted like it was the most natural thing in the world for him to cross the ocean to go and pick her up at his boss's orders, an attitude Emma appreciated.

It also bothered her a little.

Did Marco regularly go on runs to fulfill Vanni's companionship requirements?

Marco stowed the bags in the trunk of a sedate, black luxury sedan and then opened the passenger door for her. "Vanni's schedule has been pretty booked up with last-minute planning for the race on Sunday and a bunch of pre-racing events. Do you like racing?" Marco asked conversationally once he'd gotten into the driver's seat and started the engine.

"I'm afraid I don't know all that much about it," Emma admitted. "But I've been listening to Vanni. I gather he's going out on a limb a bit, using stock cars instead of the Formula Ones?"

Marco nodded as he fleetly maneuvered out of the parking facility. "There was some initial resistance on the locals' part, but that's all in the past. Vanni's got himself a world-class race on his hands. He assured that by signing the best drivers from all over the world, whether they race stock cars or F1's. It helped that he and Niki are best friends. Once Niki Dellis agreed, everyone signed up just for a chance to beat him. It didn't hurt that Van also acquired the crème de la crème of society to sit on the racing committee and make crucial decisions. With that on his side, he eventually won over any local resistance. Everyone is pouring to the coast in droves, dying to see who will prevail in the race. It's American-style cars, but it's on a traditional European road-racing circuit, so both sides have something to prove. I shudder to think about all the money changing hands this week in the casinos."

"Are there clear favorites to win?" Emma asked, interested.

"On the American front, Tito Burton, Joe Hill, and Santo Howles are top runners, the three of them have over a dozen NASCAR championships between them. On the Formula One side of things, the betting favorites are Mario Acarde, a flashy Italian driver with fifteen grand prix wins under his belt, and Niki, who has six world titles. Niki drives Montand cars, but always Formula One racers in the past. He won the pole position this morning in the time trials, so Vanni's got to be pleased about that."

"Wow, I didn't realize Niki was so good."

"The best. You've met him?" Marco asked.

"Yes."

"Niki and Vanni go way back . . . family connections," Marco said.

They began to climb the rugged mountainside in the sedan. Marco took a tight turn that looked down on the stunning coastline. Emma felt like she'd left her stomach two hundred feet behind them. She trusted Marco, but she suddenly wished it were Vanni behind the wheel taking the hairpin turns with his usual effortless handling.

"It seems like all of you have to be part racecar driver just to go to the grocery store around here," she said a moment later, glancing down nervously at the steep drop-off on the side of the road.

"The French Riviera is no place for the faint of heart, that's for sure. It's a strange paradox of people living fast and furious and at the same time, being experts on relaxation. They call it a playground, and it is, but it's a fierce one. Playing on the Côte d'Azur can become an intoxicating . . . and dangerous business," Marco said amusedly.

"I'll bet."

"How beautiful," she said in awe a while later as they passed the ancient village of Saint-Jeannet set high in the mountains. It sat on a ledge between two looming cliffs overlooking the sea far below. Winding streets passed medieval-looking buildings and stunning vista terraces. "Oh, look," Emma pointed out, smiling at the red, white, blue, and black flags hanging from lampposts along the street proclaiming the Montand Franco-Américain Grand Prix.

Marco grinned. "The locals are buzzing about the race almost as much as the people pouring in to all the top-notch hotels to watch it. Vanni is considered a local boy, and not just because his father started his car company in Antibes nearby. The Montand family has deep roots in the Côte d'Azur," Marco explained.

He made his way out of the village, eventually driving onto a thickly wooded road that was so twisting, Emma quickly couldn't say which direction she was facing anymore. She kept catching a glimpse of the Mediterranean in the far distance and a burnt red slate roof nestled among lush green treetops. Finally, Marco pulled into a secluded drive and there was the villa before them, a white limestone structure with a red roof, sprawling and enormous, yet nestled quite comfortably in the forest and cliffside, almost as if it had been there so long, it had become part of the natural landscape.

"La Mer," she breathed out, staring wide-eyed at the ancient home. "Vanni loves it here."

Marco gave her a swift, speculative glance, and she wondered what he'd heard in her voice. He brought the car to a halt. "That he does," he said. "He's a little happier, when he's here. I don't understand why he doesn't live here all the time, but . . . that's not for me to decide."

Emma glanced at him. She had an uncomfortable suspicion of why Vanni refused to give up the Breakers—the site of so much tragedy.

A minute later, a dark-haired, aproned, middle-aged woman who introduced herself as Mrs. Denis led them into a circular, sunlit entryway that featured a white alabaster grand staircase and windows that went up for three stories. Such a lovely, bright, airy home, Emma thought admiringly as she stared around in awe. Even though the finishes were ornate, there was an openness to the rooms that she spied off the entryway, an approachability. Emma inhaled deeply of fresh sea air and . . .

"Is that bread baking?" she asked Mrs. Denis.

The housekeeper smiled. "I am always baking something."

"Lucky for us," Marco said amusedly.

Down a hallway, Emma saw a huge terrace that was open to the interior. Fresh sea air wafted into the elaborate entry hall. Bright flowers in huge clay pots waved in the gentle breeze on the terrace. Mrs. Denis noticed where Emma looked.

"Come," she said in her French-accented English. "You'll sit on the terrace and I'll bring you some refreshment. Vanni has told me you drink tea. Some chamomile, perhaps, so that you can rest after your flight?"

"Thank you, that'd be nice."

"I'll just put your bag upstairs and see you later," Marco said.

"Thank you so much," Emma replied warmly. "For everything, Marco."

"Not a problem. You enjoy yourself. I have a feeling you might be able to get Vanni to relax a little, despite the whirlwind of the race," the pilot said.

"I'll try," Emma said, returning his friendly wave before she followed Mrs. Denis outside.

"I'll just go and get your tea and make sure Marco gets something to eat before he goes. He *always* has an appetite. I wish I could get him to share some of it with Vanni," Mrs. Denis said with a grin before she bustled inside.

Emma walked out onto the terrace, her mouth falling open in delighted awe. The stone terrace was huge, running the entire length of the house. It was filled with fruit trees, flowers, and seating areas. In the distance, rocky cliffs sharply dropped off, but she caught sight of a white staircase. It must meander down to the sea. Far below them, the brilliant blue Mediterranean took up the entire horizon. It was the most breathtaking view she'd ever seen. She soaked in the sunshine and the stunning view for several minutes, standing next to a three-foot-tall stone wall covered in vines and blooming roses. She inhaled deeply of the sea air. The smell of gardenias and roses wafted into her nose. She could almost see Adrian and Vanni on the terrace as children . . . Adrian staring at the magnificent landscape dreamily while Vanni excitedly described some new adventure for them to undertake. Adrian would have calmed his fire, and Vanni would have infused Adrian with energy and purpose. How was it that she could picture Vanni so easily as an animated, happy child when she'd only ever known him as sober and controlled?

Resigned to his sadness?

Perhaps it was because of the trace of wistfulness in his tone when he'd talked about Adrian and him at La Mer as boys. Maybe it was because of the glimpses she caught of him when he made love, and she saw beneath the aloof surface to his fierce, savage soul.

Her thoughts weighed on her. Why couldn't he make La Mer his permanent home? Why couldn't he completely reclaim the happiness he'd once felt there?

And . . . tell Vanni . . . to forgive himself. I know he thinks it's his fault.

Some of Cristina's final words rose to haunt her at that moment, a sad, poignant reminder in such a sunny, beautiful, peaceful place.

"It's lovely, isn't it?" Mrs. Denis said from behind her. Emma turned from the stone wall and saw the housekeeper laying a tea service on one of the wrought iron tables. Formerly, "tea" meant a bag and hot water in one of Emma's mismatched mugs, but since Vanni had entered her life, it was an event.

"I've never seen anything to compare to it," Emma agreed as she walked over to the table. "How long have you worked at La Mer?"

"It'll be twenty-five years this winter," Mrs. Denis said, setting the delicate antique teapot on the table along with a tiered plate filled with cakes, slices of aromatic, thick whole-grain bread, and a dish of butter. Emma's mouth watered. "It's hard to believe, especially since La Mer hardly ever changes. It's the same old house I remember from my first weeks here."

Emma smiled and sat when Mrs. Denis pulled back a chair at the table for her. "Some things should always remain the same. La Mer is definitely one of those places. I can see why Vanni loves it so much." She started to pour, but Mrs. Denis beat her to the task.

"He does love it here. I only wish he'd be in residence more," Mrs. Denis said. Her gaze sharpened on Emma as she set down the teapot. "I've never heard the tone in his voice before—the one I hear when he speaks of you."

Emma's fingers fumbled the silver cake knife she'd picked up. She looked at the housekeeper in surprise. "Really?"

Mrs. Denis shook her head, a sparkle in her black eyes. "If I had to guess, I'd say that Vanni thinks you're special."

Emma felt her cheeks heating. "That's so nice, but it's not as if . . . that is . . . Will Vanni be away for the entire day?" she fumbled, changing the topic because she didn't know how to respond to the news. Mrs. Denis's kind observation warmed her to her very core, but she didn't know how to tell Mrs. Denis that she'd likely never return to La Mer, given the parameters of her relationship with Vanni.

"Yes, but I just called to tell him you'd arrived," Mrs. Denis said, stepping back, her hands folded at her waist. "He asked me to tell you to rest up after your trip. He's going to take you to Cannes this evening for a dinner planned for the drivers, their teams, and the racing committee at the Hôtel et Casino 'Le Majestueux.' We just call it Hôtel Le Maj, for short. It will be *très glamour.* All of the surrounding villages are very excited for the race, too," she said, her toothy grin making her look years younger. "We're having our own little celebrations at the café in town tonight, although it will be nowhere near as fancy as the one you'll be going to with Vanni. Vanni has a special reason to celebrate, too, since Niki won the pole position for the Montand car today. Is everything all right?" Mrs. Denis asked, obviously noticing the shadow that crossed Emma's face.

"Yes, of course. Thank you for the tea."

"I probably shouldn't have spoken about Vanni's feelings. What do I know? It's not as if he ever says anything of significance to me. Still, an old woman gets used to reading a man when she's known him since he was this high," she said, indicating a place on her leg below her apron. Emma smiled. "Forgive me if I made you uncomfortable," she said. Emma was moved by her sincere, warm manner.

"You didn't. You've made me feel very comfortable here, in fact," Emma assured.

"I'll keep an eye out for you. When you're finished, I'll show you to Vanni's suite. He said to put you there."

"Thank you," Emma said, watching as the housekeeper left her to her tea.

In truth, she hadn't looked worried because she was thinking of what Mrs. Denis had said about Vanni's tone of voice when he spoke of her. It'd been the mention of the dinner they'd be attending tonight that reminded her uncomfortably that she'd told Vanni to return all the clothing he'd so generously bought her. Had he carried out her request or ignored it? He'd told Amanda in his message that she needed to only bring herself, and he'd have everything arranged for her. She'd taken him at his word, bringing only some bare necessities and toiletries. Now that she was here in these glamorous surroundings, however, she started to "get" just how truly out of place she'd be wearing one of the sundresses she'd brought.

A half hour later, Mrs. Denis led her down an arched-ceiling, whitewashed stone hallway to a closed door.

"Oh, how lovely," Emma breathed out when she followed the housekeeper into the room. Like the rest of the house, it was flooded with sunlight from an entire wall made of French doors. It was a large, wide-open room, simple in design, containing a huge iron bed with pristine white bedclothes, two armchairs, and a sofa situated before an ancient-looking fireplace and a fantastic carved antique armoire made of dark stained wood. She saw the large trunk Marco had brought from the plane next to the armoire. Flowers were everywhere, cut ones arranged skillfully on the mantel, bedside, and on the table in the seating area. There were also living ones outside on the shallow terrace beyond the French doors, waving in the sunshine. In the distance was the brilliant azure sea.

"Do you have everything you need?" Mrs. Denis asked her after she'd showed her the bathroom suite and how to regulate the temperature in the room.

"Yes, thank you."

"Vanni says it'll be a late night. Why don't you rest?"

"I'll definitely try."

The housekeeper smiled and left her. Emma took a quick shower and freshened up in the bathroom, then changed into a pair of shorts and a tank top. Instead of drawing the drapes like Mrs. Denis had showed her, she opened a pair of French doors and crawled into the sumptuous bed. She pressed her cheek to one cool down pillow and inhaled deeply. Not finding what she craved, she switched pillows, smiling contentedly as she nestled deeper.

She fell asleep to the sound of the wind rustling in the trees and the sea in the distance, the scent of Vanni filling her nose.

Chapter 29

"What are you smiling about while you dream, *mon petit ange*?"

Emma's eyes sprung open at the sound of his deep, resonant voice in her head.

Vanni looked down at her from where he sat at the edge of the bed. He wore a blue-and-white striped shirt and cobalt blue tie along with a pair of gray pants. The bangs of his brown hair had fallen forward, parenthesizing his sea-colored eyes. She'd never been so glad to see anything in her whole life than she was his face in that moment.

She reached up and touched the scruff on his lean jaw, assuring herself he was there.

"You," she replied with sleepy honesty.

The small smile faded from his firm lips. He leaned down and kissed her, his slow, patient cadence quickly turning faster and more forceful. His hand trailed down her side and cupped her hip, rolling her closer to him. She moaned into his mouth and delved her fingers into his hair, losing herself in his taste.

"I don't appreciate you depriving me of this," he firmed his hand on her hip and plucked at her lips, "for four whole nights."

"I was . . . mad at . . . you," she reminded him, kissing him back hungrily.

"Are you still?" he murmured, biting gently at her lower lip. Emma shivered in delight, and he pulled her closer into his arms.

The truth was, it was nearly impossible to stay mad with him nibbling at her mouth and his scent filling her nose, especially when she hadn't seen him for days. "Sort of," she mumbled, returning the favor and scraping her teeth along his lower lip, her actions completely at odds with her words. He gave a low groan and swept his hand along her waist and ribs, stopping next to her breast. He cupped her side. "I don't like being manipulated, Vanni."

"I wasn't manipulating you," he said, glancing up to meet her stare. "I only have you for so long, Emma. Do you really blame me for wanting you every minute I possibly can? I was trying to ensure that by calling Mrs. Ring in advance. You say I did it for myself, and maybe I did. I told you I was selfish from the beginning."

For a moment, she didn't speak. She understood he wasn't used to being in relationships. He handled her like he would any other task in his busy world.

"I'm not something to check off your work list," she said quietly. "But I do understand that you were doing it with good intentions. It's just that my work is . . ."

"Your domain. I understand," he said soberly. "I won't do anything like that again. But I can't regret it this time," he said pointedly, his nostrils flaring slightly as he looked down at her. His hand slid down to her ass. He cupped a buttock and kneaded it with his large hand, making her thoughts scatter. "I wanted you here."

"And whatever Vanni wants, Vanni gets?" she asked dryly, although she knew full well it was the absolute truth most of the time.

"Obviously not, or you would have been here sooner. But yes, I was willing to do whatever was necessary to make it happen. It didn't happen as quickly as I would have wanted, but you're here now," he said, his gaze narrowing on her face as he squeezed her buttock and stroked the slope of her hip, his manner intent and thrillingly possessive. "I'm too happy about it to apologize."

"Congratulations on the Montand car winning the time trials today. Marco told me," she said softly.

"Luck came with you," he said, leaning down to capture her mouth with his. By the time he lifted his head from their kiss a moment later, her flesh had gone warm and tingly, her sex soft and liquid.

"I do regret one thing about my protest, now that I'm here," she said, scraping her fingernails along his neck and feeling the slight shudder that went through him. It was intoxicating, knowing how her touch affected him. She saw his dark brows go up in a query when he noticed her anxious expression.

"Mrs. Denis told me about the dinner tonight," she explained. "You said not to bring anything in the message you sent through Amanda. Is the wardrobe you bought me here in France?"

"You said you wanted me to return it all, so I did," he said, his expression deadpan. Her heart seemed to plummet into her belly. She hadn't actually expected him to say that. She'd never regretted her angry outburst more. "Isn't that what you told me you wanted?" he prodded quietly.

She nodded, trying to look happy about his decision. She couldn't be *both* miffed at his heavy-handedness and desirous of his gifts at once. But she didn't want the glamorous clothing for herself, she wanted them because she didn't want to embarrass him . . . or *herself*, she added fairly in the privacy of her mind. His handsome mouth quirked slightly in amusement.

"You don't really think I'd leave you without resources after insisting that you attend the race with me, do you?"

"What do you mean?" she asked, confused. "Did you return the clothes, or not?"

"I did," he said briskly, straightening. He took her hand. "But I had Marco go to the Breakers and get something else for you there. My aunt Michelle—Dean's wife—helped me arrange it. And this *something* I'm referring to truly is yours. You won't have to worry about accepting anything from me."

"What?"

"Come here," he said, tugging on her hand when she just stared up at him in amazement. She followed him across the room to the trunk Marco had taken off the plane. He flipped it on its side and opened it. Inside, there were several garment bags that had been folded once, one on top of another. He drew some keys out of his pant pocket and grabbed several of the garment bags.

"Follow me," he said, turning. She trailed him to a door. He used a key to unlock it and swung it open. He flipped on a light, and Emma followed him into a large walk-in closet. Very quickly and efficiently, Vanni unzipped the two garment bags, scooted aside some of his neatly hung suits, and placed what appeared to be dresses upon dresses on the rack.

"Oh, they're *gorgeous*," Emma whispered, stepping forward to touch a stunning, gold evening gown, then a showstopping black textured gown with a fitted white bodice and cutout back, followed by a darling red day dress . . . they went on and on. She looked up at Vanni in confusion.

"Did you return the ones you bought me and buy *different* ones?" she asked.

"No. These are yours. Bequeathed to you by Cristina."

"What are you talking about?"

"Apparently, she contacted her lawyer in the last days before she died and altered her will, leaving you her entire wardrobe, shoes, accessories . . . everything. It's no small thing," Vanni said, his lips tilting in dark amusement. "Cristina was a real clothes hound, and was often named one of the best-dressed women on the planet. Most of these dresses have never even been worn."

"She and I did discuss her love of fashion," Emma said numbly, her mind trying to make sense of what Vanni was saying. She couldn't believe this was happening. Part of her was stunned, part of her deeply moved by Cristina's gesture. "She and I talked about her shop and she actually . . ."

"What?" Vanni asked when she faded off.

"She said she wanted me to have all her clothes. I didn't take her seriously, though. I only knew her for a little over a week."

"I told you she liked you," he said quietly.

His eyes looked shrouded in the dim light of the closet, but she saw the glint in them as he stared at her. Emma touched the dresses in a mixture of awe and sadness. "I probably shouldn't accept them . . . but I will," she said with breathless resolution. Cristina had wanted her to have them, for whatever reason. Emma thought enough of her not to refuse such a lavish, thoughtful gift. Cristina hadn't done it randomly, she just knew that somehow.

"It was a very personal gift," Vanni said.

"I know. Clothes meant so much to her," Emma agreed in a hushed tone.

She looked over her shoulder and met his stare, seeing the hunger gleaming in his eyes as he watched her. Her pulse began to leap at her throat.

"Come here," he said.

She swallowed, a thread in his tone making her skin prickle with awareness. Something caught her attention to the left of him as she walked into his arms.

"Oh my," she mumbled, craning to see what hung on the wall behind him. A rush of excitement went through her, hot and forbidden, something akin to what she'd felt that night in the armoire, but this time more intense.

"You know I always feel like you're out of my reach," he said quietly, ignoring her anxious stare over his shoulder.

She looked up at him slowly when he caught her chin, her fingers clutching instinctively on his hard, muscular biceps. "I'm right here," she whispered.

"Yes. But you deprived me of your presence for four days," he said, a hard glimmer of challenge and dark amusement in his eyes. An electrical shiver ran through her. "So I'm going to give you a little punishment."

"I didn't do anything wrong," she said, giving him a glare for good measure.

"That's not what this is about. It would give me pleasure to have you at my mercy. I need it, after what you did. I believe it will give you excitement and pleasure as well. That's all. Now I want you to go and choose one," he hitched his chin in the direction behind him, and Emma knew very well he'd known exactly what she was looking at the whole time.

She again looked past him. There was a built-in chest of drawers, but above, instruments of sexy punishment were hanging on the wall. She saw several leather floggers and what appeared to be a riding crop. There were several sizes of paddles—long and thin, medium and wide, short and round.

The idea of being the one to choose her method of sexual punishment amplified the forbidden thrill of the dark room, Vanni's hot eyes, and her own breathless excitement. She dropped her hands from his arms and walked past him, approaching the wall slowly. For a moment, she studied all the instruments, highly aware of his eyes on her backside. She fingered first one polished hardwood paddle and then a leather-covered one, then one with holes drilled into the wood, which looked like it would hurt. Her clit tingled with excitement. She'd didn't relish the idea of pain. The idea of being at Vanni's mercy was what excited her. Her fingers ran over the thin crop and the square slapper at the end. She touched the leather lashes on the flogger, but her hand dropped quickly away. It reminded her too much of that night she watched him and Astrid. The idea of him doing something similar to her left her feeling almost unbearably sexually excited, but also intimidated, because she'd felt so cast out at sea on that night, like she was a novice watching two professionals in gaping wonder and confusion.

But she was learning a few things . . .

She reached, removing the polished, long wood paddle that was about two and a half feet long and four inches wide. Heat scalded her cheeks when she saw Vanni's small smile as she handed it to him. Was that a glint of triumph in his eyes? It suddenly felt impossible to meet his stare.

"You'll have to take your strokes on a paddling bench with that large of a paddle," he said gently. "Is that all right?"

"What's a paddling bench?"

"It's a padded bench that you kneel on to receive the punishment. I could have you bend over with that paddle, but I'd prefer the bench today. You will be completely exposed to me, but you'll be comfortable." He seemed to notice her hesitation. "You can choose another paddle if you prefer. With a shorter one, I could paddle you across my knee."

She shook her head, her throat too constricted to speak.

"Go out into the bedroom then, and get undressed. I'll join you in a moment." He reached up and swept his forefinger along her cheek and jaw, his actions striking her as very tender. She walked past him, not taking a full breath until she stood by the bed. A shadow was cast on the balcony outside the French doors now, leaving the room cool and comfortable. In the distance, the Mediterranean sparkled like a jewel in the bright sunshine.

The sea breeze tickled her sensitive nipples and the skin of her belly and thighs a moment later when she removed her panties—the last item of clothing she wore. She swept her hand along a buttock, imagining how hot it would soon be from the paddle. She dropped it guiltily to her side when she heard Vanni's step, and turned to face him. Her eyes widened when she saw him carrying a wooden bench in one hand, and the paddle in the other. The wooden stool was about two and a half or three feet tall. It was unique, with a long leather center cushion at the top to lie on and a cushioned ledge on either side, where the knees and hands would rest. She would be spread if she took that position, her bottom at the edge of the bench, an easy target . . .

"We'll make this very simple," he said quietly, his gaze lowering over her as he came closer, making her already tingling skin prickle in awareness. He set down the bench. She realized he held more than the paddle in his other hand. She glanced down nervously and saw he held the dual vibrator he always used on her. Her clit twanged with excitement, her body having become conditioned to the pleasure that would follow the vision of the little device.

"I'm going to put this in you," he said, holding up the vibrator. "I enjoy giving you little punishments, but I only want them to arouse you. Do you need lubrication?"

His question mortified her. True, she'd gone soft and wet for him when he'd kissed and touched her earlier, but it'd been choosing that paddle while he'd watched her with that hawklike gaze of his that had truly got her ready. She shook her head, staring at his tie.

"I've told you that's a good thing, Emma," he chided quietly. "It pleases me, that choosing your mode of punishment excited you."

She gave him a dry glance and rolled her eyes to diminish her embarrassment. His smiled widened as he went to set the paddle on the table.

He held up the vibrator expectantly as he returned, and she recalled what he'd told her to do whenever he did that. She parted her thighs, her heart starting to pound in her ears. He stepped closer and reached between her legs, the vibrator in his hand. "Look at me so I can read your expression," he murmured when she continued to stare blindly at his shirtfront and tie. She looked up and felt his fingertip touch her entry. His jaw went hard. "Yes, nice and wet." He pushed the vibrator into her several inches, wedging the other end against her clit. "Okay?" he asked, reaching up to touch her shoulder. The feeling of his fingertips skimming across naked skin caused her skin to roughen in excitement.

"Yes," she whispered.

"Then come over to the bench," he instructed. "Kneel here," he said, indicating the two padded ledges on either side of the raised center portion. He guided her down, but upon seeing the bench Emma had instinctively understood the position required. When she settled, she straddled the raised cushion, belly and breasts and cheek resting on the elevated portion while her knees and hands were at the outer, lower ledges. Her ass was at the very edge.

"How does it feel?" Vanni asked, bending down and reaching under her hips. She realized he was adjusting the vibrator, making sure the clitoral end was in place.

She assessed what she was feeling, spread like that on the bench, her bare ass in the air. "Very . . . vulnerable," she admitted breathlessly.

"Yes," he mused. She turned her chin, trying to see what he was doing, and saw him reach into his pant pocket. He withdrew the remote control for the vibrator and pushed a button. She moaned softly in excitement. He'd put it to a medium setting, she'd guess. Instinctively, she pressed down with her hips, grinding her pussy and the vibrator against the cushion. "What else are you feeling?" he asked her.

"Excited. But I'm nervous, too," she said in a muffled voice.

"I'm not going to hurt you, you know that. It'll just sting and burn a little," he said, walking across the room. He picked up the paddle from the table and walked toward her. He looked very tall and large from her position on the paddling bench. She couldn't pull her eyes off the vision of him holding the paddle and the bulge in the front of his trousers. "Too much nervousness will ruin your pleasure. But just the right amount will give your pleasure an extra edge."

He came around the back of her to the opposite side. She couldn't see him anymore and started to turn her head.

"No," he said sharply. "Keep your eyes turned away."

"Why?" she asked, anticipation and excitement making her voice shaky.

"This will excite me very much," he said thickly. Her eyes went wide and her heart seemed to stop when she felt him press the end of the paddle against her ass. "You're very beautiful. If you look at me, I might find myself taking you before I turn your sweet ass pink. But

I'm determined to give you fifteen good strokes. I want to know that when we're out together tonight that your ass is sensitive under your new dress. I want your pussy to be, too. I want you to feel it when you're sitting down next to me or if we see each other from across the room. I want you to remember being at my mercy. I want you to remember me."

She moaned softly, aroused by his words and the persistent buzzing on her sex caused by the vibrator. He lifted the paddle.

"Mrs. Denis has gone to a racing celebration in the village. You needn't worry about anyone overhearing. The villa is empty except for us," he said.

Emma found herself hugging the center portion of the stool in almost unbearable excitement.

Smack.

He'd paddled her. She jumped slightly, not because it was terribly painful, but because she'd been so tense in anticipation, not knowing what to expect. His hand was immediately there, soothing the sting, shaping her flesh to his. "Such a sweet ass," he said. "You picked the exact paddle I've fantasized about using on you."

"I did?" she asked shakily, highly distracted by his massaging, molding hand on her ass and the increasing burn on her clit. She ground her hips down instinctively against the bench. She couldn't seem to help it—

"Yes," he said, and his hand fell away. "But that doesn't surprise me. Almost everything you do seems predesigned to drive me crazy."

"I'm sorry," she whispered, her entire focus on the sensation of him pressing the paddle against her ass again and circling it slightly. She wished she could see him.

"No, you're not," he said in a hard tone. "You love having me at your mercy as much as I love having you that way." The paddle was gone and she knew it was swinging. She braced herself, but a small *oh* popped out of her throat when it landed with a thwack. It stung, but she'd managed not to jump this time. Then the paddle was gone again and she gripped the bench with knees and elbows. *Smack.* She suppressed a whimper.

"If it's too much, you have to say so," Vanni said, his hand on her ass, rubbing the stinging flesh.

"It's not too much," she insisted in a high-pitched, choked voice. His soothing hand paused. Spreading his hand on the crack of her ass, he lifted and spread her buttocks. She almost felt his gaze scorching her sex. She squirmed in excitement. Suddenly his hand was gone. He swatted her again.

"Keep your ass still for the paddle," he warned. His voice sounded strained. Was he as excited as she was? She doubted it, considering the wicked little dual vibrator that was turning her to a bundle of sizzling nerves. A breeze from the open French doors wafted into the room, tickling her burning bottom and clit, the contrast of sensation pricking her senses even more. "Take one more and we'll pause a moment," she heard him say.

He landed the paddle with a popping noise. She moaned, the heat and sting from her ass transferring somehow to her clit.

"You're doing very well," he said from behind her, and she realized from the direction of his voice that he'd knelt behind her. She felt his hand between her spread thighs, reaching. He moved aside the end of the vibrator on her clit and pushed a blunt fingertip between her labia. She moaned uncontrollably as he pressed and circled the sensitive piece of flesh until she sizzled and her feet flexed as she started to crest. Then his hand was gone and she sensed he stood again. "You're extremely wet," he said in a hard tone. "But you're doing very well by keeping still." He stroked her ass. "You're getting nice and warm. Can you take ten more?"

"Yes."

"I thought so," he said, and she heard the warmth in his tone. She gritted her teeth in anticipation, and the paddle fell again and again. He paused after three strokes. She jumped slightly when she felt the hard wood of the paddle rub against the sole of one of her feet.

"You're curling up your feet. Do they burn?" he asked.

"Yes," she gasped. How had he known how sympathetic the nerves on her feet were to her sex? He tapped very lightly with the tip of her paddle on her heel. She didn't know why, but arousal shot through her. Her toes curled inward. She couldn't stop grinding her hips down on the bench in order to get more friction on her sex. He cursed softly, and suddenly the power on the vibrator diminished. He'd put it on a lower setting.

"You have to have the most sensitive little body in existence," he said, and she suddenly pictured the slant of his handsome mouth and the sharp glitter of arousal in his eyes as he took position behind her again and swung back the paddle.

"Ooh," she breathed as he gave her two more brisk swats, the exciting sound of polished wood against skin reverberating around the room and echoing in her head when he'd paused.

"Are you going to remember this tonight?" he asked her, reaching between her thighs. Moving aside the vibrator, he stimulated her again with his finger. She cried out, unable to stop herself. He was so much more precise than the vibrator, applying an eye-crossing pressure and succinct glide against her lubricated flesh.

"Yes." *Always*, she added in her lust-heavy brain.

"Would you like to come now, or would you prefer to wait until my cock is inside you?" he grated out. She clamped her eyes shut and scrunched her face tight, her body so tight and hungry for release.

"Emma?" he prodded, still rubbing her clit in a bull's-eye fashion.

He removed his hand suddenly and used it to part her thighs several inches. She sensed his gaze on her like a touch. Had he lowered behind her? she wondered, her heart racing madly. Her inner thighs were damp, more than likely glistening from her juices. She gave an agonized moan, knowing he was a close witness to her blatant arousal. A thrill went through her at the low, growling sound that emitted from his throat.

She shrieked when his mouth was suddenly on her, licking and sucking away the juices from her pussy.

"Oh God, Vanni . . . no . . . *yes*," she moaned, not even sure what she was saying. Then his mouth was gone, and her whole body was straining tight for him.

"God you're sweet. Answer me," he grated out. "*Do* you want to come now, or would you prefer to wait until my cock is inside you?"

"Wait for your cock," she whispered, the effort of restraint ripping at her. "Or try to?" she added on a high-pitched note.

"Good girl," he snarled, and suddenly his hand was gone and the paddle was landing on her ass. He rubbed a buttock, squeezing the burning flesh lewdly into his palm. "Nice and hot and pink," he muttered. "Keep trying, baby. This is killing me, too," he said almost desperately.

He smacked her once lightly with his palm. She moaned, undone by the tense eroticism of the moment and his stark declaration of need. She had a wild urge to touch her ass, to feel what he was feeling. He peeled back her prickling cheeks suddenly. Emma whimpered in suspense in the tense seconds that followed. She felt completely exposed to him, her asshole and sex tingling beneath his stare. He made that low, growling noise deep in his throat, menacing and thrilling at once. Then he released her. Her panting breath paused when she heard the unmistakable sound of a belt buckle jingling, then a zipper lowering.

"Can . . . Can I please see what you're doing?" she asked him shakily.

"Not yet," he said. He paddled her again. She cried out, trying to stop herself from grinding her pussy against the vibrator and the bench, but only partially succeeding.

"Three more," he said. "Keep still."

She gritted her teeth to stop herself from writhing. It was very difficult. He'd known what he was doing by inserting the vibrator. The combination of burning pleasure on her sex and the sting of her bottom was unbearably exciting. The paddle landed with a crack. She whimpered. He hadn't paddled her harder, but her ass was growing more tender and sensitive with each stroke.

"Does it hurt?" he asked, and she could tell that he'd knelt behind her.

"A little," she admitted, even though the pain was already fading to a hot burn as he rubbed her ass with his hand. Again, he peeled back her cheeks. Again, Emma held her breath in the weighty silence that followed. He cursed quietly, and then the vibrator was sliding out of her. She gasped at the deprivation of the stimulation. "Oh," she cried out when he inserted a thick finger into her pussy and plunged it back and forth.

"I couldn't resist, even though you've got two more coming," he said. "You're so juicy . . . so warm. God, it's going to be so good to explode inside you."

She almost begged him to just take her then. The suspense was killing her, and she wanted him so much. He withdrew his finger and rubbed her clit. Her eyes sprung and she gripped the bench tighter, every muscle in her body bunching tight. "You're on the edge, aren't you? Yet you remain so quiet. Why?"

"Why what?" she gasped.

"Why do you always stop yourself from screaming?" he asked, sounding almost angry.

"Because I thought that's what you wanted."

His circling finger slowed on her clit.

"Why would you think that?" he asked tautly.

She ground her hips against his hand. She couldn't stop herself. "That's what you told Astrid that night. You said you didn't like her hysterics," she said, too aroused to be anything but completely honest at that moment.

"Emma," he said, his tone almost angry even though she didn't really think he was. He began rubbing her clit again. She moaned in agonized pleasure. "I wish I could erase that memory from your brain. It has nothing to do with you and me. Do you understand me?"

She blinked her eyes open at his hard tone.

"Yes," she managed, biting her lip because his circling fingertip was keeping her skating right on the edge.

"Tell me what you want me to do now, Emma," he rasped, and she heard his rabid arousal as easily as she heard his voice. She clenched her eyes tight. What she wanted to do was come.

But she also wanted to please him.

"I want two more," she said, her entire body trembling with the effort it took for her not to come against his hand.

His rubbing finger stilled, and then fell away. She bit her lip to stop from moaning in agony. The bench under her still provided a source of pressure, however, and she found herself squirming against it.

"You're so incredible," he said thickly, and Emma could tell from the sound of his voice he'd stood. "And after I give you your punishment and sink my cock inside you, what are you going to do for me?"

"Scream?" she replied shakily.

"That's right," he said darkly. "Don't ever think I won't want to hear you scream in pleasure for me." He placed the end of the paddle on her ass and circled it slightly, getting her attention. "Raise your bottom off the bench for the last two," he said. "It will help you to keep still. And I *do* want you to stay completely still."

She pushed off slightly with her hands and knees, raising her ass several inches off the end of the bench.

"That's right. Such a good girl," he murmured. The paddle fell, biting at her ass. She choked off a cry. He gave a rough moan. The urge to look at him overwhelmed her. She turned her head and opened her eyes. He held the paddle in his right hand and fisted his enormous erection in the other. His fiery stare met hers. He was the very image of primal sex in that moment, a leashed storm straining to break. Her lips parted in awed arousal.

Her gaze lowered to his cock and pumping fist. His pants and underwear were bunched below his jutting erection and balls. He was furiously erect; the fat, tapered crown of his cock was flushed dark pink . . . so delicious looking. "I'm not that good, Vanni," she whispered heatedly, the tip of her tongue brushing the inside of her lower lip. He groaned and pumped his cock harder.

"Yes, you are," he grated out. "And because of it, you'll get another stroke."

She watched him as he cracked off the last two. The image of him was so powerful, she barely noticed the sting of her ass. He held her stare as he leaned the paddle against the bench near her hand.

"You can lower your ass to the bench again." The last glimpse she had of him, he was walking behind her, cupping his erection from below. A thrill of anticipation went through her when she sensed him lower behind her and he put his hands on her burning ass. "Brace yourself," he said. "I'm going to fuck you. Hard."

She bit her lip, waiting . . . burning. He didn't make her wait long. The hard crown of his cock parted her channel. He tightened his hold on her bottom and thrust. She dropped her forehead to the bench and screamed. It was a good thing she was so wet, because he clearly wasn't in the mood to wait. His growl was rough and feral as he immediately began to fuck her. The evidence of his rabid need only fueled her arousal. She hugged the bench, keeping herself steady for his onslaught, pushing back even, wanting more of him . . . craving all of him. His pounding cock was merciless. She felt herself cresting.

"Scream for me," he rasped behind her. "Scream again for me, Emma."

She wasn't sure if she screamed or not. All thought left her as she finally succumbed to the burn, igniting gloriously. She came back to herself at the sensation of an almost uncomfortable pressure. She glanced around and whimpered. He'd come up on to his feet and had lifted her hips, serving her pussy to his cock in a relentless frenzy of need. He was so beautiful, it felt like something was going to burst inside her. She put her cheek back on the bench, helpless in the clutches of the storm. Her fingers brushed across the paddle he'd leaned there and she gripped it tight, the smooth wood grounding her for some reason. He cursed. She grimaced at the sensation of him swelling huge inside her. His low growl amplified to a roar.

He began to pour himself into her. She stared blindly, her mouth hanging open at the amazing sensation . . . the sacred one. He kept coming for what felt like an unprecedented period of time, sinking his cock again and again into her depths while he gasped and grunted.

His fucking motions eventually slowed, until he just held her fast against him, and the only sounds in the room were their erratic panting and in the distance, the sound of the sea breaking against the shore far below.

He lifted her and carried her over to the mussed bed. While she snuggled into the softness, he stripped off the rest of his clothes. When he lay on his back a moment later with Emma's head on his chest and the cool breeze drifting across his heated skin, he experienced a rare, profound sense of peace. He trailed his hand up Emma's supple back and along her arm, relishing in her shape and the silkiness of her skin.

Her presence.

"Thank you for coming," he said.

She lifted her head off his chest and looked at him. Her hair was a mess of gilded waves. Her cheeks and lips were still stained pink. She was adorable. Sexy as hell. He didn't used to think those two things could go hand in hand so perfectly until he'd met Emma.

"You're welcome," she said, her soft brown eyes moving over his face.

His gaze narrowed. "There's nine of them," he said distractedly.

She raised her eyebrows in a query.

"Nine freckles on your nose," he clarified.

"I hate every one of them," she said, rolling her eyes and covering her nose with her hand.

He sat up partially, turning her in his arms so that she lay pinned beneath him. Her hand fell away in her surprise at his abrupt action. "I love every one," he growled ominously. He kissed her nose repeatedly, stilling her wriggling, the sound of her laughter making him smile. "One kiss for each adorable freckle," he said before he leaned down and tasted her lips. She was so sweet. Everywhere, he thought as his tongue dipped into her mouth. He'd like to kiss her like that in the soft bed forever, with the refreshing breeze cooling him, desire banked but glowing inside him like a warm ember that would leap back into a flame at any moment. When he lifted his head a moment later, her liquid brown eyes had gone sober as she looked up at him.

"I know what you meant now," she whispered breathlessly. "When you said once that you could do exactly what you did to Astrid to me, and it would be completely different."

A pain went through him at the idea of her still thinking about what she'd seen in that armoire. He meant what he'd said earlier. If only he *could* erase that night from her memory. If only he could eradicate it from his. He realized he was so caught up in his shame about what she'd seen that perhaps he hadn't fully understood her.

"What do you mean?" he asked, his fingers brushing against the delicate line of her jaw. "Don't tell me you thought that"—he glanced in the direction of the bench—"was remotely like what you saw that night."

"No. It wasn't. That's my point," she said softly. "I mean, some of the actions might have been similar, but . . ." She faded off, seeming to struggle with finding the right words.

"I was making love to you, Emma," he said starkly, exposing himself in an uncommon way because he hated to see her uncertainty. "I know I told you I wasn't cut out for the long term, and then you set the time limit on our time together. Maybe you think that means that what we do together doesn't matter, in any lasting sense . . . that it's just sex. Just gratification. I disagree. I could be doing the kinkiest thing in the world to you, and I'd still be making love to you," he said, trailing his finger over her flushed cheek. He saw amazement creep across her expression and raised his eyebrows. "Do you understand?" he asked, stroking her temple and the shell of her ear and relishing her tiny shiver.

"Yes," she whispered before she touched his cheek, her simple caress and the expression in her eyes sweeter to him than anything he could ever recall in his life.

Chapter 30

Emma was not thrilled at the idea of rising from the comfortable bed and leaving Vanni's arms in order to prepare for the dinner at the Hôtel Le Maj. The only consolation she had was that Vanni seemed just as reluctant to leave the bed as she was.

"At least after the race on Sunday, I'll have you all to myself for nearly a week," he told her later as they stood in the bathroom together, naked and entwined. He kissed her softly and she felt herself melting against his solid, warm length. His open hand trailed over her ass and she shivered. "Are you sore?" he asked, breaking their kiss but still nibbling at her lips.

She shook her head, brushing her mouth against his. "It stings a little." She glanced up at him humorously. "Certainly enough for me to think about it all night . . . again and again. That was your plan, right?"

His smile was a wry flash of brilliance. "Great. I set myself up for that one. Now I'll be thinking about it all night, too, knowing you are." He ducked his head, kissing her again, his hunger palpable. He grimaced when he stepped away a moment later. "I'd like to shower with you, but it'll lead to other things."

"That doesn't sound so bad."

"No, it sounds fantastic," he said grimly. "*Too* fantastic, because we're running late. I'll go and shower and get ready in the room next door." He released her and stalked toward the bathroom door. She just stood there for a moment, befuddled by the vision of his long legs, strong back, and jaw-dropping ass. He opened the door and passed through it.

"Wait!"

He paused and looked around the edge of the door.

"What should I wear? I mean . . . how formal is this dinner?" she asked.

"It's black-tie."

She nodded. He gave her a small smile and walked out of the bathroom.

With him gone, it was admittedly easier to attend to the task of getting ready. With him gone, it was also easier to feel a few flutters of nervousness at the idea of attending a glamorous, high-profile dinner with the world's racing elite. Luckily, their lovemaking—not to mention some of the sweet things Vanni had said afterward—went a long way to shield her from too much anxiety. The vision of the way he'd looked at her while they lay in bed together just now—*I was making love to you*—went a long way to armor her against worries.

The flush of her cheeks and brightness of her eyes didn't dissipate much after she'd showered and blow-dried her hair. When she left the bathroom, Vanni was nowhere to be seen. She recovered the rest of the items that Cristina had left her from the trunk and carried them to the closet. A feeling of warmth and gratitude swept through her yet again when she finally fingered the full array of dresses and other items that had been in the trunk. It was almost like the older woman was her fairy godmother, assuring her she would not only belong at the ball, but shine at it.

Heartened by the thought and by Vanni's focused lovemaking, she chose a dress that was meant to be worn by a sexually confident woman, a female who was comfortable in her own skin. She thanked

Cristina mentally yet again as she found some shoes and accessories to go with it.

Fifteen minutes later she examined herself in the bathroom mirror. Cristina had been right. They must have been the exact same size at the time Cristina had bought the dress. Emma had chosen a stunning teal green halter dress that emphasized her coloring nicely, but did absolutely amazing things for her figure. It clung to her curves like it'd been tailor-made, making her waist look especially small and her breasts more . . . significant. It managed to look sinfully sexy while still being elegant, Emma thought with amazement as she studied herself. She'd had no idea she possessed such an hourglass figure. She'd combed her hair behind her ears in a simple style and wore only a pair of dangling gold chandelier earrings and the Prisatti angel along with a pair of fierce black pumps. Her eye makeup was good, considering Emma had done it and not Amanda, making her eyes look large and smoky.

She turned and looked over her shoulder, flushing with pleasure and sheer amazement at what the dress did for her hips and ass. No wonder stars and models always looked so fantastic, if they could afford to buy dresses like this one. Her bottom felt tingly and slightly abraded beneath the fitted fabric of the dress. Vanni had accomplished what he wanted. She'd be thinking about those exciting, illicit moments with him all night.

She heard a sound out in the bedroom and grabbed the clutch that matched her shoes. Feeling both self-conscious and excited, she exited the bathroom. Vanni was across the room at the huge, carved armoire, standing behind an open door. He closed it a second later with a bang and was in the process of fastening a gold watch around his wrist, when he glanced up and noticed her. He did a double take. Emma stood there, her heart throbbing, as his blue-green gaze dropped over her. He wore a classic tux with a white shirt, a textured vest that was low enough to show off his tie—a classic black one versus a bow tie. He wore the garments, as usual, with insouciant ease, his long, lean body the ideal frame for such finely made, elegant garments.

"Well," he said after a pregnant pause, clicking the watch into place and walking toward her. "Cristina knew precisely what she was doing in at least one thing. You're stunning. You do incredible things for that dress."

She smiled. "Isn't it the other way around? If anything, the dress is doing it for me."

He grabbed her hand and gracefully turned her. Emma stared at him in surprise over her shoulder as he regarded her backside. One dark eyebrow quirked up and his mouth went hard.

"No," he said grimly, spinning her back around. "I had it right."

"Then why do you look so unhappy about it?" she teased him as he led her toward the door.

"I'm not so sure I like the idea of you in that dress and a roomful of racecar drivers," he said. "They're the worst kind of womanizers, you know."

"Like it would matter."

He glanced back at her swiftly, giving her a hard, blazing look, before he swept down and kissed her mouth. His hand cupped her hip and then a buttock, the warmth and pressure on her tingling flesh making her shiver in his arms.

"Just remember," he said next to her lips a moment later.

"As if I could ever forget," she whispered.

Much to her surprise, there was a chauffeured sedan waiting for them on the back drive when they exited La Mer. Perhaps it was best that Vanni hadn't talked too much about what to expect for their evening, because it likely would have ratcheted up her nerves. As it was, she was too amazed by the stunning scenery as they descended from the mountains, too overwhelmed by everything she was seeing. She stared out the window, enraptured as they traversed down the Boulevard de la Croisette, that famous stretch of road that ran between the exclusive Cannes beaches and luxury hotels and casinos. It wouldn't grow dark for a while yet. People still lounged on the beach, swam in the turquoise waters, or strolled along the promenade. Others who passed were prepared for the evening, however, beautiful men and women dressed to the hilt as they headed toward the glitzy casinos.

It took Emma a little bit to realize *she* was one of those glamorous people as she alighted from the sedan and Vanni took her hand. As they headed toward the entry of the Hôtel Le Maj, several men took their picture. A few who didn't have their cameras at the ready seemed to come to attention and scurry when they noticed it was Vanni.

"Just ignore them," Vanni said quietly as he escorted her up some white marble steps. "The race is local headline news."

Emma had a feeling *Vanni* was the news even more than the race, but she didn't say anything as he opened the gilded doors for her.

The restaurant where they dined was right out of a movie set. A room had been reserved for the racing party. Although they would be eating inside, an entire wall of glass doors had been opened to a terrace and the sea, giving the impression of eating al fresco. A five-piece band played out in the open air. It took them a while to reach their assigned table, as so many people came over to greet Vanni and to be introduced to Emma. A few of the people spoke French, but several spoke English. The drivers were eager to discuss the circuit conditions with Vanni following their early morning practice runs.

Vanni was holding her hand as they crossed the room a few minutes later, so she felt him tense slightly when a tall, handsome man with longish dark brown hair, swarthy skin, and electric blue eyes intercepted their progress.

"How is it that you always manage to have the most beautiful creature in the room on your arm?" the man asked with an Italian accent and a heavy-lidded look at Emma.

"How is it that you always manage to make a grown woman sound like a pet bird, Mario?" Vanni replied. The man gave a slashing grin, as if Vanni had been joking. Vanni sighed irritably. "Emma Shore, this is Mario Acarde. He's a driver."

"*The* driver," Mario assured her, taking her hand and caressing the edge of her palm. "Montand just doesn't like to admit it since he picked that rooster Dellis to drive Montand cars. But Niki isn't going to win on Sunday . . . despite the preferential treatment."

"All of the drivers had the exact same opportunity to practice on the circuit, Mario," Vanni said, his bored, weary tone implying this wasn't the first time he'd told the Italian driver something similar. "The racing officials have strict orders from the local governments to shut down the route by eight a.m. Maybe you should consider getting to be bed early tonight so you can get your full practice time," Vanni said, his dry tone implying that the idea of Mario going to bed early was as likely as a snowy Christmas on the French Riviera.

Mario smiled, never removing his gaze from Emma. "He never could take a joke," he told her in a confidential manner.

Vanni successfully pulled Emma away from Mario, saying something about dinner starting. She was relieved to see two faces she recognized when they approached their table—Niki Dellis and Vanni's uncle, Dean Shaw. Niki sprung up from his seat, taking her hand and leaning down to kiss her cheeks as if they were the best of friends. She grinned as she greeted him, privately thinking to herself how perfectly Niki matched the glamorous, romantic setting with his dark good looks, easy manners, and classic tuxedo.

"The rose has bloomed," Niki complimented her warmly, dark eyes roving over her dress in clear male appreciation.

"But is still firmly attached to the stem," Vanni replied dryly, giving his friend a half-warning, half-amused glance. "Give it a rest, Niki, she already had to endure Mario."

"Then she especially deserves my attention. She'll think all drivers are swine." She saw the merriment in Niki's glance at Vanni. Clearly, Niki was an established flirt, but he'd been mostly ribbing his friend by admiring Emma so blatantly. Niki certainly had no cause to ogle other women. He introduced her to his date, a stunning blonde named

Georgia who wore a white gown that displayed showstopping breasts. When she spoke, it was with a cool, regal English accent that was a fascinating paradox to her gilded good looks and the lack of a tan line anywhere in evidence on her plunging neckline. The paradox was only amplified when Niki referred to her casually as "George." Vanni introduced her to Dean Shaw's wife, Michelle, a friendly, middle-aged woman who seemed especially pleased to be introduced to Emma.

"I see I chose well," Michelle enthused with a smug grin, glancing down over Emma's dress as they shook hands.

"You chose impeccably," Vanni said. "But as you can see, it would have been hard to choose poorly given the wearer."

"Without a doubt," Michelle said warmly.

Vanni noticed Emma's bewildered look. "Michelle was kind enough to go to the Breakers and choose your wardrobe for your stay here," Vanni said under his breath.

"Oh, thank you!" Emma said. "You did an excellent job."

"Have you actually seen your inheritance?" Michelle asked her with a dry smile. Emma shook her head. "It would have been hard to go wrong. That closet is as large as our bedroom," she told Dean, "and stuffed to the brim with clothes, most of which still have tags on them, and shoes and every geegaw you can imagine."

"Vanni's aunt—Vera, that is—seems very fashionable. She must have been a good assistant to help you choose," Emma said.

"Oh, Vera wasn't at the Breakers," Michelle said. "She was here, in fact."

Emma blinked. "Will Vera be here tonight?" she asked Vanni. She wasn't sure she was so wild about the idea of socializing with Vera Shaw for the next week, but perhaps it'd give her an idea of how to break through the woman's dislike of her? Vanni glanced at Dean, a vaguely annoyed expression breaking through his typically impassive one.

"Vera has left," Dean said quickly, as if trying to fill the uncomfortable pause. "She had a great deal of work she needed to attend to back in Chicago."

Another woman at the table, who Emma learned was named Estelle Fournier, listened to this exchange with a shrewd, narrow-eyed focus. Her husband, Simon, sat next to her. Estelle was a good deal younger than Simon, who appeared to be in his late fifties. Nevertheless, both husband and wife were stunning. As Vanni seated Emma and took his place next to her, Emma found herself wondering idly if the exotic Mediterranean coast somehow sprouted splendid-looking people to inhabit it.

Not only Vanni, but Niki, Michelle, and Dean were all very attentive to her during the dinner, something that went a long way to increasing her comfort level. Niki seemed very unconcerned about the upcoming race, and instead described to Emma and Vanni his adventure in catching an enormous sea bass that afternoon. Meanwhile, the woman named Estelle kept trying to engage Vanni in conversation in French, which seemed to annoy her husband, Simon. Knowing Emma didn't speak the language, however, Vanni kept reverting to English, something that clearly annoyed the French beauty. At various times during the four-course meal, Emma noticed Estelle watching Vanni from across the table with a hungry look in her eye. She glanced at a nearby table and saw Mario Acarde stare at her—Emma—in much the same way Estelle looked at Vanni.

Apparently, not only did good looks thrive on the French Riviera, so did raging libidos, Emma thought dazedly, blinking and looking away from the amorous driver.

As the waiter cleared away the remains of their meal and couples began to dance out on the terrace, Georgia regally excused herself to go to the ladies' room. A dark haired man with a mustache drew Vanni away to clarify some question that was a point of contention at another table. Estelle and Simon Fournier were twirling together on the dance floor, and Dean and his wife were off socializing at another table. Only she and Niki remained.

"Did I mention that you look amazingly beautiful tonight?" Niki asked her, smiling.

"Only once or a dozen times," Emma replied, blushing despite his light, teasing tone.

"Something in France seems to be setting you alight," Niki said, glancing pointedly across the room to where Vanni stood. "And I'm not the only one who's noticed. You've caught the attention of almost every male in the room. Vanni is a fool to leave your side. Mario Acarde looks like he wants to eat you alive," Niki said derisively under his breath, nodding subtly in the direction of the dark-haired man with the startling blue eyes. Mario was now talking to two women not twenty feet away. When Emma glanced in his direction, she saw him looking at her over the two women's heads. He raised his highball glass as if in a private toast and took a healthy swallow of liquor.

"Drunken, horny bastard has been circling ever closer to you ever since he noticed Vanni was called away," Niki muttered darkly under his breath.

"He's one of your rivals, isn't he? Marco told me a little about the race and the frontrunners," she explained when he glanced at her in mild surprise.

"Acarde wishes."

Emma chuckled. "I heard you won the time trials earlier. Congratulations. Are you nervous about the race on Sunday?"

"A little," Niki admitted. "I'm usually not nervous before a race, but no matter how much I've practiced on the stock car, it's still my second language, so to speak."

"Do you think it'll make a difference in the outcome of the race?"

"The Americans have the advantage as far as the car. But we," he said lifting his highball glass and giving her a pointed, mischievous glance, "have the advantage of the road. No perfect little oval racetracks here—narrow roads, tight hairpin curves, and plunging shifts in elevation down the mountainside."

"Will it be dangerous?" Emma asked warily.

"Without a doubt," Niki replied, as if she'd stated the obvious.

She caught the gleam in his eyes and laughed. He smiled. "I realize you probably don't know much about road races in the South of France, but they are traditionally the gladiator arena for drivers seeking their fame." He noticed her alarmed look. "Don't worry. It's much better nowadays, and the local governments have assured we put together a safe race." He shrugged. "Relatively safe, anyway."

He flashed her a grin when she gave him a teasing "don't mess with me" glance. "If anything, it'll be a test of our basic driving instincts. We've only been allotted two early mornings of practice in addition to the time trials before raceday, given the constraints of the surrounding villages. It'll be exciting, that much is certain. It started out as a lark between Vanni and me. But the level of competition has grown fierce in the past several months. We all craved the unique challenge, apparently. I'm glad," Niki said, setting down his glass. "It was a gamble on Vanni's part to attempt it, but he's got a phenomenon on his hands. Excellent publicity for Montand Motorworks and Automobiles Montand. The race is going to become an annual, highly anticipated event, mark my words. Bit of a shame for Vanni, though," Niki said, casting a hooded glance across the room to where Vanni stood at a table, flanked by two men in tuxes. "He actually hates high-profile events and being the center of attention, despite understanding the need for publicity owning the type of businesses he does."

Emma recalled what he'd said that first time she'd officially met him about the "vampires" at press events. "Yes. Has he always been so reserved?"

Niki turned his highball glass distractedly. "No. He was a hotheaded teenager. It wasn't that he wanted to be the center of attention or anything, but it was like he couldn't stop it from happening . . . a little like expecting a raging inferno to be dim," Niki said with a rueful sideways glance. Emma nodded in understanding.

"What happened to change him?" Emma asked quietly.

"Life. Death. Then . . . Meredith," Niki said simply. He met

Emma's stare, and she could tell he was curious as to whether she knew who Meredith was. She didn't, technically, but she made a guess.

"His wife?" she asked.

Niki nodded, looking a little relieved that she knew. "He was only twenty-two when she died. First he lost his mother young to leukemia, then—"

"Adrian," Emma finished soberly.

Niki blinked. She had a feeling Niki Dellis didn't look surprised often.

"Vanni told you about Adrian?" he asked, shock ringing in his quiet voice. Emma nodded. Niki's gaze sharpened on her as if he'd truly seen her for the first time. "Well," he said after a moment, looking away. "I knew you were having *some* kind of unprecedented effect on him, but I didn't guess . . ." He seemed to come to himself and sat up straighter in his chair, taking a deep breath. "It was Adrian's death that hit him the hardest, being as young as they were and the tragic circumstances," Niki said grimly. He took another idle sip of his bourbon. "His mother's and Adrian's death turned him into a blaze of trouble. Nothing mattered to him. Nothing *meant* anything. As a teenager, he was on a one-way road to hell, and anyone who got in his way on the journey was going to get burned. Unfortunately, I was a hotheaded teenager myself and on a similar clueless path. Fire can't burn fire," Niki said, all remnants of the mischievous charmer vanished. "So I was no help. I was too stupid to realize where that trip was going to take him. Us. Then, while Van was in college, a miracle happened."

"He met Meredith?" Emma asked through a tight throat.

Niki shrugged. "I never really knew if it was Meredith who did it, or if Vanni was just ready to stop grieving and get on with his life." He shrugged. "Whatever the reason, he seemed to find a purpose . . . a focus, even before she came along. When his dad protested against the marriage, it only firmed his resolve. It was during those months before he met Meredith and after they were married, when Michael Senior and Cristina had cut him out—both from their lives and financially—that Van designed the revolutionary intake manifold and carburetor for racecars that made him his personal fortune. Those inventions became the linchpin for his own company, Montand Motorworks. Everything seemed like it was falling into place for him. He seemed content for the first time in his life. Then . . ." He faded off, shaking his head.

"What did Meredith die of?" Emma asked in a hushed tone.

"Thyroid cancer. It spread very fast, once she was diagnosed."

Emma found herself staring at Vanni's tall, striking form across the room, her heart heavy.

"After Meredith passed, he seemed to completely shut down emotionally. He turned cold and methodical—ideal for eventually being the head of two separate multibillion-dollar companies, but not so much for anything else. He eventually built that new house in the place where Adrian died, almost as if he wanted to . . ."

"Punish himself?" Emma asked, dread filling her chest cavity. She turned to Niki and met his stare. He was looking at her with blank incredulity.

"You've guessed that? Surely he'd never tell you—"

"No," Emma mouthed, swallowing thickly. "I guessed from something Cristina said, when she was dying. And just . . . intuition."

Niki didn't respond for a moment, but then he set down his glass with a thud. Vanni couldn't have heard the sound from far across the crowded, music-filled room, but he turned suddenly and looked directly at Emma. She felt his stare in the pit of her belly.

"Vanni was the stronger of the twins," Niki muttered next to her when someone said something to Vanni and he turned away. "For whatever reason, Adrian was smaller and much frailer. Michael Senior used to goad both Vanni and Adrian when they were little by joking that Vanni had stolen all of Adrian's strength in the womb, and Adrian had stolen Vanni's kindness."

Emma stared at Niki, stunned. "What a horrible thing to say to children."

Niki nodded thoughtfully. "You don't need to tell me that. Michael was not the kindest of men, although he was a force to be reckoned with. He did have his moments . . ."

Neither of them spoke for a moment when Niki drifted off, both seemingly lost in their own thoughts.

"They were both caught up by the riptide, you know," Niki said quietly. "From what I gather—because Vanni never talks about it—Vanni tried to save Adrian, but couldn't."

"He could only save himself," Emma whispered, shivers crawling across her skin.

"He was all of nine years old," Niki said, his mouth pressed into a grim line. "He was lucky to have accomplished that."

"He believes the opposite. He thinks he's cursed," Emma said softly.

Niki sighed and met her stare. "There's one thing I can be thankful for. Tragedy hasn't struck him in years. If he *was* cursed, so to speak, hopefully the storm has passed. Sometimes I think if something else horrible happened to him, it'd end him."

Emma swallowed thickly, trying to ignore the spasm in her chest cavity.

Chapter 31

A little while later, the restaurant started to clear. Emma was leaving the ladies' room, when someone caught her hand and halted her. She looked around and saw Mario Acarde standing there.

"I've been trying to find you all night," he told her, the thickness of his speech making her think he'd had a bit too much to drink.

"Really?" Emma asked in a friendly, neutral tone, removing her hand from his. "I've been sitting in the same place the whole time." Another hand enclosed the one she'd just dropped. She looked over her shoulder.

"Hi," she said, smiling.

"Hello. Sorry for leaving you like that. Everyone has something to say about the race," Vanni replied, his gaze running over her face and then flicking over to Mario. "But I promise I won't leave your side for the rest of the night. Excuse us, Mario."

"Are you off to the tables?" Mario called, but Vanni didn't respond. He just led Emma onto the terrace, which had cleared out. It was a warm, starry night, a full moon in the sky making a swath of the sea gleam and wink. The band had stopped playing and was starting to pack up their instruments. Vanni left her, approached one of the men, and exchanged a handshake with him.

"*Encore une chanson, s'il vous plait*?" Vanni asked quietly.

The man looked down appreciatively at his palm. "*Avec plaisir, monsieur.*"

The musicians all took up their instruments again and at a signal from the leader began playing. Vanni came toward her, a small, devastating smile shaping his mouth. A thrill went through her when he took her into his arms and they began to dance. She looked up at him as he pulled her closer, her smile matching his.

"Do you always do things perfectly?" she asked softly.

"What do you mean?"

"They're playing 'Moonlight Serenade,'" she said with a small laugh, glancing significantly out at the moonlit water.

"It's not me who is perfect tonight," he murmured. Her breath caught when his lips closed gently over hers and lingered as they spun to the music. Her flesh tingled next to his solid length. It was pure magic.

"I'm sorry for leaving you. It seems every time I turned around, someone had a question or something to say about the race," he said a moment later.

"Don't worry. I understand. This is your work. Niki kept me company."

"I saw. I asked him to watch out for you."

"Did you?" she asked, entranced by the image of his angled, bold face etched in shadow and moonlight, and the feeling of his body moving in subtle rhythm next to hers.

He nodded, his expression sober. "And then I got jealous when I saw him doing it," he growled softly, capturing her lips again for another kiss. She felt his body harden next to hers, and the kiss deepened.

"You have absolutely nothing to be jealous of," she told him breathlessly a moment later. "All I can see is you, Vanni." One dark brow rose in a wry expression.

"For these weeks and days and hours?" he asked, a thread of sarcasm in his tone. One of his hands lightly skimmed over her lower back and the top of a buttock. Emma shivered.

"For these weeks and days and hours."

"You're mine."

She smiled and pressed closer to him. "You know it's true," she chided.

"I still like to hear you say it."

"I'm yours," she whispered. His head lowered, and their mouths fused again.

"Almost everyone will have gone into the casino," Vanni said as he led her through the mostly deserted restaurant after the memorable dance was over. "Would you like to stroll through before we leave, or would you rather not?"

"I'd like to at least have a look," she said as they entered the palatial grand lobby of the hotel, and Emma glanced around eagerly. Vanni's stare stuck on her face.

"Of course. I keep forgetting you haven't been here before," he said.

"I've never even been to Europe," she said.

"What?" he asked, his stride breaking slightly.

"It's my first time. I have a passport because I was supposed to go to London for a trip arranged through my college after graduation. But then my mother died, so I never got to go. She had a small life-insurance policy, but funerals are a lot more expensive than I'd realized."

He didn't say anything as he led her to the entrance. There was a line to enter the casino, but Vanni surpassed it. The burly man wearing a tuxedo guarding the entrance nodded once at them and murmured, "Mr. Montand," before releasing a velvet rope for them to enter.

When they entered the bustling casino, Vanni squeezed her hand.

"I'm sorry about how busy I am. I'll be a better tour guide, I promise," he said quietly. "As soon as the race is over. And tomorrow, we've been invited onto Niki's yacht. You'll get a nice view of the local country from the sea."

"We have been?" she asked excitedly. She noticed how sober he looked and squeezed his hand back. "Don't worry, Vanni. You're treating me to the experience of a lifetime. Don't you know that?"

He gave her a small smile and they proceeded into the casino. The atmosphere was electrical and chic. She recognized many of the faces she'd seen at the dinner, people looking around and greeting Vanni as he passed. It wasn't just a casino, Emma realized. In the distance, she could see a crowded club where people were dancing and lounging in deep, cushioned booths and drinking exotic-looking beverages. If a patron chose, they could escape the sounds of music and slot machines and music by walking out onto a wide veranda that faced the Mediterranean. Unlike other closed-off, stuffy casinos she'd been in in the States, the opened patio doors made the atmosphere open and sea-air fresh.

"Do you gamble?" she asked Vanni, watching gamers as they passed a row of roulette tables.

"Not much anymore. Would you like to play?" he asked her politely, noticing her curiosity.

"Can we just watch?"

"Of course."

They paused behind a table that was a little less crowded than the others. Vanni ordered them drinks from a passing waiter as Emma observed. She wasn't familiar with the chip denominations, but she had a feeling from the extremely well-heeled and bejeweled players around the table that this was a high-limit table. She'd been to Las Vegas once, but had never played roulette. The game hadn't been all that popular in the States, but roulette appeared to rule here in the Cannes casino. Vanni patiently answered some of her questions about how it was played, before three men appeared—two of which Emma recognized as American drivers she'd been introduced to at dinner—and drew him into conversation about the race.

"He's a fool to keep ignoring you," a man said near her ear in an Italian-accented voice. She glanced aside reluctantly and saw Mario standing very close. Emma stepped back to a more appropriate distance.

"The race is a pretty big deal," she said lightly, turning her attention back to the table and the spinning wheel. "He's just doing his job."

"If you were mine, I'd make *you* my job," he said quietly. He leaned closer yet again and whispered in her ear. "Do you know what I think? I think you're lucky. I can sense luck from a mile away and I saw it in you the second you walked in to that restaurant tonight. I know you have no reason to believe me, but I have been utterly captivated by you since that moment."

Emma's eyes widened in amazement. Mario must play the part of a Lothario frequently, because he managed to make the corny statement sound completely genuine.

"Do you even remember my name?" she asked him with hushed incredulity.

He looked offended, but she had the distinct impression he was in fact fumbling for her name mentally. She resisted an urge to laugh, glancing anxiously to her left, where Vanni stood. His back was partially turned to her as he spoke with the three other men. Mario seemed to notice his preoccupation and moved in for the kill, sliding his hand suggestively against her forearm. She thought for a disbelieving second he was reaching to hold her hand. Instead, he pushed something against her palm. Emma's hand instinctively cupped the objects.

"Take a chance with me," Mario whispered hotly. "Luck should be with a winner."

She held up her hand and stared blankly at what she held.

"Close your hand, you little fool," Mario hissed, covering her hand with his, but not before Emma noticed what he'd given her . . .

A casino chip and a hotel room key. She stared from the items to Mario in stark disbelief. Had he really just propositioned her with Vanni standing right next to her? *Narcissistic swine.* Mario had frozen and was looking over her shoulder, his eyes glassy from too much drink, his expression stiffening with anxiety. Emma glanced around, and did a double take. Vanni stood next to her and was facing them both. She started when he shoved Mario's arm and Mario's hand fell away from Emma's. Holding Mario's panicked gaze with a glacial stare, Vanni lifted her hand. He looked down at what she held, his jaw going rigid. Emma glanced up and saw a startled expression on Mario's face as he looked at her hand as well. He recovered quickly.

"I was just inviting her to play roulette, giving her a little gambling money. She looks as if she wanted to play, and I was trying to be a good host, since you were so busy," Mario said, his anxious expression belying his cocky tone.

"Funny, I hadn't realized the Hôtel Le Maj had roulette tables in their hotel rooms these days," Vanni bit out.

Sensing his cold, sharp fury at Mario and not wanting there to be a scene, Emma tried to intervene. "It was just a misunderstanding," Emma assured, putting her hand out to give the chip and the hotel keycard back to Mario. The men who had been talking to Vanni were starting to look over at them, obviously sensing the rising tension between Mario and Vanni. Mario put out his hand to take back the key and chip, a relieved expression on his face.

"Damn straight, it was," Vanni said, halting her action with a hand on her arm. He stepped past her toward Mario aggressively.

"No, please," Emma said. She put her hand on his shoulder. "Let's just go, Vanni." Vanni looked down at her touch, his icy, focused anger fracturing slightly. His face settled into a determined mask. He put his hand on her upper arms and turned her in front of him. The next thing she knew, he was urging her up to the table. People were laying down their chips.

"Vanni . . . what—"

"Bet it," he said quietly from behind her. She looked over at her shoulder, shocked. Was he so furious at Mario, he'd gone crazy? His face was still stiff from anger, but when she met his stare, he gave her a small, imperceptible smile. "*Bet* it," he repeated, placing his hands on her waist.

"What do I do?" she asked, turning back to the table.

"Pick a number on the inside and put the chip directly on it," Vanni instructed. She thought she understood what he meant by emphasizing *directly*. Some people were setting their chips between and at the corner of numbers. He wanted her to bet it all on one roll of the wheel.

She bit her lip uncertainly. A thought struck her. "What's the Montand racecar number?" she asked impulsively.

"Fourteen," Vanni said from behind her.

She placed the chip on the velvet-covered table directly on fourteen. She heard someone curse bitterly and glanced around to see Mario standing there, his handsome face pale.

"You said you were playing host, Mario," Vanni said with false calmness. "You certainly were being a generous one."

Mario bared his teeth, and the wheel was spinning. Emma looked on, her heart beating fast with rising excitement. Somehow, she knew what was going to happen before it did. The ball rattled to a stop as if in slow motion. The croupier called out something, but Emma couldn't discern what for the roaring in her ears.

The ball had landed on fourteen.

She spun around in Vanni's arms.

"I *won*?" she asked with excited disbelief.

"You won," Vanni said, a smile breaking free. He caught her against him when she jumped, his deep laughter adding to her sense of euphoria. Over Vanni's shoulder she saw the men Vanni had been talking to laughing and congratulating her.

"I've never won anything in my life!" She told them ecstatically. Then she caught sight of Mario's desperate, angry expression and immediately sobered. "Oh . . . but it was Mario's chip, of course . . ."

"Nonsense," Vanni said briskly, setting her back down. "Take your winnings. It's time to go." He shot Mario a dark glance. "Mario knows the rules of the house. Maybe he won't be quite so *hospitable* next time."

Mario opened his mouth to protest, but seemed to think better of it under the influence of Vanni's glare. He turned and disappeared into the crowd.

"Take your winnings," Vanni directed again gently. "We're leaving."

Emma scooped up her chips and followed Vanni through the crowded casino. This time, when people tried to stop him to talk, he politely put them off.

"Do you want me to cash them for you?" Vanni asked her a moment later when they approached a desk that looked like it might be casino services.

"Are you sure we should?" she asked doubtfully, handing him the chips. "Mario seems pretty drunk. It doesn't seem fair."

"He didn't realize he'd given you such a big chip," Vanni said succinctly. Emma blinked in surprise. "He gets sloppy when he drinks. Trust me, I've seen it before. And if you think I'm going to feel sorry for that idiot for propositioning you right in front of my face, you're sorely mistaken. You *do* realize he was trying to buy you for the night—or an hour or two—with that chip?"

"Yes," Emma admitted.

"And you're still defending him?"

She sighed. "No. I guess he got what he deserved. I just feel bad that I'm the one to benefit from his stupidity."

"Who else should? You were the one he insulted. I'll be right back," he told her, turning to the desk. A minute later, he returned and handed her a receipt.

"I had them convert it into American dollars. They'll be sending the check to your address at home," he said, grabbing her hand. Completely undone by the strange turn of events, Emma just followed him out of the casino and hotel lobby. As the doorman opened the gilded doors for them, however, she glanced down at the receipt. Stunned, she stopped dead in her tracks at the top of the marble stairs. Vanni looked back at her when she broke his hold, his brow furrowed.

"Vanni . . . this says that they'll be sending a check for one hundred forty-one thousand seven hundred and fifty-one dollars to my apartment in Evanston," Emma said, shock making her voice sound hollow.

Vanni gave her a bland glance and took her hand again.

"Mario has never been one to bet small. I'm sure he's bet a king's ransom in the casinos that he'll win the Montand cup on Sunday, for instance. Maybe this will teach that stupid sod not to bet on what isn't his."

Week

SEVEN

Chapter 32

Adrenaline, happiness, and Vanni's seemingly unquenchable sexual appetite assured that Emma only got three or four hours of sleep that night. Nevertheless, when he awakened her by nuzzling her cheek and ear the next morning, Emma immediately buzzed with alert sensual excitement. She opened her eyes to a room infused with pale gold morning light and fresh, sea-infused air.

Who had time for sleeping when being awake was so sweet? Who had time for sleeping when they were falling in love?

Don't think about that, a voice in her head warned. *Don't be stupid.*

"Would you like to start our day with a swim?" Vanni asked her, his voice a sexy, sleep-roughened rumble near her ear, and she promptly forgot her dire mental warnings.

"Yes," she replied, turning her head to find his lips with her own. "I still can't believe I won all that money," she sighed a moment later when he lifted his head and she stared up at him, muzzy and warm from his kiss. "Did it really happen?"

"I'm sure Mario is wishing it didn't, but it most definitely did," Vanni said, smirking slightly. "You couldn't have shoved his idiocy in his face any more forcefully. What are you going to do with your winnings?"

"I don't know," she said blankly. "I suppose Amanda could use some of it. Medical school isn't cheap."

His brows slanted. "You are not giving found money to your sister," he said darkly.

"Why not?" she said, although she thought she already knew the answer. "Vanni, I don't have a vendetta against Amanda. We're working on things in our way. I wish you'd stop imagining me victimized. I love my sister. My mother would have wanted—"

"What do *you* want, Emma?" he interrupted as he coiled a tendril of her hair around his finger. She looked up at his face as her heart throbbed an answer. He looked beyond beautiful to her in the morning light, his thick hair tousled and bracketing his sea-colored eyes, whiskers sexily darkening his lean jaw. She touched his shoulder, wondrous yet again at the delicious denseness of muscle covered so tautly in smooth skin.

"I want to be happy," she whispered.

"Are you?"

"Yes," she said without reservation. His small smile made her happiness swell.

Yes, for these diminishing weeks and days and hours, she was nothing short of ecstatic.

Instead of swimming in the terraced pool area to the right of the villa, Vanni led her to the cliffside, where they descended the long, meandering white staircase, the bright sun shining off the Mediterranean blinding her. There was a small beach when they reached the bottom and a floating dock forty feet out from the shore.

"Heaven," she whispered several minutes later when they'd crawled onto the suspended dock and they lay side by side, panting slightly from their swim, the hot sun quickly drying their wet skin. The sea surrounded them like a rippling, sparkling blue-green gem. "Were the beach and the dock here when you were a child?" Emma asked, turning on her hip to face Vanni.

"Yeah," he said. He turned toward her as well, bending his arm and using his hand to prop up his head. She stretched her right arm above her and laid her cheek on top of it, letting his solid body block the sun for her. It was heaven in and of itself, to gaze up at him against a backdrop of a clear, robin's-egg blue sky, the waves rocking the dock gently. His small nipples were tight from the cool water, his ridged abdomen moving in and out slowly above his low-riding swim trunks. She wanted to touch him everywhere, but couldn't decide on what delectable spot, so she just ate him up with her gaze. Vanni, on the other hand, was more decisive. He put his hand on her naked hip and moved it back and forth ever so slightly, gliding it against her damp skin. "It used to be Adrian's and my favorite spot," he said. "We had an au pair from Switzerland who came down here with us every day during our summer vacations. She was very dedicated and patient with us," he mused. "I didn't realize until years later she was one of my father's lovers."

She didn't respond for a moment.

"When he died, were you still angry at him?" she finally asked.

He blinked and cupped her hip tighter in his palm. "Do you mean did I forgive my father for all of his infidelities? For his constant disapproval of me? For bringing Cristina into our life?"

"For being who he was," she replied. "Nothing more. Nothing less."

He inhaled slowly. "No. I don't suppose I have." He stared into the distance behind her, his eyes seeming to glow between the narrowed slits of his eyelids in his shadowed face. "Maybe it's time I did. Maybe." She gave in to her urge and touched a hard pectoral muscle. Something about his quiet thoughtfulness in regard to his father caused her conscience to prod and poke at her.

"Vanni?"

"Hmmm?" he asked, rubbing her hip lazily.

"There's something I know you don't want to talk about, but I feel obligated to bring it up," she said reluctantly.

She felt him stiffen slightly beneath her stroking fingertips. He looked down at her.

She inhaled for courage. "When Cristina was dying, she made me promise that I'd tell you something. The problem is, I wasn't sure how long you were standing there behind me. I wasn't sure how much you heard."

His rubbing hand stilled. His mouth pressed into a hard line. For a few awful seconds, she thought he was going to turn away from her, shut her down like the last time she'd tried to broach the topic with him.

"Please," she whispered. "Try to understand. It was her dying wish, and I promised. If you don't let me tell you, I'll feel the weight of that promise forever."

He bowed his head slightly. "When I walked in, she was saying something about how a child shouldn't have been left to feel so much . . ."

"'No man forced to feel so little,'" Emma finished when he faded off. "She meant you, Vanni. She knew that . . ." Emma swallowed thickly, trying to gather herself. "She knew that you blamed her for Adrian's death, but she also knew you blamed yourself. She begged me to ask you to forgive yourself."

He just stared down at her. Emma's throat ached with emotion.

"She was highly aware of her shortcomings," Emma continued, knowing it was too late to turn back now. "She understood that she was petty when it came to your father, that she couldn't stand sharing the spotlight with you and Adrian. She felt she was meant to be a mistress, that she wasn't good enough to be a wife or mother. I think she was sadly realistic about the fact that her personality was cast in stone. I think she grieved over the fact that she wasn't made of better stuff. She couldn't change, she couldn't make herself less selfish, but she regretted that truth. Deeply, I believe."

"That makes no sense," he stated with quiet forcefulness, his hand dropping from her hip. "If she truly regretted her actions, she would have chosen to take responsibility for them."

"I don't think she thought she was strong enough. She thought very little of herself."

"There are very few women on this planet who think as *well* of themselves as Cristina did," he stated bitterly.

"Maybe it looked that way. On the surface," Emma agreed. "A woman like Cristina wasn't the type to ever show her vulnerabilities. She hid behind her looks and glamorous life and beautiful clothes. She didn't trust enough to let anyone see the truth. But I think she regretted not only Adrian's death more than either of us can ever begin to understand, she hated her inability to help you deal with your guilt and grief after Adrian died. She was *incapable*. She *knew* it, and that absence in her character haunted her. She knew that because she didn't claim blame for what happened to Adrian—because she *couldn't* take responsibility—that you shouldered a heavy portion of that guilt. Illogically and unfairly, true, but that didn't stop you from carrying that burden. That's why she begged for your forgiveness at the end above all others."

"She begged for my forgiveness because I was the only one left standing!"

"No," Emma said firmly. "She understood that because of the circumstances, you were the one whose forgiveness meant the most. Not just to her. To you. And not just *for* her. For *you*."

He jerkily started to sit up, and then stopped himself just as abruptly. Emma's heartbeat started to pound in her ears. He reminded her very much of a trapped animal in those seconds.

Yet he didn't move. He didn't flee.

"I told Cristina once I wasn't her judge," Emma said softly, reaching to caress his whiskered jaw. He flinched slightly at her touch, but then he stilled. He clenched his eyelids shut. "I'm not your judge, either, Vanni. What's between you and Cristina is your business. But I promised her I would tell you. And for my sake, I hope you do forgive that little boy you once were. You were a child. It *wasn't* your fault. And . . ." She hesitated. "Adrian may have died, but part of him is in you. It always has been, Vanni."

"Enough," he bit out quietly through a tense jaw. He slowly opened his eyes and she saw the fierce maelstrom of emotion frothing inside him. She held his stare, difficult as it was.

"I'm sorry," she said. "I felt obligated to say it. I *have*, ever since she passed."

"Then you've met your obligation," he said.

She nodded, her concern for him and her love and so many other unspoken things shining in her eyes. She couldn't stop it.

"Dammit, Emma," he grated out, and then suddenly his mouth seized hers and he was pulling her against him. She gasped at the impact of him, all of his chaotic emotions finding an outlet in physical need. She'd never felt his desire to be so sharp, so focused. His hunger was furious . . . single-minded. She moaned into his mouth as he rolled onto his back on the dock, bringing her on top of him, their fused mouths never breaking. His hands were everywhere, kneading her back muscles, squeezing her ass, pushing her tighter against him. She moaned, her desire sparking to full flame at the sensation of his cock swelling against her belly. He pulled her higher against him, rubbing her pussy against the long column of his cock, using his hold on her bottom. She held on to his shoulders, overwhelmed by the sudden storm of him, tangling her tongue with his, knowing she was drowning in her need and unable . . . *unwilling*, to save herself.

His hands moved at her back and he was drawing off her bikini top. He slid her farther up his body until she planted her hands above his head on the dock, bracing herself. Then his mouth was on her nipple, his stiff, wet tongue laving furiously, his mouth applying a sinful suck that made her whimper and flex her pussy against his hard midriff for relief. She stared out at the glittering blue sea, too overcome with pleasure and emotion and need to actually absorb what she was seeing.

His head fell back as he cupped both of her breasts in his hands. She saw the snarl that shaped his mouth as he watched himself touch her, his fingers plucking at the sensitive flesh, urging it to grow harder and stiffer until she wiggled her hips against him to get relief on her sex and called his name.

He glanced up at her briefly, the hard glitter in his eyes stealing her breath, and then he was sucking her other breast, drawing on her until she cried out sharply as desire stabbed at her from clit to her deepest core.

He rolled her onto her back and came on top of her.

"I'm going to fuck you," he grated out ominously. "I'm going to fuck you hard for making me feel so much."

Emma's mouth dropped open but she couldn't inhale. Her lungs had stopped working. It was like being pressed against the outer limits of an inferno that stole all the oxygen in the vicinity.

"Vanni! Van!" someone yelled.

He started to reach for her bikini bottoms as if the voice hadn't penetrated his furious lust.

"Vanni," she said shakily, her eyes burning with emotion. "Someone is calling you. I think it's Mrs. Denis."

"*Vanni*," Mrs. Denis called again from on top of the cliff, her voice drifting and eddying in the sea breeze. A muscle jumped in Vanni's clenched jaw as he scored Emma with his stare. He turned slightly, still shielding her naked breasts, and waved. Emma strained to see over his shoulder. At the top of the cliff, she saw Mrs. Denis standing there, her white apron showing up starkly against a dark blue dress.

"I'm coming," Vanni bellowed.

Mrs. Denis waved back and turned toward La Mer.

"We'd better go," he said after a tense moment. "She wouldn't have called if it wasn't important."

Emma nodded, still finding it difficult to catch her breath.

He reached for her discarded top and handed it to her. He waited until she'd replaced it and then jogged and leapt, making a perfect dive off the dock, knifing through the sea. Emma followed him. Despite his obvious disquietude, he waited for her to surface before they swam back together toward shore. The cold water was a slap to her hypersensitive nerves and dazed arousal, forcing her into alertness . . . forcing her to consider what had just happened.

When they climbed onto the shore together, however, and Vanni made a point of avoiding her gaze, her uncertainty mounted.

She knew deep down she was right to have spoken about Cristina's dying words, but that didn't make her regret Vanni's emotional turmoil in regard to them any less. Not that he was behaving tumultuously at the moment, she acknowledged later as she watched him in the distance, talking to a racing official as he paced on the terrace. During the walk back up to La Mer, his typical controlled façade had seemingly rebuilt itself. He'd calmly listened to Mrs. Denis's news that a driver had crashed during the early morning practice session, and then immediately dived into action making phone calls.

"Don't look so worried," Mrs. Denis said soothingly as she opened a covered dish, revealing eggs and bacon. The housekeeper had had breakfast ready for them on the terrace when they returned, but Vanni had told Emma to go ahead and eat while he attended to some phone calls. "The race official who called said that the driver wasn't hurt. His car was all right, too, but the course was damaged."

"Will it be ready for tomorrow?"

"If Vanni has his say about it," Mrs. Denis said with a smile before she poured some tea for Emma. "And he does, so that means the race will go on."

When she'd finished a light breakfast, Vanni was still on the phone, so she went upstairs to shower. She was sitting on a stool and applying some lotion to her legs, when a brisk rap sounded on the door. Vanni stepped into the room, looking both casual and chic in a pair of dark blue shorts and a white short-sleeved shirt with a single dark blue stripe across his powerful chest. His somber expression made her freeze.

"Is the damage to the course bad?" she asked.

"It isn't good," he admitted. "But it'll be fixed in time. There are crews there now working on it. We'll stop by and inspect it on the way back from Niki's. Are you almost ready to go?" he asked, checking his sports watch.

"Yes. I just need to dress." His gaze flicked down over her when she stood. She wasn't wearing anything but a towel. His mouth hardened slightly and he started to leave the bathroom. "Vanni?" she called out abruptly. "Is everything . . . okay? Are you all right?"

He nodded once, unsmilingly. "Yeah, I'm fine."

Then she was staring at the back of the door.

Chapter 33

During the drive to Nice in a convertible Montand sports car, Vanni pointed out highlights of the area and gave her a general idea of points on the racing circuit. Still, Emma recognized as they left the car in a lot at a private boating club and walked toward the sea, the things she'd said about Cristina out on the dock that morning continued to simmer inside him. No one could fault his manners, but she felt his withdrawal. She wanted to apologize for upsetting him, but didn't quite know how, given his reserve. Besides, she *wasn't* sorry she'd spoken up. It'd needed to be said. She was just regretful of his reaction and worried about him.

Niki had a small motorboat waiting for them at a dock at the club. Already there were Simon and Estelle Fournier, whom she'd met last night at dinner, in addition to three other people. One was an attractive American racer named Joe Hill that she'd met briefly last night at the Hôtel Le Maj. The other two were a couple—a stunning dark-haired woman named Vitoria Franco and her husband—also a racecar driver—Miguel. The couple was from Brazil, and seemed friendly enough, although Emma could have done without Vitoria's sharp, assessing glance and tiny, knowing smile when she shook Vanni's hand. Vitoria had been sunbathing on the dock while they waited for Emma and Vanni's arrival and had greeted them with sublime nonchalance even though the bikini she wore was so tiny, she might as well have been naked. Fortunately, the reserve and preoccupation Vanni had displayed all morning was not just for Emma. He was cool but polite in both the voluptuous Vitoria's greeting as well as Estelle's warm kisses and lingering hand on his arm as she queried him about the crash that morning.

Emma had learned last night that Estelle and Simon were on the racing committee. When they first got into the motorboat, the drivers, Simon, Estelle, and Vanni all talked about the accident and the extent of the damage, Vanni filling in details in regard to repairs. As they exited the harbor, Vanni pointed out Niki's awaiting yacht to Emma. She just stared in incredulity at the approaching one-hundred-foot-long, many-tiered behemoth. Did one get that degree of wealth from being one of the best racecar drivers in the world? she wondered as they began to disembark a moment later. *I don't think so*, she thought as Niki greeted them, looking every bit the prince of his small floating kingdom despite the fact that he was wearing only a pair of khaki-colored swim shorts, flip-flops, a deep tan, and a flashing smile. She thought it because of that hard-to-define grace he possessed—the ease of an aristocrat—an elusive quality that Vanni also seemed to embody without conscious thought. There was a confidence that came from money, and there was one that came from power, and there was perhaps another, deeper assuredness that ran in the blood. That was the quality she sensed in both Vanni and Niki, but had also recognized in Cristina without previously putting it into words.

Niki led them to a flight of stairs on the yacht, looking over his shoulder and talking to Vanni the whole time about the wreck he'd witnessed that morning during practice trials. Emma hardly listened to him. She was distracted partially because she was busy gaping at the lush interiors they passed as they rose up the yacht—a sumptuous living room on one level, an indoor saloon on the next—but mostly because Vanni had taken her hand into his. It'd been the first time he'd touched her since their interrupted, torrid clench on the dock that morning. Had he noticed how awed—and anxious—she was in these decadently luxurious surroundings in the company of all these beautiful people? She thought that might be the case. Either way, she was thankful for his touch.

They rose at last onto the upper deck that was open to the sky. It was enormous, featuring a sun-bleached wood-planked floor, multiple cushioned lounging chairs and deep sofas, a bar and dining table. A Jacuzzi and shower were located on one end, while on the other, the bridge was located within a glass compartment. Emma could see that someone captained the yacht, a convenience for Niki, she supposed, who was hosting the party and wouldn't have to think about piloting. Niki led them over to a group of lounging people.

"Emma, you met George last night and this is Cici, her friend, and my cousin Ari," Niki said.

Emma blinked the brilliant sun out of her eyes as she greeted the two women and the man, who were lounging on cushioned chairs, their feet on ottomans. "Hello," she said, her voice a little high because of surprise. Both women sunbathed topless, and they were disgustingly gorgeous. The man was yet another specimen of Mediterranean beauty. Ari was drying off a broad, naked chest with a towel. She thought she saw a trace of Niki's charm in his smoky dark eyes and smile as he greeted Vanni familiarly and Emma with warmth. As for the females, it was the strangest feeling for her to witness such an opulent display of nudity while standing next to Vanni, knowing he was looking at the same thing. No one seemed to think twice of it. Georgia stood when Niki put out his arm for her. Emma was very relieved when she shrugged on a beach tunic and walked with them under the shade of the canopy.

"We've got food and plenty to drink, so get whatever you like," Niki said generally to everyone, but looked specifically at Emma as he took her hand, leading her over to the bar. She smiled her thanks at his warmth. She appreciated his trying to make her comfortable.

She was a fish out of water, and everyone must see it. Georgia, too, took pains to draw her into conversation as the bartender served ice-cold champagne and martinis to the newcomers. Emma doubted she could ever feel any sense of true friendship toward the statuesque blonde—her cool aloofness seemed impenetrable—but Emma appreciated her efforts.

The small party took their seats on the open deck, sipped their drinks, and ate delicious, light appetizers. The captain headed the yacht out to sea, keeping the coastline in their view. When they sat, Vanni urged Emma to a sofa that was shaded. He must have realized that despite the sunscreen she'd applied earlier, she'd burn like bacon on a griddle all too soon in the glittering Mediterranean sun. She was as white as a ghost compared to the group of sun-bronzed gods and goddesses. Even Joe Hill, who was fair-skinned by nature, had a good base tan.

Maybe it was the relaxing movement of the boat and sea beneath them or sitting next to Vanni on a couch while his long leg brushed against her thigh—or possibly it was the two glasses of champagne she drank—but she started to feel a little more comfortable. By the time they'd all finished eating, she had drawn up her feet onto the couch and sat leaning against Vanni, his arm draped loosely around her. He'd taken off his shirt, but thankfully the women had kept on their beach wraps while they ate. She felt a little drowsy from the sun and the champagne, and pressed her check against Vanni's warmed, hard chest. She looked up when he pushed his fingers into her hair and rubbed her scalp. It felt delicious.

"Sleepy?" he asked quietly while the others talked.

She smiled and shook her head.

"Come over to the rail and I'll show you some of the coast."

She nodded, wishing he wasn't wearing sunglasses so she could better judge his mood. He helped her up and they stepped away from the chatting party, hand in hand. They stood at the railing a good distance from the others while Vanni pointed out the picturesque mountainside town of Villefranche-sur-Mer, where a good part of the road circuit meandered. Niki brought them both glasses of champagne after a while, but didn't stay. Vanni's arm came around her as they sipped their drinks, and the stunning landscape of Monte Carlo began to unfold. She glanced up at his stark profile as he stared toward shore and wondered if he was finally starting to calm after what had happened on the dock this morning.

She was so lulled by Vanni's company that when they returned to the gathering, she'd nearly forgotten her discomfort. It made a lunging comeback, however, when she saw that all of the women in their party—Estelle, Vitoria, Georgia, and Cici—were all lolling about lazily in the sunshine, topless once again, their golden-brown, smooth skin gleaming in the hot sun. Niki looked to have fallen asleep in a lounger near Georgia, although it was hard to tell since he wore sunglasses. Simon, Miguel, and Joe were talking quietly. Vanni guided her over to a cushioned double chaise lounge that was near the rail and several feet away from the others.

"Did you put on sunblock this morning?" Vanni asked her.

"After my shower," she replied.

He nodded and sat, patting the cushion next to him.

Self-consciously, she whipped the tunic she wore over her head. She felt like it was flashing a neon sign in everyone's eyes, she was so pale. Certainly Miguel and Ari glanced around. Wearing just her bikini, she came down next to Vanni. She noticed the handsome Ari smiling at her from across the deck. Determined not to show her awkwardness, she lay back and closed her eyes, pretending to soak up the sun with as much regal insouciance as the rest of the party.

Chapter 34

Emma said she'd put on some sunblock, but he grew concerned looking at her flawless, smooth skin as she lay next to him with her eyes closed. Even with his sunglasses on, she looked vulnerable to the ruthless Mediterranean sun. He could even see a few delicate blue veins just below the pale skin at her exposed hip bone. And the skin on the plump upper swells of her breasts—the skin that rarely saw sunlight—looked especially pale and creamy. He thought of how she'd looked this morning on the dock while he'd held her beautiful breasts in his greedy, dark hands, the mouthwatering pink nipples poking between his pinching fingers.

In a flash, all of his anguish, all of his lust reared up like a striking snake. His cock stiffened. He jerked his gaze off of her and stood. He knew Niki kept an assortment of sunscreens and oils in a cabinet in the bar area. It wouldn't hurt to put more on her. He didn't want to see her burned and uncomfortable, but it didn't seem fair to insist she stay in the shade on such a gorgeous day. Emma opened her eyes and shielded them with her hand when he returned and lay back next to her.

"I'm worried about you," he murmured, holding up the bottle of sunblock.

"Are you?" she asked softly. He glanced into her face while in the process of pouring some of the white lotion into his hand. "That's funny, I thought I should be worried about *you*."

He reached, rubbing the lotion onto a smooth, sun-warmed thigh. He found himself staring at the small, red triangle of cloth covering her mound. "I'm fine," he muttered.

"Really?"

"Do you think I'm going to burn?" he asked dryly, glancing up into her face. He looked away when he saw her slight annoyance and worry at his flippant reply. As he rubbed lotion into her other thigh, he glanced up and saw Ari Carboni watching him with fixed intent as he massaged lotion into Emma's hip. *Lecher.*

But what could Vanni expect, really? Ari carried the Carboni hot blood. He was a relation to Cristina, after all.

He gritted his teeth at the reminder of the things Emma had said that morning, doing his best to ignore his swelling erection. It annoyed him, but he understood perfectly why the men were either glancing their way or staring, in Ari's case. Emma looked more naked than the other women, somehow. There was an illicit quality to her bikini-clad, lithe, curvaceous body, like the jolt that went through a man when he accidentally caught the sight of a woman undressing. The other women were beautiful, yes, but there was no mystery to their gilded skin and exposed breasts, no challenge. Whereas Emma's innocent beauty held some secret, some sexual enigma he couldn't quite grasp with words.

He knew firsthand what it was like to thirst for the answer, though, aching to find it in her deep, warm depths.

He glanced up and saw Ari's rigid expression as Vanni cupped her waist and rubbed lotion along the sweet swell of her hips that he prized so much . . . that his cock adored.

"Vanni?" Emma asked, her voice just above a whisper.

He glanced up at her face. She blinked in surprise. He realized he'd been snarling a warning at Ari.

"Yes?" he asked, forcing his face into impassivity.

She bit her lip in a gesture he recognized as an anxious one. "Should I take off my top?" she whispered.

He blanched, his gaze unerringly lowering to her breasts. Her nipples were erect against the relatively insubstantial fabric of the bra. Was she growing as aroused as he was, touching her? Or did she enjoy Ari's attention on her? The thought scalded him. He poured more lotion onto his hand and began to apply it to her arms.

"Do you want to?" he asked evenly, rubbing up and down on both her upper arms at once, the rhythmic movement striking him as sexual. Everything was striking him as sexual. His cock swelled tighter. Dammit. What was wrong with him? The hot summer air surrounding him suddenly felt thick and electric. He couldn't get enough oxygen in his lungs.

"I don't know. I just feel . . . so *American*."

"You *are* American," he replied drolly.

"I've never equated the word with feeling like a Puritan until now," she said under her breath.

"I like your Americanness just fine," he said stiffly, rubbing some lotion on her chest, "but if you want to go topless, do it. As you see, it's the custom."

He didn't know what was wrong with him. Why didn't he just tell her to take off the top? He'd sunbathed with girlfriends going topless hundreds of times while he was in the South of France, never thinking more of it than Niki did about Georgia.

Emma was no different.

The emotion he'd been tamping down since this morning threatened to swell higher. He gritted his teeth. She *was* different. He liked *everything* about her. He adored her freshness and sexy sweetness and otherworldly wisdom. So how come he wanted to punish her for those things she'd said this morning? How come he wanted to hurt her a little for hurting him? He knew she hadn't meant to cause him distress. He knew she was kinder and just . . . *better* . . . than anyone he'd known since he was an adult.

Ever known.

But he still wanted to see her undone, just a tad anxious . . . not to mention writhing with excitement, whimpering in pleasure.

His fingertips brushed across the tops of her firm, thrusting breasts. He felt the pulse in his cock. In the distance, he noticed Niki get up and ask everyone if they wanted refreshers on their drinks. He didn't look around even when his friend called, "Van? Emma?" Vaguely he was aware of Emma shaking her head. He stared fixedly at the pale mounds of her breasts as he rubbed them with his fingertip. Her nipples were growing more and more erect beneath the fabric. He glanced up to her face and saw that her lips were parted as she stared down at him. She was so exquisite.

Too exquisite. She was a threat, somehow.

He reached up abruptly and untied the strings at her neck. "It's not a big deal," he lied. He lowered the fabric, exposing her creamy, firm breasts and tight nipples. The vision taunted him. They looked so delicate . . . so *naked*. In the periphery of his vision, he noticed Ari start slightly and place his hands on the arm of the lounger as if in preparation to spring up. Every muscle in Vanni's body tensed.

"Fuck," he muttered savagely, jerking the strings back up around her neck and tying them off hard. He'd been willing to expose her to assure himself it didn't matter . . . to convince himself *she* didn't matter.

"Vanni?" Emma asked, clearly bewildered by his actions. He flung himself off the lounger and grabbed her hand. She rose and he headed with a single-minded purpose toward the stairs. He ignored the others when they looked around. They didn't exist. Only Emma did, and this strange, boiling need inside him that was about to erupt.

Emma's gaze skimmed across the others' startled faces as Vanni pulled her to the staircase. Estelle whipped off her sunglasses and followed their progress across the deck with a livid scowl. Her husband, however, looked pleased.

"Van?" Niki stood at the bottom of the stairs, holding a bag of ice. He looked from Emma's dazed expression to Vanni's rigid, furious one. "Oh," he said, blinking in amazement. "Downstairs, first door on the right."

Heat flooded her cheeks when without another word, Vanni pulled her down the next level of stairs. Emma looked back at Niki.

"I'm sorry," she said.

A strange expression broke over Niki's handsome face. He looked pleased. "Don't be," he said emphatically.

Vanni marched across the living room, a man on a mission. Her heart was about to pop out of her chest, it was thundering so fast against her breastbone when he pulled her into a room and slammed the door shut behind her. The snick of the lock in combination with his burning gaze sounded ominous . . . thrilling.

Emma had a fleeting impression of a luxury suite with gleaming mahogany wood and a king-sized bed. Then Vanni was reaching behind her neck and tearing open the knot he'd just made up on the deck. He jerked the bikini top down over her breasts and pushed her toward the bed. Emma spilled backward, her knees at the edge of the mattress. He came down over her, his hands planted next to her shoulders, elbows bent, his lower body pressing her down into the bed. One second she'd been standing, and the next his mouth was enclosing her breast. She gasped at the impact of him, his hot suck on her sensitive flesh, his rigid, laving tongue on her nipple. Liquid heat flooded her, answering his fierce, wild demand. She felt his cock jump against her thigh. He flexed his hips, grinding himself against her, unapologetic in his need.

She understood this was the same fire that had raged in him on the dock. It leapt up even stronger now, more furious because it had been banked and forced to simmer under wraps. She was more than willing to be the focus of his distilled desire and chaotic emotions. She wasn't afraid of him; her own need more than matched his.

He gathered both of her breasts in his hands and plumped them for his ravening mouth. He lifted his head after a moment and switched his target, latching on to her other nipple and drawing on it so precisely, so sweetly, that she clutched at his head in rising desperation and flexed her hips, pushing her sex into the bed to get an indirect pressure on it. As if he felt the give in her flesh, he ground against her, his cock feeling like a long, heavy poker throbbing beneath the thin layer of his trunks.

He lifted his head a moment later, still squeezing her breasts in his hands. She stared down at him, panting. He seemed transfixed as he stared at her, his thumbs rubbing her slick, erect nipples. Her clit pinched in arousal at the vision, and she whimpered. His avid stare transferred to her face.

"Why are you doing this to me?' he asked quietly.

"I don't know," she whispered, overwhelmed by the question for some reason. His nostrils flared, his mouth slanting as if he found her answer wanting. He shifted his weight to the side of her and reached for the bikini top, which was still fastened below her breasts. He whipped the material off her a second later and pushed himself off the bed.

"Come here," he said, his mouth hard but his touch on her hand gentle enough as he pulled her into a sitting position. "Stand up. I'm going to tie your hands behind your back."

She stood, eyeing him warily. Nevertheless, she turned her back to him and let him bind her wrists at her lower back with the skimpy fabric and strings of her bikini top. He spun her back around with his hands on her shoulders. She opened her mouth to ask him what he planned, but suddenly his mouth was covering hers and she was enveloped in his angry, hot consumption.

"Are you mad at me?" she asked him a moment later when he abruptly ended their kiss.

"I don't know. Maybe," he snarled. "Yes. You're making me feel so damn . . ."

"What?" she whispered when his deep voice caught.

"Alive," he grated out, his eyes a little wild. "It . . . *hurts*."

"Vanni—" she whispered, confused and concerned by his words, but he was having none of her compassion. He was single-minded in his desire to burn. He pushed lightly on her shoulders.

"Go down on your knees," he said.

She blinked, considering denying him. But then she looked into his eyes and saw all the anguish and confusion and white-hot need exposed there. She'd done that, by insisting they talk about Cristina and her dying words. His feelings were natural. What's more, they were as right as a storm letting loose after all that pressure built for so many years.

She let her weight go. He felt it and tightened his hold on her shoulders, guiding her to her knees. She stared at his crotch. Only his swim shorts covered his cock. It was tenting the fabric, trapped by it, straining to be released. Vanni liberated it with a vicious jerk of the shorts out over his cock and down to his thighs. His erection sprung free, heavy and tumescent. He stepped toward her, his hand cupping the back of her head. She looked up at him as he fisted the thick shaft and lifted it to her lips. What she saw in his blazing eyes made her want to cry. There was an apology shining through all that feral heat. He needn't be sorry. She understood his exposed pain, maybe more than he did.

She opened her lips and he guided his cock between them. They stretched around his girth as he pushed the fat, turgid crown across her tongue. A rough groan rattled his throat when she polished the head with her tongue. He flexed his hips back, withdrawing, only to pierce her mouth again. She strained to bathe the shaft with her tongue, but he tightened his hold on her head, gripping at her hair.

"Stay still," he rasped. She did as he asked while he plunged the first several inches of his cock in and out of her mouth rapidly. Heat spread in her cheeks. Her pussy tingled. She kept her lips a rigid ring around him, but otherwise, he wouldn't let her do much . . . except be the target of his desire. For some reason, being forced not to move made her crave his cock more. Her tongue pressed hard up against that delicious, quarter-inch-thick ridge below the fat crown. He groaned and his fingers flexed tighter in her hair. She clamped his cock so hard her mouth hurt and sucked until her cheeks collapsed from the vacuum.

"Holy . . ." He said something else, but it was on a groan and she couldn't make it out. Holding her head firmly, he flexed, sending his cock further into her mouth, filling her. Overfilling her. Her eyes opened wide, but then he was granting her a reprieve. He was back almost immediately, though. This time, she continued to suck hungrily, needing him. The tip touched her throat and she gagged reflexively. He withdrew, but she craned forward, not letting him escape so easily. He loosened his hold slightly on her hair, and she felt it. She ducked her head back and forth, taking him a fraction of an inch further each time, her craving overcoming her body's instinct to reject him. She found it grew easier with each pass.

"Dammit, Emma," he bit out above her, and then he was holding her still again, but his cock kept coming, driving into her mouth, wild and ruthless. She let herself be the center of the storm for a stretched moment, surrendering to his need.

A vicious curse ripped out of his throat, and his cock was sliding out of her mouth. It was jarring, to be so suddenly empty of him. She opened her eyes and stared up at him, confused. His mouth was slanted in a thin line. He reached down, lifting her with a hand beneath her elbows. His jutting, damp cockhead pushed against her belly when he leaned down over, untying her top and freeing her wrists.

"Why do you always have to test me?" he growled, jerking impatiently at the strings.

"I thought you said I always seemed out of your reach," she said dazedly, her throat raspy from taking his cock so deep. "I was just trying to show you I'm not."

He ripped the top over her hands. "We'll talk about it later," he said. "Right now, take off the panties and go lie on the bed."

Panting softly, she did what he said, her anticipation and wary excitement building by the second. She lay on her back on the mattress, her head on the pillows.

"Move to the center of the bed," he said. "And spread your thighs."

He waited until she'd taken the position before he shoved his shorts off his legs. Cupping his jutting erection from below, he stalked toward the bed. He flicked his hand over the length, sending a hot stab of excitement through her, before he came onto the bed on his hands and knees, kneeling over her. He reached between her thighs and palmed her outer sex, almost immediately sending his middle finger into her slit. She gasped, staring up at him, helpless in her desire as he finger-fucked her.

"You're soaking wet," he grated out, white teeth flashing.

"I told you I was no angel," she choked wryly.

"But you are," he snarled, withdrawing his finger and grasping his cock. "Sent here to test me. Now . . . spread your thighs farther."

He placed one hand on her inner knee and pushed back firmly so that her thigh rose and her hips rolled back on the bed. He presented the head of his cock to her slit, flexing, forcing her to part for the swollen tip. His hand made a swiping motion, scattering the pillows next to her head off the bed before it settled next to her head. He held her stare, his gaze blazing, as he slowly thrust his cock into her. She clenched her teeth at the hard, relentless pressure. A muscle jumped in his cheek. His balls pressed tight against her outer sex and she bit off a scream.

"Put your hands above your head," he said. "Hold on to your wrists. You're not allowed to move them. I can't take your hands on me right now."

She did what he'd directed, feeling full and incendiary. She held her breath; there wasn't room for air and Vanni's furiously throbbing cock in her body.

"I'm going to fuck you hard. I can't help it, Emma," he said, his voice breaking slightly.

"I know," she whispered. "I want it."

His face collapsed for a brief second, the vision making her heart squeeze in anguish. Then he was drawing his cock out of her to the tip and thrusting deep again, and then again, a wave pounding at the shore relentlessly. She bit her lip to stop from screaming. His intensity and arousal were such that it was slightly uncomfortable. But she lifted her hips for him nevertheless, wanting this. Needing it. She held her breath as the headboard began to rock against the wall as he drove into her, and she stared up at the wild, fierce expression on his face. Rabid lust had turned his already supertoned body into a rigid coil. Lean muscle bulged against smooth skin, only adding to her impression that he was about to explode. She bobbed her hips, matching his fast tempo. Slowly, the uncomfortable pressure morphed into a sizzling burn.

"Fuck," he snarled, feeling her excitement. He switched his hands to her wrists, pushing her hands into the pillow. He extended his long legs on the mattress and reared up over her. Emma clenched her eyes shut, intuiting what was coming. He came up on his toes and the balls of his feet, driving his cock into her with the power of his whole body. He fucked her like that for several heart-stopping moments, the headboard clacking loudly against the wall, Emma keening uncontrollably. The friction he built in her sparked and flared. She shook in climax as he power-fucked her, seeking his own relief with blind desperation.

He roared as he came, the harsh sound blistering her ears and echoing in her skull. He caught his breath and thrust into her again, another shout tearing out of his throat. She'd never witnessed him more savage.

She'd never seen him so beautiful.

He collapsed down over her after a moment, gasping wildly for air. In his momentary weakness, she broke free of his hold on her hands. She put her arms around his neck, pulling him to her. Something swelled in her chest, something sweet and huge and agonizingly sharp.

"Shh," she soothed, rubbing his back muscles, feeling his ribs expand and contract as he fought for air. His head fell between her neck and shoulder. She could feel the puffs of his warm breath against her skin.

"I'm sorry," he groaned.

"It's okay," she whispered, her fingers delving into his thick hair. "I wouldn't be here if I didn't want to be."

His panting ceased, his rib cage convulsing, before he exhaled again roughly. "I want more time."

"What?" she asked, her hands freezing.

"Give me more time," he bit out between clenched teeth.

"I . . . We can talk about it later," she fumbled. He lifted his head and scored her with his stare. "Don't, Vanni. Don't make me decide right now."

"Why?" he asked, still panting. She felt cornered by the single word and all its meanings.

"Because it's already happening . . . what I didn't want to happen," spilled out of her throat. It was hard to withhold the truth after his fiery, honest lovemaking. He stilled.

"What? What's happened?"

"I'm starting to fall in love with you," she said desperately. "It may already be too late."

His expression flattened.

"Emma," he whispered fiercely. He shook his head incredulously. "How can you say that to me after what I just did to you?"

She shrugged helplessly. "I think that's what popped it out of me."

He stared at her, his face rigid with shock. Then his mouth twitched. His smile broke free at the same time hers did, a brilliant radiance after a storm. An unpleasant thought intruded, but it couldn't entirely erase her grin.

"What your friends must think of me . . ." she whispered, trailing off as she mentally answered her own question.

"If anything, they'll think *I'm* the rude caveman, hauling you off like I did. Rightfully so. You didn't do anything wrong," he added darkly under his breath. "And they really aren't my friends, except for Niki. And he'll only be glad something has broken me out of my funk."

Emma thought of how stunned Niki had looked when Vanni charged down the stairwell just now, dragging Emma after him, then how pleased; how he'd called out "don't be" when she'd apologized for their rude exit from the party.

"You know, I think you're right," she mused.

"Of course I'm right. Emma, the whole idea of you walking away at the tick of a clock is ridiculous."

She opened her mouth to say he was supposed to be walking away, too . . . that he'd taken pains to warn her that he *would*, but then he was kissing her, deep and sweet, and her thoughts flew away like scattered moths.

She knew only one thing for certain. Despite her thoughts about feeling compelled to the truth just now, she'd lied.

She wasn't *starting* to fall. She'd already landed.

Good and hard.

Chapter 35

The next morning Emma rose early when Vanni did. He would go down to the racing circuit to make sure everything was in order, take care of last minute-details, and do a last-minute check of the Montand racecar with Niki, then return to La Mer to pick up Emma for the race itself. She'd showered, thrown on a sundress, and gone downstairs before him. It was another perfect day on the French Riviera. Emma wondered if there were ever days that weren't sun drenched and infused with the sweet breezes off the Mediterranean.

Mrs. Denis was in high spirits for raceday. She led Emma out onto the terrace and proudly displayed a breakfast table laid with china, silver, colorful flags, and what appeared to be a miniature version of the Montand racecar.

"They're selling them in the village. I thought Vanni would like to see it," Mrs. Denis said, laughing as Emma picked up the little black, red, and blue car with *Montand* and the number *14* painted on the side in white. She heard a sound behind her and turned to see Vanni walking onto the terrace. Her gaze dipped over him appreciatively. No one could wear a tuxedo with such masculine, careless grace as him, and then morph into a casual resort mode with equal comfort. He was clean-shaven this morning and his eyes looked cool and sharp and focused . . . until they landed on her, Emma realized with a rush of warmth. She held up the little car as he approached, smiling.

"Look what Mrs. Denis got you. Lucky boy, you get to play with the real thing."

"And she better play nice for Niki today," he said, his uncommon, brilliant smile warming her even further.

"Happy Raceday. *Bonne chance,* Montand!" Mrs. Denis enthused, waving her hand with a little flourish. Emma laughed. She was adorable. Vanni must have thought the same thing, because he leaned down and kissed the housekeeper on both cheeks. Mrs. Denis looked extremely pleased, giving Emma a pointed glance.

"What have you done to my gloomy Vanni?"

"She's beat him into the shadows, where he belongs," Vanni said without pause, meeting Emma's stare, a smile lingering on his lips. Emma felt herself color at the potent compliment.

"I knew you were luck to us," Mrs. Denis enthused, patting Emma softly on the arm.

Vanni chuckled and leaned down, kissing both of Emma's warm cheeks and then her lips, where he lingered. Mrs. Denis cleared her throat. "I'll get your breakfast." Which seemed to be a signal for Vanni to pull her closer and kiss her in earnest.

"You smell delicious," he said a moment later, nuzzling her neck. "Maybe I should skip breakfast and eat you instead."

"You already did," she murmured, her eyes fluttering closed as his lips brushed against her pulse.

"Two meals is a lucky tradition on raceday, especially when they're as delicious as you." He kissed a patch of skin just below her ear and then scraped it lightly with his teeth. She shivered in excitement. He transferred his mouth to the opening of her ear, and she felt herself melting.

"You just made that up," she said.

"I'm entitled. It's the first Montand grand prix. I have to start raceday traditions sometime."

"You're not really thinking of going back to bed, are you?" she asked weakly.

"Of course I'm thinking of it," he said, straightening his head and pinning her with a lambent stare.

She smiled. She was thinking of it, too, and he knew it.

"We shouldn't," she said in a hushed tone. "I can still look Mrs. Denis in the eye without blushing, unlike Niki. And the rest of the people on the yacht."

His mouth tilted in amusement. They both heard Mrs. Denis's footsteps inside, bringing them their breakfast. Vanni's dark brows went up in a silent message of resignation. He seated her at the table instead of leading her back to the bedroom. She knew he was thinking about what happened yesterday after he'd hauled her off to bed. She was thinking about it, too.

After they'd made love that first time so explosively, Vanni had made love to her again, the second time still heated, but soulful and poignant. Afterward, they'd talked quietly, touching each other, the afterglow so sweet that she'd forgotten where they were.

When reality had finally struck, anxiety came with it.

"Is that really the time?" she'd asked, her gaze landing on a bedside clock. "Oh my God, Vanni, we've been down here for hours. Niki must think we're so rude. The others must wonder what we're doing," She'd started to scramble up from the bed, but Vanni had halted her with a hand around her wrist.

"They know what we were doing. We're all adults. Besides, the yacht has been anchored for the past twenty minutes. Most of the guests have probably already gone back to shore."

She'd blinked in surprise. "Really?"

"Really," he'd said dryly. "Besides, I told you it doesn't matter what any of them think, Niki aside. And he'll be happy."

She'd fallen back on the bed, bracing herself with her elbows.

"Because you are?" she'd asked hopefully.

He'd pulled her to him again.

"Because I am."

She glanced at Vanni's profile now, drinking in his newfound peace as Mrs. Denis served them Raceday Bellinis, coffee, tea, fruit, toast, and freshly made pastries with cute little racing-flag toothpicks.

"Who will I sit with at the race?" Emma wondered after Mrs. Denis had bustled back inside.

"Me, I expect."

She smiled and popped a grape in her mouth. "I thought you'd be away doing important racing things."

"Anything that isn't done before the race begins isn't going to get done period."

"And what should I wear?"

"I'm wearing what you see," he said, spreading marmalade on some thick wheat toast.

"So it's casual? I thought maybe we were supposed to wear our Sunday best and big hats or something."

"This is the Montand grand prix, not the Kentucky Derby," he said dryly.

"Right. A prince's version of casual," she said, glancing down over him with a smile.

She imagined Cristina was guiding her as she fingered through the clothing she'd inherited. Of all people, Cristina would have known she needed help. Feeling the festive mood of raceday, she settled on a flirty, fresh red halter sundress that fell just above her knees, along with a pair of black sandals. She looked through some of the accessories Dean Shaw's wife had sent but couldn't find anything in blue to accessorize in the Montand colors. She settled for a chic black-and-white watch. If she was to judge by Vanni's warm, appreciative stare on her when he returned to pick her up later that day, she thought she'd hit the mark just right. He stood at the bottom of the stairs, waiting for her.

"I dressed in the Montand car colors," she told him with a grin.

His eyes had sparkled before he swooped down and kissed her surprisingly hard, taking away her breath. "You look like luck walking," he'd said. She blinked when she felt him slide a velvet box into her hand. He just raised his brows expectantly when she gave him a surprised look.

"Oh my God, they're gorgeous. And perfect! It's the Montand colors," she exclaimed when she opened the box and saw the sapphire, diamond, onyx, and ruby bracelet lying there along with a vintage-looking, flower-shaped sapphire ring. Vanni picked up the bracelet and looped it around her wrist.

"You dressed as if you knew you were getting them," he said, fastening the clasp.

"I knew no such thing. Oh, it's so pretty," she said, twirling her wrist in the sunlight. He reached, immobilizing her hand, and slid the ring onto her finger. Her heart came to a dead stop.

"Thank you," she whispered feelingly. He smiled. She put her arms around his neck. He pulled and she came off the stairs, fully into his arms. Their kiss left her breathless.

"I thought they would bring me luck," Vanni said near her lips a moment later.

"For the race?"

He shook his head, his gaze warm on her face. "I bought them the day before you agreed to come to France. It worked. You came."

Everything from that day struck her as a colorful, exciting, bright blur. Mrs. Denis rode with them to the main grandstand for the race, located on the outskirts of Villefranche-sur-Mer. As they drew closer to the circuit, the crowds of people walking, riding their bikes, and attempting to drive grew thick. Vendors with carts sold everything from sorbet to water to race flags. The atmosphere was electrical, and Emma couldn't help but be caught up in the excitement. As an event organizer, Vanni had a pass to drive on the road to the huge grandstand that was erected at the starting and finish lines. Most of the people would watch the race at various sites along the route, roadside locations that had been designed with spectator safety in mind.

Mrs. Denis kissed Vanni and Emma, excitedly bidding Vanni good luck when they walked up the steps to the grandstand a while later; she would watch the race with some friends and family members elsewhere.

Vanni led them to a prime box located in the grandstands, one that was canopied and directly in front of the white finish line of the main arena racetrack. Apparently, the box was designated for the racing board and their friends and family. Estelle and Simon Fournier were already there, seated not in the metallic benches featured elsewhere in the grandstand, but in comfortable-looking deep chairs. Next to each chair was a table with an attached video screen. Determined to follow Vanni's easy manner and not betray her embarrassment over what had happened on the yacht yesterday, Emma returned the couple's greeting warmly. Vanni introduced her to the mustachioed man she'd seen at the dinner along with a regal-looking woman in her fifties, both of whom greeted her cordially. Emma almost immediately forgot their names, she was so distracted and excited by the energy in the air. A bar was set up in the back of the box, and caterers were busy laying out what appeared to be a lavish, gorgeously displayed lunch.

"Sit here," Estelle Fournier insisted while Vanni went to get them drinks. Feeling she had no other choice, Emma sat in the chair Estelle indicated next to her. Estelle looked extremely beautiful in a sophisticated yet simple ivory sundress that set off the tan she'd gotten yesterday on the yacht. "The South of France agrees with you," Estelle said, her gaze dropping over Emma's figure shrewdly.

"Or something does," Simon agreed with a warm, knowing smile and a glance back at Vanni.

"Do be quiet, Simon," Estelle snapped coolly. "You're embarrassing the girl."

Emma was more embarrassed for Estelle's sharp tongue than she was for anything Simon had said. She was glad when three or four others joined the group in the box, distracting her from the Fourniers' marital discord. Vanni appeared a moment later with their drinks—a punch they had prepared at the bar—and took a seat next to her.

"Feeling lucky, Van?" Simon asked briskly.

"Very," Vanni replied, his gaze on the track, his hand closing briefly on Emma's thigh.

"I don't think I ever heard how you two met," Estelle said, sipping her drink.

"Emma is a nurse. She cared for Cristina," Vanni said, his clipped tone and the manner that he continued staring out at the arena track not inviting further inquiry. Emma looked out to the track, too, when she heard some applause and the roar of engines. The drivers were taking their marks. Vanni pointed and she saw the red, blue, black, and white Montand car.

"You want to be down there, don't you?" Estelle asked, studying Vanni's profile as an announcer began to speak in French on the arena sound system and the noise level increased from the crowd.

"Down there?" Emma asked, confused.

"Leading Niki's team. In the pits," Estelle said.

She turned to Vanni. "You're usually down in the pits?" she asked him.

Vanni threw Estelle a vaguely annoyed glance. "Sometimes. Not always."

"Usually," Estelle said pointedly, taking a bite out of the lemon from her drink with flashing white teeth.

At that moment, her concern about what Estelle had said was dampened by Dean and Michelle Shaw's arrival. They rose up the steps to the box, both of them out of breath and looking very eager. They greeted Emma and immediately took their seats. The drivers were being announced. Emma recognized the names of several drivers she'd met in the past few days, trying to take note of the number and car announced with their name. She clapped extra hard when she heard Niki's name, the manic excitement of the event spreading to her. The stands were now packed. She could see that the road leading off the center arena to the main circuit was packed on both sides with people.

"The pace car is off," Vanni said quietly next to her, obviously remembering that she didn't speak French. Emma sat forward in her seat, following the car at which Vanni pointed. "It'll lead the drivers through the circuit once," he said, "getting them up to pace. The drivers can't leave their lanes or pass the pace car until the pace car leads them across the starting line and the flag is waved," Vanni explained, pausing to switch on the video monitor next to him as the drivers exited the main arena. His manner was intent and focused.

"How long will the race last?"

"The best clocked time so far was two hours, fourteen minutes, thirty point two seconds set by Niki during time trials," he said, staring at the screen. Her heart went out to him when she recognized his barely leashed excitement.

"Vanni," she said softly.

He glanced up at her.

"Is it too late for you to go to the pits?"

"No, but what's—"

"I think you should go," she interrupted softly. He gave her an incredulous glance. "You're usually in the pits when you're around for one of Niki's races, aren't you?" she said, giving him a fond, remonstrative look.

"Don't pay any attention to Estelle," his said with quiet disdain, his voice muted by the cheers of people for miles around reverberating off the mountainside.

"I'm not. I'm thinking of you. I should have realized you would have wanted to be in the thick of things. You came to the stands today because of me, didn't you?" She saw the slight give in his expression and knew that said she'd spoken the truth. "Go on," she urged. "It'll do Niki good to know you are there. And Dean and Michelle are here. They'll keep me company," Emma added when he opened his mouth to protest.

"All right," he said suddenly. He saw her smile and leaned over to kiss her. "I'll come back here to get you after the race," he said quietly near her lips a moment later.

"Good luck, Gearhead," she whispered.

"One more shot of it," he growled quietly, kissing her hard once more. He met her stare when they broke apart a moment later.

"You're sure it's okay?"

"Yes. *Go*," she laughed.

In the distance, she heard the roar of the approaching engines. The crowd in the main stands began to stand and cheer. Vanni's small but unguarded smile and the spark of excitement in his blue-green eyes made the sacrifice of his presence more than worth it.

Everyone in the box began to stand as the cars tore into the main arena, zooming toward the starting line. Vanni said something in Dean's ear and Dean nodded. The cars began their first lap to a deafening cheer, and Vanni was jogging down the flight of steps. Emma watched him go, a dazed, happy feeling swelling inside her.

"Potent stuff, isn't it?" Estelle asked quietly from beside her, taking a large swallow of her drink. The beautiful French woman nodded in the direction where Vanni had just disappeared. Emma gave her an arch look.

"Maybe you should go easy on it, then," Emma said, nodding significantly at the potent raceday punch in her hand. Estelle was on her second glass.

Estelle laughed. "So . . . there *is* a little more to you than the girl next door?" she said as they sat again. "I figured there must be, to keep Vanni interested for more than an hour. He's notoriously dissatisfied with women, you know."

"Did it take him all of an hour with you?"

Estelle snorted into her drink. This time when she smiled, Emma thought it was genuine. A cheer went up in the distance. She turned on her monitor, too excited about the outcome of the race to be overly concerned by Estelle taking a bat at her with her claws.

The drivers were on their third lap. Several cars flew past the picturesque harbor. Niki appeared to be in second place with a green and gold car she recognized as Mario Acarde's just inches ahead of him. It seemed the Formula One drivers were having a blazing start. Her heart seized slightly when they took a harrowing turn, seemingly not slowing down at all. The car in third place tried to use the turn to gain position on Niki, but scraped against the inside wall, bumping Niki. Emma gasped and placed her hand on her heart as if to contain it in her chest as she watched Niki regain control masterfully.

"Miguel Franco," Estelle said. She'd leaned over and was watching Emma's monitor with her. "You'd never guess he was so ruthless having met him, would you?" she asked drolly. Emma shook her head, recalling the polite, quiet-spoken Brazilian driver she'd met yesterday on Niki's yacht. Then again, Miguel Franco would have to have some fire in him to deal with his gorgeous, flirtatious wife Vitoria on a daily basis. Niki hadn't only recovered from Miguel's aggressive move, he'd managed to inch up on Mario. By the time they roared into the main arena, he and Mario were neck and neck.

Emma watched the next several laps with Estelle in quiet awe, getting a feel for the tricky course and gaining a huge respect for the subtle skills and monumental courage of the drivers. Her heart was beating very fast, just watching on the monitor. She'd thought Niki had been teasing her when he was so cavalier about the dangerousness of the sport, but she now realized he'd been downplaying just how harrowing this road race really was.

"Do they crash a lot on these type of races?" Emma asked Estelle shakily.

"All the time," Estelle said, taking a drink.

"But they're not usually . . . deadly?"

"Not *usually*, no," Estelle said offhandedly.

Emma didn't find that very reassuring.

"You don't have to worry about me, you know. In regard to Vanni, I mean." Emma blinked in surprise, realizing Estelle was casually returning to their earlier topic. The twentieth lap had just finished. People in the box were starting to stand up and get food, and Simon had joined them at the back of the box. "Vanni would never look twice at me. He's very particular that way."

"What way?" Emma asked blankly.

"He doesn't . . . associate with married women. I have a cousin who knows him well. Apparently he's fastidious about avoiding married women because his father was a philanderer. He's dead set against interfering in marital bliss," Estelle said, her mouth curling derisively. "No matter how unblissful the marriage. Very moral."

"Very inconvenient. For you," Emma added with a rueful smile.

Estelle looked a little startled at her honesty, but then met her stare. "*Definitely* not the girl next door," she murmured speculatively. "Still, I'd watch myself. Vanni isn't the type to settle down any more than he's the kind to get involved with a married woman. I know that for a fact from my cousin as well." She glanced distractedly toward the arena as the cars rounded the main track again. "Oh . . . here she is now," Estelle said suddenly, smiling and waving. Emma looked at what had caught her attention, her mouth dropping open in disbelieving recognition.

"Astrid," Estelle called excitedly. Men and women alike in the stands did a double take at the stunning woman with the long, flowing black hair as she ascended the steps. In the four-inch platform sandals she wore, she must have been close to six feet tall. She definitely could have stopped traffic wearing a short blue-and-white-striped dress that optimally showed off tanned, smooth legs and full breasts straining against tight cotton. Against her will, Emma had to admit that the statuesque beauty and Vanni must have looked amazing together.

She'd seen them together, Emma realized, feeling a little nauseated. She'd seen them together at a very private moment. And they *had* looked amazing.

That only increased the roiling sensation in her belly. Vanni had said their relationship would be exclusive during their five weeks together, and she'd believed him. She hadn't thought about what that implied—if anything—to Astrid.

Astrid entered the box, her gaze skimming over Emma and clearly finding her insignificant. She stepped right past her to embrace Estelle. Emma stood, all too glad to move over into Vanni's seat next to Michelle Shaw and give Astrid the one next to her cousin. Michelle greeted Emma warmly and moved her monitor so they could share. Emma was growing accustomed to Estelle's frequently vicious tongue, but she didn't have to always be on her guard with Michelle.

She was uncomfortably aware of the two women chattering away in rapid French next to her, especially when she specifically recognized Vanni's name mentioned by Astrid. Estelle replied. Out of the corner of her eye, she noticed Astrid whip her head around and glare pointedly in Emma's direction.

"Just ignore her," Michelle said quietly. Their heads were close together as they leaned in to watch the same screen. Emma looked up with just her eyes and saw the older woman was regarding her with a small, knowing smile. "I noticed how you tensed up when you saw her just now. She's about as important to him as what's on the dinner menu. And at least until recently, Vanni had a take-it-or-leave-it attitude about food."

Emma gave her a grateful smile. She appreciated the show of support. But it wasn't that she was worried about Vanni being overly interested in Astrid. She'd heard him tell the fiery beauty firsthand, after all, that sex was all he could give her. The reason she was troubled by Astrid's appearance was that she was reminded in a jarring fashion that *she*—Emma—was in the same boat as Astrid. She'd agreed, just as Astrid had, to a sexual affair. The only difference in her case was that she'd put the time limit on it. Otherwise, she and Astrid had more in common than it was comfortable for her to think about.

She hadn't *forgotten* the practical reason for her and Vanni's entering into the agreement. It was just that under the influence of the romance and excitement of the French Riviera and Vanni's masterful lovemaking—and her own foolishness—it was easy to mask the truth. It was convenient to *escape* it.

Something she was infamous for doing, Emma realized with a sinking feeling.

Now she'd allowed things to progress to the point where she'd told Vanni she was falling in love with him. His response to her confession had been fierce and sweet and had swept her off her feet completely.

But he'd never returned the words. Why had it been so easy while in his addictive presence to not focus on that glaring fact?

She blinked when Michelle touched her arm. "I meant to make you feel better," Michelle said in a hushed tone. "But from that look on your face, I've made things worse."

"No. No you haven't. Thank you for saying what you did."

Michelle didn't look convinced, but at that point a roar went up in the distance. The announcer exclaimed excitedly in French.

"Niki just took the lead on the mountain turn," Dean yelled as the crowd in the main arena began to cheer.

She and Michelle turned their total focus back to the race. By the time the fortieth lap was complete, one of the NASCAR champions had spun out in a frightening, fiery crash at the harrowing harbor turn, and the caution flag had gone up, slowing down the race considerably. Miraculously, the driver escaped from the crash unscathed. Meanwhile, Joe Hill had come back fighting strong for the Americans, nudging out Mario Acarde and gaining on Niki. She, Michelle, and Dean went to get a plate of food, but Emma could barely eat it, the danger level of the competition was growing so fierce. The announcer had taken to yelling nonstop into the microphone as drivers took greater and greater risks to gain supremacy on the road.

"Can I ask you something?" Emma asked Michelle during one of the more relatively placid moments in the race. Michelle nodded. "Did Vera leave the French Riviera because I was coming?"

Michelle's friendly face collapsed slightly. "Did someone tell you that?"

"No," Emma said. "But she did, didn't she? Leave as a sort of protest to my coming?" Emma saw her answer on Michelle's honest face.

"Vera can be very idiosyncratic at times, especially when it comes to Vanni," Michelle said apologetically. "She imagines herself as a mother figure to him, although I've never noticed Vanni reciprocating the sentiment. To be honest, I've always thought he's so forbearing when it comes to her because she resembles his mother a bit, and he loved his mother so much."

Emma nodded in agreement. "I just don't understand why Vera hates me so much."

Michelle shrugged. "Isn't it obvious? She sees you as a potential threat to her comfortable little world. I'm afraid Vera's feelings for Vanni's father complicate things even further." Emma gave her a puzzled glance. What did that mean? Michelle waved her hand. "Trust me, the internal workings of my sister-in-law's mind are not worth thinking about. I won't be so cruel as to call her delusional, but she gets pretty close to that description. She's an odd one, but relatively harmless."

Emma wasn't sure she agreed, but she didn't think it was worth pursuing at the moment. The end of the race was fast approaching, and just like every spectator for miles, it captured her full attention. The fierce competition escalated to a barely controlled desperation as the drivers took the final lap. A communal gasp went up to the heavens as Niki, Mario, and Joe Hill seemed to fall straight down a steep mountain pass, and Joe maneuvered around Mario on the bottom turn in a breathtaking feat of pure skill and daring. Now he was gaining on Niki as the cars plunged toward the main arena and the finish line.

Emma stood like everyone in the arena, the roar of the engines growing louder by the second making her skin tingle with mounting excitement. The sound was deafening as the frontrunners stormed into the arena. Her vision obscured by people's heads and waving flags, Emma turned the monitor and watched the finish there, holding her breath. There didn't appear to be an inch difference between the Montand car and Joe Hill's. Just yards before the finish line, however, Niki surged. Still, Emma wasn't sure who had won, it'd been so close when they crossed. Above all the wild shouting and screaming, she heard the announcer yell Niki's name. Emma shouted triumphantly, turning and hugging Michelle, both of them jumping up and down. Then Dean was hugging her, too.

One thing was for certain, Emma thought later as she watched Niki do his victory lap. She could understand why Vanni loved the sport so much.

Chapter 36

Emma had been flushed with excitement and beaming when Vanni arrived back at the box to claim her for the award ceremony. She'd been unusually quiet on the car ride home, however, and Vanni thought he knew why.

They'd stayed to drink champagne with Niki, the Montand crew, and friends and family at a private room on the arena grounds. After taking one look at Emma, whose expression appeared strained and her face pale, he'd bowed out for the celebratory dinner at a local seaside resort. He'd had enough of crowds and champagne and the hoopla for an entire year. Besides, despite the fact that Emma had enthusiastically said she'd go if he liked, she looked a little relieved when he said he'd rather have dinner alone with her at the empty villa.

He brought the car to a halt in La Mer's circular back drive and looked over at Emma.

"I'm sorry she came," he said simply. "I was shocked to see her sitting next to you."

"It's okay. I know you didn't have anything to do with it," she assured.

He reached over and grabbed her hand. She folded her fingers into his. Why did the way she curled up to him always strike him as so much sweeter than when anyone before had done it? "She doesn't mean anything to me. You know that, right?"

She met his stare. "I know that firsthand. I was *there*, remember?" she asked softly.

He stiffened. Emma was right there, holding his hand. So why did he have the feeling she was drifting away from him? His gaze narrowed on her.

"Are you all right?"

"Yes." She must have noticed his doubtful expression. "I'm just really tired. I . . . I started my period this afternoon," she said, grimacing slightly, her pale cheeks coloring. She gave him a reluctant glance. "I'm sorry."

"For what? Biology?" he asked, relieved that her being out of sorts wasn't associated with something he could have controlled but hadn't. She gave him a rueful smile. "Do you have difficult periods?" he asked.

She shook her head. "I just get tired and headachy on the first day. I'm usually okay by the second."

He squeezed her hand. "Come on. Let's get you inside. How about a hot bath and a glass of wine?"

"Make it tea and it sounds like heaven."

She padded barefoot out of the bathroom, wearing a short, pale blue button-up nightgown, pausing when she saw Vanni standing next to the bed. He folded back the sheet and comforter and motioned for her to get in.

"You're being very sweet. I'm not an invalid, you know," Emma told him amusedly. She'd thought the bath and cup of chamomile had made her sleepy until she walked into the bedroom and saw Vanni. It appeared he'd showered in the other bathroom. He wore a pair of black cotton lounging pants that hung low on his trim hips and a simple white T-shirt. He was barefoot. The hair around his neck was still damp.

Her entire body perked into instant awareness. He looked good enough to eat.

"I don't think you're an invalid. It wouldn't hurt to rest, though. And for once, we have nothing else to do. For a whole week," he added with a significant glance as she sat in the bed.

"A whole week. Amazing," Emma murmured, staring out the open French doors to the sea in the distance. It was evening, and a cool breeze made the room very comfortable and ruffled the potted flowers on the terrace. She'd thought a lot about the concerns Astrid's appearance had reawakened in her at the race. No matter how she dressed things up, she and Astrid were definitely in similar situations when it came to Vanni. The only difference was that Emma had his attention now. There would be someone else to follow her. She'd decided the wise thing would be to bail on this whole thing now, before she fell even further in love with him.

But the simple matter was, she wasn't *wise* when it came to him. If she only had days to live, she wouldn't hasten death. She'd cherish and savor every second she had.

It was the same for her in this thing with Vanni.

She turned toward him. "I'll lie down for a bit if you come with me."

"I was planning on it."

She smiled at that and scooted over for him. After a moment, he spooned her from behind beneath the soft cotton sheet as both of them stared out at the terrace and the sea beyond.

"Are you cramping?" he asked quietly, opening his hand at her lower belly and stroking her soothingly. It felt sublime.

"Not much," she said, caressing his forearm. She was being honest. She wasn't so much cramping as she was suffering from a constricted, slightly achy feeling at her core. After several minutes, however, his stroking hand close to her pelvis and his long, hard body pressed so close to her backside evoked a different feeling than comfort. A thick, warm feeling settled in her sex. She felt his cock twitch against her backside and her stroking hand stilled.

"Was it a good day for you, Vanni?" she asked in a hushed voice.

"No. It was the best," he said, continuing to stroke her with his magical hand. She wriggled her hips slightly.

"That feels good," she said in a tight voice.

"Does it?" he asked, and she heard the pointedness of his tone.

"Very," she said, her head still turned away from him. "I'm sorry about starting my period. Bad timing. Your best day, and all," she finished on a hesitant whisper.

"Today isn't going to be ruined by something like that. Impossible."

Her heart seemed to grow beyond its space in her chest. She turned her chin toward him. His elbow was bent and his head propped against his hand. Evening whiskers darkened his jaw. He looked down at her with a lambent stare, and she felt his cock swell behind the thin fabric of their clothing. Her lips parted to ask him . . . what, exactly? But then he was there, his mouth moving coaxingly over hers, shaping their flesh together, his tongue penetrating her lips.

"Do you want to make love?" she whispered when he lifted his head a moment later.

"Of course," he said, as if that was a foregone conclusion. He studied her face for a moment. "If you do."

"I do, but . . ."

His brow quirked in slight puzzlement when she faded off, but then understanding dawned. He began to stroke her again on the strip of skin just above her mons. She felt her clit pinch in acute arousal.

"I see. You usually don't have sex when you're on your period," he said quietly.

"No. I don't think most women want to, do they?" Emma asked, glad he'd put her dilemma into words. He gave her a bland expression. She laughed softly. "Oh, I see. Most women *do* with *you*."

"I didn't mean that," he said soberly.

"What did you mean then?" she asked, not dissuaded from her initial belief—what woman wouldn't want him, even on her deathbed?—but she was still curious.

"I meant," he said, continuing to watch her as he lifted the hem of her nightgown, "that there are certain things that happen to a woman's body when she's on her period. If she feels up to it, it's very good to take advantage of those things. Are you wearing a tampon?" he asked so matter-of-factly, she blinked. She nodded. Her eyes widened and she gasped when he burrowed a finger between her labia and began to rub and press on the sensitive flesh. "Do you feel that?" he murmured. "There's increased blood flow to this area during your period. Climaxes can be much more powerful and frequent. Plus, orgasms can help alleviate the discomfort of cramps."

"Really?" she managed because he was continuing to rub her. She bit her lip and flexed her hips slightly, feeling his erection, now full and heavy next to her ass. "Never mind," she gasped as pleasure and arousal inundated her. "I see what you mean."

A smile shadowed his lips. "Your body is so sensitive. I've been looking forward to this . . . to seeing whether or not you'd become even more sensitive during this time."

She opened her mouth to exclaim in disbelief over the idea he'd been looking forward to her period, but then he pressed harder with his rubbing finger and all she got out was a moan. Heat rushed into her cheeks. Her nipples prickled against the fabric of her gown. His touch had a charge to it tonight—forbidden and taboo. She'd never even masturbated when she was on her period, let alone allowed a man to pleasure her during it. God. What had she been missing out on?

"I can see you're going to exceed my expectations, as usual," he rasped, his gaze flickering over her breasts, before his mouth closed on hers. She came a moment later while he kissed her deeply, shuddering against his hard, primed body.

"There," he said quietly as her trembling eased. "Nice?"

"So nice," she panted, smiling slightly because he continued to play her sensitive clit, and it was abundantly clear to both of them how creamy she'd become in the cleft between her labia.

"Would you like to feel nice again?" he asked, holding her stare.

"Yes," she mouthed wordlessly.

"I thought so," he replied with a small smile. Like the sea, the muted evening light was turning his eyes into a smoky blue. She winced slightly at the deprivation when he removed his hand from her panties. "Let's just unbutton this," he said calmly. His long fingers moved down her chest, unfastening her gown to above her belly button. He peeled back the fabric, exposing her breasts. His nostrils flared slightly as he looked down at her, and she felt that telltale leap of his cock against her ass. She circled her bottom against him, and she saw a muscle jump in her cheek.

"Would you like to be spanked?" he asked.

She stilled her wiggling, stunned by his serious, intent question. She just stared at him a moment

"No," she lied.

One dark brow rose in a doubtful expression, but he didn't argue. He just slid his hand beneath her underwear again and began to rub her well-lubricated clit. She whimpered as heat and sensation rushed through her anew. He lowered his head and spoke near her ear. "Because the next time you wiggle your ass against my cock like that, I'm going to consider it an invitation." Her hips twitched at the dark promise. His head started up, but she stilled herself at the last moment. He gave her an amused look of warning.

"How does it feel?" he asked a moment later, ungluing his gaze from her naked breasts.

"It burns so . . . *good*," she gasped. Her clit had never sizzled like this before. The soles of her feet started to heat in sympathy to his touch on her sex. "You were right about the advantages. But what about you?"

"What about me?" he asked, his mouth hard as he stared at her breasts fixedly. Her nipples prickled at the delicious contrast of the cool breeze feathering across the sensitive crests and his hot stare.

"Don't you want to come, too?" she asked in a strangled voice. She was restraining herself mightily not to grind her ass against his flagrantly swollen cock.

"Yes," he replied in a hard voice. "But not until we explore the advantages more. Squeeze one of your breasts," he bit out.

She was surprised by the taut demand, but didn't hesitate. She cupped her breast from below and massaged it, watching his expression darken. Her skin felt surprisingly soft in her hand, silky and smooth.

"Hold it up for me," he said.

The words sent a hot thrill through her. She burned. Everywhere. She longed to bob her hips against his hand, but thought he might consider that a tease to his cock. She cupped her breast from below and lifted the firm flesh as if in offering. His cock batted against her ass. She held her breath when she saw the feral flash in his eyes, and then his mouth enclosing her nipple, giving it a firm, hot suck. It was too much. She bobbed her hips up and down, circling against his straining erection and wicked, stirring finger, and exploded again in splendid climax.

She opened her eyes a moment later when she felt his mouth unclamp from her nipple. He stared down at her with a rigid expression, his finger still moving subtly against her slick clit, sending an occasional post-orgasmic shiver through her. Slowly, he withdrew his hand and drew her panties down to her thighs, holding her stare the whole while. His hand skimmed over her naked hip, and she felt the moistness of his finger. He held her steady and ground his cock against her ass. She bit her lip and whimpered at the feeling of his heavy, engorged flesh.

"I'm going to have to give you a little spanking, Emma."

She shivered at the impact of his low, gruff threat.

"I know," she whispered.

"Look out at the sea or I won't be able to do it," he said, white teeth flashing in a restrained snarl.

She turned her head, staring out the terrace doors onto the gently falling summer night. He moved back slightly. She missed the feeling of his pressing, throbbing cock. His hand skimmed across her bottom, caressing her. She held her breath in anticipation. His hand lifted and fell, lifted and fell, giving her upper buttock two crisp smacks, the cracking sound of flesh against flesh ringing out in the air. He paused and rubbed the stinging skin.

"Bring up your knees some and roll over on your hip," he said, guiding her with his hands so that when she'd settled, she was still lying on her side and staring blindly out at the Mediterranean, but her waist was twisted slightly and her right knee was higher than the left, making her entire bottom more exposed. "That's right," he muttered, his hand making little circles on her ass. He cupped both cheeks in his palm before he landed several spanks in a row, peppering her skin with stinging slaps. She moaned and shifted her hips in arousal.

"Does it hurt?" he asked her tensely, massaging a buttock.

"No," she whispered.

"Then hold still," he ordered quietly. She bit her lip as he smacked her bottom several more times, his last spanks concentrating on the lower curve of her buttocks. He slapped up on the cheeks slightly, and she had the impression he was watching her flesh quiver from the small blows. The moan she'd been holding in escaped her throat when he suddenly pulled back one buttock.

"Stay still," he said sharply when she flinched.

She forced herself into immobility despite her uncertainty. The cool evening air brushed across her asshole, but she imagined she could feel the heat of his stare in that intimate place more acutely. She waited, holding her breath.

He groaned roughly, and the next thing she knew, he'd wrapped both his arms around her middle and was pulling her against him. His long legs curled up to bracket hers from the back, and he was bouncing her in his lap.

"Oh God," she moaned feverishly, because he'd pushed his pants to his thighs. His cock was exposed, and he was bouncing her ass against it. It was a tense, lewd, ridiculously exciting thing to do. Half-wild with arousal, she tried to reach around to grab his cock, but he caught her wrist.

"Fuck me," she gasped, panting erratically. She ground down with her ass, making it clear what she wanted.

His groan this time sounded like it tore at his throat. He released his restraint on her wrist and put it on her hip, where he used it to circle her ass against his straining erection. "Have you ever done that before?"

"No," she moaned.

"Are you just offering it because you think I need it? I can come with your hand or your mouth. Just by doing this a minute more," he muttered bitterly as he jerked her into his lap again as her ass popped his cock and thighs.

"No," she insisted desperately, looking over her shoulder. "I want it . . . if you do?" she finished the last on a shaky question.

He rolled his eyes, his beleaguered, "you've got to be kidding" expression making a laugh jump to her throat. He rolled away from her for a moment, reaching for the bedside table. She realized in his absence that a sheen of sweat covered her body and that things were very sticky between her thighs. He'd brought her to untold raptures since she'd known him, but she'd never before felt this hot. This raunchy. When he rolled back, he held a bottle of lubricant. She strained around to see what he was doing. He was pouring some of the clear liquid onto his fingers. He let the bottle fall to the bed between them and met her stare.

"You're sure?" he asked.

She nodded, excitement trumping her wariness. By far.

"Then look out at the sea again and try to relax," he urged. She turned slowly, the image of his hot stare lingering in her mind. He peeled back a buttock and pressed his finger to her ass. It felt blunt and warm and hard against that sensitive flesh. Her eyes sprung wide when he breached her. "Press back against my hand. Gently," he instructed. His finger slid into her. "There we go," he said soothingly. She stared blindly out the terrace doors as dusk fell in the hushed quiet while his finger moved in and out of her ass. Her clit began to sizzle again, as if his finger stimulated those nerves as well. He leaned down and spoke near her ear, his gruff voice an illicit caress. "Does your clit burn?" he asked.

"Yes," she whispered feverishly.

"Then rub it. Make yourself feel good, because you're so tight and hot, this is going to be heaven for me."

Panting softly, she did what he said, rubbing her burning clit. He squeezed another finger into her, and she pressed and circled more rigorously. He moved his hand back and forth, finger-fucking her, pleasuring her, preparing her. She'd never been this aroused in her life. She craved that dark possession. It seemed as if it was the only thing that would satisfy her, she burned so badly.

"Slow down," he ordered sharply. She blinked, realizing her fingers were moving faster and more forcefully between her thighs. He withdrew his fingers from her ass. Then he was parting her buttocks and presenting the fleshy, tapered crown of his cock to her asshole. She gasped. He'd obviously spread the lubricant on his cock, but he felt enormous in comparison to his fingers. "You can only come when I'm all the way inside you."

"Will it work?" she asked in a choked voice.

"It'll work," he replied, and from the sound of his voice, she thought he was clenching his teeth. "Just flex into it. It might hurt for a second, but—"

He grunted when she pushed her ass back onto his cock. The thick head penetrated her. She cried out as a sharp pain went through her.

"Stay still," he ordered, recognizing her cry for what it was, but in an agony of arousal with just the head of his cock clamped like a vise in her warm ass. "Is it better?" he asked after a tense moment.

"Yes," she said in a small, muffled voice. He cursed silently. He really was an animal to be subjecting her to this when she hadn't been feeling well. Yet he'd recognized her feverish arousal for what it was. He'd been right. Her unusually sensitive body was even more primed tonight than usual.

Or maybe you're just telling yourself that to make yourself feel better? a nasty voice in his head taunted.

Her muscles tightened around him, and he grimaced as he tightly bound down the promise of white-hot bliss. "Touch yourself again," he hissed. "Is the pain really gone?" he asked when she resumed rubbing her clit.

"It doesn't hurt," she said.

"Good." He leaned down and kissed her shoulder. "I'm going to go deeper."

"Yes." She faced away from him, but just the sound of her whisper feathered across his hypersensitive skin. His entire body felt prickly with life, his cock like a live, exposed wire. She felt decadently good. It wasn't going to take much before he was exploding in her, which was a blessing for her. He didn't want to make her more uncomfortable than she had been before they started making love.

"Then push back again," he instructed grimly, firming his hold on her hip. He was in her now. There was no going back. No way in hell.

They moaned in unison when he gained another inch. He waited for her flesh to become accustomed to him. "Okay?"

"I'm fine," she squeaked. For a second, he thought she was lying, until he noticed how rapidly her hand moved between her thighs.

"Hold still then," he instructed. He began to fuck her with just the tip of his cock. She moaned loudly, and this time, he knew for certain it was in arousal, not pain. Jolts of pure, electrical pleasure went through him. *Yes*, this is what he'd needed ever since he noticed her slight withdrawal earlier. He hadn't thought twice of it when she'd said she was on her period, but maybe on some level, he'd been disappointed. He'd needed to fuse with her in some way, feel her there with him on some deep, elemental level.

There was nothing more primal and poignant than this.

He fell down behind her, his head on the pillow above hers. He held her against him, absorbing the heat of her skin and her subtle shudders and the sweet, sharp whimpers that fell from her lips as he slowly burrowed deeper into her with each pass. A lavender dusk had fallen, the sound of the waves hitting the beach far below the cliffs sounding hushed and expectant. He stared out at the sublime night, holding her tightly, a feeling swelling high inside him. He wanted to let it out, to speak it, but he'd never felt it before—not to this degree. The incendiary quality of it made him wonder if it wasn't dangerous, something to be held in, just like he strained to bind his mounting desire.

His resources failed him, though. His entire body tightened, his need ripping and tearing at his restraints when his pelvis bumped against her bottom. He took a moment to catch his breath.

"Can you come for me, Emma?" he asked on a ragged exhale.

"Yes," she said in a high-pitched, quivering voice.

"Then do it. Let me feel you shake around me," he grated out, hovering on the crumbling ledge of his restraint, bliss bubbling and boiling just beneath the surface, tempting him to fall. He waited, unable to breathe, his lungs burning in anticipation. When she cried out and shook, a rough groan scored his throat. He flexed his hips, fucking her in short, firm strokes, his pelvis slapping against her ass. He was a pure savage in those electrical moments, but Emma took him eagerly, absorbing his furious need . . . mounting it until he couldn't contain it anymore.

Climax hit him, brutal and slashing.

It was like being ripped open by a slicing flood of feeling. For a crazed moment as pleasure buffeted him, he seemed to look down at himself from outside of his body. Laid open as he was, he saw there was more inside Vanni Montand than he'd realized.

But was it enough?

Week EIGHT

Chapter 37

The following week with Vanni consisted of one halcyon day after another, golden and peaceful, achingly sensual and sweet. He took her to the picturesque village of Saint-Jeannet one late afternoon, where they strolled to the Place St. Barbe and dined while staring out at the stunning view of the sea and surrounding rocky cliffs. In Cannes, they walked through the open markets and chose food and flowers for their evening dinner at La Mer. In Cassis, they took a boat out and toured the calanques, massive limestone walls that enclosed inlets and bays resulting in the most jaw-dropping scenery Emma had ever imagined.

Mostly, however, they opted to stay at La Mer and indulged in each other's company in the beautiful, peaceful surroundings. Vanni hired two men to come to the villa and erect a blue-and-white-striped pavilion on the private beach by the sea. They also brought a cushioned double lounger that was divided at the top only, so that two people could either sit up or lie down side by side, and tables and two chairs.

"You'll burn easier than you think if we spend hours on the beach every day," Vanni had explained.

He'd been right, of course. With the pavilion in place, they spent entire mornings or even days on the beach swimming and napping and making love. Mrs. Denis never came down to the beach, but upon some sort of prearrangement with Vanni, she brought them lunch at one o'clock. Vanni would jog up the hundreds of steps to claim it and bring it down to Emma.

Emma had brought a historical women's fiction book with her on the trip and took it to the beach the first day when the pavilion had been set up. The vision of Vanni returning from a swim took her attention off the pages as he arose from the azure waters like a bronzed Greek god and came to collapse on the lounger next to her. She swatted him playfully with the book when he intentionally dripped cold water all over her. Grinning, he grabbed it from her. Water drops clung to his long eyelashes as he narrowed them and read the back cover.

"Read out loud to me?" he asked, handing her back the damp book.

She thought he was kidding, but began to read aloud where she'd left off. He stretched out next to her, and Emma tried to keep her attention on the page instead of on the long, glorious expanse of wet male next to her. Realizing it was a hopeless cause, she carefully set aside the book on the table next to her.

"What are you doing?" he asked, watching her with a quirked brow as she straddled his midriff and lowered over him.

"I'm having a salt craving," she told him before she licked a warm, solid pectoral muscle and tasted the sea and Vanni on her tongue. He smiled, watching her for a moment as she kissed and licked his shoulder and chest, experimenting with the feeling of crisp chest hair, hard muscle and smooth, warm skin with her lips, teeth, and tongue. She hovered for a moment over a small dark brown nipple. His hand went to the back of her head, cupping it, and she kissed the disc, laving it delicately with the tip of her tongue. She looked up at him, feeling his nipple pebble. He lifted his head off the lounger and was watching her with a tight focus. Suddenly, his ridged abdomen muscles flexed as he sat up slightly and pulled the back of the lounger up, so that he was in a sitting yet partially reclined position. His fingers tightened in the back of her hair.

"Go on," he told her, one eyebrow going up in a gentle dare.

She smiled before she scooted back slightly over his damp body, her inner thighs and bottom coming into contact with his wet trunks and the growing fullness behind them. She took a bite out of the side of him, just over his ribs, and he grunted softly, his fingers tightening in her hair. Her tongue soothed the sting. She lowered farther, straddling his thighs. A thrill went through her when she felt his abdominal muscles jump as if her lips and tongue sent an electric current through them. His muscles were so dense and delightfully defined, his skin taut and smooth. When she reached the narrow path of hair that led from his belly button below the waistband of his swim shorts, she pressed her lips and face against it and twisted her head slightly, loving the sensation of the silky hair against her mouth. He made a hissing noise above her. She glanced up and saw that his eyes glittered with arousal as he stared down at her. He pulled slightly on her hair, urging her without words, and she let him guide her in his need. He pressed when she was over the bulge of his cock, and she came down over him, finding the rigid column with her seeking lips and biting at it gently through the damp fabric of his shorts.

"Emma," he muttered, and it was both an endearment and a taut warning on his tongue. She looked up and held his gaze while she held the girth of his cock between her bottom and top teeth and slid them back and forth in a gentle sawing motion. His face tightened in a grimace. She reached up and cupped his full, firm testicles, squeezing them gently while she found the succulent cap of his cock beneath the fabric and scraped her teeth across it as well. The feeling of him always aroused her, but he so rarely let her touch and play with him at will. He was like a forbidden treat she relished. By the time he jerked his trunks downward to his thighs, exposing his naked, swollen cock, she was starved for him.

"Slow down," he murmured as she took him into her mouth and pulsed him just below the head, applying a hard pressure against her rigid tongue and lips and sucking hungrily. She looked up at him lounging there, the image of his bronzed, naked, cut torso and rigid face from this angle decadently beautiful. His fingers tightened in her hair. "We have all day," he told her softly.

She closed her eyes, overwhelmed by the fullness of the moment, and tried to push the memory deep into her consciousness: the soft sigh of the waves hitting the beach behind them, the seabirds calling in the distance, Vanni's taste and the hard pressure of his cock filling her mouth, hurting her a little because her hunger was so great. Instead of running from her hunger, however, she submitted to it fully, taking him deeper than she ever had before, his patient instructions assuaging her anxiety, the golden day stretching out before them and his gentle hold in her hair assuring her there was time . . . always time.

It was so easy when she was there with him in that magical little world they'd built together to forget that their time was running out.

He'd never experienced something as sweet or so arousing as Emma making love to him with her mouth on that warm summer afternoon. Her unselfishness surprised him, and yet it didn't. She always gave freely. Completely. He could feel her sexual hunger, a pure, untainted desire to provide him pleasure and joy. But there was something more that he sensed. Her submission to his desire sparked her own arousal. When her heat escalated, his did. Several times, he pulled her back from the brink, urging her to soften, wanting her to be comfortable with this manner of lovemaking . . . wanting it to last.

He lay there, swimming in pleasure and sensation, watching her with a rapt focus. Her blond hair was turning lighter under the influence of the Mediterranean sun; it fell in wind-tousled waves around her face and felt so soft in his gripping fingers. The sprinkling of freckles on her nose that he prized so greatly were growing slightly more prominent under the sun, but he'd never tell her that, knowing how much she hated them.

She was a sexy, unmade bed, innocent and brazen at once. Every time they made love, he discovered a new height to how aroused she could become . . . how aroused she could make him. Her cheeks were rosy, whether from the sun, the heat, or arousal, he didn't know. He watched as she wet the entire stalk of his cock with her pink tongue, her velvety dark eyes shining as he met his stare.

"Suck the balls into your mouth," he instructed quietly. "Now use your hand on the staff." He grunted when she did what he asked, proving again she wasn't only an eager student, but also an apt one. He winced in pleasure, his head falling back against the recliner. Her small hand fisted him tight. She was a little ruthless on the lubricated, blood-engorged flesh, but he liked it.

He loved it.

After a while, he urged with his hand and she rose over him, holding the base of his cock with her fist and inserting the head into her mouth again.

"Use your teeth on the head, but lightly," he instructed, watching and tensing in pleasure as she followed his direction. He grasped her head with both hands, urging her to take him into her mouth again. When she sucked him so hard that he grimaced in stark pleasure, he warned her yet again.

"What's your hurry?" he asked, his fingers tightening in her hair. She paused, looking up at him, her cheeks hollowed out as she sucked. He snarled at the potent image she made.

"All right," he conceded. "Have it your way, *mon petit ange*."

He groaned as she sucked him deep and he felt her throat tighten around the tip. Agonized pleasure seized him. He didn't want to hurt her. He did, a little. He never *would* in any real sense of the word, and those paradoxical desires made his need sharp and cutting. He pulled her back, gasping, a coat of sweat breaking out on his skin. She took him deep almost immediately again, her nostrils flaring for air. He grunted in disbelieving pleasure, his need roaring in his veins. Through the blur of his raging lust, he saw a tear fall down her cheek. He gasped and pulled back on her hair, but she was having none of it, bobbing her hard over his lap, the friction of her taut lips and pumping fist killing him.

He felt that familiar tingling in his balls and urged her to use more force. "You've done it now," he grated out, watching her fixedly as she pumped his cock with mouth and fist. "I'm going to come in your hot little mouth," he said, the ferocity in him breaking free.

He gasped at the sensation of her taking him deep and began to shudder in orgasm. He came into her throat, but dislodged his cock as the second shudder tightened him. Pleasure continued to wrack him as he ejaculated powerfully on her tongue, and she sucked and swallowed.

An ecstatic moment later, he opened his clenched eyelids. Had he hurt her?

Her eyes were open and fixed on him as she continued to bob her head over his cock. There was a blazing quality to her gaze as she sucked him clean, and he was reminded yet again that he was foolish to think his flashes of savageness could ever degrade her. She was as deep as the sea and every bit as mysterious.

"Come here," he said, holding out his arms for her. He held her against him, his hand moving between her thighs. He squeezed her tighter when she climaxed against him a moment later, eating the small whimpers that fell across her lips, treasuring her pleasure as much as he had his own.

More.

The thought of losing her felt like hot knives piercing him, stealing his breath. But he *would* lose her. All things that he treasured left him in the end. Emma had been wise—as she was in a lot of things—for setting the limit of parting. Not knowing when the ax of loss would fall was worse.

Wasn't it?

He flipped her onto her back on her side of the recliner and came down partially over her, burying his face in her neck. He closed his eyes and inhaled her fragrance, letting it chase away his pain until it was only a dull, throbbing ache.

Chapter 38

Despite her distraction that first time, she did read to him sometimes while they lay together next to the sea. She'd wondered at first if he wouldn't fall asleep after a while, given the steady cadence of her voice and the hypnotic, rhythmic waves hitting the beach, but when she'd glance aside occasionally, she'd see the aquamarine crescents of his eyes as he stared up at the top of the canopy or out at the sea . . . or at her face.

She set aside the book once and picked up the glass of lemonade Mrs. Denis had sent down with their lunch, taking a sip and setting it down again. "She was a lot more calm than I would have been, meeting a queen," Emma said, referring to the passage she'd just finished reading in the book where the heroine of the book, a sixteenth-century peasant unaware of her royal roots, had been presented to the monarch of the land.

"You were pretty calm when you met royalty," Vanni said from where he lay next to her, his own glass of lemonade perched on his taut belly and seeping moisture onto his skin. He was turning even more golden brown and beautiful with each passing day in paradise.

She laughed, and then did a puzzled double take when she saw his serious expression. "When did I meet royalty?" she asked.

He reminded her of the couple she'd met in the racing box—the mustachioed man and the sober, polite woman sitting next to him. She just stared at him. "They were *not*," she scoffed after a moment.

"Well, granted, he's several steps away from the crown, but still . . ."

A shiver of amazement mixed with outrage and amusement when she realized he wasn't kidding. She slapped him on the shoulder. "Why didn't you *tell* me?" she demanded, trying desperately to remember the details of the couple and what she'd said and done. "Did I make a fool of myself?" she demanded anxiously. "Wasn't I supposed to address them in a certain way?"

"No," Vanni assured, chuckling. "He's enough steps away that a formal address isn't required in non-ceremonial settings."

"He seemed so nice and . . . normal."

"I'm sure he thought the same of you," Vanni said drolly, grinning as he set aside his drink.

"You know what I meant," she chastised. He reached, pulling her against him. She nestled against his chest and stared out at the wide, sunlit sea.

"Royalty isn't all it's cracked up to be. They're just people, like anyone else. You couldn't pay me to have their jobs, though." She sighed as his fingers brushed in her hair. "Niki is normal enough, don't you think? And Cristina? They both belong to offshoots of the same family."

"Really?" she asked, stunned. She listened while he described the lineage. It all sounded very convoluted and confusing to her. Still, she was glad to hear him speak of Cristina. He hadn't said her name since that volatile morning out on the dock.

"Vanni?" she asked after a moment, turning her face and kissing his chest.

"Hmmm?" he purred, sounding supremely relaxed.

"I know you didn't like Cristina. But . . . was she *ever* kind to you and Adrian?"

She held her breath, wondering how he would react to the question. Maybe it was foolish of her, but Emma didn't abide by the idea of keeping things locked tight inside. The things Vanni had avoided discussing for most of his life had ended up taking their toll on him . . . hurting him.

"To Adrian, she was more frequently kind," he said at last. "But Adrian was very easy to be kind to. Me . . . not so much. Very rarely, she was kind to me, though. It'd come upon her in fits."

"Fits?" she asked, lifting her head and looking at him.

He nodded, his fingers falling out of her hair. "It was like she'd see the light one day and want to do better, mothering us, taking care of us . . . noticing us." His mouth flattened at the last. "It wouldn't last."

She just stroked his chest, saying nothing. She wanted to bring up the topic of his guilt for Adrian's accidental death, but she felt she'd already pushed her luck enough by bringing up the topic of Cristina and not ruining their peace.

One morning she awoke in bed to find Vanni gone. She showered and dressed in her swimsuit and a tunic and grabbed her book before going downstairs to breakfast. Mrs. Denis directed her to "his workshop," as she called it, and provided her with a tea tray. Vanni's workshop turned out to be a garage that, while not as large as the one at the Breakers, was large enough for four cars and a huge table where various car parts and machinery sat. She found Vanni wearing a pair of coveralls, similar to the ones he wore in Chicago, with one hand inside what appeared to be an engine that sat on the table. He'd glanced around when she greeted him, the small smile on his lips telling her he was pleased to see her.

"Don't stop working on my account," Emma insisted when he

withdrew his wrench and picked up an oil-smudged towel to wipe off. "I'll just sit here and drink my tea and read."

"You're sure?" he asked, and she could tell by the way his gaze drifted back to the engine that he wanted to continue with his task.

"Of course, if you don't mind."

He shook his head with certainty. She sat on a stool near the table and poured some tea.

After that, she joined him in his workshop several more times while they were at La Mer. At first, she read while he worked for an hour or so, but once she realized he was quite glad to tell her what he was doing and what his goal was, she forgot the book and just observed him while they talked, learning more about the workings of a car than she'd ever imagined was possible. She recalled what her friend's father, Mort Forrester, had said about Michael Montand Sr. and Vanni both being brilliant mechanical engineers. She started to understand just the very edges of Vanni's genius during those visits with him while he worked, and he gave her a rough blueprint for comprehending the advances he'd made in mechanical technology. She respected him even more with that understanding.

She loved him impossibly more.

Of course days and nights as special as those couldn't last forever. They planned to fly back to Chicago on Sunday morning, and Emma was due back at work on Monday. As their time together drew to an end, neither of them seemed willing to be apart even for a short time. Vanni asked her what she'd like to do on Saturday, their last day at La Mer, and she replied without hesitation that she wanted to spend it on the beach with him next to the sea.

They made love after eating the delicious afternoon tea Mrs. Denis had prepared for them, and afterward, Emma drifted off to sleep in Vanni's arms, lulled by the sound of the waves and his strong, steady heartbeat in her ear. When she awoke, it was evening and the sun was beginning to set. She sat up, disoriented because she was alone. For some reason, a prickle of unease went through her as she stared out at the sea and didn't see a sign of Vanni.

"Vanni?" she called, but there was no answer.

Then she caught sight of him. He was farther out to sea than she'd ever seen him swim, his head appearing small in the shimmering waves. He was going farther away still.

"Vanni!" she yelled, panicked for some reason at the sight. She shoved aside her beach cover-up, which had been draped over her while she slept, and stood naked, staring fixedly at the black spot in the sea that was Vanni's head. For several seconds, she couldn't breathe.

She exhaled with relief when she realized he'd changed directions and was headed back to shore. When he was just past the anchored raft, he stopped swimming, his head breaking the surface. Her naked skin prickled with awareness, and she knew he stared at her standing there, just inside the pavilion. He resumed swimming with gusto toward the beach. He stood when the water was waist-deep and began walking toward shore, his stride unbroken by the rolling waves. The roughening of her skin and that strange sense of tension mounted. He was naked, the evening sun casting a golden-reddish light onto his skin. Her gaze lowered over him, her breath catching.

He wasn't only naked, he was fully aroused.

As he drew closer, she saw the glint of fire in his sea-colored eyes as they lowered over her naked body with a hot, possessive look. She just gaped at him in rising wonder. What had happened? Why did he look so fierce?

She didn't have time to put the question to words, because he was taking her into his arms, pulling her against his body and sweeping down to cover her mouth with his. His heat resonated beneath the cool sheen of water, the degree of it shocking her since he'd just been submerged in the sea. He almost felt feverish. He lifted her, her feet coming off the beach, and set her down at the end of the lounger.

"Scoot back and open your thighs," he said, hovering over her, his face rigid. She hastened back on the lounger, sensing his urgency. He straddled her and came toward her on his hands and knees, the primal vision he made sending a thrill of wariness and anticipation through her. She didn't know what was happening, but the moment was taut with unspoken, thick emotion.

He stared at her pussy as he approached, a slight snarl shaping his lips. Without any preamble, he fisted the stalk of his cock and arrowed it into her slit. She was still moist from their previous lovemaking, but the abrupt entry still made her wince.

He fell down over her and flexed his hips, driving his cock deeper. She gave a shaky cry. "Let me in, Emma," he commanded quietly, staring down at her with a scoring stare. She opened her legs wider. Her flesh melted around his hard length at the same moment that he grasped her wrists and pushed them above her head. He began to fuck her with long, hard strokes, holding her stare the whole time, his face tight, his eyes blazing. He was telling her something, screaming the truth, but his mouth remained closed the whole time.

She heard him in the quiet, though; heard his pain and his confusion.

She lifted her hips, driving her pussy along his thrusting cock, absorbing his unrest and anguish, breaking it like a wave that pounded on the beach.

"That's right," she whispered heatedly. "Fuck me."

A convulsion of emotion broke across his face. A groan rattled his throat. He took her harder, lifting his face and wincing in an agony of pleasure. She felt his cock swell in her and jerk viciously. A shout erupted from what seemed like his deepest part. It escalated to a stark howl, the sound causing her neck and forearms to roughen and prickle. She felt him convulse inside her, then the warm rush of his semen as he ejaculated.

He removed his hands from her wrists, bracing himself with his hands on either side of her head, and sagged, panting raggedly for air.

The heaving of his chest and ribs slowly eased. He made a rough choking sound, and she reached for him, bringing him down against her.

The sound of his ragged breath eased under the rhythmic surf surrounding them. She furrowed her fingers into his thick, damp hair and stroked his back. Eventually, he came up off her and fell onto his back. He reached for her and she rested her cheek on his chest.

"I was married before."

She went still at his unexpected words.

"I know," she whispered against his chest.

"How did you know?" he asked, his fingertips feathering down her spine.

She told him about what Mort Forrester had told her, and also mentioned Niki. He didn't say anything for a moment when she fell silent.

"She was a special girl, but I met her at a time in my life when I was ready to . . . to give it all another try. I was tired of being bitter. After Meredith died, it seemed like all the pain came roaring back, even worse than before," he said starkly. "I used to swim past the spot where Adrian drowned at the Breakers. I'd swim far out in the lake. When I was here, I'd swim far out to sea. I never told anyone before."

Her lungs ached, and she realized she was holding her breath.

"I didn't think of it as wanting to die. It was a kind of compulsion. I just . . . wondered what would happen. I wondered if I went far enough, if I'd be taken, too. I should have been the one who went on that afternoon. Not Adrian."

"No," she said steadfastly. "*Neither* of you should have been taken. It was a horrible accident. And you were fortunate to live through it. Blessed. I'm blessed, because you're here," she said, kissing his skin. She exhaled shakily when she felt his fingers in her hair.

"You never told me what happened," he said. "When you died." His hand opened at her back, and he made a soothing motion. He must have felt her tremble. His hand stilled. "I'm not asking because I'm curious to find out for myself, Emma," he said wryly. She lifted her head, hungry to see his face. He met her stare calmly. "I'm not suicidal."

She studied him closely, then nodded, sighing in relief at what she saw in his eyes.

"There was a feeling like floating . . . no, flying," she said. "I was weightless. Comfortable. In control. But mostly, there was just a *feeling*," she whispered, her voice cracking slightly with emotion. "A *knowledge*, and I knew even better than I know my own name that all was well . . . and that . . . things were *bigger* and deeper and wider than I'd ever begun to imagine, so big that all my fears were like a drop in the ocean of it."

"Do you think that's what Adrian experienced?" he asked quietly. "Because when he was struggling, and I was trying so hard to keep him above the water . . ." He closed his eyes, and his pain was like a knife in her side. "He was *very* afraid."

"Vanni."

He opened his eyes slowly.

"When the time came, he wasn't afraid. *Please* believe me."

He stared at her face, rapt.

"I'm sure enough for both of us," she said in a pressured whisper.

His rigid expression broke. He pulled her closer in his arms, and she slid farther up his body so that her head nestled in the hollow between his shoulder and neck. She touched her lips to his pulse and closed her eyes at the feeling swelling tight in her chest.

"When you swam out all those times, what made you turn back?" she asked him in a hushed voice after a moment.

His hand cupped the back of her head.

"I never knew," he replied gruffly, a far-off look in his eyes. "Until now."

Emma's eyes sprung wide. She hid her face in his chest, hoping he hadn't noticed her flash of hope at his words or the pulse that had begun to throb at her throat.

"Emma?" he said quietly, his fingers massaging her scalp.

"Yes?"

"When we return to the States . . . I don't want any more of this talk about the weeks and the days. Do you understand?" he asked, his fingers stilling.

"Yes," she whispered against his chest, although in truth, his statement had brought up a dozen questions, all of which made her wildly anxious—but also intimidated—to hear his answer.

Chapter 39

Emma said good-bye to Mrs. Denis that night. When tears sprung to her eyes as they hugged, Mrs. Denis noticed.

"There's no need for that," she soothed, smoothing Emma's hair fondly. "You make Vanni happier than I've ever seen him, even when he was a boy. We'll see one another again."

Emma nodded, but perhaps Mrs. Denis noticed the brittleness of Emma's smile, because her expression fell. These days and nights with Vanni had been heaven-sent and poignant. Although wild, desperate hope had sprung into her breast out there on the beach when he'd insisted he wanted more than their total time of eight weeks together, he'd never returned her admission of caring. He certainly never suggested that their affair was anything beyond the sexual variety.

He'd certainly never spoken the word *love*, as Emma had, and that absence was beginning to haunt her. Would he ever be capable of anything more than an affair—a sweet, sublime one, yes, but a sexual affair at heart nonetheless?

It was only a matter of time before these days became hellish memories because he was no longer in her life. She was beginning to regret saying yes to an indefinite extension of their affair. At least doubt would slink in when she wasn't in his immediate presence. When he was there next to her, stroking her, touching her, making love to her with every glance, Emma felt woefully incapable of saying no to him even for an additional second.

Yet she also knew perfectly well every additional moment would just tear at her spirit more.

The rude intrusion of reality onto their happiness came earlier than she'd expected, however, during their last night at La Mer. It was still dark out when Emma was awakened by the sound of a phone ringing. She blinked, disoriented, her eyelids heavy with sleep. If she had to guess, she'd have said she and Vanni just drifted off to sleep an hour or two ago. Vanni didn't turn on a light, but she sensed him leave the bed. Was there a house phone in here? She'd never noticed one, but that wasn't a cell phone that had been ringing so jarringly.

"Hello?" she heard Vanni say, his voice rough, but alert. "Yes," he said, and she sensed the tension in his tone. She sat up in bed, pulling the sheet up over her bare breasts. She started getting worried in the silence that followed. "Was anyone hurt?" he asked. Her concern escalating, Emma rose from the bed, turned on the light in the bathroom and retrieved a robe. "Well, that's something. And it's definitely out? Any idea of the damage yet . . . Yes, I'll be there as soon as I can. In the meantime, please call Sheldon and Devitis and inform them, and of course the insurance company. We'll cease any operations until we can better assess the damage and determine whether it's safe or not. I'll be there as soon as possible."

"That was the night security officer at the Montand plant in Antibes," Vanni said, walking toward her in the dim bedroom. "There's been a fire."

"Is everyone all right?"

Vanni nodded, but looked worried. "Yes, there was no crew on duty except for night security, and they're fine. But it looks as if the damage might be extensive to the property and equipment."

"Should I get ready and come with you?" Emma asked.

She saw him squinting at the bedside clock. "No. Two of my vice presidents will be meeting there to assess the damage. Besides, it'll be dawn soon. Marco will be here in a few hours to take us to the airport."

"We can call him and postpone."

Vanni shook his head, distracted. "He has the flight scheduled with the airport, and you have work tomorrow. I'll ask him to try to delay it for an hour or two and try to catch up with you at the airport."

"Let me know if there's anything I can do," she said.

"I will," he stepped forward and kissed her, his hand cupping her head. "With everyone safe, it's just a matter of figuring out what needs to be done to get operations up as quickly as possible," he said against her lips. "You just go with Marco, and I'll tell you about it later."

She nodded, looking up at his shadowed face. He touched her jaw.

"I'm sorry," he said.

"Don't be. I'm just glad no one was hurt."

He kissed her once more on the mouth and entered the bathroom to shower.

She had a strange prescience as she waited on the plane later that morning that she wasn't going to see him anytime soon. Sure enough, her phone rang at a little after ten o'clock and she saw it was Vanni.

"Hi," she said, staring out the window of the luxurious private plane. "It's bad, isn't it?"

"It's worse than I thought," Vanni admitted. "The insurance adjustor won't be here for an hour still, and the fire inspector is still trying to figure out the cause and assess any structural damage. We're also trying to figure out what parts we need to order to get things up and running as soon as possible. Marco can't stretch things out any longer with the tower. I told him to go ahead and take off and get you home. I'll follow you as soon as I can."

"Of course. I'll be fine. I'm so sorry about the fire."

"Crap happens," he said grimly.

Emma smiled sadly. "I guess our little jaunt into paradise is at an end."

"Our time together isn't done just because of an accidental fire. Call me as soon as you reach Chicago?"

She assured him she would. He was right. There was every reason to anticipate more hours in his arms and by his side in the days and nights to come. They had time left.

Still, she hated the idea of flying away from that golden, azure coastline where she'd known paradise with him.

On Tuesday morning, she was leaving a patient's house in Lake Forest, when she saw that Vanni had called. They had spoken both when she'd gotten home and last night, when Vanni had wearily told her he would be returning to Kenilworth most likely this evening. Before she even got into her car, she eagerly listened to the message, her heart jumping when she heard he planned to land tonight.

"Can you meet me at the Breakers at seven?" he asked. "I don't know how much I'll be good for, but I'll try to sleep on the plane. Maybe I'll get a second wind," he added more quietly, and it'd almost been like he was there, speaking the words to her intimately, his words gruff and warm in her ear, his aquamarine eyes gleaming a promise.

She walked on air the rest of the day, having to take pains to tone down her euphoric mood while in the somber atmospheres of her patients' homes. On the way to her apartment, she stopped at the grocery store and splurged on an expensive bottle of champagne to commemorate Vanni's homecoming. It was expensive for *her*. She was sure he had much more expensive, premium bottles of the stuff at the Breakers, but Emma wanted to give him something she'd purchased.

Amanda wasn't home when she returned to the apartment at five thirty, so she left a note not to expect her back tonight. She carefully got ready, packing a few items so that she could go straight to work from Vanni's tomorrow morning. She donned a sundress that showed off the light gold tan she'd received in the French Riviera. At a few minutes before seven she arrived at the Breakers, her heart pounding with excitement.

All was silent in the massive garage when she entered. As she passed the large, elaborate kitchen, she noticed it was empty. An idea struck her. She looked around in for an ice bucket, opening several cupboards, but didn't find one. She'd just put the champagne in the refrigerator and come back for it after it'd chilled.

"You certainly know how to make yourself at home."

She paused with her hand inside the open refrigerator. Mrs. Shaw stood in the entryway of the kitchen, wearing a chic, dark blue pantsuit and scarf and looking at Emma with a cold, furious expression. She clutched some papers in her hand, as if the sound of Emma moving around in the kitchen had interrupted her while she did some filing. Emma set down the champagne in the refrigerator and closed the door. Taking a deep breath, she faced Vanni's aunt.

"Vanni asked me to meet him here. Has he arrived yet?"

"He called a moment ago to say he was delayed."

"For how long?" Emma asked, concerned. Instead of answering her, Mrs. Shaw's thin lips clamped tight. "Is he still arriving tonight, just later than his scheduled time, or is he still in France?" Emma prodded, irritated by the housekeeper's surly uncooperativeness.

"He won't be home tonight," Mrs. Shaw said. She stepped over the threshold of the kitchen as if crossing some invisible line. Inexplicably, the hairs on Emma's forearms stood on end.

"I understand that Vanni has become quite taken with you. From something Niki told Dean after the race, I'm getting the impression

Vanni has told you all about his life up to now . . . things he's never opened up about to another woman."

Emma lifted her chin, sensing a storm brewing but unable to guess the direction it would take.

"And now you've been to La Mer," Mrs. Shaw said, lifting her upper lip slightly when she said the last words.

"Yes. It was beautiful there. I've never seen anything like it."

"Of *course* you haven't."

Emma blinked at the undiluted acid in the other woman's tone. Her sense of trepidation increased as Mrs. Shaw began to slowly walk in an arc around her. She couldn't help but think of a predator circling. Warily, she turned, keeping Vera Shaw in her sights.

"Michael—Vanni's father—loved La Mer. So did I. Laurel didn't *get* it like *we* did," Mrs. Shaw said quietly, referring—Emma knew—to Laurel Montand, Vanni's mother. Vera's pale blue eyes glittered like fractured glass. "Michael appreciated my love for his ancestral home. Of course Adrian and Vanni loved it, too. Now *you've* been there as well. Dean and Michelle insinuated that you and Vanni were supremely happy together there. That's why I left, so I wouldn't have to witness you in a place that was so special to Michael and me. You should congratulate yourself. For a nurse, you've been flying high. But despite what you may think," she said with a contemptuous glance at the refrigerator, "despite Cristina's favoritism toward you and Vanni's infatuation, you are far from *belonging* in a place like this. You will never belong in Vanni's world."

Emma exhaled with effort, finding it difficult to breathe in the woman's presence. What had freed her hatred? It wasn't as if Emma hadn't felt it before, but Vera Shaw had kept it carefully contained.

Not anymore.

She turned again and faced the unpleasant woman full-on. "What do you have against me, Vera?"

Vera didn't try to disguise her snarl this time. Emma knew why she was infuriated. Calling her "Vera" had been a subtle way of putting them on equal footing. The New Horizon nurses had been instructed to address her as Mrs. Shaw. Vera came to a halt in her circling prowl.

"I know your type. I recognized you *right* away. Sweet, pretty little martyr. Sure enough, you immediately caught Vanni's attention. Men can be so predictable when it comes to lust. Michael was drawn to the type, just like Vanni is. That's why Michael asked my sister to marry him. He needed a saint to watch out for the boys. Oh, he wanted Laurel, but he wanted a lot of women. Michael had many *types*. Don't kid yourself that this thing with Vanni will last. The appeal of the saint is very short-lived when it comes to the appetites of a Montand."

Emma arched her brows in a show of patient contempt, but the skin of her forearms had roughened even more. Vera was seriously unbalanced. "You seem confused. Maybe you should rest. First off, I'm no saint. Secondly, Vanni and his father are two *very* different men. And lastly, Michael didn't ask *Laurel* to marry him in order to watch out for the boys. He asked *Cristina* to do that."

"That's what you think," Vera spat, her eyes alight with malice. The prickling on Emma's forearms transferred to her spine.

"What's that supposed to mean?" Emma asked with forced calmness.

"Michael pulled a switch, that's what I mean," Vera said, looking madly pleased by her enigmatic statement. Emma remained silent, not wanting to stir the pot. Still, Vera bizarrely seemed unable to resist releasing the venom of her secret.

"No one knew, save Cristina, Michael, Laurel, the doctor . . . and *me,* of course. I knew because Laurel confessed it to me before she died. She wanted me to take over, looking out for Vanni and Adrian in her place. Mothering Michael's sons. *I* was the only one who could do it. Certainly that slut Cristina wasn't up for the job."

Emma had gone very still now. The tingling in her body had amplified, feeling like ice-cold water dripping down her spine. "What are you talking about, Vera?" The woman really *was* delusional, despite what Michelle had said. Emma knew firsthand from

Vanni that he endured Vera because of her relationship with Laurel, but he hardly considered her as a substitute mother. His attitude toward Vera Shaw was at best respectful, at worst forbearing and vaguely impatient.

"I'm talking about the truth," Vera said, shrugging. "It was Cristina who was Vanni and Adrian's real mother."

"What?" Emma asked, disbelief making her voice sound hollow.

"Michael got Cristina pregnant when they met in Italy. But of course, Cristina was too selfish to ever settle down. She was furious at Michael for getting her pregnant, worried about what motherhood would do to her figure and her social status. Cristina Carboni, glamorous socialite who used to run fast and furious with that movie star sister of hers and their elite crowd of golden people; Cristina Carboni, who settled for no man: forced into motherhood, her wings clipped for good, tied to just one man? Never," Vera said scathingly. "She flat-out refused Michael when he proposed after she became pregnant with Adrian and Vanni."

"You're crazy," Emma whispered.

"No," Vera said triumphantly. "I'm telling you the *truth*," she stated, punching the air with the hand that clutched the pieces of paper for emphasis. "When Cristina refused to marry Michael, he was able to convince her to give him the children. It wasn't hard. *She* didn't want them. He tucked her away in a resort in the Adirondacks while she was pregnant. When Cristina continued to refuse to marry him, he grew desperate. He caught sight of my sister while he was in New York. It was pure chance . . . pure *luck* on my sister's part. She was the administrative assistant to one of Michael's business associates, and Michael imagined himself smitten. It could have been me. It *should* have been me." Vera straightened her spine and lifted her chin in a bizarre gesture of imagined self-importance. "I was always the stronger sister, much more suited to be Michael Montand's wife and mother of his children. But no . . . Michael wanted a pale little saint. And so he married my sister, who was biddable enough . . . *weak* enough to agree to have him, even once she learned about the children. Of course Michael forgot about her once they were married. He took up with Cristina again. He took up with any number of women. But none of them meant anything to him."

"And you?" Emma asked coldly. She was having difficulty absorbing all this. The only thing that seemed clear and evident was Vera Shaw's mad hatred. "Did *you* take up with him? Did *you* mean anything to him? Or is all of this some fiction you've created in your head because you know deep down you never meant anything to Michael Montand, and that you only hold Vanni's affections because of loyalty to his mother?"

"Laurel *wasn't* his mother," Vera shrieked. "Haven't you been listening? And Michael's and my relationship was above sex. He seduced women with ease. His conquests meant nothing to him, just like you mean nothing to Vanni. Sleeping with all those women—with that *bitch* Cristina—didn't earn women the respect Michael gave *me*."

Emma shook her head, staring at the woman in mounting wariness. She felt nauseated. All she wanted at that moment was to be away from Vera Shaw. She was a twisted, hateful woman who clearly saw Emma as some kind of threat to her ordered but delusional world. She'd somehow morphed Vanni into some bizarre mixture of Michael Montand and the son she'd never had with him—the man she'd desired above all else.

"I'm not really sure why you're telling me this . . . this *story,* but I think I should be going. You don't seem—" *Right in the head*, Emma stopped herself from saying at the last minute. "*Well*," she finished with a glare. She started toward the door.

"I have proof!"

Emma was caught off guard when Vera shoved the piece of paper in front of her chest. She hauled up short and found herself staring at what appeared to be an official document.

It was Vanni's birth certificate. Vera snapped away the top document, revealing the one beneath it. She shoved both pieces of paper closer to Emma's face. "And here is Adrian's birth certificate as well. You see? *Who* does it say Vanni's mother is? Who does it say is Adrian's? *Cristina Elizabeth Carboni*!" she spat, spraying some saliva into Emma's face. "I found these after she died, hidden away at the bottom of one of her shoeboxes when I went through her closet to see what she'd left you! That whore *would* put something so sacred in such a place. That's how much Adrian and Vanni meant to her. Only after she started to age a little, only when she began to suspect she couldn't remain the prima donna of the European social circuit forever did she finally listen to Michael. After Laurel died, he begged her again to marry him. He was blind with lust when it came to Cristina. She finally agreed, probably seeing nothing better in her future, and came. You should have seen it!" Vera laughed. "You've never seen a woman less suited to be a mother. Vanni *hated* her from the first, and Cristina couldn't stand the sight of him. What do you think it would do to Vanni to find out *Cristina* was his mother?" Vera shouted.

Emma staggered back as if she'd been shoved, the force of Vera's vitriolic excitement was so great.

"He hates her with a white-hot passion. Cristina killed Adrian—her own son, Vanni's twin. He's never loved anyone like he did his brother. Vanni has never—*will* never—forgive Cristina for that, and yet it's her cold, selfish blood that runs in his veins! What do you think it would do to him?" she demanded again.

"It would kill him," Emma gasped, too shocked and set off balance to say anything but the truth.

Vera's smile was an ugly thing. "Perhaps he deserves to know the truth."

"No," Emma said forcefully, anger fortifying her. She stepped toward Vera, meeting her stare in preparation to fight. "You say you care about him. You know very well finding out Cristina was his real mother would . . . unhinge him. Do you really want that for him?"

"No," Vera said, her chin going up. "Do *you*?"

Emma inhaled slowly, reading the truth in the woman's glittering eyes. "Just tell me what you're planning," she bit out angrily.

"I'll keep the secret until my grave. If you promise never to see or speak to Vanni again."

The refrigerator hummed on in the tense, horrible silence that followed.

"You must realize this thing with Vanni won't last forever," Vera reasoned. "How long do you have before this affair between the two of you is over? Weeks? Days? All I'm asking—"

"All you're doing is blackmailing me," Emma interrupted coldly. A fury started to build in the pit of her belly, melting her icy shock over the bizarre unfolding of events. "You know as well as anyone how much Vanni has suffered. You claim to care about him. Yet you would make him suffer in this way, out of spite toward me?"

"You claim to care about him as well," Vera challenged, showing her teeth. "Would you make him suffer, just so that you can satisfy your lust for a few more nights? Don't try to tell me Vanni has promised you more. I know him. He's unfailingly honest when it comes to what he'll give a woman. Well . . . *has* he promised you more? Has he professed any other emotion but lust for you?"

Emma refused to answer, but perhaps Vera saw the flash of doubt in her eyes. Vera smiled.

"I didn't think so," Vera said in a low, victorious tone. "You'll have to tell him that you decided to end it now, since you know it'll end sometime soon, anyway. A girl like you, so sweet and fragile . . . it'd pain you too much to keep things going until they inevitably end."

Emma snarled in a very unfragile manner and lunged toward the disgusting woman. Vera's eyes widened in momentary alarm.

"How do I know you won't tell him anyway, even if I agree to this? How do I know you won't harm him in another way, you crazy bitch?" Emma demanded.

For a few seconds, Vera looked like she was ready to resort to violence, but Emma was ready. She waited. Vera inhaled, regaining her composure.

"He's like a son to me," Vera said. "I've never done anything to harm him. Has he ever mentioned that I have?"

"No," Emma said. "He doesn't *think* about you much at all, let alone talk about you."

Her arm went up instinctively, blocking Vera's striking hand. She gripped her wrist tight when Vera tried to jerk it away. Vera's attempted blow at her face had brought her closer. Emma stared unblinkingly into Vera Shaw's eyes while her heartbeat roared in her ears. A memory came back to her in that harrowing moment: Niki Dellis staring at her, sadness and concern in his dark eyes as he spoke of Vanni. *Sometimes I think if something else horrible happened to him, it'd end him.*

She couldn't bear the idea of him learning that Cristina was his real mother. Just imagining his pain felt as if it took her breath away.

"Promise me you won't tell him about Cristina," Emma grated out. "Promise me you won't do anything to harm him."

"I promise it easily," Vera hissed. "If you promise to walk away now."

Emma shoved the other woman back with force. Vera stumbled back, looking outraged. She started to lunge toward Emma again, but suddenly came up short when their stares met.

"I know someone who will keep an eye on you," Emma said fiercely, channeling all of her fury into her gaze. "If I hear you've run to Vanni with this information, I'll find out. I'll tell Vanni what you did, just in case you convince him that you were only telling him for his own good."

Vera laughed. "Are you referring to my stupid sister-in-law, Michelle? Or maybe my annoying brother, Dean? Yes. I hear you've become quite the darling with them as well. Fine. Check on Vanni's well-being, if need be. But if you intrude too far into his life again, all bets are off. Do you understand me?"

"Unfortunately, all too well. You're pitiful," Emma said, casting a glance of cold disdain over the woman before she walked out of the kitchen.

* * *

Previously, Emma hadn't allowed herself to imagine too greatly what it would be like when she eventually was forced to walk away from Vanni. Maybe it was best that she was doing it unexpectedly.

When she reached the garage—that place where she'd first spent time with Vanni, peered into the private world of a man who had suffered and lost and was ever so cautiously starting to live again, where she'd first felt her heart pound with boundless passion—what had just occurred in that kitchen suddenly struck her with force.

She stumbled slightly, gasping, and braced herself against the Bentley, her gaze landing on the backseat window. Pain swept through her. The thought of Vanni eventually arriving home and expecting to see her there felt unbearable. She choked on the air she'd just gulped as if her lungs didn't know how to process it.

Don't do it. You can't abandon him!

But the truth was, Vanni wouldn't feel abandoned. Not really. Her absence would confuse and annoy him. He'd definitely made it clear he didn't like the idea of things ending on her terms. He wanted and needed her. For now. But *abandoned*?

No. That wasn't realistic.

Was it?

It didn't matter, in the end. The thought of him learning that Adrian had died while under the watch of his true mother, that Vanni carried the blood of Cristina in his veins, was an even worse agony for Emma to consider. He *despised* Cristina. He guarded the memory of Laurel Montand above all else. She was a pillar of goodness in his tainted, pain-strewn world.

I wondered if I went far enough, if I'd be taken, too.

She clamped her eyes shut and gasped at the impact of recalling Vanni telling her about his dangerous, fate-tempting swims. She recalled his tired cynicism and hopelessness when she'd first witnessed him with Astrid. He carried such a heavy emotional burden with him always. The news about Cristina could so *easily* be the straw that broke the camel's back.

No. She couldn't allow it.

After taking a moment to compose herself, Emma straightened and slowly walked out of the garage.

She suddenly had an inkling of how Vanni must have felt all of these years, numbing off the heart and taking one difficult, reluctant step at a time into an empty, cold future.

Chapter 40

His hand was throbbing with pain, but still, he beat on the door with it. Suddenly, the wood was no longer there and he was beating on air. Amanda Shore was standing inside the threshold, looking panicked and furious.

"I'm about to call the police, Vanni."

"Is she in there?" Vanni demanded, stepping over the threshold. Amanda stepped in front of him, blocking his way. He looked down and met her stare. He blinked and came to a halt. He realized—reluctantly—that she was a human being and not merely an obstacle to Emma. Amanda's blue eyes looked fierce, but beneath her anger, he saw her worry.

"You can't just come bursting in here, Vanni," Amanda bit out. He took a step back. He'd been about to knock over a woman, for Christ's sake.

"Why won't she see me?" he asked. Despite his earlier recognition that he couldn't force his way past Amanda, he kept his hand on the open door. He wasn't walking away, dammit. How was it possible that he'd last seen and touched a soft, warm woman who was as eager for his presence as he was for hers, and suddenly be faced with an Emma who was telling him she'd decided not to see him again? It didn't compute in his short-circuiting brain.

When he'd arrived home at the Breakers an hour later than his scheduled flight, he'd found it empty. He'd immediately tried to call Emma, assuming she hadn't received the messages he'd left on her voice mail or the one he'd left with Vera that he'd be late. He'd reached her by phone, but what she'd said in her uncharacteristically cold, flat voice was still being rejected by his spirit wholeheartedly.

After France, she'd decided that it was too painful to continue seeing him.

Had she been planning on walking away when they'd kissed good-bye that last time in his bedroom at La Mer? No. That truth hadn't been on her lips or tongue or in her warm, supple body pressing against his.

What was *his* truth when it came to Emma? He only knew he didn't want to let her go. Life without Emma? Could he go back, once he'd known her indescribable warmth, her sweetness and touch?

He suspected he *must*, at some point. He feared it. Needing her was such a horrible, sweet risk. The only thing he knew for certain was that there, in that moment, the thought of losing her was like having his lungs ripped out of his chest.

"What's happened to her? It doesn't make any sense," he told Amanda angrily.

"Really?" Amanda asked sharply.

He stilled and peered at Emma's sister. "What's that supposed to mean?"

Amanda crossed her arms at her waist and drew herself up, giving him a very hard look. He'd never been a huge fan of Amanda, given what she and that jerk Colin Atwater had done to Emma, but at that moment, he saw a resemblance between Amanda and her sister.

"Emma told me what you proposed: an affair of a purely sexual nature. She told me all about it." He felt himself withering a little under Amanda's condemning, disgusted gaze, but he didn't flinch. "You proposed something like *that*? To a woman like *Emma*?"

"That's only how it started out," he bit out.

"You're right. That's how it started out, but it's not how it ended. Not for *Emma*. She's not built like that. Surely, despite your . . . *cold-blooded* plans for her, you must have realized she's not cut out for this kind of thing."

"That's rich," he said with quiet, building, helpless fury. "*You* preaching to me about not being sensitive enough to Emma."

Amanda paled. Regret and helplessness swept through him in equal measure. "Dammit, Amanda, just let me see her. I know I can clear this up."

"How? By professing your undying love for her? By promising her you'll always be there for her?" He met her stare, a snarl shaping his lips. In his unguarded state, her pointed words had felt like piercing missiles. Amanda's eyes closed for a moment. "I'm sorry, Vanni. I know that you care about her, in your way." She opened her eyes. "A person would have to be a complete robot not to care about Emma, right? But I saw when she came home tonight. She was . . . beyond belief. I've never see her like that before."

Her trembling voice still ringing in his ears, Vanni started to walk past her again, intent only on one thing: seeing Emma.

Amanda was suddenly in front of him, looking royally pissed. "She's not even here!"

He came to another halt, helplessness and fury now boiling inside him. "I pleaded your case to her before, Vanni, when you called me while you were in France. That was before I knew what you proposed to her. That was before I understood that you aren't capable of offering her more. Unless you're prepared to say you've completely changed your tune about that, unless you can give more of yourself to her than that selfish crap you dribbled out to her, I want you to turn around and go!"

The silence was deafening.

"Because that's what Emma realized tonight," Amanda continued shakily after a few seconds. "That she can't be with a man who has so little to offer. Do the right thing, Vanni. Think of Emma, not yourself."

For once.

Amanda hadn't said the words, but they pulsed in his blood and his brain as if she had.

Do the right thing *for once.*

He inhaled, the air scalding his lungs, and walked out of the apartment.

Emma listened through the pounding of her heart. She heard the door slam. A few seconds later, Amanda walked down the hallway to where she stood, leaning against the wall. She'd needed the support, listening to Vanni out there. For a few seconds, they just stared at each other.

"You heard it all?" Amanda asked in a hushed tone.

Emma nodded. She felt sick to her stomach. "He left," she whispered. "I . . . I didn't think—"

Amanda was suddenly pulling her off the wall and walking her down the hallway, her arm around her.

"He left," Emma repeated again dazedly when Amanda urged her to sit on the edge of her bed and sat down next to her.

"I know," Amanda said, looking miserable. "But I thought . . . I mean, after everything you told me earlier about how he proposed this no-strings-attached affair with you, did you really expect he wouldn't?"

Emma just stared at her sister, her mouth gaping open. The truth hit her full force.

No. *I didn't really believe he'd walk away, in the end. I still held out hope. I'm such an idiot.*

"Oh, Emma," Amanda said miserably, obviously seeing the truth displayed on her face . . . the crushed hope. She hugged her tightly.

When Emma had arrived home earlier after that toxic encounter with Vera Shaw, Amanda immediately knew something terrible had happened. Emma had only to open her mouth and a partial explanation came spilling out, her agreement to an affair with Vanni, her caveat of a specific time limit to keep her safe, and her tearful admission that it hadn't worked. She was far from safe. She'd fallen in love. Deeply and irrevocably. Emma hadn't told Amanda about Vera Shaw, though, or any of the specifics about Vera's threats or Cristina. That all seemed like too tender a topic to expose.

In truth, it'd shocked her to the core that Vanni had listened to Amanda's reasoning. She was willing to do her part to make sure that Vera didn't spill that poison truth to him about Cristina, but she hadn't thought he would walk away so easily.

Here it was: firsthand proof that his feelings for her hadn't altered since he'd first suggested a sexual affair. Or if they had changed, Emma realized with a wave of dizziness, they hadn't altered enough to make him fight for her. His suffering and his fear of letting another person get close had triumphed. It left her stunned, her entire being vibrating with shock.

Emma wasn't used to letting doubt and fear triumph. But it had. That victory was not sitting well with her. It was constricting her spirit . . . dimming it.

"Maybe it's best," Emma said after a moment through numb lips. The pain would have come sometime. She knew that now for a fact. Whether Vera Shaw had made her ultimatum or not, Emma would have eventually sat here, bereft and empty. She now knew firsthand that he wouldn't have fought for her, because his fear of losing another was too great.

There was nothing to act as a stopgap. Loss crashed into the vacuum that had opened inside her with tidal wave force, stealing her breath.

For the next several days, Vanni went through his waking hours like an automaton. The feeling wasn't entirely unfamiliar to him. He'd gone through a good part of his adult life on automatic mode, after all. He hardly slept, but he was alert and he responded when people spoke to him. When a few crucial issues came up associated with work, he'd responded decisively and coolly.

On the inside, however, some sharp kernel grated, causing the ice inside him to splinter. Finally the pressure grew too great, and he felt the cracking of his brittle control.

He rose from his bed one night about an hour before dawn and walked down to the beach, naked.

He stood at the edge of the lake as the waves lapped around his bare feet. The water stretched out before him, as black and eternal as the night sky. The contrast between the thick, suffocating darkness of this shore and the warmth and brilliance of the beach at La Mer struck him . . . Emma standing on the beach, naked and beautiful, waiting for him . . .

He plunged into the frigid water. It hit him like a slap, ruthless and stinging. The farther away from shore that he swam, the clearer his brain got. Ever since he'd heard Emma's flat voice on the phone so many days ago, he'd been fogged. Now shards of memory cut through his awareness like slicing glass.

Emma's deadened voice on the phone: *I thought I could do this, Vanni, but I can't.*

Amanda: *Because that's what Emma realized tonight. That she can't be with a man who has so little to offer.*

Cristina's dying words: *No child should have been left to feel so much. No man forced to feel so little.*

A man who has so little to offer.

Those words taunted him most of all. He cut through the black water angrily now, swimming farther from shore. When he sensed he was just past the breakers, he paused, lifting his head. Water surged up and hit him in the face.

The memory of Adrian's pale, frightened face leapt like a lion into his consciousness.

Help . . . Van . . . I can't . . .

And then Adrian was sinking beneath the slate-blue, churning water, and so was Vanni, pulled under by the strength of his hold on Adrian's hand, sucked beneath by the force of his love for his twin. He and Adrian were one there. Under the waves, it'd been shockingly peaceful.

He hadn't been afraid.

Vanni never understood what had happened next or how. He hadn't let go . . . but suddenly he'd broken the surface, oxygen burning his lungs as he gulped it greedily.

And they were two.

He gasped and sputtered in the present, the lights of the Breakers sparkling on the distant horizon. He had a crystal-clear image of Emma with the Mediterranean sparkling behind her, an ocean of compassion in her dark eyes.

Adrian may have died, but part of him is in you. It always has been, Vanni.

And then . . .

When the time came, he wasn't afraid. Please believe me. I'm sure enough for both of us.

He remembered Adrian's hand letting go . . . releasing him. For the first time, Vanni realized it hadn't been a weakening gesture, but a firm, decisive one. He'd grasped for Adrian desperately, but only water filled his hand, and he was rising to the surface like a buoy.

Why hadn't he recalled that until now?

Vanni realized he could make out the outline of the bluffs and his house now. Dawn was breaking behind him. He took a shuddering gasp and plunged into the water again, swimming toward shore.

He walked back into the Breakers, soaking wet and naked. His mind was clear, though. He'd find Emma. He'd make her understand. It was different now than it had been when he'd tried to see her and Amanda stopped him several nights ago.

He was different.

He was shivering when he stepped into the kitchen to make

himself some tea for fortification. It was Emma's drink, and just that thought warmed him.

What if I can't convince her that I really can offer her more?

You'll do it. One step at a time.

He took heart from that steady, patient voice in his head. It was new, and yet it was achingly familiar.

Part of him is in you. It always has been, Vanni.

He opened the refrigerator to get some milk while the kettle heated on the stove. His gaze landed on the bottle of champagne on the shelf. He withdrew it and just stared at the label for several seconds, his brow furrowed.

A moment later, he flipped off the burner on the stove and strode out of the kitchen determinedly.

Realizing it was too early to go to Emma's yet, he stopped at a coffee shop in Evanston. He dialed Vera's number as he sat at a booth.

"Vanni?" his aunt answered on the second ring.

"Did you see Emma? Last Tuesday night?" he asked without a greeting. "Did you talk to her at the Breakers before I got home from France?"

There was a long, pregnant pause. "Why?" Vera asked finally. "What did she say to you?"

"I asked you the question, Vera. Did you see Emma or not?"

"Yes. We spoke briefly."

"Why didn't you tell me that when I asked you on Wednesday? You claimed you hadn't spoken to her at all, that she'd never arrived there to your knowledge. What did you say to her?" he seethed.

"Only the truth, Vanni."

"What particular brand of the truth are you referring to?" he bit out, vaguely aware that the waitress cast a concerned glance his way. Anger was making him inappropriately loud.

"I told her I didn't think things would work out between you two. Emma seemed to agree, after she'd given it some thought."

He froze.

"*You* told her . . . *you* didn't think things would work out?" he finally got out in disbelieving fury.

"She wasn't right for you, Vanni."

"Who the hell are you to decide that? Isn't that for Emma to decide? And me?"

"I was just trying to be realistic. I thought—"

Vanni turned toward the window, trying to block the rage that blasted through him like an inferno from the other customers in the restaurant.

"I don't care what the hell *you* thought. Emma told me you didn't like her, but I never actually thought you'd do something this outrageous. You had no *right*. Stay away from her," Vanni grated out, barely containing his wrath. "And stay away from me, too. It's going to be a while before I can take looking at your face again."

He hung up, immune to the muted sounds of Vera's pleas and protests.

Emma?" Amanda called, halting Emma's exit from the apartment. Her sister caught up with her in the front entryway. Emma looked over her shoulder, her hand on the knob. Amanda's hair was tousled and she looked sleepy and alarmed at once. "I thought I heard you out here. You're not leaving already? It's not even seven yet, and I heard you up last night. You can't have slept much. Again," Amanda added pointedly.

"I'm sorry if I kept you up," Emma apologized woodenly.

"Don't worry about it. But why are you leaving so early?"

"I have some paperwork I can get a jump on at the office," Emma said. She reluctantly met Amanda's stare. "It's better than just lying in bed . . . thinking."

Amanda's mouth tightened. Amanda knew what her sister was thinking about, but Emma doubted Amanda knew how she was feeling. At times, she just felt numb, but at other times when she wondered if she'd ever see Vanni again, a great wave of pain would surge into the empty hole inside her.

And what if that witch told him about Cristina and Laurel, despite it all? The thought made her physically ill.

"It's just better for me to keep busy," Emma said, feeling that wave of misery rising even now. She turned and twisted the doorknob.

"But you look so tired," Amanda protested.

"This is better," Emma assured before she plunged out the door.

Much better than just lying there, stewing in my misery.

Ten minutes later, she paused at a stoplight in a right-hand-turn lane, preparing to turn onto the road where her hospice was located. She'd driven briefly on this very same road on the day she'd been with Vanni going to Cristina's funeral. It must have been a hell on earth for Cristina to spend those final weeks in Vanni's home, knowing her son was there in the house, living off his charity, knowing he refused to see her because of their tragic history. It'd literally been a hell, and yet she'd chosen her fate. Did she think she deserved to be punished? Is that why she'd done it? She needn't have gone to the Breakers if she didn't want to. She could have spent her last days alone in her condominium with someone like Emma or one of her coworkers dropping in on her for an hour or two every day.

No, Cristina definitely had chosen to spend her last days near Vanni, knowing it would be bittersweet and painful. She hadn't been weak, in the end. She'd embraced the pain.

Was embracing the pain what Vanni did every day of his life? He certainly hadn't run from it. If anything, part of him had thought he'd deserved that pain.

Because when he was struggling, and I was trying so hard to keep him above the water . . . he was very afraid.

The memory of Vanni saying those words made her flinch in agony. He'd blamed Cristina all these years for the loss of his other half, but he blamed himself perhaps even more elementally. His unrelenting anger at Cristina had been the surface, obvious emotion, a shadowy reflection of the deep fury he had for himself for not being able to save Adrian.

Tears filled her eyes. She couldn't seem to control them for the past few days and nights. They sprung up at the most inopportune moments.

The light turned green. She'd pull into the parking lot just past the intersection and wait until her tears had passed.

She didn't know what hit her. One second, she'd been turning right, and the next she was jarred forcefully. She heard a loud bang, and everything went black.

Chapter 41

Vanni jogged up the stairs to Emma's apartment and looked over the ledge on the second floor of the stairwell, getting a bird's-eye view of the parking lot. He grimaced, not seeing her car. Had she already left for work? He rethought his strategy for finding her. He'd talk to Amanda first. This time, he was better prepared to talk to her than he had been several days ago, when he'd still been sideswiped by Emma's refusal to see him again.

This time, he knew what Amanda needed to hear in order to become his ally in getting Emma to talk to him, and Vanni was ready to say it.

He approached Emma's apartment and drew back his fist in order to knock. The door flew back before he'd ever made contact. Amanda stared at him, shock plastered all over her pale face.

"Oh my God, *Vanni.* How did you know?"

Alarm roared into his awareness, making his flesh tingle. He edited himself at the last second from saying *How did I know* what?

"Where?" he demanded tautly instead, his buzzing, shocked brain tightening its focus on Amanda's leggings and T-shirt, haphazard bun, and clutched purse. She was clearly running out the door in crisis mode.

"North Shore Hospital. She's in the emergency room." He stepped back when she walked out and slammed the door. "Colin is coming to get me—"

"*Emma?*"

Vanni realized he'd yelled and that he was clutching Amanda's arm. He loosened his grip with effort.

"Emma?" he repeated tautly, a cascade of chills going through him. Oh no. *Please don't let this be happening.*

"Yes. The hospital just called. She was in a car accident. They've brought her there." Vanni's grip loosened when Amanda gave a desperate lurch. She started to jog toward the stairs.

Oh, Jesus. He'd dared to care about her. He'd fallen in love with her. Was this the inevitable result?

"*Amanda*," he shouted sharply. "What did the hospital say?"

She turned, still jogging "I don't know anything, Vanni. I have to go!"

The examining doctor said good-bye to Emma and pulled the curtain closed. She was in some kind of makeshift examining room in the emergency room, a square ten-by-ten-foot space set off by curtains, not walls. She could hear the doctor talking to Colin and Emma on the other side of the curtain, telling them what she'd already told Emma.

"She's fine, but we'd like to keep her overnight for observation . . . just to make sure there's no concussion. There isn't any observable wound to the head. The air bag deployed, but she lost consciousness for nearly ten minutes following the accident. Her vitals are all good, but we'd like to watch her for the next twenty-four hours for any signs that there might have been a blunt head trauma."

"Do you suspect there's a brain injury?" Amanda asked anxiously.

"No, the stay overnight is just a precaution, I assure you. Your sister is going to be fine."

"Can I see her?" Amanda asked.

"Of course. We're running a little short-staffed today. She might not be moved to a room for an hour or so."

Ever since Emma had regained consciousness, she'd experienced a strange sort of desire for action, an inexplicable restlessness. In fact, when she'd first come to in the ambulance, the first thing she did was swing her legs off the stretcher and start to get up.

"Whoa, whoa, where are you going?" the stunned EMT had asked her, urging her to lie down again.

Emma hadn't been able to reply logically. She only experienced a deep, profound need to be *somewhere*. That sense of an inner push—or an outer pull—continued. She'd almost screamed in frustration when the doctor told her a few minutes ago they'd be keeping her overnight for observation. Her silent reminders to herself that she was being ridiculous, that she had nowhere to *go* with such a sense of urgency, were only minimally calming to her.

Was she disoriented? Had she hit her head harder than she thought?

She heard a murmuring as Colin and Amanda conferred, but couldn't make out what they were saying.

A second later, Amanda was coming around the curtain. She and Colin had been there earlier, but had vacated the space when the doctor came to examine her. She gave Emma a bright smile.

"Where'd Colin go?" Emma asked when she absorbed that Amanda was alone.

"He, uh . . . went out to the waiting room," Amanda said, setting her purse down on a chair and coming up next to the triage bed where Emma stiffly reclined. Energy surged through her. The last thing she felt like doing was lying around. Suspicion flickered through her at Amanda's forced neutral tone and the way she avoided Emma's eyes.

"Why'd he go out there?" Emma asked. "Amanda?" Her sister met her stare hesitantly. "What's up? Why are you acting so weird?"

Amanda sighed and glanced reluctantly at the closed curtain and then back at Emma.

"He went out to the waiting room because Vanni is out there."

"What?" Emma said incredulously, sitting up straighter on the bed, her skin tingling, her muscles shouting at her to *move*.

"I'm sorry . . . I didn't want to bother you with it, but—"

"That's all right, just tell me why he's here," Emma interrupted hastily.

Amanda explained about running into him as she left the apartment earlier. "I assumed he knew about you somehow, because of the timing and well . . . I was in shock myself. I told him what hospital you were at before I realized he wasn't there because he knew about your accident," Amanda admitted ruefully. "He arrived here just after Colin and me, but of course, they wouldn't let him back. A couple security guards actually had to restrain him, and they threatened to call the police before Colin and I intervened," Amanda said worriedly, her blue eyes huge. "Emma . . . he's a wreck."

"A *wreck*?" Emma asked in alarm. She swung off the sheet that covered her lower body and looked around the tiny space frantically. "What did they do with my clothes?" she demanded.

"Emma, lie back down! I knew I shouldn't have told you."

"What are you talking about? Of *course* you should have told me. Is Colin—"

"*Yes*," Amanda said, her hand on Emma's medical-gown-covered shoulder, urging her back onto the bed. "He went out to tell him you'll be fine!" Amanda insisted.

Emma grabbed her sister's wrist, forcing her to meet her stare.

"Amanda, listen to me. Go and get him," she directed. "Go and get him and bring him back here."

"But—"

"There's no 'but' about it. You don't know everything about Vanni. He's lost a lot of people in his life. This must be hell for him. He *needs* to see for himself that I'm fine."

"But *you're* the one I'm concerned about," Amanda argued.

"If you *are*, then you'll go get him," Emma said firmly. "Because *I* need to see that he's all right, too."

"But what about—"

"Damn," Emma said, flipping back the sheet again in preparation to go herself.

"All right, I'll get him!"

"Hurry," Emma directed succinctly.

Amanda blanched. She looked highly uncertain as she grabbed her purse and left the curtained-off space, and Emma knew why. She was concerned because Emma had said she would never see Vanni again. She and Emma had both agreed it was for the best, given the situation. But Emma didn't care about that at the moment. She didn't care about caution, or Vera Shaw's threats, or her vulnerable heart.

She only wanted one thing with every fiber of her being: to see Vanni's face again.

It felt like an eternity, waiting, but Emma knew it was probably only a matter of seconds. She held her breath at the sound of rapid, firm footsteps approaching on the tile floor. She jumped slightly when the curtain whipped back.

He looked far too tall and large for the cramped little space when the curtain fell back into place behind him. She recognized the soft gray T-shirt he wore with faded jeans; she'd seen him wear it during their golden, heaven-sent days at La Mer. He looked both wonderfully familiar to her and fantastically new, like she was witnessing a miracle firsthand. Her gaze traveled over his tense, bold features with a frantic hunger. Something wild leapt into his sea-colored eyes.

"It's okay. I'm fine—" she sputtered, but she was cut off, because suddenly he was stalking toward the bed, a blazing look in his eyes, and he was bending down and squeezing her against him.

"Don't leave me, Emma," he said roughly, his face pressed

against her neck. Her face scrunched tight with swelling emotion. She dug her fingers into his thick hair and fisted it.

"No. I *won't*," she vowed shakily. She'd seen the truth there, bold and harsh and big as day on his anguished face just now. *This* was hurting him even more than she'd imagined the truth about Cristina would. She'd have to find a way to break the news to him. Better her than Vera Shaw. At least when he knew, she'd be there with him to help shield him from the pain.

She wasn't sure how long they clung together like that in their desperate embrace. He did pull back after a stretched moment, however, his gaze searching her face. He palmed the back of her head gently, a tear spilling onto her cheek at the familiar, prizing gesture.

"They said you're going to be okay?" he asked.

"I'm fine," she insisted. "They're keeping me overnight, but it's just for routine observation. I wish I could go now . . ." She swallowed thickly as she stared into his rigid, handsome face. She hadn't understood until now that he'd been the target of her restless anguish since awakening from the wreck. She touched his whiskered jaw, and then smoothed back his longish, finger-strewn bangs from where they'd fallen on his forehead.

"I'm *so* glad to see you," she whispered.

He shook his head, his gaze narrowing on her face. "You have no idea how glad I am to see you." He leaned down and covered her mouth with his. Her heart seemed to seize and then renew its beating, stronger and faster than before. His taste and the sensation of him filled her like an elixir, sublime and wonderful because she'd thought she'd never experience it again. Warmth suffused her. When he broke their kiss, she held him against her, forehead to forehead.

"I'm so sorry," she said in a pressured whisper.

"No. I am. I know Vera said something to you to upset you. I'm sorry I was so dense when you talked about how much she hated you. I know she can be difficult at times, but I usually just disregard her fussiness and territoriality. I've grown used to it, even if I don't love it. I've built up a layer of protection against her, I guess. I had no idea she'd purposefully try to hurt you or sabotage something because I cared. If something worse had happened to you this morning," he said, his voice cracking slightly, his gaze glacial, "I would have held her personally responsible."

"No, Vanni," Emma said. "The accident was just that: an accident. A stranger ran a red light. I know because the police officer investigating the crash told me the man who hit me had been treated at another hospital's ER. He's not seriously hurt, and is admitting he ran the light."

He leaned back and peered at her closely. "So you didn't wreck because you were upset or from unfocused driving?"

"No," she said, sidestepping the truth a little and not feeling too guilty about it because she didn't want to burden him further with rage. The fact of the matter was, she might have been hit whether she'd been distracted by thoughts of Vera, Cristina, and him or not. There wasn't much you could do when someone barreled through a red light. Besides, she was going to have to tell him the truth about Cristina and how it related to Vera's threats, she realized with a sinking sensation. He didn't need any extra fury and helplessness in addition to that. "It was rotten luck and timing, that's all."

He nodded after a moment.

"Sit down," she whispered, scooting over slightly on the cot. He perched his hip on the edge of the mattress. Emma curled around him, still holding his hands fast in hers, but wanting to feel him with as much of her body as she could.

"You're sure you feel all right?" he asked quietly.

"I'm fine, Vanni. Please believe me," she assured.

"And you meant what you said earlier?" he asked cautiously.

"About not leaving you?" she asked, squeezing his hand. "Yes. I meant it. That's all past. I'll stay with you, for as long as you want me."

Her heart started to thrum in her ears as he looked down at her with a lancing stare.

"Forever," he said.

She blinked in shock at his steadfast demand.

"Forever is a long time," she whispered.

"It won't be long enough," he stated grimly before he was leaning down, and she was lost again in his kiss.

The golden-pink light of sunset was peaking around the closed curtains in her hospital room when Amanda and Colin stood to say it was time for them to go. Emma had studied the couple closely during the last few hours, seen the way they communicated with only a glance, the warmth in their eyes when they looked at each other. Maybe it was just her new, profound happiness because of what had happened with Vanni earlier, but Colin and Amanda really did seem *right* together. It made her feel both glad and heart-sore. She'd assumed *she* was the wronged party when they'd gotten together despite her realization that she didn't want to be with Colin herself. Maybe, in fact, she'd been the one in the wrong for keeping them apart for all these years, all because she needed the security of Colin.

But all of that was over now, and in the past. When it came time for them to leave, Emma hugged Amanda extra hard.

"I love you," she said earnestly in her sister's ear when their heads were close.

Amanda pulled back and studied her face. Tears filled her blue eyes.

"I love you, too," Amanda said.

Emma put out her arms to Colin, who looked shocked by the gesture. She noticed Vanni's eyebrows go up in doubtful wariness across the room, but he didn't say anything. As she watched him over Colin's shoulder, his guardedness and skepticism slowly faded and was replaced with a small smile.

The couple left them alone. Emma had been placed in a private room—a fact that she firmly believed Vanni was responsible for, even though he'd merely shrugged and changed the subject when she'd asked him about it earlier.

Vanni pulled up a chair close to her bed. A nurse's aide knocked and entered. She poured a glass of ice water for Emma and left the pitcher on her bedside table. After the aide left, Vanni leaned forward and grabbed Emma's hand. Emma hadn't been able to keep her eyes off him all day. He was a miracle to her. The feelings she was having were miraculous, too. Yet all the while in the background, a black, heavy threat hovered. She was going to have to tell him about Cristina, and soon. From what he'd told her about his confrontation with Vera on the phone earlier, Vera might be vindictive and pounce the truth on him at any time.

"How are you feeling?" he asked, the low, gravelly sound of his voice making her skin prickle with awareness.

"Fine. Ready to go home," she replied with a sigh because he was lazily stroking the skin of her inner forearm, and it felt so good.

"Well you're going to have to be patient," he replied, giving her an amused, pointed glance. "Since we have plenty of time, why don't you tell me what's bothering you?"

She tensed, her gaze sharpening on him. "What do you mean?"

"There's something weighing on you," he said matter-of-factly, still stroking her arm. "You're not very good at hiding things, baby," he chastised her when she gave him a forced look of surprise. She grimaced and he gave a gruff laugh. He stood and she scooted over for him to sit on the edge of her bed. He squeezed her hand. "Just say it, Emma. I'm not going anywhere."

"No?" she asked, attempting to smile but not succeeding very well, given the way his gaze narrowed on her face with concern.

"Not a chance. I've told you I'm not letting you go. I'm willing to face death again, if I have to, that's what today taught me . . . that's what last night did."

"Last night?" she asked curiously.

He gave her a stern glance. "I'll tell you about it another time. Right now, you talk about what's on your mind. Does it have to do with something Vera said that night you came to the Breakers to meet me, and I asked her to find you and tell you we were landing a little late? I wasn't sure you'd picked up my phone messages."

"A *little late*?" Emma asked, surprise temporarily making her forget the anxious topic. "She told me you wouldn't be returning that night."

"She lied," he stated flatly. "She was likely lying about whatever it was that she said to spook you as well."

Emma recalled the official-looking birth certificates. "I wish she was lying," she whispered. An image of Vera waving those pieces of paper in front of her face sprung up in her mind's eye. For the first time, she realized Vanni's aunt had gone and gotten the birth certificates on purpose. She'd known Emma would be at the Breakers, alone and vulnerable, and she'd prepared for battle. Maybe Vanni saw something on her face, because he squeezed her hand. Her gaze flickered to his face.

"Tell me," he said.

"It's just . . . you're . . . you're not going to like it, Vanni."

"Does it have to do with you?" he asked, his blue-green eyes looking like gleaming crescents as he peered down at her through narrowed lids.

She shook her head, looking away from his stare.

"Emma, as long as you're fine and you've given up on this crazy idea about not seeing me anymore, I can take it," he said. "Everything else is a breeze compared to thinking something had happened to you, worrying I was never going to have the chance to see you again." His finger brushed across her jaw. "Touch you. Tell you how I really felt about you," he said more quietly.

She went still beneath his caress. "And . . . *how* is that, again?"

"Are you trying to sidestep the issue?" he asked quietly, humor quirking his mouth.

"Maybe a little," she admitted, meeting his stare earnestly.

A smile quivered on his firm lips. Her love for him swelled like a balloon expanding in her chest, threatening to burst.

"Maybe you're right," he said, his fingertip brushing across the bridge of her nose. "There's nothing more important than what's happening between us."

"Really?"

He looked at her, his heart in his eyes, and shook his head. "You've hauled me into the world of the living again, Emma . . . kicking and screaming in protest at first, maybe . . . but still . . . here I am. I'm going to stay here, too, as long as you'll have me."

"Forever," she mouthed, smiling. His fingertip brushed across her lips, and she felt that familiar tug at her core.

"I love you," he said simply. "I never thought I'd tell another person that. I thought I knew what that word meant. But I've never known *this*."

She stared at him, unable to draw breath.

"What? Don't you believe me?" he asked, his brows knitting together.

"Yes," she said emphatically. "I love you, too."

He cupped her jaw before he leaned down to kiss her. She'd been wrong to think they'd left behind that golden, unfurling sweetness on the sun-drenched beach at La Mer. It spread inside her now in the unlikely setting of a hospital room, all because he was here next to her, taking a risk.

He lifted his head and plucked softly at her lips with his.

"Now. Tell me," he urged.

And with his breath mingling with hers, and that golden sweetness running thick in her veins, she gathered her strength, knowing his pain would be hers.

She couldn't read his expression as the truth spilled out of her, no matter how desperately she tried.

". . . and Vera showed me the birth certificates, Vanni," she finished, her voice having gone high as her concern mounted. He just continued to look at her, an unreadable, vaguely stunned expression on his face. "Vanni, I think it's true," she whispered, touching his face. "But is it really that terrible? Yes, Cristina bore you, but that doesn't take away a tiny bit of the love you have for your mother. If anything, I'd think you might love your mom more, knowing how she dedicated herself so completely to you and Adrian, despite the fact that you weren't hers biologically. And *you're* still the same person. Vanni?" she asked, her desperation mounting. "*Say* something."

"That *bitch*," he bit out. Emma started at the venom in his tone. "I can't believe she did that!"

"I told you, she hated herself for not being capable of being a good mother. Cristina suffered more than you'll ever know with the knowledge of her lack—"

"I don't mean Cristina," he interrupted. "I mean Vera. She spewed all that at you, and then told you that if you saw me again, she'd tell me about Cristina and . . . what? I'd go into a tailspin? The truth would ruin me forever? And you *believed* her?"

Emma's face went slack. "I believed her, but with good reason. She had the proof. Are you telling me you think she was making it all up? Cristina wasn't really your biological mother? I was being gullible?"

An expression of pure frustration and fury tightened his face. "No, I didn't mean it like that. *You* didn't do anything wrong. Vera *was* telling the truth. Cristina was . . . *is* Adrian's and my blood mother. My father told me before he died. *That's* not why I'm in shock. I can't believe that Vera has known all these years, and that she used the information to blackmail you. What a fucked-up bitch."

He shook his head distractedly, obviously lost in thought. His gaze eventually landed on Emma's face. He blanched.

"Jesus," he muttered heatedly under his breath. He stood and poured her more ice water. "Here. Drink this. You've gone white as a sheet," he said grimly, handing her the water and sitting back on the bed next to her. He waited until she'd taken a swallow. "I'm sorry," he said, taking the cup and setting it back on the bedside table.

"You *knew*? You knew all along Cristina was your biological mother?" she asked, shock ringing in her voice.

He sighed and shut his eyes briefly. "Just since my father died five years ago." His gaze sharpened on her. "It wasn't the most welcome of news, and I can't say I took it well. Still . . . it didn't *ruin* me, even if it did confuse my feelings for Cristina all that much more," he admitted bitterly. "But that's not the point. You were willing to keep this from me because you thought it'd hurt me that much? You were willing to sacrifice what's happening between us because you thought that would hurt me more than losing you?" Stark pain flashed in his eyes. "Nothing could be further from the truth."

Emma shook her head, clobbered by the turn of events. Relief swept through her, escalating her emotional state even more.

He shook his head, clearly as incredulous as she was. "And the worst of it all?" he asked. "It almost worked, what Vera did."

"No. Don't think about that," Emma said firmly, finding her voice. She reached for him. "It *didn't* work. We're here together." He held her fast and she squeezed him back. "You know what I'm thinking?" she asked him with a bark of hysterical laughter after a moment, her voice thick with emotion.

"What?" he asked as he pressed his lips against her neck with feverish intensity.

"Maybe that car wreck today wasn't such a random accident, after all."

He stilled. His hand rose to cup the back of her head. He pulled her back slowly. Before his face lowered next to hers, she saw the fierce light in his eyes.

"It wouldn't surprise me. I may have said I doubted you at first, but I was kidding myself. It couldn't be more clear to me now that you can make miracles, Emma," he said with grim finality before his mouth claimed hers.

Epilogue

ONE MONTH LATER

Emma curled up on her side on the cushioned lounger and looked out at paradise. Vanni noticed her smug smile as she stared at him, and raised his eyebrows in an amused query.

"I think I'm becoming extremely selfish," she murmured, her voice pitched just above the silken, rhythmic cadence of the waves hitting the beach.

"I'm trying to imagine how and coming up short," he replied dryly, moving aside the tray and remnants of the delicious lunch Mrs. Denis had made them. He rolled onto his side facing her, his head perched in his hand. She reached out and traced her finger along his ridged, taut abdomen with languorous sensuality.

"Really?" she murmured, turning her hand and brushing the stunning ring he'd given her just last night after they'd arrived at La Mer against his belly. His stomach muscles leapt against the gently scraping diamond. They shared a smile. Since Vanni had insisted upon a very short engagement, *she'd* insisted she didn't want a ring until they exchanged their wedding vows on the cliffside terrace of

La Mer four days from now. Vanni had had other plans, however. Almost as soon as she'd agreed to marry him three weeks ago, he'd hired Angelo Prisatti to design her ring. It was a breathtaking symphony of meticulously wrought platinum and diamonds. *Suited for an elven princess*, Vanni had teased warmly last night when he'd slid it on her finger and she'd gaped at it in wonder.

"I think you spoil me rotten," Emma told him pointedly.

His lips tilted in amusement as he reached out and delved his fingers into her hair. "Most women would think I was selling them short by not giving them a huge wedding at the Villa Ephrussi de Rothschild or the Château de la Napoule."

"You showed me those places, and several besides," she reminded him, running her finger over the soft, thin trail of hair that led from his belly button below the waistband of his swim trunks. "You gave me the choice. You know as well as I do that none of them is as beautiful as La Mer."

"Certainly none as special to us," he said, sobering.

"Vanni?"

"Yes?"

"Do you think that maybe we could live here most of the time?" she asked in a hushed voice.

She thought he'd be surprised or nonplussed, but instead, a small smile tilted his mouth, as if he'd been expecting her to say it. He pushed slightly on the back of her head and she leaned forward, meeting his kiss.

"Do you really love it here that much?" he asked next to her lips a moment.

"You know I do," she whispered. "But more importantly, I think you do. I know we'll have to stay at the Breakers at times, with your work." Emma was even more prepared to stay at the Breakers now that Vanni had insisted upon shunting Vera Shaw away from his home and private life and over to a lower management position at Montand Motorworks, where she supervised the janitorial and cleaning staff. As Vanni had put it, in that position she could do relatively little harm and was directly under the eye of her brother, Dean. Both Dean and Vanni agreed after what had occurred with Emma that Vera *needed* watching.

"And what about *your* work?" he asked, cradling her jaw with his hand.

"I've thought about it a lot. There are a few English-speaking nursing agencies here. I'll find work. Nurses are always in demand."

"And you're sure you want to work?" he asked, nuzzling her nose.

"Of course."

"Being a nurse is part of who you are," he agreed quietly, meeting her stare. She raised her eyebrows in a silent query, waiting for what he'd say about La Mer. Again, he smiled. "Yes," he said. "I think it's time I made La Mer my home. *Our* home. I don't feel as tied to the Breakers anymore. I don't feel like part of me is trapped there."

"I'm so glad," she whispered.

He dipped his head and covered her mouth again. Warmth swept through her at the sensation of his firm, moving lips. She'd have thought their intense sexual attraction for each other could mount no higher, but she'd been wrong. It seemed to escalate every day, the fire fed by their increasing trust and feelings for each other. When they'd been together during that amazing, magical week at La Mer before, they usually made love after lunch. It was a habit she was looking forward to making a tradition.

"I'm definitely selfish about one thing. I'm dreading the fact that people will start to arrive tomorrow for the wedding," she said against his plucking lips a moment later, highly distracted by the feeling of his hand moving along the curve of her hip and ass. "Dean, Michelle, Amanda, Colin, Niki—"

Something struck her and she rolled back, staring at Vanni's face.

"What?" he asked.

"*Niki.* I don't know why it didn't occur to me before. Because of Cristina, Niki is a relation to you, isn't he?" she asked.

Vanni nodded, and she was glad to see how calm he looked. Since he'd revealed to her that he'd known Cristina was his biological mother, her name didn't come up often between them. Still, Emma didn't consider Cristina to be a taboo topic for Vanni, like she had before, and she was glad to observe firsthand that she'd been right in her assumption. He seemed quite comfortable as he pulled her back into position close to him, resuming his caress on her naked hip.

"Cristina was Niki's great-aunt, so I guess that makes us second cousins or something?" he said, glancing down and watching himself rub her hip.

"Does Niki know?"

Vanni shook his head. "I've never told another soul about Cristina."

"Do you think you'll ever tell him?" Emma asked quietly, cupping his shoulder.

"Maybe. Probably," he amended after a moment. He met her stare, looking pensive. "There's something I've been meaning to ask you."

"Okay," Emma said, sensing his intensity.

"Take off your bikini first."

"What?" she asked, surprised.

"Just do it," he directed, the quirk of his brow a subtle challenge.

She laughed, but did as he asked, then lay on her side next to him again. His gaze moved over her naked body with warm appreciation.

"Okay?" she asked amusedly.

"Better than okay," he murmured, caressing the side of her breast and sweeping it downward over her sensitive side, making her shiver. His hand opened on her hip and he met her stare. "Do you think it was wrong of me, not to grant Cristina forgiveness when she asked it of me?"

Emma tried to mask her surprise at the unexpected question.

"No," she said honestly. "Forgiveness is a state of mind. You know what I've told you all along about Amanda and me. If you weren't feeling it, if they were just words, it would have been wrong to lie about it."

He stared out at the sea as he rubbed her hip, the sun-infused water turning his eyes into brilliant cerulean crescents.

"Vanni . . . do you *want* to forgive her?" Emma asked.

His mouth quirked slightly. "It's too late now."

She touched his whiskered jaw, and he looked at her.

"It's never too late."

She saw his throat convulse as he swallowed.

"I've been thinking a lot about what you said out there." He nodded toward the floating dock. "About me carrying a good load of the guilt for Adrian's death, and how Cristina knew that, and how she asked for my forgiveness not just for her . . ."

"But for you," Emma said, tears burning her eyes. It was a miracle to her, to see him tackling his demons . . . to watch him heal. "That's why it's never too late to forgive, Vanni. Because in the act of forgiving another, the forgiver is changed . . . lightened. But it's not something that you can just *say*. You have to—"

"Feel it," he said, nodding. "I understand it's not black and white, like I thought. And I *do*. Feel it, I mean. I'll never love Cristina, but I understand that she was doing all that she was capable of, coming there to mother Adrian and me . . . never really feeling or wanting that role. She was wrong for her neglect, but she was trapped by her selfishness. I think she *wished* she could have been different."

"I know she did," Emma agreed, stroking his shoulder.

His gaze flashed up to meet hers. "I never told you this, but the night before you were in that accident, I swam out again."

Her caressing hand stilled. She knew what he meant by "swam out." He meant that he'd tempted fate again, tested whether or not he would ever be taken like Adrian had been.

"Something happened to me out there," he admitted starkly.

"What?"

"I remembered more than I'd ever recalled about the day when Adrian died. I'd always thought that I'd let go of him, that I hadn't held on tight enough, that I wasn't strong enough to save him . . . but that's not what happened."

She waited, her naked skin prickling with amplified awareness. He looked into her eyes, and a shiver coursed through her.

"I didn't let go," he said. "I was ready to go down with him. *He* let go of *me*," Vanni stated succinctly. "His hand didn't slip away. He pulled his hand out of mine, and I zoomed to the surface like a balloon."

"You mean . . . he intentionally released you?"

Vanni nodded, a strange, awed expression creeping over his face. "It was like he was telling me to . . ."

"Live," Emma finished for him.

His glance at Emma was a mixture of doubt and longing and hope. "Maybe I'm wrong. But that's what it *felt* like, when I remembered it out there that morning."

"You weren't wrong. Adrian released you all over again, and this time you *felt* it. Vanni, that's amazing," she whispered.

His gaze sharpened on her. He cupped her jaw. "No. *You're* amazing."

"Me? What have I got to do with it?" Emma asked, stunned.

"*Everything*."

Her lips parted, and suddenly his mouth was covering them, his tongue sliding between them, and he was rolling her on her back and coming down over her, his heat and arousal stunning her. She hadn't realized as he'd spoken that desire had coiled just below the surface. He was heavy and hard when he lowered his trunks a moment later. He entered her, filled her completely, his fierce gaze on her the entire time. She gasped as he ground their pelvises together, circling slightly with his hips, applying a delicious pressure on her clit.

"If it wasn't for you—for your grace, and your kindness, and your example—I would have never gotten here, Emma," he stated gruffly, keeping his hips still. He leaned down and kissed her parted lips gently while his cock pulsed high and hard inside her.

"I would have never even considered forgiving Cristina," he said next to her trembling mouth. "I *certainly* never would have forgiven myself. I would have kept on, a dead man walking in the world of the living. It's all down to you, *mon petit ange*. You've pulled me into the world of the living, and now that I'm here, I'll never let you go," he assured her heatedly.

He braced himself with his hands on the cushion and began to move.

Keep reading for an excerpt from
Beth Kery's novel

GLIMMER

Available from Berkley Books

Alice Reed was used to hiding her nerves. She was used to hiding almost everything. Today was different though. She could have disguised her anxiety about her upcoming interview as easily as she could have ignored a provocative mathematical challenge.

"Don't worry about it. It'll be a piece of cake. Just focus on what you know. You're pretty damn awesome when you do that," Maggie Lopez said soothingly as she stood over Alice and gave her a friendly, but critical once-over. Maggie was her graduate advisor at Arlington College's executive MBA program. After a series of initial screwups that now looked like serendipity, Alice rented the apartment above Maggie's garage. Most importantly, Maggie and Alice had become friends. She respected Maggie's opinion, so her anxiety ratcheted up even higher when she saw her mentor's slight frown as she stared down at her. A horrible thought hit her. She plopped her hand palm down on the top of her head.

"*Shit.* My roots. They're showing, aren't they? I forgot to color them. I got so caught up in running those numbers last night, I forgot about everything," she moaned as she flung herself out of her chair and rushed to the mirror mounted on the wall in Maggie's office. She was a decent athlete, but unaccustomed to wearing anything but combat boots, flip-flops, or tennis shoes. She nearly took a header in her new interview pumps.

Maggie sighed in amused exasperation behind her. "Only you would forget an interview for a chance at the most coveted executive training program in the United States—the *world*—because of some inconsequential calculations."

Alice stared wide-eyed into the mirror. Her face looked especially pale due to her anxiety and the contrast between her short, near-black hair, navy suit, and lined dark blue eyes.

"You were the one who asked me to run those inconsequential numbers," Alice mumbled distractedly. She flattened the hair next to her part and peered furiously into the mirror, as if she held her reflection responsible for all her many shortcomings. Sure enough, there were the telltale glimmering, reddish-gold roots. "Fuck it," she muttered through her teeth. "This is a joke anyway. Durand has never sent a recruiter to Arlington College's MBA program before. Is this another example of famous Durand *charity*?" she demanded, rounding on Maggie.

Maggie had grown immune to her frowns and sharp tongue in the past two years, however. She knew damn well that Alice's bark was much worse than her bite.

Usually, anyway.

"Don't you dare put down this program," Maggie warned with a pointed finger and an ominous expression. "I happen to be extremely proud of it and everything we've accomplished in the past few years, thanks in large part to *your* brilliance, hard work, and groundbreaking research. Am I surprised Durand asked to recruit from our graduating class? *No*. I'm *not*," Maggie added with finality, when Alice gave her a half-hopeful, half-doubtful look. "The philanthropy and profit article sent shock waves through the business community. Now stop feeling sorry for yourself," she said as she dropped into her desk chair, making the springs protest loudly.

Alice's pique deflated.

"I *am* proud of the P and P study," she said honestly, referring to the groundbreaking business article she and a few other grad students had published with Maggie as the lead researcher several months ago. "Did Sebastian Kehoe tell you he was coming to Arlington because of the study?" she asked. Kehoe was the vice president of human resources for Durand.

"No."

"Then why *is* he?" she grumbled.

Alice halfway wished Sebastian Kehoe had continued to ignore her little college. She performed best in solitude. It grated to have to sell herself to interviewers as if she were both a commodity *and* the pitchman for that commodity. To say she didn't interview well was a gargantuan understatement.

"Durand is coming because they're searching for talented, top-notch executives, I expect."

Alice snorted. "You told me to look at this interview as good experience for future interviews. Even *you* don't actually believe anyone at Arlington stands a chance with Durand."

"I don't know what I think, to be honest," Maggie said stiffly. She snapped several tissues out of a box and held them up for Alice to take. "Now wipe off some of that crap you insist on putting on your eyes. Comb your hair back from the part to hide the roots. Put on a little lipstick for once. And for God's sake, stiffen up the spine, Reed. I expect you to rise to the challenge, not wilt in the face of it."

Alice's spine *did* stiffen in reactionary anger for a few seconds before the truth of Maggie's words penetrated. Her mentor was right. As usual.

"I'll go to the bathroom to wash up a bit," Alice agreed in a subdued tone. "I have ten minutes before the interview starts."

"Good girl," Maggie said bracingly.

"Alice," Maggie called sharply as Alice reached for her office door.

"Yeah?" Alice asked, looking over her shoulder. She went still when she saw the unusually somber expression on Maggie's face.

"There's been a little change of circumstances as far as your interview. Sebastian Kehoe became ill a few days ago and had to send someone else in his place."

A perverse, savage combination of disappointment, triumph, and relief swept through Alice. *So*. They'd sent some low-level stooge in Kehoe's place? Figured. She knew Durand would never take anyone in her graduating class as a serious contender for "Camp Durand." The four-week-long program on the shores of Lake Michigan was where the brightest and best business school graduates went every summer to show their stuff. Sixty percent of the Camp Durand counselors were chosen to become the highest-paid, most elite young executives in the world. Through a combination of team-building exercises, intense observation, and a highly reputable children's camp held on the lake, Durand culled the chosen few, ending up with the best of the best.

Those selected for Camp Durand were paid a hefty sum for their weeks of service, whether they went on to become permanently employed or not. Alice coveted that chunk of money, even if she didn't dare to hope she'd ever be offered a regular corporate position at the highly successful international company. She had student loans that would come due soon, and no solid job leads. Still . . . she was torn about being forced to prove herself to the slick, influential company.

"I *knew* Durand couldn't be serious about Arlington," Alice said.

Or me.

Maggie must have noticed the smirk Alice strained to hide. "They're so *unserious* about Arlington College that their chief executive officer is coming in place of Sebastian Kehoe," Maggie said.

Alice's hand fell from the knob of the door and thumped on her thigh.

"What?"

Suddenly, Maggie seemed to be having difficulty meeting her stare. "Several Durand executives were on a business trip here in Chicago recently. When Kehoe got ill, Dylan Fall agreed to fill in for his remaining appointments." Maggie glanced at her warily. Or was it *worriedly*? "I . . . I didn't want to tell you because I thought you'd get more nervous, but I didn't want you to walk in unprepared, either," she said miserably.

A wave of queasiness hit her.

"Dylan Fall," Alice stated in a flat, incredulous tone. "You're telling me that in nine minutes, I'm going to be interviewed by the chief executive officer of Durand Enterprises?"

"That's right." Maggie's expression of stark compassion faded and was replaced by her game face. "This is the opportunity of a lifetime. I don't expect you to get a spot at Camp Durand, necessarily—that might be too much to hope for, all things considered. But you're a unique, smart girl, and you're kick-ass with numbers, and . . . well, you're the *best* Arlington has got. You're the best I've ever known," she added with a defiant look. "At the very least, you had *better* walk in there, hold your head up, and do Arlington College proud."

Maggie's proclamation still rang in her head while Alice waited on hot coals in the waiting room of the dean of business's offices. The dean had apparently cheerfully vacated his office for Dylan Fall.

Of course.

Fall probably had people regularly lying across mud puddles so he could cross without soiling his designer shoes.

Maggie had been right to call her out earlier. Alice didn't stand a chance of getting into Camp Durand—let alone getting hired as an elite Durand executive. But that didn't mean she would cower. Alice had stood up to bastards and lowlifes that were a hundred times scarier than a suit like Dylan Fall.

She'd stood up and walked away, pride intact.

"He's ready for you," Nancy Jorgensen, the business department secretary, twittered as she stuck her head around the corner of the door leading to a hallway. Alice stood, clutching her new vinyl portfolio and trying not to sway in her heels. She cast Nancy Jorgensen a dark glance. The middle-aged, typically gray little woman looked suspiciously flushed with color and excitement. She suspected she knew why: Dylan Fall. *Traitor,* Alice thought bitterly as she stalked past Nancy.

Just get this damn thing over with.

Instead of walking into the office Nancy specified, Alice charged. The door was lighter than she'd imagined from its formidable, oak-paneled appearance. She pushed at it too aggressively and it thumped against the wall inside the office. Alice started at the loud noise and froze on the threshold. The man sitting behind the large oak desk looked up and blinked.

"Is there a fire?" he asked quietly.

"No," Alice said, frowning, wary because she wasn't sure if he was kidding or not. Funny he had mentioned fire. She hadn't been this nervous since she'd locked herself in her bedroom and her uncle Tim had ignited some of her mother's meth-cooking chemicals in order to smoke her out of it. He hadn't succeeded, but he'd very nearly killed Alice—and himself—in the process.

Nancy closed the door behind her with a hushed click. Dylan Fall studied her while Alice's lungs burned for air.

He suddenly whipped off the glasses he wore and stood. Alice willed her ungainly limbs to move. He reached out his hand.

"Alice. Dylan Fall. I can't tell you what a pleasure it is to meet you," he said, his voice low with just a hint of gravel to it. Her spine flickered with heightened awareness at the sound.

"Thank you for taking the time to see me," she said, gripping his hand firmly and giving it a perfunctory pump. He held out his other hand in an elegant "please, sit" gesture and lowered into his seat. She sat in the leather chair before the large desk, feeling like her arms and legs were glaringly out of sync with her brain . . . worse, like she were a beggar supplicant at the polished altar of the god of wealth and power. She absolutely refused to be impressed or cowed by Dylan Fall.

You can refuse all you want. You are.

"I'm glad to have the opportunity to meet with you. From what I've gathered, much of the statistical brilliance from the philanthropy and profit article in the *Journal of Finance and Business* is owed to you," he said, picking up a pen and tapping it on the desk. He moved the pen in an absentminded fashion, running long fingers over the smooth metal cylinder, flipping it, and repeating the process.

Alice ripped her stare off the vision and focused on his face. Her heart had started to beat uncomfortably fast. He played with the pen in a distracted way, but his gaze on her was razor sharp. The thick drapes were drawn, blocking out the spring sunlight. The contrast of shadow and glowing lamplight made his strong jawline and near-black eyes appear even more dramatic. Enigmatic. She'd already known what to expect from his looks, or at least that's what she'd told herself. He had dark brown hair that was smooth, despite its thickness. It was longer in the front than in the back. He wore it combed back, the style suiting his business attire, even if it did look like it could be sexily disheveled in a heartbeat by a woman's delving fingers. A pair of lustrous, drilling eyes advertised loud and clear you better give Fall exactly what he wanted, or he'd freeze you to the spot. Dark lashes and slanting brows added to a sort of sexy gypsy-gone-corporate-pirate aura about him. His face was handsome, but in a rugged fashion—full of character and strength. He was far from being a pretty boy. There was something rough about him, despite the expensive suit and epic composure. The cleft in his chin only added to the sense of hard, chiseled male beauty.

The media loved him. She'd seen photos of him clean-shaven, sexily scruffy, and even once with a beard and mustache. Currently, he wore a very thin, well-trimmed goatee. His skin wasn't pale, but he didn't look like the type of man who tanned as a matter of course, either. Alice imagined that, like her, he spent a lot of his time reading reports and squinting at numbers on a computer screen, or else sitting at the head of a boardroom table.

Durand Enterprises was well known for not only its strong philanthropic practices, but its financial robustness. Alice herself had suggested it right off the bat for their multifactorial, longitudinal study about the correlation between company philanthropy and profit. Alice had pored through journal and magazine articles, collecting relevant data on Durand, so she'd seen photos of Fall.

She'd stared at those photos a lot. So much so, in fact, that she'd started to think she was getting a little obsessed with the business mogul.

She was pretty unimpressed by men as a rule. She'd had to deal with her share of strutting, bullshitting, worthless, and dangerous males in her life. Good-looking men usually had even fewer redeeming qualities than the plain or ugly ones, in her opinion. The ugly ones had to compensate somehow in order to compete for women. She didn't usually blink twice when she met a hot guy, but Dylan Fall was the kind of rough-and-tumble gorgeous that had all sorts of involuntary chemical reactions sparking in her body.

At the moment, she damned him straight to hell for it. Didn't he possess an unfair amount of advantages as it was?

She straightened her spine and cleared her throat. "I was one of four research assistants on Dr. Lopez's project. We all did our share of research and running numbers."

His sliding fingers slowed on the pen. His gaze narrowed on her. "You're a team player, then?" he asked quietly.

"I'm just stating the truth."

"No. You're not."

Her chin went up. She almost immediately ducked her head when she felt how muscle and skin tightened, making her thrumming pulse probably more obvious to him, exposing her vulnerability.

"I spoke to Dr. Lopez about it in person before arriving here today," he said. "She says that most of the innovative statistical analyses run on the project were not only completed by you, but designed by you."

She couldn't think of what to say, so she just held his stare.

"You don't want to brag about your accomplishments?" he asked.

"Is that what you'd like? A little dog-and-pony show?"

His long fingers stilled, holding the silver pen mid-flip.

Shit.

Her cheeks flooded with heat. "I'm sorry. I didn't mean that," she said, flustered. "I'm just a little confused as to why Durand is here at Arlington College. We *all* are, to be honest. Did you come because of the article?"

"Does that surprise you?" he asked, tossing the pen on the blotter. "Durand was one of the main companies featured. You single-handedly vindicated our strong philanthropic principles using hard statistics to do it. I'm impressed," he said starkly. She swallowed thickly when he leaned forward, elbows on the desk, and met her stare. "Very."

"Did you need vindication?" she couldn't stop herself from asking.

He shrugged slightly and leaned back again, the action bringing her gaze downward to broad shoulders and a strong-looking chest. He knew how to wear a suit, that much was certain. Powerful. Elegantly dangerous. On Dylan Fall, a suit was transformed into the modern-day equivalent of a warrior's armor.

"Not really, no. Durand is a privately held company, as I'm sure you already know. There are no stockholders to whom I need to justify my actions."

"What about to other officers on the board?" she asked, curiosity trumping her anxiety.

His stare narrowed on her. "I was under the impression *I* was the one interviewing *you*."

"Sorry," she said quickly. Is that all she was going to do during this interview? Apologize? And was that a tiny smile tilting his mouth? Somehow, she'd rather it wasn't, as unsettling as she was finding this whole experience. She wasn't wilting, like Maggie had worried she would, but she *was* blowing this. Not by a slow burn, either.

More like death by blowtorch.

"I was just curious about Durand's reaction to the article," she backpedaled. "I worked on that project even in my sleep for fifteen months straight. It sort of gets into your blood."

"As someone who sleeps, drinks, and eats Durand, I'm inclined to understand completely," he said dryly. "Actually, Durand's philanthropic goals are built in to Alan Durand's—the company founder's—directives. Durand has a long tradition of community projects, people-building, and charitable programs. After completing the study, were you convinced it's a worthwhile goal for a company to have?"

"Sir?"

"Do you think most companies should include philanthropy in their operating directives?"

"The statistics certainly indicate they should."

"That's not what I asked."

She stared at her interlaced fingers, lying on top of her folder. A small patch of perspiration wetted the vinyl. "If a company can increase its profits by doing good works for the community and its people, it seems like a win-win situation all around, doesn't it?"

She looked up at his dry laugh. "That's certainly a politically correct answer. Now give me an honest one, Alice. Do you think companies like Durand should continue with philanthropic community efforts?"

The silence stretched taut.

"Alice?" he prodded quietly.

"Of course. It's just . . ."

"What?"

"It's nothing." His dark brows slanted menacingly. "It's only . . . It seems . . ." *What the hell, you've already blown the interview anyway. Everyone knows you never stood a chance from the get-go.* "A little patronizing, that's all." She cringed a little when he went eerily still. "Aside from that, I think the answer is an obvious yes. I think large corporations should have charitable directives."

"Patronizing?" he asked, his quiet voice striking her as similar to the deep purr of a misleadingly calm lion. "Like Durand is grandstanding, you mean. Making itself look good in the public's eye for the sole purpose of selling widgets . . . or candy bars, soda, energy drinks, and chocolate milk, among other things, in Durand's case."

"All of the things your campers at Camp Durand—low-income urban youth from poverty-infested neighborhoods—consume," she couldn't stop herself from saying. Heat rushed into her cheeks.

She forced herself not to flinch under his boring stare, but her defiance definitely wavered. To call his eyes merely "deepest brown" or "almost black" vastly understated their impact. They shone like polished stones with fire in the depths. Somehow, his eyes managed to startle her on a constant basis instead of a quick rush.

"Do you consume those products, Alice?"

"Once in a while," she said with a shrug. In truth, she was a chocoholic. Durand Jingdots, Sweet Adelaides, and Salty Chocolate Caramels rated among her favorite guilty pleasures while sitting at her computer running numbers. Not that she'd confess that weakness to Dylan Fall. "Why?" she asked warily. "Is that a prerequisite to be chosen for the Durand training program?"

"No," he said, picking up a piece of paper from his desk. Her heart raced. He was going to tell her any second the interview was over. *Let him.* The sooner she was done here, the better. He idly perused what she realized was her resume. "But I happen to know that Little Paradise—where you grew up—is one of the crime-infested, low-income urban areas you just described."

Her heart jumped uncomfortably against her sternum. She unglued her tongue from the top of her mouth.

"How did you know I grew up in Little Paradise?" she rasped, mortified that Dylan Fall, of all people, knew about the infamous place where she'd grown up—Little Paradise, the grossly inaptly named, sole remaining trailer park within the Chicago city limits;

a grimy, mangy little community tainted by toxic-smelling fumes from the nearby factories of Gary, Indiana. The address wasn't on her resume. She wanted no part of Little Paradise. She'd used a local address ever since she'd left for college nearly six years ago.

"Dr. Lopez mentioned it," he said without batting an eye. "Are you ashamed of where you grew up?"

"No," she lied emphatically.

"Good," he said, dropping her resume to the desktop. "You shouldn't be."

He was probably only ten or so years older than her almost twenty-four years. She resented him for his air of experience and unflappable composure, despite his relative youth. What were the circumstances of him becoming CEO of Durand at such a young age? Wasn't he related to the company founder or something? She struggled to recall. It'd been extremely difficult to find personal details about both Alan Durand and Dylan Fall. She'd never found many details about Fall's meteoric rise in the powerful company.

It suddenly struck her full-force how out of place she was in the face of his polished, supreme confidence. He was no doubt amused by her gauche defensiveness and confusion.

"Are you going to ask me any relevant questions in regard to business, my interest in Durand, or my qualifications?" she asked through a tense jaw.

"I thought that's what I'd been doing." Her rigid expression didn't break. He exhaled. "Fine." He briskly put on the charcoal-gray glasses he'd been wearing and picked up some papers from the desk. He looked extremely sexy wearing those glasses.

Of course.

"I have some questions for you in regard to your research decisions on the philanthropy and profit research."

She began to relax slightly as he launched into a series of pointed queries regarding her statistical analysis. Alice knew mathematical models backward and forward. She was also a workaholic. In this arena, he couldn't fluster her. Even so, she sensed after a period of time that Fall not only understood the nuances of the statistics as well, if not better, than her, he was light-years ahead of her in knowledge about what her conclusions *meant* in the practical workings of the business world. She was envious of his knowledge, but also curious. Hungry. Tantalized by the glittering promise of power that those numbers might grant her when paired with knowledge and experience like Fall's.

After nearly an hour of intense question and answering, he tipped his forearm and glanced at his watch.

"You're a statistical trend spotter, aren't you?" he asked casually, referring to her ability to absorb data and quickly break it down into meaningful trends, spot anomalies, and even predict outcomes.

"I suppose you could call me that," Alice said.

"Are you a savant?"

"No," she denied tensely. The word *savant* labeled her as a freak. All she wanted was to go unnoticed. Freaks didn't blend in. "I just have a decent feel for numbers and what they mean."

"You have a *phenomenal* feel. A rare gift," he corrected, his deep voice making her spine prickle again in heightened awareness.

"I think you've informed me of just about everything I need to know," he suddenly said briskly, his gaze on the papers on the desk. Alice eased forward in her chair, recognizing the end of the interview. "I *was* wondering—were you interested specifically in Durand Enterprises before you began the philanthropy study?"

She shook her head. "No. I mean . . . I knew about it, of course. I was familiar with both its corporate success and philanthropic emphasis."

"Ah. I was under the impression from your advisor that you were the one who first suggested Durand for the study," he said.

"I might have been. I'm a business major," she said shrugging. "Durand Enterprises is one of the most successful businesses in the world."

He took off his glasses, his gaze on her sharp.

"Are there any questions you have for me?" he asked after a pause in which Alice had to force herself not to squirm.

"How many people will be chosen as Camp Durand counselors?"

"Fifteen. We try to keep the camper-to-counselor ratio as low as possible, while offering scholarships to as many of the kids as we can. New-participant numbers remain fairly steady, but the returning campers have to keep a clean legal record and pass several random drug tests if they have a history, in addition to maintaining an acceptable grade point average. As you probably already know, the camp focuses on junior high and high school-aged kids. Each counselor usually has around ten kids on his or her team."

"So only nine counselors make the cut to become a Durand manager," she reflected. "Do you honestly think that this setup—a summer camp on the shores of Lake Michigan for three weeks—*really* gives Durand the information it needs to hire top-notch executives?" she asked skeptically. "It seems a little"—*silly*, she said in the privacy of her brain—"odd to expect business graduate students to have the necessary experience. We're not social workers or teachers. Or babysitters."

He flashed her a glance when she mumbled the last under her breath.

"You're not expected to be any of those. Well . . . maybe teacher, but not in the classic sense. There are regular, experienced staff at Camp Durand—cabin and grounds supervisors around the clock. It's true, though, that the counselors play a crucial role in the campers' experience. The Durand counselors are, essentially, the face of leadership and support to each individual camper. We offer a week-long training period to the counselors, so they know what to expect. That training program is similar to many management retreats utilized around the world by companies to hone leadership skills. But that's only the beginning. Then the kids arrive, and the challenge *really* begins. What's required to succeed as a counselor—and as a Durand executive—is a large measure of ingenuity, leadership, people skills, and humanity. Those are qualities we've been unable to measure adequately from a resume, recommendation letters—which are almost always glowing—and a few interviews. Camp Durand works for us, no matter how unconventional it may seem. It's worked for us for decades. The executive contestants are under nearly constant observation for four weeks: one week of training and the three weeks while the children are there. Their schedule is arduous. They're considered to be on the clock from seven thirty in the morning until nine p.m., when the night supervisory staff takes over for them. They're expected to work Saturdays until three, with only Sundays off. It's not enough to brag about qualities of leadership, planning, intelligence, innovation, salesmanship, compassion, determination, hard work, and courage: The counselors have to *demonstrate* those skills daily with a group of children, some of whom have been labeled as criminal, uncooperative, manipulative, lazy, or unreachable. It's a lot harder than it sounds at first blush," he said, his mild tone in direct contrast to his lancing stare.

"So Durand does it again. It combines philanthropy—no, it *uses* it—to optimize the bottom line."

His smile was closemouthed, slashing . . . *dangerous*.

"Yes, I understand. That's the way you would view it," he mused as if to himself, sounding not at all concerned by her pessimism as he leaned back in his chair. His stare on her made her feel like a wreck he was considering making into a project. It was a cold, sharp knife, that stare, so Alice couldn't figure out why it made her sweat so bad.

"Would you be adverse to accepting a position at such a seemingly mercenary organization?" he asked.

"No," she replied without pause.

His gleaming brows arched. "Ah. So you're a little mercenary yourself."

"I don't know about that. I'm not stupid, if that's what you mean."

He gave a gruff bark of laughter. "No one could accuse you of stupidity," he said with a swift glance at her paperwork spread across the desk. He stood abruptly. Alice jumped up like she'd been released after being held down on springs.

"This has been enlightening," he said briskly, holding out his hand. They shook. "We'll be making our decision on finalists for Camp Durand within the next two weeks. Chicago-area colleges and universities were Sebastian Kehoe's last stop on the recruitment tour. We'll be in contact."

"Right."

His eyes flashed. She grimaced. She hadn't meant to sound sarcastic, but recognized she had. Well, at least this fiasco was over with. Now she had all the valuable interviewing experience either she or Maggie could ever want for her. Everything after Dylan Fall would be trite. She had a future full of cakewalk interviews before she landed her new, realistic job.

Probably a boring, entry-level, menial one given the current job market.

She turned to go.

"Alice."

She came to an abrupt halt, pausing in the action of reaching for the door. She didn't care for the fact that she looked over her shoulder with a measure of eagerness. It was hard not to crave every glance she could get of Dylan Fall. Despite the fact that he intimidated her, he was one hell of a sight.

"I know a man—he's a member of the Durand board, in fact—who grew up in the Austin neighborhood on the west side of Chicago," Fall said. "Are you familiar with that neighborhood?"

She studied him narrowly, trying to see his angle and failing. "Yeah. It's one of the worst in the city."

"Worse than Little Paradise."

She barely repressed a snort. Mr. Slick, Gorgeous CEO in his immaculate Italian suit had a lot of nerve, presuming to know about Little Paradise. He noticed her flash of disdain, because his brows rose in a silent, pointed query.

"There's nothing worse than urban hillbillies, Mr. Fall," she explained with a small, apologetic smile. "I don't know how much you actually know about Little Paradise, but that's a pretty apt descriptor for who lives in the trailer park there. It's just that in our case, the 'hill' is a giant garbage dump."

She'd been trying to use levity. She must have only sounded flippant, though, because he looked very sober.

"My point is, Durand doesn't just offer philanthropy to needy kids to get publicity and prime photo ops, and then drop them off on the streets and forget about them. The man I'm speaking of rose through the ranks, starting as a Camp Durand camper when he was twelve years old. People-building isn't an empty philosophy at Durand. We want the best, no matter where the best comes from."

She realized belatedly she'd turned and was staring at him now full in the face. Searching. Suspicious.

Hopeful.

Against her will, her gaze flickered down over his snow-white tailored dress shirt and light blue silk tie. A vivid, shocking impression popped into her head of sliding her fingers beneath that crisp cotton and touching warm skin, her palm gliding against the ridges and hollows of bone and dense, lean muscle. Her gaze dropped to his hands.

Just the thought of his hands sliding across *her* skin made her lungs freeze.

I'll bet he could play me perfectly. He just looks *like he knows his way around a woman's body. He'd do things to me I've never even imagined.*

They were completely inappropriate thoughts, but that didn't halt her instinctive reaction. Need rushed through her like a shock to the flesh, leaving a trail of heat in its wake. Her thighs tightened, as if to contain that unexpected flash fire.

Maybe it was because her few former lovers suddenly seemed young and clumsy in comparison to Dylan Fall?

Her stare leapt guiltily to his face. His dark brows slanted dangerously, but he also looked a little . . . *startled*? His eyes flickered downward, just like hers had. She hunched her shoulders slightly at the webwork of sensation that tingled the skin of her breasts, tightening her nipples against her bra.

The whole scoring, nonverbal exchange lasted all of three ephemeral seconds.

Her hand curled into a fist when she recognized she'd let her guard drop.

"I'm happy for your friend. But *I'm* not a charity project," she said.

"Neither was he."

She flinched slightly at the stinging authority of his reply. Dylan Fall was a little scary in that moment.

"We'll be in touch," he repeated, looking down at the desk in a preoccupied fashion, and she knew she'd imagined not only that spark of mutual lust, but his cold, clear anger at her pitiful display of insubordination.

Be on the lookout for the follow-up
to Glimmer *by Beth Kery*

GLOW

Available December 2015
from Berkley Books

About the Author

Beth Kery lives in Chicago where she juggles the demands of her career, her love of the city and the arts, and a busy family life. Her writing today reflects her passion for all of the above. She is the *New York Times* and *USA Today* bestselling author of *Because You Are Mine.* Find out more about Beth and her books at BethKery.com or Facebook.com/Beth.Kery.